AT
WOLF
RANCH

A MONTANA MEN NOVEL

JENNIFER RYAN

AVON

An Imprint of HarperCollinsPublishers

This is a work of fiction. Names, characters, places, and incidents are products of the author's imagination or are used fictitiously and are not to be construed as real. Any resemblance to actual events, locales, organizations, or persons, living or dead, is entirely coincidental.

AVON BOOKS
An Imprint of HarperCollins*Publishers*
195 Broadway
New York, New York 10007

Copyright © 2015 by Jennifer Ryan
Excerpt from *When It's Right* copyright © 2015 by Jennifer Ryan
ISBN 978-0-06-233489-3
www.avonromance.com

First Avon Books mass market printing: March 2015

Avon Trademark Reg. U.S. Pat. Off. and in Other Countries, Marca Registrada, Hecho en U.S.A.
HarperCollins® is a registered trademark of HarperCollins Publishers.

Printed in the U.S.A.

10 9 8 7 6 5 4 3 2 1

"Tell me to go and leave you alone."

"I don't want to be alone. I want to be with you."

He wanted to ask her for how long, but stopped himself, because soon she'd leave and go back to that life she thought she'd outgrown, but would want back because it was familiar. She'd need it back to regain some of the normal from her past in her new life without her sister.

He let loose the reins on his need and pulled her close. He dipped his head, his gaze on her rosy lips. He pressed his mouth to hers for a deep kiss and held nothing back this time. He swept his tongue along hers, melding his mouth to hers. His fingers gripped her hips, let loose, and swept up inside her sweater and up her smooth spine. When his fingertips touched her skin, she sighed and pressed closer.

She rocked her hips against him and he groaned, breaking the kiss to move down her neck and kiss that sweet spot between her neck and shoulder. "God, you always smell so good."

Her head fell back, and he kissed his way back up her throat to her lips again for another searing kiss.

"Don't stop," she said against his mouth. "Don't ever stop."

"I'm just getting started."

By Jennifer Ryan

At Wolf Ranch
Dylan's Redemption
Falling for Owen
The Return of Brody McBride
Chasing Morgan
The Right Bride
Lucky Like Us
Saved by the Rancher

Short Stories
Can't Wait
(appears in All I Want for Christmas Is a Cowboy)
Waiting for You
(appears in Confessions of a Secret Admirer)

For my husband and children. Thank you for always supporting me and hardly ever complaining that dinner is late and the house is a mess. Kids, I hope I've shown you that with courage and a lot of hard work you can make your dreams come true, whatever they may be.

Thank you to my amazing editor, Amanda Bergeron, and my incredible critique partner, Lia Riley. I appreciate all you do. I'm so blessed to have you both in my life and along for this amazing ride.

Thank you to my fans, who make this all possible. I hope you love my Montana Men—Gabe, Blake, and Dane—as much as I do.

AT
WOLF
RANCH

CHAPTER 1

Three long days without a word. No call. Not even a text. Ella stared at her phone, willing it to ring. She tapped her finger on the screen and stifled the urge to call Lela for the hundredth time that morning.

The coffee shop buzzed with activity. People headed off to work with their lattes and scones. She sipped at her caramel macchiato, reading over the newest projections on her laptop for the cosmetics line debuting in March. The numbers looked promising.

Ella jumped when her phone vibrated on the table. She snatched it up and read the caller ID.

"Finally." She swiped the screen to accept the call. "Lela—"

"Where have you been?" Uncle Phillip's demand surprised her.

Why did Uncle Phillip have Lela's phone?

Ella opened her mouth to answer her uncle's question, but he spoke first.

"I oversee the estate. You answer to me."

"Twisting the truth again, Uncle. Ella and I sign off on everything," Lela said, her tone unusually sharp. "You're just a watchdog, there to ensure we adhere to the terms of the will. You have no real power, but you'll do anything to steal it away, won't you?"

What? Ella had never heard her sister talk to their uncle in such a disrespectful and spiteful way, or anyone for that matter. Why did her sister call and not say anything to her? Maybe she'd pocket dialed?

"Lela, it's me. What is going on?" Ella got no response. Uncle Phillip continued to speak over her.

"You have no idea what you're talking about, my dear." Uncle Phillip's soft voice belied the steel in his words. "Don't make me ask again. Be a good girl and tell me where you've been."

This time, her sister answered, but didn't explain a damn thing. "Uncovering your dirty secret. I know what you did," her sister accused.

Secrets?

Butterflies in Ella's stomach fluttered like a flock of birds taking flight. The uneasy feeling she'd carried with her these last days intensified.

Ella gathered up her laptop and notebook, stuffing them into her oversize tote. She dumped the dregs of her coffee in the trash on her way out the door. The penthouse was only a block up from her favorite café where she had breakfast every Tuesday when the house staff had the day off. She kept the phone to her ear and headed home to find out what the hell was going on.

"You won't get away with this." Lela's voice rose in pitch. It took a lot to rile her sister. Whatever Uncle Phillip had done touched a nerve.

"Whatever you think you know doesn't amount to anything without proof." Her uncle used that chilling, yet utterly calm voice.

Ella picked up her pace, sensing the escalation of the

situation into something more than just an argument about company business. She pulled her bag close to her side under her arm and ran for her building, knocking elbows and shoulders with other pedestrians. No time to apologize, she ignored their outraged remarks.

"Oh, I have the proof."

Proof of what?

"You're lying." Uncle Phillip let out a nervous laugh.

"You wish."

Ella passed her building's doorman and ran for the elevator, pushing the button three times, frantic for the doors to open.

"Where is it? Show me."

Come on. Come on. The elevator doors finally opened and she rushed inside and pressed the button for the penthouse. Ella prayed she didn't lose the cell signal and drop the call. She only ever got one bar in the elevators.

"You think I'd be fool enough to bring it here? To you? I'll see you in jail before this day is over."

"I'll see you in a grave first."

The ice in her uncle's tone frosted Ella's heart. The evil laced there erased all trace of the man she knew. He meant those ominous words.

Lela gasped and let out a startled shriek. Ella didn't want to believe her uncle actually struck Lela, but that's what it sounded like.

"What. Did. You. Find?"

"Everything," Lela sputtered.

What? What are you talking about?

"If you're lying to me—"

"Let me go. It's over. There's nothing you can do. I can prove you did it."

Did what?

"Don't look at him," Uncle Phillip snapped.

Him? Who else is there?

"Please, do some—"

"He's not here to help you, you stupid girl. He works for me. Everyone works for me. You should have left well enough alone."

Lela shrieked again. Ella's heart dropped into her stomach.

"This is your final chance. Tell me where it is and I'll make this quick. Refuse and I'll take my time. You'll know the meaning of the word 'pain' when I'm done with you."

Touch her and I will make you pay.

"Go to hell."

"Where is it, you little bitch?"

"You will pay for what you've done. I'll never cave."

"Tell me what I want to know, and *maybe* I'll show you mercy."

"You won't . . . get . . . away . . . with this," Lela stammered, something choking off her words. "The truth will . . . roll out. Come out."

Something about the way she said it the first time struck Ella, but her mind couldn't process anything right now. She slammed her palm against the elevator doors, wishing the damn thing would hurry up.

Please, Lela, get out of there.

"Last chance. Where did you hide it?"

The intensity in his voice sent a shiver up Ella's spine.

The elevator doors finally opened. She ran down the hall to her door, shoved it open, and nearly tripped over the suitcase Lela left in the middle of the foyer. Where had she been?

Ella shoved the cell phone in her purse and turned toward the voices coming from the other room.

"If you won't help me, I'll find someone who will."

Who is she talking to?

"Uncle Phillip, please. Put the gun down."

"Where. Is. It?"

"I'll never tell you where I hid it."

Ella ran across the living room toward the open library doors. Her gaze locked on her uncle's out-stretched arm, the gun in his hand level with her sister's chest. Her father's bloodred ruby pinky ring winked in the morning light streaming through the windows.

"Tell me," her uncle yelled.

"Never."

"Then you're of no use to me anymore."

The crack of the gunshot stopped Ella in her tracks. Her sister's eyes went wide when the bullet plowed into her chest. Blood blossomed over her cream-colored sheath dress, like some gruesome poppy. Lela wilted in slow motion into a heap on the floor. Her legs kicked in a quick jerk, and she never moved again.

Ella stood frozen, rooted to the spot just outside the library doors, her gaze fastened on her sister's lifeless green eyes.

"Damnit, we needed her alive," a man she couldn't see said from inside the room. It took her a second to place the voice. Detective Robbins.

What is he doing here? Why didn't he help?

Self-preservation kicked in and she scurried to the side of the door before the men off to the side saw her. Hands shaking, her stomach in knots, a whirlwind of thoughts circling her mind, but nothing explained why her uncle killed her beautiful sister. It couldn't be, she denied the stark reality. She leaned over and spied through the crack between the open door and frame.

Uncle Phillip knelt next to Lela and touched his finger to her bloody neck. "If I'd had more time, I could have gotten her to talk."

"You mean if you hadn't lost your temper."

Ella's heart broke into a billion sharp pieces that slashed her soul to shreds. Her other half—gone. The emptiness engulfed her. She covered her mouth with both hands to hold back the scream of pain rising up her aching throat. Her eyes filled with tears, and Lela's face, the same one Ella saw in the mirror each morning, swam in front of her.

Uncle Phillip stood, tugged at one shirt cuff and then the other to straighten his crisp white shirt. Her father's ruby cuff links sparked with a glint of light from the overhead chandelier. He ran a hand over his more gray than dark brown hair, smoothing it back. Composed again, he turned to the door. Her breath hitched and stopped. She thought he saw her. His next words startled her even more.

"The stupid girl doesn't know when to quit." He pulled a handkerchief from his gray slacks pocket and wiped his sweaty face, devoid of wrinkles thanks to his many trips to the dermatologist for Botox injections.

"You're lucky she called me. That she saw me as a friend."

"Did she tell you what she found?"

"No. She asked me to meet her here. Her confidence in whatever she had on you convinced me to take her seriously. If she actually had something and shared it with anyone, you'll go down for everything."

"Don't think you won't fall with me," her uncle threatened.

The detective moved forward, blocking her view of her uncle, and stared down at Lela. "What do you want to do with the body?"

Lela was a body. Bile rose in Ella's throat.

Her uncle clinked open a crystal decanter at the bar across the room, pouring himself a drink of the expensive bourbon he preferred. She prayed he choked on it.

"Give me a minute to think." The ice in his voice melted and turned less definitive and more hesitant.

"We need to find that evidence. If it falls into the wrong hands—"

"Shut up." Her uncle sounded as out of control as she felt. Her insides in chaos, not a single thought of what to do taking shape in her mind.

"We need to retrace her steps over the last few days. Find out where she went. Who she saw. We'd have the state attorney and FBI banging down the door if she gave the evidence to anyone. She hid it somewhere. We need to find out where and get it."

"Easier said than done. She was smart."

"Not smart enough to pull this off. She contacted you without ever considering your association with me. She was naive." He toed Lela's still body with his Italian leather shoe.

"Our business arrangement has been mutually beneficial, but if you think I'll be your patsy, you're wrong. So, think, damnit, where would she hide the evidence?"

"I don't fucking know." Her uncle slammed the empty glass down on the desk. "But Ella might."

"Do you think Lela told her what she uncovered?" Detective Robbins asked.

"No. Ella asked me and the staff several times if Lela came home or called. I'm almost certain Lela worked this out on her own and left her recalcitrant sister out of it."

"Almost certain isn't good enough. Why the hell didn't you cover your tracks better?"

"I did."

"If you did, we wouldn't be here right now."

Ella needed to call the police and have them arrest these two for killing her sweet, gentle sister. But the police were standing right there, helping destroy her life.

The room was silent for a moment, and Ella was certain they'd hear her ragged breathing. She jumped when her uncle spoke again.

"Detective, let me tell you a story." Uncle Phillip's voice went eerily calm. "Our studious, prim Lela earned her master's degree and worked as an executive at the company to satisfy the terms of the will and earn her place at Wolf Enterprises. Sadly, her Princess Party Girl twin sister barely made an effort, working in the mailroom and every other odd job at the company. While it satisfies the general terms of the will for them to inherit and take over the company on their upcoming twenty-fifth birthday, Lela's carried the weight and shouldered all the responsibility for the business.

"Lela finally had enough and confronted her sister right here in this room. Ella, party girl that she is, had been out all night and was high, not at all in her right mind. The fight escalated. Ella knows I keep a gun in my desk drawer. She grabbed it and shot Lela. She panicked, but somehow had the wherewithal to try to cover it up, making it look like a robbery gone wrong. With Lela gone, she will inherit the company and other Wolf assets.

"It's heartbreaking, isn't it? Such a pity. Lela had such a promising future. I couldn't be more heartbroken.

"Set the scene, Detective, and then find Ella. Take her to a hotel. Not a dump, but not extravagant either. She's hiding out. Make the place look like she's been on a bender, drinking, doing drugs. The pain and grief send Ella over the edge. She ODs. No one will question it. Use your contacts in the police department and morgue to prove what happened . . . make the evidence show Ella murdered Lela."

"This is more than I signed on for," Detective Robbins said.

"Don't think you're so indispensable. There are plenty of others on my payroll in this town, higher up the food chain than you, that would do my bidding without blinking."

"I'll get it done. I'll need to use some of those contacts to pull this shit off."

"You know who to use to make this clean. I want all the evidence, reports, and public perception to corroborate the scenario I've outlined."

Uncle Phillip knelt by Lela and used his handkerchief to remove her diamond stud earrings. The ones their mother always wore. He unclasped Lela's bloody necklace with the pendant of a heart made out of roses that matched Ella's. Ella reached up and wrapped her trembling fingers around the one against her chest and sighed. Lela's ring came next. Ella had given her the emerald encircled with diamonds for their twenty-first birthday. The night they shared a quiet dinner in an exclusive uptown restaurant and planned their future and fulfilling their parents' wishes and dreams for them.

She took a step forward to snatch back the ring and everything else her uncle took from them. She wanted to claw his eyes out and see him in a grave. Not her sister. Not Lela.

Uncle Phillip handed the bundled items to the detective, except the bloody locket.

"What are you going to do with that?" The detective indicated the gold necklace her uncle tucked away in his pocket.

"Don't worry about it. Do your job. The one I pay you extremely well to do."

Her uncle went to the bar, grabbed a towel, and wiped down the gun. He wrapped it in the towel and handed it to the detective. "The household staff knows I keep this gun in the top drawer of my desk. Unlocked. Easy enough for Ella to take it and use it on her sister. Plant it, along with the drugs and alcohol, at the hotel room. Make sure the report shows Ella's prints are on the gun and it is a ballistic match to the bullet in her. Tomorrow morning the staff will arrive for work and discover the body. You've got until then to find Ella and kill her."

Ella had wasted enough time. She needed to get away. Fast.

Her gaze fell on her dead sister. Her soul pleaded with Lela to wake up and make this all just a bad dream. But Lela remained motionless on the floor.

Ella backed away from the door, walked a wide arc around the living room to stay out of their line of sight, and rushed back to the foyer.

"What the hell is that?" the detective asked.

"Lela called someone."

Oh God, they found her phone.

"Shit. She called her sister."

The panic squeezed her gut tight. If they discovered her, she'd be dead. Ella grabbed her sister's suitcase, coat, purse, her own tote, and slipped out the door, closing it with a quiet snick of the latch. Maybe she'd find a clue in her sister's things.

She rushed to the elevator, hoping to outrun the detective before he came after her. She took the elevator down and walked through the lobby and out the door. The doorman took the coat draped over her arm. "Let me help you with that, Miss Wolf."

She mechanically stuffed her arms in the sleeves of Lela's favorite cobalt blue coat—she'd forgotten her own in her rush out of the coffee shop. Her sister's scent brought tears to her eyes. She blinked to keep them at bay. The doorman hailed her a cab, and she tossed her stuff in the backseat and slid in, checking the front of her building to be sure the detective hadn't come down and spotted her escape.

"Where to?"

Ella couldn't think past the fear and grief eating away at her insides. She didn't know where to go or who to turn to that she could definitely say wasn't in her uncle's pocket. Detective Robbins would check with all her friends. She couldn't risk going to one of them and putting them in danger.

Her gaze fell on her sister's suitcase and the baggage tag still on the handle. She didn't know the BZN airport code. The purse lay on her lap, her fingers clutching it in a death grip. She made herself relax and unzip the bag. She found the airline ticket voucher inside. Bozeman.

Why did you go to Montana?

They hadn't been back to the family ranch since their father died in a plane crash when they were fourteen.

"Where are we off to?" the driver asked again, pulling her out of her dark thoughts. A plan started to form.

"LaGuardia airport." She barely choked out the words.

She'd retrace her sister's steps, find out what she'd been doing the last three days, where she went and who she saw. She'd find the evidence Lela died for, and God help her uncle when she did.

CHAPTER 2

Three Peaks Ranch, Montana

Gabe Bowden put the quarter horse through its paces around the corral, stopping him short to make an abrupt turn, then pulling on the reins to make him back up. All in all, he liked the horse's attention and readiness to follow commands. His brother Blake trained the animal well. The horse would be a fine addition to his new ranch and a big help with the cattle due to arrive in six weeks. Gabe couldn't wait to take over Wolf Ranch. He'd worked his ass off to earn the money to buy the place. Once the deal closed, he'd have everything he ever dreamed: the huge spread with wide-open meadows, rolling hills, rivers snaking out over the land, grass as far as the eye could see for the cattle. A livelihood he could depend on, and a legacy he'd leave to his kids. If he ever found a woman and had some kids.

After Stacy left him standing at the altar all alone, turning her nose up at his little ranch, the plans he had to build it into something more, and a quiet life as his wife and the mother of his children, it couldn't be just any woman. He needed to find the right woman. One who wanted the same kind of simple but meaningful ranch life he wanted. Since he bought Wolf Ranch, he had a hell of lot more to offer now than he did when Stacy left him.

Finished getting a feel for the horse, he rode over to the rail and stopped next to Blake and dismounted. He ran his hand over the horse's flank.

"You did a fine job with this one. Where'd you find him?"

"He's one of Ross's."

"Something about that guy puts me off. Don't get me wrong, his horses have the bloodlines, but I don't like the way he runs his ranch."

"Me either, but you asked for the best I could find. Sully is gentle, attentive, a hard worker, and a fast learner. He'll suit you."

"Sully? You named him already."

"I've spent the last six weeks training him. I couldn't keep calling him horse." Blake grinned and patted Sully on the white patch on his brown forehead. The horse leaned in and closed his eyes, completely enamored and content with Blake. Gabe had to admit, his brother had a way with horses.

"How do you like it here at Three Peaks Ranch?" Gabe asked.

"I love it."

Though Blake trained quarter horses for cutting cattle, he was making a name for himself training Thoroughbred racehorses.

"The partnership with Bud working out? It's been a few years, you ready to get your own place?"

"Naw, I like it here. I've found exactly what I wanted and more."

"I'm glad you're happy, man."

"You must be chomping at the bit to get into the Wolf place."

"I can't wait."

"I still can't see you rambling around that huge house."

"It's the stables and pastures I'm more interested in."

"Please, that house is beyond awesome."

Yeah, it certainly would appeal to that elusive wife he kept looking for.

"Did you get it cleaned out like the owner asked?"

"Get this, I've dealt solely with Phillip Wolf, but Lela Wolf showed up the other day."

"What's she like? Spoiled rich girl?"

"Hell if I know. I only spoke to her for a couple of minutes. I met her in the driveway. She wanted to know what I was doing there. When I told her Phillip requested I put the contents of the house in storage, she told me to leave the place alone and tore out of there. You'd have thought the hounds of hell were after her."

"So you didn't pack the house?"

"No, I did. Moving trucks showed up fifteen minutes later."

Blake frowned. "Why didn't she want you to touch anything in the house?"

"She didn't say."

"Did you tell her you own the place now?"

"I don't own it until escrow closes in nine weeks. That's the deal."

"Did you tell her that?"

"She didn't give me a chance. Come to think of it, she thought her uncle sent me to find her."

Blake frowned and narrowed his eyes. "That's strange."

"I had my orders from her uncle and delaying the inevitable seemed stupid. The stuff sat in that house for the last ten years untouched. People like them, from the city, more money than they know what to do with, they don't care about all that land. Hell, Travis Dorsche took over running their prime cattle, and that guy's just this side of worthless, and they don't give a shit. So, yeah, I cleaned out the house. When the deal goes through they'll still have all that stuff sitting in the lockers Phillip rented. With those people, it's out of sight, out of mind."

"Too bad you didn't get the cattle as part of the deal. That would have saved you some big bucks getting the place set up."

"Tell me about it." Gabe rolled his shoulders to ease the ache.

"Still sore."

"I'm too old to be riding bulls and roping calves. I'll leave that to Dane."

"You won the bull-riding championship. Again."

"It felt good to beat our little brother one last time. I got the last of the seed money I needed to pay for the cattle."

"When do you expect delivery?"

"The day I move in. Things will be tough the first year. I sank everything I have into this deal, but after that, sky's the limit."

"You're on your way." Blake gave him a thump on the shoulder. "Come on, let's load this guy and get you moving. The snow will pass us by here, but you'll meet it head-on. It'll be sunset in another hour."

Gabe led Sully to the gate Blake held open and walked him straight to his truck and trailer. He unstrapped the saddle and pulled it off, handing it over to Blake, who took it inside the stables to put it on the rack. Blake walked out carrying a brush and handed it to him. Gabe tossed the saddle pad Blake's way, and his brother caught it and took it back inside too. Gabe shook his head and thought of them back on their parents' ranch, always working together to get the chores done. He missed those days. Now that they were all scattered—Caleb down in Colorado with his new wife, Summer; Dane traipsing all over Texas, Arizona, and Nevada riding rodeo; and Blake here—it wasn't often they all got together at one time. He missed being with his brothers. Maybe Blake was right about him rambling around that big house alone.

He thought often these days about having a wife and kids. Seeing Caleb last month with his pretty bride, how happy they were together, made him think of finding someone special, instead of someone just for tonight, or this week, or this month. Tired of roaming, he wanted to settle down to a normal ranch life like his parents shared and Caleb found with Summer. The life he planned to have with Stacy before it all fell apart.

Blake slapped him on the back, bringing him out of his thoughts.

"Go anywhere interesting in that mind?"

"Just thinking about Caleb and Summer."

"Never seen two happier people."

"Me either. Maybe that will be us someday."

"Let's hope," Blake said, surprising him with his candor. Whenever they talked about women it was to razz each other or brag about some conquest. They never talked about getting married and settling down.

Gabe brushed Sully down before leading him into the trailer and changing out his bridle for the halter.

With the horse settled into the trailer, Gabe stepped out, closed the gate, and faced Blake.

"What do I owe you for the feed and training?" Gabe pulled out his wallet, but his brother put his hand on his arm.

"Call it a housewarming gift from me to you."

"It's not necessary," Gabe tried to argue.

"It's a gift. I can't wait to come out and see your new place once you get settled."

"I'll probably need some help when the cattle arrive to get them into the right pastures."

"I'm there. Just give me a call, and we'll set it up."

Gabe gave his brother a hearty hug and smack on the back. He wanted to stay, take his brother out for a beer and some food, but sunset came early this time of year. Just after four in the afternoon, it'd be dark in another hour.

Gabe sat in the cab of his truck and started the engine, cranking the heater to ward off the cold. Thirty-three degrees, the temps would plummet come dark. With the snow coming, he needed to get home without delay.

"Hey, drive careful. Sorry you're getting off to a late start."

"My own fault. I wanted to spend time with you."

"I'll see you soon. If not, definitely in six weeks when you take over the Wolf spread."

"See you then."

"Was she pretty?"

Taken off guard, Gabe narrowed his gaze and asked, "Who?"

"Lela Wolf."

He didn't even have to try to recall that heart-shaped face, those green eyes, the sweep of her light brown hair over her eyebrows and tucked behind the curve of her ear. She smelled like a field of lilies.

"Yeah, she's pretty." Gorgeous. Stunning. Unforgettable. Fragile, but he caught a glimpse of steel when she found out about him clearing the house and ordered him to stay out.

"Maybe she'll come back."

Gabe smirked at his brother and shook his head. Blake gave him a lopsided grin, obviously reading that Gabe indeed thought she was more than just pretty. Gabe hit the gas and left his brother in the dust, but not the thoughts he'd had of a beautiful woman in a blue coat with a face he couldn't forget.

Gabe concentrated on the slick road. Due to the earlier rain, he slowed down considerably on the back roads. When he hit the highway farther north, rising up toward the pass, the rain turned to snow and slowed him even more. Way past schedule. The sun had set nearly an hour ago and visibility was getting worse by the minute along the two-lane road. If he didn't have to worry about the horse and trailer, he'd make better time. By morning, he'd need a snow plow to clear the roads if this kept up all night. Right now, it didn't look like the snow would stop anytime soon.

Tired after a long day and in need of a hot drink, he scratched at his rough jaw and thought about all he needed to do when he got home. Settle Sully into the stall he'd prepared in the stables that morning. Crack open a couple of cans of stew for a late dinner and make a pot of coffee. Grab the clothes he kept tossing over the seat and take them to the laundry room. Tomorrow, he'd do all the laundry. He'd get the guest room cleaned up in case Dane dropped in for another visit.

His phone rang, and he checked the caller ID. Speak of the devil. He hit the button on his steering wheel for the hands-free to answer.

"What's up, Dane?"

"Checked out your Black Angus beauties at my buddy's place." His brother's voice filled the truck cab. "Man, those are some prime beef cattle."

"They ought to be for what I paid," Gabe grumbled.

"Like I said, they're a bunch of beauties. Get them certified organic and you'll make a killing."

"Well, it's going to take some time, but once I get the certification and the breeding program up and running, I hope to start turning a decent profit."

"I confirmed the delivery and verified all the records and bloodlines for the cattle. You're good to go, man."

"Thanks, Dane. You saved me the trip down to Nevada. How're things going with you?"

"Rambling around, kicking ass on the rodeo circuit. I'm ranked number two behind Kurt Collins."

"You'll catch him." Gabe had all the confidence in the world his brother would not only catch Kurt but beat his ass by the finals. Dane wanted that prize money and a chance at setting up his own place.

"No doubt. Gotta run, man."

"Hot date?"

"Always. You should try it sometime. You spend far too much time alone with your horses."

"Horses are less trouble than women."

"Women smell better."

Gabe chuckled. "I've got other priorities right now."

"Doesn't hurt to have some fun."

"You're having plenty enough for me and half the men in Montana."

This time Dane laughed. "That's for sure."

"So go have your fun."

"You used to come out with me. I miss those days."

"I don't." After Stacy, he'd left his ranch and rambled around on the rodeo circuit, chasing the thrill of the ride and every woman he could get his hands on, until he woke up one morning with another buckle-bunny beside him and no idea what her name was. He didn't care. She'd scratched an itch, but left him empty. They all did. He'd used them to fill up the emptiness inside him that grew with every meaningless encounter. He'd needed the thrill of the conquest, knowing he could seduce a woman into his bed. But he woke up and realized that's all they wanted from him, because that's all he had to offer. If he wanted to build a life with a woman, he'd have to have something more to offer than meaningless, mindless sex. So he came home to build something he could be proud of, a life someone would want to share with him.

"I miss hanging with you, but not the reckless lifestyle. I'll leave that to you, bro. See you when the cows come home."

"I'll be there."

Dane clicked off. Gabe couldn't wait to see Dane when the cattle arrived. Dane promised to help him get things set up on the ranch.

Gabe didn't hold back the smile, thinking of Dane, his wild-at-heart brother, and Blake, living his dream, training racehorses. Gabe worked his ass off over the last three years to pull together the money he needed for his ranch, to buy the cattle, and finally have everything he ever wanted. Still, Dane's words rang in his head. *Have some fun.* Seemed he'd forgotten how to do that these last years living alone at his place, barely going into town for more than supplies. When it came to the women, a few new ones had moved to town, but mostly they were the same faces he'd seen growing up, and none of them appealed.

He wanted something different. Something new. Someone who challenged him.

Eyes the color of spring grass, the same ones he'd thought of ever since he saw her, floated into his mind.

CHAPTER 3

Ella spent the cab ride to the airport trying to hold herself together and devise a halfway decent plan. She dug through her sister's purse for any other clues and came up with nothing but a drawing of the heart-shaped locket they both wore. Lela had drawn tiny roses, one after another, to form the heart around their initials, L.W. and E.W. She'd drawn an arch over the heart with a rosebush on both sides. Lovely. Her sister always had a talent for doodling.

Ella held the paper to her heart, closed her eyes, and let the overwhelming sense of loss engulf her. She'd never see Lela again.

Aside from the slip of paper, her sister's wallet, keys, her favorite scarlet lipstick, a half-eaten bag of airline peanuts, and mints, nothing told her what her sister had done over the last three days, except rent a car. She carefully tucked her sister's things back into the purse.

Why Montana, Lela?

She squeezed the bag to release her pent-up anger. Something odd pushed against her fingers. She set the bag back on her lap and checked inside again. Nothing accounted for what she felt, so she ran her fingers over the lining and felt the outline of a rectangular card. Her sister had carefully slit the seam by the zipper and used double-sided tape to hold it closed. She pulled the lining free, revealing the fake ID tucked inside. Her sister had pilfered Ella's fake driver's license, which she'd bought off an artist friend who turned out to be an excellent forger of paintings and documents when the money was right. Eighteen and looking to get into some of the more exclusive clubs in the city, she'd bought the ID under an assumed name. It came in handy when she didn't want to be Ella Wolf.

If her guess was right, her sister used Ella's license to buy a plane ticket under the false name and rent a car. Why the secrecy? Why the need to be someone else and not leave a trail?

Whatever her sister was up to, Ella vowed to finish what she started. She too would see her uncle behind bars—or in a grave—for killing her sister, and whatever other heinous crimes he'd committed. The man deserved a hell of a lot worse for what he'd done.

She thought of all those things she and Lela had talked about doing now that the next chapter of their lives was about to begin. Run the company. Travel to distant lands and explore the world. Fall in love with the right man. Get married. They'd serve as each other's bridesmaids. Have babies. Live full lives until they were old biddies drinking tea and sharing photos and stories of their grandchildren.

She swiped the tears away as easily as her uncle had taken away that future.

In six weeks, she turned twenty-five, and if she didn't put her uncle behind bars, and he succeeded in framing her for Lela's murder, he'd take over the company and holdings her parents left to Ella and Lela. He'd get everything and have the power and money to get away with murder.

Never going to happen. Not as long as she still had a breath in her body.

"We're here. What airline?"

Ella checked her sister's ticket stub, the one bread-crumb she'd left. "United."

The cab pulled up in front of the departures terminal. Ella didn't hesitate. The sorrow filled her, but with her grief she felt a profound sense of purpose. She marched up to the ticket counter, handed over her fake ID, and booked a flight to Bozeman, using the cash she gathered between her bag and her sister's, which left her with little more than five hundred dollars.

The flight didn't leave for two more hours, but she'd get to Bozeman by three in the afternoon. She hoped to get to the ranch to begin her search for whatever her sister discovered before it got dark.

The monotony of the security line only gave her more time to think. She didn't want to let her mind take her back to the penthouse library and her sister's lifeless eyes, but the scene played out again and again in her head. She couldn't stop it.

So many what-ifs came to mind. She second-guessed everything she did and didn't do. What if she stepped in to help her sister? Why didn't she call the police? What if she found the evidence her sister said she had and it still wasn't enough to arrest him? What if he got away with killing her sister?

She passed through the security line in the automatic fashion everyone else did, following the person in front of her. She ignored the stares and whispers. If the grief felt this heavy to carry, surely it showed on her face, because she couldn't even muster a fake smile to make others believe she was okay. She'd never be okay. Not ever again.

Shoes back on, cell phone and her laptop packed back in her bags, and free to roam the terminal and walk to her gate, she made one last stop at the ATM. Between her debit and credit cards, she managed to withdraw twenty-five hundred dollars. If her uncle tracked her to the airport with the withdrawals, he still wouldn't know which flight she took, thanks to the fake license.

After ignoring the other passengers on the plane and crying herself to sleep, she awoke just as the plane touched down in Bozeman. She exited, ignoring the stewardess's sympathetic look, and followed the other passengers to baggage claim, where she picked up her sister's bag. Without the ability to use her credit card to rent a car, she hopped into a cab.

"Where you headed, miss?" The older man gave her a concerned glance in the rearview mirror. She caught her haunted reflection. She should have stopped at the restroom to clean the smeared makeup under her eyes from crying.

"Home." The ranch had been her favorite place as a kid. Large, looming mountains stood as the backdrop to the stone and timber house with the huge windows. She'd loved the rustic, comfortable feel of the house compared to the elegant penthouse her parents kept in New York.

"What's the address?"

"Uh, sorry. Forty-two Wolf Road." Since her father bought the property and paid for all the utilities and the road they built out to the house, he used his favorite number for the address and named the road after the family.

"I'm not familiar with it," the driver said, punching the address into his GPS. "That's quite a drive. There's a storm up past the town of Crystal Creek. I can get you there, but you'll need to stay overnight in town, or find someone with four-wheel drive who can get you through the back roads."

Resigned and at the mercy of the gathering storm clouds in the distance, she nodded her agreement.

She used the long drive out of Bozeman's wide valley to clean herself up with the makeup wipes she found in her sister's toiletries that she dug out of the small suitcase. Eyes puffy and red, she'd never win a beauty contest, but she looked and felt better.

The drive relaxed her, unlike the turbulent flight. She hadn't eaten since last night, lost her appetite completely this morning seeing her sister murdered, but now her hollow stomach ached. Maybe if she took a minute, had some coffee and a snack, she could think straight, take the edge off her raging headache, and figure out what to do next.

How far would her uncle go to find her?

Easy, he'd hunt her down.

"Where can I drop you, miss? This rain'll turn to snow up where you're headed."

Lost in her own dark thoughts, she hadn't seen the rain pouring down in sheets, or heard the fierce wind whipping against the car. She checked out the small town around them and spotted a coffee shop next to a motel. If she couldn't find someone to take her to the ranch tonight, she could at least get a cup of coffee, a meal, and a warm room.

"Please drop me at the coffee shop. I'll find my way from there."

"You got it."

She paid him the sixty-two dollars for the ride, plus a tip, and collected all her belongings.

"I'll help you out, miss."

"No, don't get wet on my account. I'll manage."

Grateful, he smiled at her in the rearview mirror. "Suit yourself."

Lucky for her, he pulled up close to the front door, but even in that short distance, her hair and shoulders got drenched. Thanks to the deep puddle she stumbled in, her suede ankle boots were not only ruined, but soaked through. A gust of wind pushed her through the front door. She shoved it shut and turned to face the room; many of the patrons' gazes found her. She felt like a bedraggled wet cat with her hair dripping down her face and neck. She wiggled her freezing toes inside her wet socks and took a deep breath and let it out. Nothing she could do about it now.

She took a seat at the nearly empty counter and dumped her tote and purse on the seat beside her. A waitress bustled over from the two older gentleman at the other end and asked, "What'll it be, honey?"

"Coffee, please."

"Special's the meat loaf and mashed potatoes. We got a pot of broccoli cheddar soup and some nice warm bread if you'd like."

"I'll take the soup and bread. Thanks."

"You okay, honey?"

"No. No, I'm not. But I will be," she vowed, thinking of taking down her uncle. Better to think about that than her sister's cold, dead body lying on the library floor.

The waitress, Bev according to her name tag, poured her a mug of coffee and set a bowl filled with creamer cups in front of her. "I'll have your order in just a minute. You just sit there and get warm."

Ella slumped in the chair and wrapped her frozen hands around the mug, hoping that one day soon her insides would warm again and she'd feel something other than frozen fear and cold hate for her uncle.

Bev set a steaming bowl of soup in front of her and a plate of warm bread rolls with a plastic cup of butter. Ella slit the side of the roll and slathered butter inside to melt. She did the same with the second roll. By the time she scooped up a spoonful of the soup, the smell had started to work on her. One bite of the sinfully thick and rich, creamy concoction and she nearly felt human again. Her insides warmed. She took a big bite of the roll. Melted butter dripped down her chin. She wiped it away with her paper napkin and quietly worked her way through her meal, the loss of her sister keeping her head in a mind-numbing daze.

Finished, she looked around for the first time. Besides the seats at the counter facing the cooking area, a row of tables draped in red-and-white-checked tablecloths with four chairs around each ran behind her down both sides of the diner. Past those and along the outside wall were booths with worn red vinyl seats. Overhead pot lights cast a soft glow over the room. Above her and along the rest of the counter were drop pendant lights with red glass shades. Nice. Country cute.

While she ate, customers trickled in, filling nearly every table and booth. Only a handful of seats remained available at the counter. She needed to decide what to do for the night.

Bev dropped by and held up the coffeepot. "Refill, honey?"

"No thanks. I need to get home, but in this weather I'm not sure there's a taxi or other means to get me there."

"Where you headed, honey?"

"Wolf Road out off 191."

"You're going way out there?"

"Yes, but I don't have a car. Do you know how I can get there?"

Bev looked over her head at a gentleman paying his bill at the small counter by the door. "Hey, Travis. You headed home?"

"It'll be slow going in the snow, but yeah. Why?"

"This nice lady needs a ride out to Wolf Road. Can you take her on your way?"

"Well, now, it's past my way, but I can certainly take the pretty lady where she needs to go."

Ella eyed Bev with apprehension about leaving with a stranger. Especially one with unwashed hair, four days' worth of beard stubble, and a rip down the front leg of his grease-stained Carhartts.

Bev patted her hand on the counter. "Don't you worry none. He's mostly harmless."

"Come on now, Bev, you know I've been sweet-talking you for years."

"It's never worked with me, or any woman I know," she shot back, laughing.

A few of the other customers barked out a laugh and a crude comment about Travis's nonexistent love life. He smiled and took the good-natured ribbing in stride.

"Trust me, honey, he won't bite. If you don't go now, who knows how long it will take you to get there, what with the way the weather changes around here."

Bev had a point. The rain had given way to a soft but steady snowfall. Pretty; Ella wished her sister was here to see it. They'd so loved the snow and coming to this part of the country. They'd sit in the huge living room window at the ranch and stare at it for hours, playing with their dolls or a game of chess. She'd loved to beat her sister at Chinese checkers. The memory made her eyes glass over. She blinked the tears away. Plenty of time to grieve later. Right now, she needed to get to the ranch and find out what her sister had been doing here.

"If you don't mind, I'm happy to pay you for your trouble."

"No trouble at all to drive a pretty lady wherever she wants to go."

"Thank you. I really appreciate this."

She gathered her belongings, paid her bill, leaving Bev a generous tip, and followed Travis out of the diner into the frosty weather. The sun had set and the snow fell against the backdrop of the dark night, highlighted by the diner and city lights. The snow quickly covered her hair and clothes. She shook as much off as she could before climbing into Travis's truck cab. The smell of sweat, dirt, and manure, along with the stench of tobacco from the beer bottle in the cup holder filled with chewing tobacco spit, assaulted her nose. Her stomach lurched. She wrinkled her nose and cracked the window to let in some fresh air.

Travis slid behind the wheel and gave her a leering smile. She sat up straight and folded her hands in her lap, her bag and tote stuffed at her feet. She sighed out her relief when he pulled out of the parking lot onto the main road and headed out of town. Though the heater in the old truck worked, it barely took the edge off the crisp air coming in through the cracked-open window. She gave up the fresh air in favor of warmth, especially with her wet hair and feet.

She finger-combed the wet strands away from her face, trying to get the last of the ice out. Travis took his gaze from the road to roam it over her from head to foot.

"So, what brings you to these parts? You don't look like you're from around here. Where are you from?"

She wondered if he'd shut up and let her answer. Not that she wanted to, but if keeping him talking kept him from staring at her breasts and his eyes on the icy roads, she was all for chitchat.

"I flew in today from New York City."

"I took you for a city girl."

What gave her away? The suede boots. Her too thin slacks and sweater. The full-length coat more suited for a night out to dinner in the city than a snowstorm.

"Why are you headed out to Wolf Ranch? Wolfs haven't been back since the plane crash. I heard they might sell the place. Is that why you're here?"

The pain of her parents' death felt as raw today as it did when she was fourteen. Today, though, that pain mixed with the loss of her sister and the dreams they'd had for their future together, finally taking the helm of all their parents left behind.

"Um, yes," she choked out. "The company sent me to check on the house. For the family."

"Are they thinking of selling?" he asked again.

No way would she ever sell the house. In her mind, it held all the memories of her and Lela with their parents. Those were the happy days when her father didn't work and her mother didn't rush off for luncheons with friends. At the ranch, it was just family.

God, how she missed those simpler times.

"No. The ranch will always belong to the Wolf family." Well, to her. She was the only one left.

"That's what I thought. So, how long are you staying? Did they ask you to check on anything else besides the Wolfs' home?"

That sounded odd, but she didn't know what else her family owned here besides the house. If memory served, they'd only ever come to spend vacations together, riding the horses in the spring and summer and skiing in the winter.

"Right now, my only concern is the house. Why?"

"No reason. Just making conversation."

The tires rolled on over the road and she focused on the fluttering snow and hoped they didn't hit a patch of ice and crash. That would make her uncle happy, and the last thing she wanted to do was please him in any way. No, she planned to destroy him one way or another. He thought she'd spent the last years of her life fooling around and playing the party girl. Well, he didn't know who he was up against, and his ignorance and indifference to her would serve her well.

"I am so tired of the cold. Once the sun goes down, temperatures plummet this time of year."

"I guess I should have packed my warmer coat," she said lamely, turning to the side window and rolling her eyes. Nothing about this guy appealed to the senses. Unpleasant to look at, his gut hung over his waistband, and his overstretched shirt rode up on his hairy belly. His ruddy cheeks and nose made the rest of his face look pasty white. If that wasn't enough, he needed a shower.

Bad. But the way he kept looking at her made the creepy crawlies dance up her spine and over her skin. She hoped the roads stayed clear enough for them to make it to the ranch quickly. "How much farther is it?"

"Only about another twenty miles. Don't worry. We'll make it. I drive through thicker stuff than this all the time."

"It's just I'm cold and I can't wait to be inside so I can warm up by a hot fire." She only hoped the house still had the electricity turned on and wood for the fireplace. Either way, being at the house would be better than sitting next to Travis.

"If you're cold, come on over here, darlin'. Ol' Travis will keep you warm." He reached over and traced his fingers over her shoulder and down her arm.

"Really, thank you, but I'm fine."

"You're all wet, ain't ya?"

She didn't like the suggestive way he said "wet." It made her feel as dirty as the look in his eyes.

"Best way to get warm in weather like this is to use each other's body heat. Lord knows this old truck's heater can't keep you as warm as I can."

While she thought of a response, he reached over, grabbed her thigh, and pulled her leg closer to him. Too intimate and totally inappropriate. Fear washed through her chest, and she gasped, swatting his hand away. "Stop that."

All he did was chuckle, but she didn't find any comfort in the creepy sound.

"Come on, honey, scoot on over here and give ol' Travis a little somethin', somethin'."

"Look, I'm not interested in anything but a ride."

"I'll give you the ride of your life."

After the day she had, her trepidation turned to anger. "Really. This is how you think women want to be treated?"

"The way I see it, honey, you've got two options, me and this truck, or that there snowstorm."

Trying to appeal to his sense of decency, if he had one, she said. "What will sweet Bev and all those other customers back at the coffee house say when they find out you dumped me on the road?"

"All they'll know is what I tell them. That I fucked the hot chick in the front seat of my truck."

"Not a single one of them will believe I gave into your *charms*, big guy."

"Think you're something special, do you?" He reached for her again, but she smacked his hand, stinging her fingers and hopefully his hand as well. He pulled back from her, but checked the mirrors and slammed on the brakes in the middle of the deserted road.

"If you haven't noticed, bitch, we're alone out here. No one will know if you and I did the nasty, so stop all this fussing. Come here and show me some appreciation."

"All I want is a ride. I'm willing to pay you for it, but I am not sleeping with you to get it."

"Just a little somethin' for my trouble." He reached for her again. This time his fingers dug into her thigh. He pulled her closer, leaning in to kiss her.

She leaned back, out of his reach, and pushed at his shoulders with her hands. The fear returned. Her heart thundered against her ribs. "Travis, stop. You don't want to do this. You don't even know me."

"I know you're probably the most beautiful woman who will ever come through here, and I want you."

"Well, you can't have me, you bastard. Let me go." Her voice pitched high. Her nails dug into his hand, and his fingers clamped around her leg. Since he kept pulling at her, she unlatched her seat belt, turned her legs toward him, brought her feet up, and smashed them down into his lap, her heels digging into his groin. He bellowed in pain like a half-mad bull.

She scooted back into the door and turned back to sit in her seat properly, her feet tangled in her bag strap. *What am I going to do?* She stared out the window; nothing but empty land quickly disappearing below a blanket of white snow. Not a building or another car in sight.

Travis leaned forward, moaning and holding his nuts, rocking back and forth. "You bitch. That fucking hurt."

She didn't expect the big guy to move that fast, but he lunged across her, grasped the door handle, opened the door, and shoved her out before she could grab on to anything. She landed hard on her hip and side in the ice slush. Her foot remained stuck on the strap of her tote. Travis tried to close the door on her leg, but only managed to twist her ankle and bruise her more. Frustrated, he shoved her bag out with a grunt and slammed the door. She scrambled back farther into the snow to avoid getting run over when Travis hit the gas, spun the tires in the ice, and took off, leaving her in the middle of nowhere.

The snow fell thick and steady. She tried to stand, but slipped and fell onto her bruised side again. She needed to get help. If she was cold before, she was freezing now. No way she would survive the night in this weather. The temperature had already dropped several degrees since she arrived at the coffee shop an hour ago. With little traffic out on the roads, she'd be lucky to flag someone down. Her best hope was for a snowplow to come by.

Did they even run those this far out of town?

Her spirits dropped with each passing moment that no headlights appeared from either direction. She held out hope that someone would pass by on their way home.

She thought of her cell phone tucked in her bag. If she turned it on and the detective helping her uncle discovered where she was, she'd be alive, but she'd have to leave Montana, which meant losing her chance at learning what Lela had found—and any hope of nailing her uncle to the wall.

If things got worse, she'd have no choice but to risk turning on the phone and trying to call for help.

Probably no cell service out here anyway.

Options limited and getting worse, she limped along the road back to town. It didn't take long for her feet to freeze. Her ears stopped burning. Numb. She was numb from the inside out. She tried to keep her coat tucked around her neck and body, but the whipping wind pulled it this way and that, letting the icy breeze and snow down her neck and shoulders. If only Travis had tossed out her suitcase, too. Then she could use the spare clothes and socks to keep warm. At this point, the rain and snow soaked every article of clothing she wore.

She might not have a lot of survival skills for wilderness life, but she could add cold and wet and come up with death.

She needed a miracle. With every step she took, she prayed, "Someone, please, help me."

Over time, that prayer became more than just some-one to save her from this icy road. She needed someone to help her prove her uncle's guilt. With the cops in his back pocket and who knew who else, she was in over her head.

Her gaze wandered back up to the sky and the fall-ing snow, and she begged, "Please."

The headlights came out of nowhere. Or maybe she lost focus again as the cold sapped her energy and made it more and more difficult to take a step. Everything inside her wanted to sit down and rest, but she pushed on toward those headlights and hoped they were real and the person stopped.

Hope rose up in her chest as the truck drew closer. She waved her arms to get the driver's attention. They didn't slow down. Oh God, they didn't see her!

"Stop. Please," she screamed.

CHAPTER 4

Gabe shook off thoughts of beautiful, rich women he'd never have a chance with or see again and focused on the road. Snow danced across his windshield, swept away by his pulsing wipers. Hungry, he reached across the seat for the paper bag of snacks he picked up on the trip down to see Blake. He came up with an empty bottle of water and tossed it to the floor. His fingers brushed over the bag of pretzels, but he couldn't quite reach them. He leaned to the side, grabbed his prize, and brought the bag to his mouth, tearing the corner. He spit out the wrapper and dumped a few into his mouth. He chewed, eyes glued to the road ahead, focused on the thickening snow. He slowed even more. Caution over speed the better choice in weather like this.

A strange blue object flashed momentarily in front of his headlights on the side of the road. Surprised, he reflexively hit the brakes, but the truck slid on a patch of ice, swerved, and glided to a stop.

"Shit. What the hell was that?"

Unnerved, he hit the emergency lights and got out to investigate. He pulled his coat around his neck to keep the snow from running down his back. Cold, he stuffed his hands in his pockets and made his way on the slippery pavement back to the trailer. Sully whinnied and stomped a hoof on the metal floor.

The wind shifted and whipped the snow this way and that. He swept his gaze along the road, looking for any sign of the mysterious blue thing. Flurries obscured his view, making visibility difficult. Then, he saw it. Something flapped and fluttered in the breeze on the side of the road about fifteen feet away. Everything inside him stilled. He narrowed his gaze on the blue splotch, quickly fading beneath the dusting of snow. The wind kicked up again, pushing on his back, and making him take a step forward. In that moment, his gaze traced the outline in the snow, and he registered what he was looking at. A person.

He ran before he knew what he was doing and fell to his knees beside the crumpled figure. He reached out and ran his hand over the coat he recognized from the woman who wore it, sitting in her vehicle, telling him to stay away from her, now his, house.

"Lela." Her name barely made it past his lips. The woman with the green eyes that haunted his thoughts. He couldn't figure it out. Beautiful. He'd appreciated the way she looked, but he hadn't felt the pull the way he did right now.

Gabe ran a shaking hand over her frozen hair and pushed it away from her face, practically buried in the snow. He pressed his hand to her shoulder. She moaned and turned to her side, flinching and letting out an anguished gasp when she rolled over her hip. He helped her settle onto her back. Her ice-covered lashes fluttered and those green eyes stared up at him, though just like the strange feeling he got, they weren't exactly the same as he remembered.

"Lela, are you okay? What the hell are you doing out here in this weather all alone?"

Tears filled her eyes and rolled down the sides of her face into her hair, the moisture freezing on her face.

"Are you hurt? Can you get up?" He didn't wait for an answer and ran his hands over her arms and legs. Her thin black slacks were soaked through, along with her boots. Wet and heavy, her coat had a thick layer of ice on it. She shook all over, her teeth chattering. He cupped her freezing face in his hands and hoped she focused on him. "Lela, are you okay?"

Every time he said her name, she cried harder. He didn't know what to do, but leaving her lying in the snow wasn't an option. Her lips had gone blue along with the tips of her fingers. If he didn't act fast, she'd die of hypothermia.

He slid his hands beneath her, pulled her to his chest, and stood with her in his arms. She let out another gasp and locked her jaw in a grimace that made his chest ache. She surprised him and wrapped her arms around his neck and buried her face in his neck. Her ice-cold face pressed to his skin. He leaned into her to give her what warmth he could without pulling her close and hurting her more.

Heavier than he expected, she didn't seem that big. He took two steps and realized something kept bumping against his calf. He kicked his leg out and felt the bag hit his leg again. He glanced at her feet and the strap wrapped around her ankle. No time to free it now, he ignored the nuisance and hurried to get her into his truck. Not so easy to get the passenger door open, but he managed without dropping her. He planted one foot on the running board, shifted to the side, and hauled both of them up and slid her onto the seat so her head lay at the driver's side. With the wind blowing at the other side of the truck, the cold worked its way into the cab, but not the snow. Thank God.

Standing on the running board, he got to work, pulling her short boots off first and then her soaking socks. They landed next to the empty water bottle he tossed to the floorboard earlier. He unwound the huge purse strap off her leg and ankle and dumped the bag on the floor with a heavy thud. She lay quiet on the seat. Though he hated her crying, he found her silence even more disturbing. He didn't like the look of her pale, grayish-yellow toes. He rubbed his hands over her feet to get her circulation moving. Still, her wet pants remained plastered to her cold legs. With a shake of his head and a determination to save her, he reached up to the button on her slacks and undid them. He pulled the cold, wet material down her too pale legs and tossed the wet mess to the floor, too. His gaze swept up her toned legs to the black lace panties that made her skin look even whiter. His stomach turned over when he saw the huge splotch of red and purple on her hip.

"What the hell happened to you?"

He laid his palm over the nasty bruises and pressed his fingers into her hipbone and down the top of her thigh, feeling for anything out of the ordinary. She squirmed and moaned, but didn't really wake up.

Thank God he'd barely been crawling home in this storm, or he might not have seen her. If she spent another minute in the storm, she could be dead. The thought nearly stopped his heart. Sick with worry, he wished his cell worked out here. He'd call the police, an ambulance. In this weather, they'd take nearly an hour to get here anyway, and Lela didn't have that kind of time. He needed to take care of her and get her to the clinic. Fast.

Both his hands lay on her thighs. He squeezed and whispered, "What the hell were you doing out here, walking on the road in the dark, during a snowstorm?"

She didn't answer, so he refocused his thoughts to saving her. He needed to get the soaking wet coat off her that did nothing to keep her warm at this point. Water dripped off the ends onto his boots. He pulled the sleeves down each of her arms, trying not to move her too much. He wrapped one arm under her knees and lifted her slightly to pull the coat out from under her. Her head rolled to the side and she tried to pull her legs free. Now that he had the wet clothes off her, he reached over, turned the key, and started the truck. He adjusted all the vents to blow down on her and soon the heat pumped out at full blast. All he had to do now was keep her warm and get her to the clinic.

An idea sparked, and he leaned over the seat and rummaged through the back, pulling out two flannel shirts, a pair of sweatpants, and, yes, a thick flannel jacket he wore to his buddy's place for poker night last week.

He laid the jacket over her chest and tucked it around her arms. She still wore her gray sweater, but it wasn't thick enough for this weather. City girl. Didn't know what she was doing out here in the country during a snowstorm. He'd thought she left after he saw her at the house. Guess not. But how did she end up out here without her car? Maybe he'd find it broken down up the road. Still, she should have been smart enough to stay in it and not try to walk back to town in this weather.

He slid his hand down her calf to her ankle and took hold to push her leg into the sweatpants. A hell of a lot easier to undress a woman when she was awake and participating. Redressing one while she was passed out took a hell of a lot of work and was a lot less fun. Still, he managed to get both her feet in the legs of the sweats. Bruises marred one of her ankles, along with a mark from the strap of her huge purse. He didn't like the way it looked, but couldn't do anything about it now. He pulled the pants up past her knees, but needed to jostle her to get them over her hips. He barely got them to the tops of her thighs when her eyes popped open and the girl came to life, grabbing at his hands to push him away.

"Stop. Don't. Leave me alone," she pleaded, pushing him away and trying to kick and push him out of the truck with her feet.

To stop her from fighting and hurting herself, he lay down the length of her and took her face between his hands, making her focus on his face just inches from hers.

"Lela, it's me, Gabe. We met the other day at the ranch." Her eyes went wide, and she stopped pushing against him. Everything in her went still. Her eyes swam with unshed tears. "I found you collapsed on the side of the road. I'm trying to get you warm."

"C-c-cold."

Her body shook beneath his. "I know, stop fighting me, and I'll get you warm. I'll take you to the clinic to get you checked out."

"No!"

"You're hurt."

"I'm fine."

"No, you're not. Your lips are blue, you've got frost-bite on her toes, and your fingers don't look much better. How did you get out here?"

"He left me."

"Who?"

Her eyes fell closed. He wanted to shake her and get her to wake up and tell him who the hell left her in the middle of nowhere. She could have died. That thought pulled a tight band around his chest and made it impossible to breathe.

He tucked the coat around her again, making sure her hands were lying on her stomach and warm beneath the coat. He pulled the sweats up and over her hips and took the two flannel shirts and wrapped one of each around her feet. Hanging out the door, he pulled her legs up and turned them so her feet lay on the seat. He slammed the door shut and ran around to the driver's side and climbed in beside her. With her head at his hip, he stared down at her too pale features. Drawn to her, he traced his fingers over her beautiful face.

The urge to protect and help her pushed him to hurry. He maneuvered the truck into an odd three-point turn that took a hell of a lot more than two or three forward and backward moves due to the trailer and the two-lane road. Most of the shoulder was covered in thick snow and the last thing he wanted to do was get stuck. He headed back to Crystal Creek and the clinic that was luckily on this side of town.

Worried like he'd never felt before, he brushed his fingers through Lela's wet hair, pulling it off her face. The heater pumped out hot air, making him wish he'd taken his coat off and put it over her too, but he endured the heat because she needed it. He laid his warm hand on her cheek and hoped that little bit of comfort helped. He didn't know what else to do.

He pulled into the nearly deserted lot and hated to leave Sully in the trailer, but Lela needed to see a doctor. He shook Lela's shoulder to wake her. Warm now, her eyes fluttered open, locked on him, staring down at her from over her, and she shot up, twisted, and leaned back into the passenger door in a defensive position that made him hold up a hand to let her know he meant no harm.

"Easy, Lela, it's just me, Gabe. We're at the clinic."

"I'm not going in there. Just let me out." She looked down at the clothes he put on her and frowned, obviously not remembering him undressing and redressing her in his clothes.

"I'm not keeping you here, but you need to see a doctor before I let you go anywhere on your own."

"I can't."

"I'm not giving you a choice." He turned and opened his door, slipping out and shutting it. He made his way around the front of the truck and pulled open the passenger door. She sat with her hands in her lap, head down, a look of utter desolation on her face.

"If I go in there, and they take my name and my credit card for the bill, he'll find me."

"Who?"

"Please. I have to go. I can't be here."

Every instinct in him wanted to protect her from whoever she thought was after her, but he needed to make sure she was really okay. Her color looked better, but nothing could make him forget the horrible black and blue marks on her hip. What if she had internal in-juries? In her weak state, she didn't have much fight in her, so he took the decision out of her hands and picked her up, pushing the door shut with his back.

"Please, put me down. I have to go."

"You're not going anywhere without shoes." The shirts had fallen off in the truck when she woke up. Her small feet didn't even poke out the bottom of his sweats, which under any other circumstances would have made him smile, but not when she winced and tried to hide the pain every time he took a step and jostled her in his arms.

He hooked his finger in the door handle, pulled it open enough to get his foot inside, and kicked it open wide enough to allow him to get past without hit-ting her.

"Put me down, please."

She must be feeling better to use that uptown tone with him. She wanted down, but some part of him wanted to keep her close. She wiggled in his arms, so he held her firm to his chest. She let out another pained moan and collapsed into him, laying her head on his shoulder. She hadn't lost all her fight though.

"Please get me out of here."

"In case you forgot, my name is Gabe. Gabe Bowden. I live near your place, so the neighborly thing to do is make sure you're okay."

"I just need to get to the ranch."

"Let the doctor check you out, and I'll take you there."

"Promise?"

At this point, he'd promise her anything to get her in a room with a doctor.

"Hey, Gabe, who's this?" Tina, the receptionist, asked. He'd been in here enough times for stitches or a cold or flu bug over the years. Small towns, everyone knew everyone. Except he didn't know the woman in his arms, but he wanted to.

Lela stiffened, so he avoided saying her name in the lobby filled with a couple and their coughing kid, the older couple huddled in the corner, and a guy holding up his hand, a dish towel wrapped around it.

"I found her collapsed on the side of the road. She's got possible frostbite on her toes and a severely bruised hip."

"Anything else?" Tina asked.

"My ankle hurts," Lela admitted.

He frowned down at her lying on his shoulder. She closed her eyes, avoiding him.

Tina handed her a clipboard. "Fill these out, including your insurance information. You can take her into room three to the right. There's a gown on the table. Take off the pants and sweater and put it on, ties in front. I'll get Dr. Bell."

"I don't know him. Is he any good?" Gabe asked.

"She is young, but excellent. Super smart. Graduated medical school top of her class at twenty-two. Did four years surgical residency in Bozeman and is specializing in orthopedic surgery. Dane keeps on with his reckless ways, he may need her some day."

Gabe nodded, because she might be right about Dane needing a specialist if he kept getting thrown by broncos and bulls. Nature of the game in rodeo. Gabe had the aches and scars to prove it.

He carried Lela into the exam room, set her gently on the padded exam table, sitting with her legs out, hands braced at her back. He gave her a few minutes to rest and filled out the form himself with the pertinent information and set the clipboard on the end of the table.

Gabe handed her the gown. "Need my help to get your clothes off and that on?" he asked without the slightest trace of an innuendo in that simple but loaded question.

Ella shook her head no.

He walked back out the door, turned, and said, "I'll be back in a minute."

Ella didn't doubt he meant a minute. So far, he didn't seem the type to leave her alone for long when he insisted she get medical care for what she believed were only minor injuries.

She pulled her sweater over her head and drew the gown up one arm and then the other. She'd just managed to pull it closed in front when she rolled her aching shoulders and groaned. Everything ached after the bone-chilling cold sucked up all her energy.

A knock sounded on the door a second before it opened just enough for Gabe to be seen. He kept his eyes on the door frame and asked, "Are you decent?"

"Barely." Most people would say not at all about her lifestyle, but in this case, she was covered. She liked his manners and the way he averted his gaze until she gave him the all-clear.

He came into the room and closed the door behind him. His gaze locked on hers when he stood next to her, leaned in, and grasped both sides of the sweatpants and pulled. She planted her hands on the table and lifted her hips so he could pull the pants down her legs. His eyes never dropped to her bare skin, but remained on her face, even when he reached for the sides of the gown and pulled them down to cover her thighs. Finished, he traced a finger over her brow, drawing her damp hair away from her face and tucking it to the side. She held her breath having this big man so close she could see the flecks of dark brown in his honey brown eyes. Strange, she didn't feel the need to pull away, but wanted to get closer.

"Are you okay?"

"Stiff and sore, but I'm fine."

His frown said he didn't believe her. His warm eyes said he cared. He took a slow step back before he shifted his gaze and took a seat in the chair in the corner to wait for the doctor.

Ella bit her bottom lip and tried to think. She needed to get out of here. She needed to get to the house and figure out why her sister came here. "If you'll bring in my bag, clothes, and boots, you can go."

"You are just hell-bent on getting rid of me. Yesterday you ordered me to stay away from your palace, city girl."

"It's just a house."

"In case you didn't notice, this isn't exactly the place of mansions and luxury cars you'd find clustered around the ski resorts. Around here, we drive trucks and live in normal houses."

"My house is normal."

"Only if you've got a family of fifteen living there."

"It's not that big."

"Just over ten thousand square feet. Five bedrooms, seven baths, an apartment over the garage, and a guest cottage out back. Stables for forty horses, timberland for miles, a pond overflowing with trout, three rivers that run across the property for more fishing. Nearly seven thousand acres of prime land, including three solar-powered wells, several hundred acres of dryland hay, and thousands of acres of rangeland you haven't stepped foot on in more than ten years."

Because she couldn't go back there after her parents died. She couldn't be in that place and remember everything she'd lost. The love. The laughs. The memories they'd shared under that roof. It was too painful. Now, to return without her sister. The only one left in her family, besides her uncle and some distant cousins, it didn't bear thinking about. "How do you know all that? Why do you care?"

The door opened, preventing him from answering. Dr. Bell walked in carrying a folder. Surprised to see someone so young in her position, Ella relaxed at the sight of the doctor's warm smile and intelligent eyes.

Dr. Bell picked up the clipboard and tucked it under her folder. "Hi there. I heard you were stranded out in the freezing cold."

"Yes."

"Could you elaborate?" Dr. Bell coaxed.

"I found her on the side of the road about twenty-five miles outside of town. I don't know how long she'd been out there, but she might have frostbite on her toes, though they look considerably better now that I've gotten her warm," Gabe answered. "Her hip is banged up. Her foot was all caught up in her bag strap and her ankle hurts. Though the cold made her tired and less than coherent at first, she's got all her brain cells firing again as far as I can tell."

Dr. Bell reached out and covered Ella's hand with hers, smiling softly. The simple gesture calmed and reassured Ella that Dr. Bell would take care of her. "How did you end up on the road alone in this weather?"

"You said *he* left you there. Who?" Gabe asked.

"Some guy named Travis. Bev at the diner asked him to give me a ride, because he was going that way, I guess. Next thing I know he wants—let's see, how did he put it—'a little somethin', somethin'' for his trouble."

"You told him to go fuck himself, and he got handsy with you," Gabe guessed, a menacing look in his eyes, pulling his lips into a tight line.

"I kicked him in the nuts and he dumped me on my ass on the side of the road. Literally. He still has my suitcase, which I need back."

"Son of a bitch. We'll get it back, or I'll take it out of his hide."

The way he said it, the flex in his forearms when he clenched his hands into fists sent a wave of heat and awareness through her.

"Sorry, Doctor," Gabe said.

The doctor gave him a smile that he returned, and Ella felt a twinge of jealousy for no reason. She didn't know this man. Of course, he'd saved her life, kept her warm, and got her to a doctor. She hated to admit she needed one. Everything hurt, but nothing so much as her heart and soul, missing her sister, feeling lost and alone.

She looked up and caught Gabe studying her. She immediately turned her gaze to the doctor, who gave them both a look.

"Let's start with the easy stuff. What's your name?"

Ella swallowed hard. Moment of truth. Up until now, she hadn't corrected Gabe's assumption. Mostly because she'd been kind of out of it. Plus, she let it go because it reminded her of all the times she and Lela traded places and tricked people. This was probably the last time it would work. She hated to stop the charade and live in the reality that Lela was dead.

She took too long to answer, so Gabe did it for her. "She's Lela Wolf."

Her gaze met Gabe's. She opened her mouth to correct him, but the pain of losing Lela choked off her words. She tried to hold it together and not think that no one would ever mistake her for Lela again now that she was dead.

"Thanks, but I wanted her to answer this time."

"I didn't hit my head or anything. After being so cold, I'm tired, but my head is clear. Really, I'm fine, except for my hip and ankle."

"All right." Dr. Bell turned to Gabe. "If you'll give us a few minutes alone, I'll check her injuries."

"I'm not going anywhere." Gabe held Ella's gaze. "I want to stay while the doc checks you out and make sure you're okay."

"You don't need to stay. Just get my things from your truck. Please."

"I'm staying. Don't mind me."

"A little privacy would be nice," she shot back.

"I've already seen you half naked. Believe me, right now, all I'm interested in are your injuries."

Right now. As in later might be a different story. Maybe that was her own wishful thinking, because this man did all kinds of weird things to her insides. She wanted him to stay. She wanted him to go. And, oh God, how stupid of her, she wanted him to wrap his arms around her again and tell her everything was going to be okay.

"If you're okay with him staying, let's check you out," Dr. Bell interrupted their stare down.

Ignoring him, Ella pulled the gown away from her right side to show the doctor her side. "Travis shoved me out the door. I landed on my hip. My bag got caught on my ankle. He tried to slam the door, but smashed my foot instead. My ankle hurt, but then I walked on it for quite some time, slipping and sliding on the ice and snow, making it worse."

"Jeez," Gabe said, shaking his head, a deep frown on his face, and rage in his eyes.

"Lie back and let me take a look at this side," Dr. Bell said.

Ella settled on the table facing the wall. The gown fell down her back as the doctor ran her fingers over the worst of the bruised area, checking the bone. She bit back several yelps.

"Good, Lela. Now I want you to lie flat on your back."

Every time someone called her Lela, a fist squeezed her heart, making it hurt all over again.

Ella complied and gave the doctor an appreciative smile when she closed the gown over her breasts. The lace bra barely hid a thing. Her nipples stood out against the black material. The doctor pressed on her side and over her abdomen. Satisfied she didn't have any belly pain, the doctor clasped her hand and checked her fingers. She did the same with the other hand.

"Your hands look okay. No signs of frostbite."

"The prickly needles stopped in the car a little while ago. My feet are taking a lot longer."

"Her boots and socks were soaked through, along with her pants and jacket. Her hair was soaking wet and covered in ice. I got her into the truck, stripped off her wet things, and cranked the heater."

"Fast thinking. Keeping her in those cold, wet clothes could have made the situation worse," the doctor confirmed, working her way down her right leg, pressing on her calf, moving down to her ankle. She wrapped her hand under her heel and lifted her foot. Even that slight movement hurt when her ankle flexed. "Which way hurts more? This way? Or this?"

"Both," Ella bit out.

"Looks like you've got a bad sprain, and a couple of pulled tendons and muscles. I'll get you a brace to wear to stabilize your ankle while it heals. Your toes look okay. Do they still hurt?"

"Yeah, a little."

"I'll give you some pain meds before you go. All in all, I'd say you are very lucky. No broken bones, but that hip will ache for weeks. The bruise goes down to the bone. That will take time to heal."

"Thanks to the weather and pulling the trailer, I wasn't going that fast. I hate to think . . . man, if I'd missed seeing you out on that road . . ." Gabe hung his head and ran his fingers through his short dark hair, raking it back.

She understood just how he felt. The gravity of what happened to her sister hit her hard on the plane after she'd had time to come off the adrenaline high and everything settled in her mind. The wave of grief and guilt would come again when she had too much time to think. Gabe felt that now. He'd finished his tasks to keep her safe and make sure she didn't die on him— like she could have if he hadn't stopped and saved her.

"Gabe," she said softly, drawing his attention to her. "I'm fine."

Dr. Bell turned to the cabinet under the sink on the other side of the room and rummaged through a couple of drawers and found a black brace. She undid the straps and came back to slide it over her foot, securing the straps around her ankle. The added support did make it feel better.

"You'll want to ice your hip and ankle a couple of times a day to help with the swelling. If it's not getting better over the next week, come back and we'll take another look. I expect it will take a couple weeks before it's completely healed.

"Go ahead and get dressed. I'll grab your meds and come back with your paperwork."

The doctor left. Gabe stood and gently pulled the gown off her arms and tossed it to the top of the exam table without a word. He grabbed her sweater and pulled it over her head. At this point, she figured her hair looked like a rat's nest, so she barely ran her fingers through the shoulder-length strands to get them away from her face. Gabe's fingers lightly traced the bruises on her hip and the side of her thigh. The soft contact made everything in her go still.

"You must be in a lot of pain. I'm sorry that son of a bitch did this to you."

Taken off guard by his sincerity, she put her hand on his hard shoulder. "I'll be fine. Thank you for taking care of me."

"I'm not done yet." He snagged the sweatpants and pulled them up her feet and hips.

She read the letters down her leg. Texas A&M University. "I take it these are yours."

"Even we backwoods hicks go to college."

"I never said—never mind. Thanks for letting me borrow them," she finished, not knowing what she'd said to earn that defensive comment.

He stared at her for another long moment. "There's something different about your eyes."

She sucked in a breath and held it. People didn't really notice the subtle difference in her and Lela's eyes. They could fool just about everyone if they styled their hair the same and wore similar clothing. They resembled each other so closely, but if you looked at their eyes and noted the small flecks of yellow in hers, compared to Lela's darker green flecks against the jade, you could tell them apart.

How long did Gabe spend with her sister? She swept her gaze over his dark hair, handsome, rugged face, wide shoulders, and lean body. Not exactly her sister's type. Lela liked cute, shy, geeky guys with a quirky sense of humor.

Ella, on the other hand, liked tall and rugged. Probably why she didn't date much. Hard to find an outdoorsy guy's guy like Gabe in the city. Even now, despite everything she'd been through, she felt the tingle of attraction between them.

Dr. Bell knocked and came back in carrying a prescription bottle. Exhaustion and pain took a toll on Ella's ability to think clearly. She just wanted to sleep and forget this day ever happened.

"Take two of these tonight before bed with something to eat. You'll probably sleep late. Tomorrow, stick to one every four to six hours. This should get you through the next five days. If you need more, come back and we'll evaluate your pain level and how well you're healing."

"That's more than enough. Thank you for everything."

"Stay dry and warm. Get a good night's sleep. Tina will check you out at the front desk."

The doctor handed Gabe the paperwork and left to see her next patient. Ella waited for the doctor to leave before she addressed Gabe again. "Listen, if you'll get my bag from the car, I can pay cash for the bill. I don't want to use my insurance card."

"Why don't you want to use your insurance or credit card, because I know you've probably got ten of them—all of them platinum. Who is after you, Lela, and why?"

She opened her mouth to confess everything, but nothing came out. "It's complicated."

Gabe's brows drew together and his eyes filled with suspicions. "Right. In other words, none of my business. Fine," he snapped, irritation in his voice. "Can you walk?"

"Sure."

She slid from the table and landed on her good foot. She put her right foot down and applied some of her weight. The brace helped considerably, but her ankle still hurt. She took a step and limped, but she'd make it.

"You got it?"

"No problem," she assured him.

He held his hand out to her. She hesitated for a second, but took it. He kept his pace slow, allowed for her limping gait to keep up with him. She stood next to him at the counter. He handed Tina the paperwork, but never stopped holding her hand.

"If y'all want to use your insurance we can knock this down quite a bit."

Scared of being discovered, she grabbed hold of

Gabe's forearm. He looked down at her hand, then back at Tina. "No insurance. I'll cover it." He pulled out his wallet with his other hand and handed over his credit card.

"My money is in the truck."

He gave her a look that said, *Shut up*, so she did.

"You're all set," Tina said after processing the credit card and Gabe signed.

Gabe led her to the door. Before she knew his intention, he scooped her up into his strong arms again. She eyed him. He gave her a lopsided smile, pushed the door open with his back, and took her out into the cold again.

"Can't have you traipsing through the snow with no shoes."

The cold hit her like a slap in the face. She wiggled her freezing toes.

"Snow stopped. That'll be on our side getting back to the house, but the roads will be icy, so we'll have to take it slow."

Gabe set her in the front seat of the truck, not winded in the least from carrying her. He closed the door and went to the back of the horse trailer and disappeared from her sight in the side mirror. She waited several minutes for him to come back and get behind the wheel.

He stared down at the stack of money she'd left on the seat.

"You carry around this kind of cash everywhere you go?"

"Not really. That's what the platinum cards are for." She tried to smile, but it never really touched her lips. "Is your horse okay?"

"He's cranky, but fine. He'll be happier once I get him into a warm stall."

"I'm sorry I delayed you so long. You could have just left me here."

He started the truck, but didn't drive away. Instead, he turned that penetrating gaze on her again and stared at her for a long minute. "I'm not sure I can leave you anywhere."

CHAPTER 5

Phillip sat on the sofa in the living room, staring at the yellow police tape across the closed library doors. He didn't need to be in the room to remember the scene. The image of Lela dead on the floor was burned into his mind. The blood and Lela were gone, but he saw both clear as day.

The wave of fear and fury that swamped him when they discovered Lela's phone beneath her body rushed through him again. The call lasted eleven minutes. Ella heard everything. But how much did she really know? What could she prove? Does she have Lela's so-called evidence? Where the hell was she? Not knowing the answer to those questions twisted his gut.

Damn it, Lela, you've ruined everything.

And now he had to clean up the mess. He would, and everything would be fine again.

Where the hell did Ella go?

The plan only worked if they found Ella and staged her overdose.

The detective set the scene perfectly. Mary discovered Lela's body early this morning and called 911. Officers came to the house. Detective Robbins took over

the investigation and would mold the evidence and reports over the next couple days to fit the scenario Phillip outlined.

Phillip was properly shocked in front of the staff
when he arrived home. Full of grief and disbelief and
outrage that such a terrible thing could happen to his
niece. Yeah, he'd yelled and ranted that whoever did
this to his niece would pay.

When the detective raised questions about a possible
motive with him in front of the staff, he'd hinted about
their upcoming birthday and coming into their inheritance. That Lela had worked so hard for her spot in the
company, while Ella had done the bare minimum to
meet the requirements for her to inherit.

Phillip played his part when he was called down to
the medical examiner's offices to ID the body after he
spent the night with the woman he kept, who catered
to his specific needs. He had an alibi for the time of
the murder. Everything would soon point directly to
Ella.

Mary let Detective Robbins into the penthouse. He
walked into the living room. Phillip waited for him to
take a seat in the chair beside the sofa, so no one over-
heard them. Detective Robbins's smile encouraged him
that the man finally had good news.

"Where is she?" Phillip asked, keeping his voice low,
despite the fact Mary retreated back into the kitchen
past the dining room.

"I don't have her exact location, but she used her
debit and credit card at the airport yesterday."

"Yesterday? What time?"

"Around eleven-thirty."

"After Lela's death and that damn phone call."

"Yes."

"Did you trace her phone?"

"She shut it off."

"Where did she go?"

"I don't know. She used her cards at an ATM to get cash inside the terminal. She must have bought her ticket with cash because the machine she used is past the security checkpoint."

"Check all the airlines. Find her."

"I'm working on it. So far, I haven't found her name on any airline."

"Do you think she used another name?"

"If she did, she'd need a damn good forged ID to buy the ticket and get through security. I'm trying to get the security video from inside the terminal to track her to a gate. If I can do that, I should know which flight she took. For all we know, Ella got on a private plane with some random guy and is half naked on a white sand beach somewhere."

The lust in Detective Robbins's eyes didn't surprise Phillip. Ella and Lela were as beautiful as their mother had been.

"If she left town yesterday and didn't use her name to do it, she must know something, or at least suspect."

"You think Lela told her what she found."

"She didn't just decide to hop on a plane without reason. Did you find out where Lela went over the last few days?"

"If she took a flight the same way Ella did, I have no idea where she went. I'm still checking her credit cards. Ella took priority."

"If you're not up to the task of finding her, I'll get someone else." The implied threat that he could quickly become dispensable registered in the detective's wide eyes, which narrowed with concern.

"I've got this. I'll find her."

"Do it soon before someone else does. Like the press. She isn't exactly anonymous anywhere she goes. Someone is bound to recognize her."

"Maybe we should use that to our advantage. Instead of keeping the details from the press until we find her, let's name her a person of interest in the investigation. I'll bring her in for questioning when someone else tips us off to her location."

"Let's handle this quietly. If you don't find her in the next couple of days and things heat up with the press demanding answers, we'll have no choice." It might make things harder to stage Ella's overdose.

"Go. Find her. Now."

The detective left to do his bidding. Phillip wrapped his hand around the tumbler, his knuckles going white as he squeezed. He'd like to wrap his hand around Ella's neck for disappearing. He took a deep swallow. The bourbon burned its way down his throat to his already sour gut.

The damn girl never did anything that was expected of her.

CHAPTER 6

Ella woke up stiff and disoriented. Her ankle hurt, her side throbbed, but her heart felt broken in a way that would never heal. She gave in to a fresh round of tears. They ran down her cheeks, into her mouth, each one tasting of sorrow and pain. Uncle Phillip murdered Lela. Why? What secrets did Lela discover? What was this really about? Money, the company?

Nothing made sense.

Lela had their father's sense of trends in the marketplace. The ingenuity to take an idea and bring it to life. Ella had been the more practical of the two of them. If you ran the company and wanted to do it well and efficiently, you had to know how all the moving parts worked. She'd started in the mailroom and worked in every department from the ground floor up. Oh, she sat in all the executive meetings, listening to one pompous ass after another talk about productivity and efficiency, but not one of those asshats knew how their mail got to their desk, how the IT department kept the computer systems they relied on up and running, how shipping and receiving kept the inventory in check and the customers happy. The marketing execs had big ideas and grand plans, but they often conflicted with engineering deadlines for having the products ready and shipping's ability to deliver by the dates marketing wanted to beat the competition.

She and Lela had a plan for running the company. They'd sat up night after night talking about how they'd do things. How they'd make their parents proud.

Look at her now. Lela didn't need her tears. She needed Ella to pull herself together, avenge her death, and put their uncle behind bars.

Get up and do something.

She swung her legs over the side of the double bed and sat on the edge, letting her aching head settle and her muscles loosen. She stared down at the Led Zeppelin T-shirt and smiled. Not exactly the Kashmir she was used to wearing, but she appreciated the loan.

She stood, slowly, keeping most of her weight on her left leg, and took a tentative step. It hurt, but she'd get by. Her bag and clothes lay on the chair. Her boots sat on the floor, ruined by the snow. She'd have to get a new pair, something suited for this kind of weather. She didn't know what happened to her coat. Gabe must have hung it somewhere to dry.

Gabe . . .

She'd have to thank him for going above and beyond to take care of her, especially last night when he drove her to his place, afraid to leave her alone. She'd gone quiet on him in the truck and stared out the window, hurting and thinking about Lela. As much as she wanted to get to her ranch and investigate what her sister came here to find, she hadn't wanted to be alone last night. She didn't know Gabe, but he'd proven to be a decent guy, someone who took his responsibilities to heart. He insisted she stay in his guest room. He'd taken the time to change out the sheets on the bed his brother often used and gave her a clean shirt and sweatpants to wear for bed. She pulled them on now, smiling at having to pull the drawstrings tight to keep them on. She bent and rolled up the bottoms so she didn't trip on the too-long length.

She opened the door and hobbled across the hall into the bathroom to relieve her overtaxed bladder. She washed her hands and groaned at her reflection in the mirror. Her hair was a tangled mess, her pale skin made her look sickly, and her eyes were red-rimmed and bloodshot thanks to her near constant crying. She cupped her hands under the cold water and splashed her face a few times to take down the puffiness. Ready to face the day, she went to find Gabe.

Gabe had finished feeding the horses and his other chores for the morning. Lela still hadn't come out of her room. He hoped she finally slept. He heard her crying in the middle of the night and hated to think she hurt and couldn't find any relief in sleep. He'd wanted to go to her and offer what comfort he could, but didn't. He didn't want to freak her out by having a strange man come into her room in the middle of the night, especially after what that fucking asshole Travis did to her.

He sank down on the sofa, snatched the remote, and hit the button. CNN came on, and Lela's picture lit up the screen.

"New York socialite and heiress to the Wolf fortune, Lela Wolf, was found dead early this morning inside the library of her 5th Avenue penthouse apartment."

"What the fuck?" Gabe's heart stopped.

"Investigators left the upscale building moments ago, but they did confirm Lela's body was found around six o'clock this morning by a member of the Wolf staff with a single gunshot wound in the chest. The police have not yet released information about the scene. At this time, it is unclear if Ella Wolf, the victim's twin sister, was home at the time of the shooting.

"Inside sources say Ella is missing. A party girl, known for club hopping and closing down bars, Ella often appeared in the tabloids for much more than her fashion sense. Sources say no one has seen Ella since the night before Lela's murder.

"The Wolf family has a history of tragedy. Stuart Wolf died in a plane crash ten years ago. Rosalind Wolf, grieving for her husband, committed suicide months later. The Wolf twins are due to inherit the family fortune, estimated at four hundred and twenty million, on their upcoming twenty-fifth birthday, leading some to speculate if the inheritance played a role in this crime. So far, police won't say anything about a possible motive for Lela's death."

Gabe heard enough. He got up to confront Ella, but she stood behind him, gaze locked on the TV.

Somewhere inside him, he'd felt there was something different about her. "You lied to me. You're not Lela. You're Ella."

"I never said I was Lela."

"No. You just let me believe you were. Why? Because you killed your sister?"

"I did not kill her," she exploded, planting both hands on his chest and shoving him back.

Everything about her remained defensive, from the stubborn tilt to her head and chin, to her arms folded across her chest. The defiant gleam in her eyes turned to rage when the press shouted questions to the PR rep from Wolf Enterprises, who stepped out of her apartment building along with a detective.

"Mr. Wolf is devastated and grieving," the rep addressed the crowd. "He will not make a statement. Please, allow him the time and space he needs. When it is appropriate and more facts are available, the police or I will provide you with the information. Thank you."

The rage and desolation roiled in her gut, knowing her sister lay on a cold slab and that fucking detective did nothing to stop her uncle from putting her there. He stood before the cameras pretending to care with his pasted-on look of grave conern, and all the while he planned to find her and kill her.

The TV went back to a woman reporter outside her apartment building. "Again, to recap, Lela Wolf was found murdered this morning, a gunshot wound to the chest. Mr. Wolf has not made a statement, and Ella Wolf's whereabouts remain a mystery."

As the reporter talked, paparazzi shots flashed across the screen of Ella dressed in every sought-after designer's clothes with friends entering one nightclub after another over the last five years. She had to admit, her fashion sense stood the test of time. Simple. Classic. Provocative, but not promiscuous. Her mother wouldn't cringe, maybe frown a bit at the lack of coverage.

Gabe didn't look at the TV, but kept his steady gaze on her face. "Did you shoot your sister?" When she didn't say a word, he shouted, "Answer me."

"I already did," she yelled back. She couldn't make him believe her, but she really wanted to. "I'm sorry I didn't correct you when you thought I was Lela.

No one will ever make that mistake again. She's gone." Tears welled in her eyes, but she blinked them away. She needed to stop wallowing in the pain and do something to avenge her sister. "I need to go to the house."

She didn't wait to see if he'd take her. She turned and went back to her room and closed the door. She leaned against the wood and hung her head, numb from the inside out.

"Ella, talk to me. What the hell is going on?"

"I need to go to the ranch. Either you take me, or I'll find another way to get there." She sucked in a ragged breath and bounced off the door, determined to set her grief aside and do what needed to be done.

"We're not done talking about this." No answer. Gabe smacked his flat hand on the door frame. Short of busting down the door to get her to say something, talk to him about her sister's murder, he was at a complete loss.

Did Ella kill her? He didn't know. Not for sure. Right now, he'd give her the benefit of the doubt, because the grief he saw in her eyes was real. He hoped those tears, and the ones he heard her shed in the night, weren't hiding her guilt.

He walked into the kitchen and grabbed her pill bottle, thinking about the photos of Ella on the news and the reports about her. She lived her life on the edge, drinking, doing drugs, partying until all hours. He tried to put that together with the woman in his spare room, but couldn't make it quite fit. The woman he met last night and this morning seemed quiet, reserved, strong to endure all she had since yesterday. Not at all like the party girl they showed on TV. Strange. Intriguing.

With his mind full of questions, he waited for Ella

to change clothes. He didn't know why she wanted to go to the house, but he'd take her because it seemed important.

The TV weatherman rattled on about a storm in the Midwest. He found the remote and shut the TV off. He'd like to find out more about what happened—and about Ella and Lela.

"I'm ready." Her soft voice snapped him out of his thoughts.

"Ella, are you sure you're up to this? Don't take this the wrong way, but you look wrecked. The house will still be there after you get some rest. It's best if you stay off that ankle for a few days. Sit down. Let's talk."

"I don't have time to talk. I need to go there."

"Why? What does this have to do with Lela's murder?"

"I don't know, but I'm going to find out."

Even more confused, he wanted to push, but didn't. "Fine." He relented. For now.

She limped, heavily favoring her right foot, toward the front door. Those ankle boots didn't help in the least. The black slacks hugged the curve of her hips and her toned thighs. Some part of him had paid close attention to every line and curve when he helped her last night. In the moment, he tried to focus on the task, getting her warm and making sure she didn't have any major injuries. Last night, when his need for sleep overpowered his worry for her, he dreamed of those legs and that nothing of a swatch of lace covering her hips and sweet bottom. He stared at it now and pictured those lace panties. The matching bra had left nothing to the imagination. Her nipples stood out a soft pink against the black lace over sheer fabric. In his dream, she wasn't hurt at all, but wrapped around him, his tongue tracing the top of her breast over that fancy concoction.

Stop. She's your guest, not a fantasy come to life. So buck up and get your mind out of her pants.

She opened the front door and the blast of cold made her take a step back.

"I forgot your coat. Hold on."

He rushed into the laundry room off the back of the kitchen and grabbed her coat. "I left it on the warm dryer this morning when I washed your pants and sweater."

Ella stared down at her pants, then back at him. "Where is my sweater?"

"I owe you a new one," he admitted. He hadn't bothered to look at the tag until after it went through the washer and dryer and came out four sizes smaller. "We don't do much dry cleaning in these parts."

Her pretty mouth quirked in a rare glimpse of humor. "Don't worry about it."

"I imagine it was really expensive."

"No need to imagine. It was, but it's only clothes. You went above and beyond taking care of me last night. I appreciate it."

"I owe you a sweater."

"All I want is a ride home."

"Fine, but then we're going to have a serious talk." He held the coat up and she put her arms through the sleeves. He adjusted it on her shoulders and led the way to the door, holding it open for her to exit.

She stopped in the yard and stared at the two gray horses in the pasture. They snuggled close to each other to keep warm in the crisp morning air. Their breath came out in wispy clouds. Her eyes went soft and filled with unshed tears.

She cleared her throat and whispered, "We used to ride together when we came here. We loved the ranch. The horses. The mountains and valleys. In New York, I still rode, but she stopped. It reminded her too much of our time here with our parents."

"You rode to remember them, your sister, and everything you had here."

"We thought this place was magical. Our father spent time with us here like he couldn't in New York. Not with all the demands on him for the company and other social obligations. Here, our parents took the time to be with us. It was special."

"Who took care of you after they died?"

"Uncle Phillip is our guardian, but really, we took care of each other. We're identical twins. She is me. And I am her."

"Like your names. Same letters rearranged, but still the same."

She nodded and gave him a half smile to acknowledge how much she appreciated he got it in some small way.

"Sounds like you two were very close."

"She was my best friend. My other half. The same as me, yet different in such lovely and beautiful ways. When I looked at her, I saw all that I am and so much more that was just her. She made me believe I could be all those extra things she was, because if she could be that, so could I because we are the same."

Ella turned her back on the horses and opened the truck door, sliding inside and closing it again. She sat quietly in the car, staring straight ahead, utter despair etched on her delicate features.

Stunned by the depth of her words about her sister and how close they were to each other, he couldn't imagine Ella ever hurting Lela.

He didn't move for a moment, but stared at the horses and thought of his brothers and all the good times they'd had together as kids and now.

He walked back to his truck, got behind the wheel, started the engine, but didn't drive away. Instead, he laid his hand over hers in her lap and gave it a squeeze to let her know he understood, at least in some part, how she felt. The sigh she let out echoed through him. He didn't expect her to do anything, but she turned her hand and linked her fingers with his and squeezed, holding on.

CHAPTER 7

Ella stared out the windshield at the massive wood and stone custom home her mother designed and her father built for his beloved wife. They'd created a retreat for their family, not a lavish estate for impressing guests and business associates. Nothing like their Vail property.

Nothing had changed, except the trees looked bigger, more mature. No flowers this time of year, but in the spring the gardens would be beautiful in her mother's favorite colors. Blue camas, white asters, pink wild hollyhock, and bright yellow prairie coneflowers. The abundance of plants and flowers would bloom in a sea of color against the backdrop of the rocks and native grasses in the fields.

"Ella? Do you want to go inside?"

The feel of Gabe's hand in hers reassured her in a way she didn't want to examine too deeply. Not now, when her emotions were so raw. His comfort made it that much easier to think of the past and remember her and Lela playing in the front yard, running across the wide expanse of grass, chasing each other. A flood of happy memories rushed over her. She welcomed them

and the sense of happiness and family they brought.
She tried to hold on to that feeling and not get swept
away by the paralyzing realization they were gone, her
uncle wanted her dead, and she didn't know why.

Time for answers.

To thank Gabe for his support and understanding,
she raised their joined hands and kissed the back of
his. His eyes went wide with surprise. He reached up
with his free hand and traced the side of her face. She
couldn't help leaning into the whisper-soft caress. His
heated gaze swept down the length of her, settling back
on their joined hands. She didn't acknowledge the look,
but understood exactly what it meant. He found her at-
tractive. Lots of men did, but she long ago stopped falling for guys who looked at her that way just because
she wanted attention. With her twenty-fifth birthday
looming and the responsibilities it would bring, she'd
spent the last couple of years reevaluating her priorities
and goals. She'd worked hard to catch up to Lela, to be
the partner her sister deserved. Now, she'd have to do
it on her own. The task seemed daunting, especially if
she couldn't unravel the riddle of Lela and their uncle.

She regretted letting go of Gabe, but she did it to face
what came next on her own. She needed to be strong
for her sister's memory. She pulled Lela's purse from
her tote and rummaged through the contents for the set
of keys she discovered earlier. Determined to see this
through, she exited the truck and walked straight up
the snow-covered flagstone walkway and steps to the
front door. She inserted the key and stepped into her
past, halting in the foyer, staring at—nothing.

The house was empty. All the furniture, paintings,
rugs, knickknacks were gone. A beep sounded behind

her. She turned to punch in the alarm code, but Gabe did it for her.

Eyes narrowed, she glared. "Why do you know the alarm code?"

"I tried to tell Lela the other day. I met the movers and oversaw them clearing out the house."

"Where did they take everything?"

"Storage units in Crystal Creek."

She took a step toward him, angry he'd kept this from her. She wondered what else he knew and if he'd sold her out to her uncle. She glanced out the door, expecting a dark sedan to rush down the driveway, men spilling out to take her back to New York. Fear squeezed her lungs and made her heart stop.

"Do you work for my uncle?"

"No."

"Did he send you here to find me?" She hated that her voice trembled.

"I found you on the side of the road nearly frozen to death. I barely know the man."

"But you do know him."

"I've spoken to him over the phone a couple of times."

"Why?"

"To close the deal for the sale of the ranch."

"Are you a real estate agent?" That didn't really compute with all she knew about him. He lived on a ranch, loved his horses and treated them like children if the way he pet and fawned over Sully last night when he pulled him out of the trailer and put him into a corral was any indication. She may have been out of it, but she recognized a fellow horse lover. He kept a neat and tidy home, despite the sparse furnishings. Still, she liked the homey feel he'd created with pictures of his family on the mantel along with his belt buckles and rodeo trophies.

"No, I bought this place."

"You own my house?"

"Yes. Well, not yet."

"Which is it?"

"The deal closes on March twelfth."

Surprised, she asked, "Who signed the deal?"

"What do you mean?"

"Who signed for the Wolf family?"

"Phillip Wolf. Why?"

"That greedy bastard. How much?"

"For the house and land?"

"Yes. How much?"

"One and a half million. I put up seven hundred and fifty thousand cash and financed the other half."

She laughed, and the bitter sound echoed through the empty rooms. Pissed off and feeling surly, she snapped, "This is my house. It is not for sale."

"I have the papers. This will be my house in a few weeks."

"No, it won't."

Gabe closed the distance between them and stared down at her. She had to tilt her head way back to keep eye contact. A mere few inches separated them. His heat wrapped around her in the cold house.

"The money is sitting in the escrow account and will be paid out on March twelfth and this house and land will be mine."

"No, it won't. Unless I'm dead."

Gabe took a step back at that ominous reply.

Yes, now she saw it. Her uncle planned her and

Lela's death long before what happened to her sister. If she could think past her fear, grief, and anger, maybe she could figure all this out.

She took a calming breath to ward off the rage boiling in her gut. Gabe deserved an explanation. She hoped what little she knew explained well enough.

"When did my uncle put the house up for sale?"

"He didn't. Not really. I own the small piece of property next door as you know. I called him two months ago and asked if I could lease part of your land to run some cattle. We got to talking and he asked if I'd be interested in buying this place.

"Ella, what is going on? I see your sister here one day, she's murdered, you show up the next, and now you've got to come here. You own this place, but you don't know about the sale."

"There is no sale."

"Unless you're dead. Explain that. Explain everything you aren't saying to me."

"I can't. I thought it was here, but it's not. Everything is gone."

"It's not gone. Just packed away. Tell me what you're looking for and I'll get it for you."

She tilted her head and eyed him. "What do you mean?"

"I inventoried the entire house and oversaw the packing and moving. Everything is in storage in numbered and marked boxes. If you tell me what you're looking for, I can check the list, find the box, and get it for you."

"Did you pack up the sculpture that hung on the wall over there? My father built the intricate puzzle. I want it."

"Is that what that was? I wondered. It's in storage."

"I also want the painting that hung over the mantel."

She pointed to the river rock fireplace that went from floor to twenty-foot ceiling, with glass windows on both sides, in the great room.

"There wasn't a painting."

"Five by six foot. A field of daisies with two little girls running in white dresses, their arms outstretched to touch the flowers, their hair flying in the breeze."

"You and your sister."

"My mother painted it. I want it."

"Ella, there were no painting on the walls, just family photos."

"A Rembrandt hung in my father's office. A Manet floral in my mother's dressing room. Albert Bierstadt landscapes, probably ten of them, hung all over the house."

"His landscapes sell for tens of thousands of dollars."

"Try millions. But they weren't here, were they?"

"No. Ella, I swear to you, I didn't take them."

"I never said you did."

"Is that why you and Lela came here? The paintings?"

"I . . . I don't know." She didn't know what Lela found at the house. Was that what she discovered her uncle doing? Illegally selling paintings from their properties? Selling their properties without their signature? How many of the other houses had he ransacked? Did she have to check the Vail house? The ones in Hawaii, Paris, Milan, and the New York estate in the country where she kept her horses? Where her mother chose death over her daughters. Oh, and the house in San Francisco where he preferred to spend his holidays— away from them.

She and Lela had worked so diligently to learn the

business and earn their degrees, they'd ignored their personal assets, except to verify the bills were paid as expected by the accountants. She and Lela learned one very valuable lesson from their father: Always sign the checks. Don't trust others to handle the money. Pay them for their advice and expertise, but never give them signing authority. Which might explain why her uncle stole the paintings for easy cash. He could sell them on the black market without the provenance papers to collectors who cared less about those kinds of things and more about possessing the great works of art. Could this have been what he was hiding? Or was it just the tip of the iceberg?

"Ella." Gabe called her name to pull her out of her thoughts. "And the sale that won't take place unless you're dead, what about that?"

"I really hate talking about my death."

"I can imagine, especially since your sister's been murdered, but I need to know what you mean. My money and my life are tied up in this sale."

"There is no sale."

"I bought and paid for this house and property. The money is in escrow."

"Are you sure about that?" She hated to think her uncle might have cheated this good man out of his money.

Gabe pulled his cell phone from his pocket. She touched his hand to stop him from dialing. "If the money isn't there, tell them you'll handle the matter personally. You're in contact with Phillip, and you'll settle the matter with him directly. I will pay you back."

"If my money isn't sitting in that account, I own this place, and Phillip can go screw himself."

"You don't own this place because he can't sell it without my signature."

"He's your guardian and trustee over the estate. He told me."

"My parents made him guardian, but two lawyers are the trustees, and me or my sister are required to sign off on all checks and transactions. Without our signatures, nothing is legal. We own everything. Not Uncle Phillip. He has no power over the estate, or my sister and me."

"Unless you're dead."

"Yes." To distract him from asking anything more, she nodded to his phone. "Make your call."

It didn't take Gabe more than a minute to contact the real estate office and have them verify the escrow account closed out the day after the money cleared the bank. All his money gone. Gabe held his phone in a death grip, pressing his fist to his forehead and squeezing his eyes shut, trying to think and hold back the string of curse words running through his head.

"Fuck me!"

"Yes. He did. But I'll make it right."

"I don't want you to make it right, I want to tear his head off."

"I'm happy to let you, but first I need to see the papers he signed."

"They're at my place. The real estate agent said everything was in order. The Wolf lawyers completed the papers. How could they do that if they require your signature?"

"I don't know. My guess is that he paid them off with the money he got from selling the artwork."

"I verified the title changes into my name, but didn't

really bother to look who signed off on everything. Why would I? The house is held under the name of the trust, not in your and Lela's names directly."

"Right, I didn't think of that."

"And you're sure the sale can't go through? He has the money."

"Gabe," she said at length. "You know it can't go through. Somewhere in that bright mind of yours you thought something like this might happen, because a decent guy like you can't possibly believe my uncle sold you this house and property for one-point-five million when it's worth at least four million."

"He never meant to sell this place to me. He only wanted to steal the money."

"I'm not so sure about that."

"Why?"

"Because of the date he wanted the sale to clear."

"What about it?"

"It's my birthday."

"March twelfth."

"Yes. I turn twenty-five and everything my parents left to me is mine. No strings attached. No more restrictions. I take control of the company and all the assets."

"Unless you're dead, and he gets it all."

"He killed Lela. If you'd left me to die last night, you could have solved my uncle's problem and yours."

CHAPTER 8

"**N**o one is going to kill you." The thought turned Gabe's stomach. Her uncle wanted her dead. The bastard killed Lela, and based on the news this morning, Phillip had already subtly pointed the finger at Ella. Gabe might not want to get close to her, but he had to keep her safe. He couldn't live with himself if something happened to her. Not after all she'd been through.

This was fucked up. The money worried him. Hell, it pissed him off. All his plans just went down the drain. He had every dime sunk in this place and buying the livestock. How was he going to pay back the loan? Where the hell was he going to put another four hundred head of cattle? They'd never fit on his tiny spread. He needed the Wolf land, or he'd simply have to resell them and eat the loss.

All that money . . . His stomach soured and tightened, threatening to make him ill.

Every time he was on the verge of having everything, it all fell apart. The scale had simply changed. Before, he'd bought his small property for his fiancée, to show her he could provide for her. It was to be the start of their new life together, but it turned out to be the end. This time, he'd worked his ass off, reached higher, put everything he had into the impressive Wolf spread, and still he came up empty. Now, he might not even be able to hold on to his place.

"Will you please take me to get my bag from that asshole Travis?"

Pulled from his dark thoughts and dwindling bank account, he refocused on the woman in front of him who needed his help. "Then what? You'll go back to New York and accuse your uncle of murder and theft of the paintings?"

"I don't have a way to prove either yet, and he has God knows how many officials in his pocket. You saw the news, they are ready to pin the murder on me. But this gives me a place to start. First, I need to find the paperwork on the paintings. It's probably in my father's papers."

"Maybe that's what Lela found, too. She left the files all over your father's office. Looked like she spent a long time going through them."

"Maybe. Did she say anything to you about the property sale?"

"Based on the way she acted, I don't think she knew about it. She was in a hurry to leave."

"Maybe she found something else in the files."

"More embezzlement and fraud perhaps?"

She frowned and shrugged. "Perhaps." She turned and hobbled out the door, her gaze straight ahead. She never looked at the massive rooms. The house might be empty, but she'd filled it with her grief. He felt it like a living thing inside these walls.

He went after her, stopping in the open front door to stare at her beautiful upturned face. Tears tracked down her cheeks and onto her neck. Eyes closed, her face soft and pale. Her light brown hair glistened with gold highlights in the bright sun. Her arms hung heavy at her sides. She favored her right foot and leaned a bit, but none of that held his attention as much as the weight of utter, desperate loneliness that hung on her.

His feet moved before he consciously knew what he was doing. Instinct carried him to her. Something else made him wrap his arms around her and pull her close to his chest. He didn't think too hard about what made him want to protect and comfort her. Instead, he gave in to that need and held her and pressed his cheek to her soft hair and stood with her in the sun until her tears dried.

She gathered herself with a deep breath. Her hands slid up his side to his chest. She pushed back, but he held her close with his fingers locked at the small of her back. Her face turned up to him and her eyes finally opened again. The same shade of green he remembered from the other day when he met Lela, but just enough different to get his attention last night. Meeting Ella was different. Lela's beauty drew him, but something even more profound in Ella touched something inside him.

He'd like to see her smile. Watch the way something happy or humorous changed her eyes, brightened and lightened them, stealing away the darkness clouding them. He wondered what made her laugh. He'd love to hear it. Somehow he knew it would take away the heaviness in his chest.

"I'm sorry about your sister and your uncle and . . . everything."

Her eyes went soft with more sadness. "I'm sorry my uncle screwed you. I'll make it right. I promise."

That was the only thing keeping him off a plane and flying to New York to kill Phillip himself. Whatever was going on in the Wolf family, he needed to help Ella take her uncle down and see her take her place at the head of Wolf Enterprises. If her uncle didn't want her there, that's exactly where he wanted to put her and piss off Phillip. It'd certainly give the guy something to think about behind bars.

He stared off into the distance, the land that spread before him and might have been his.

"This place is everything you dreamed of for your life and future." She said his thoughts out loud. She stared back at the house. "This is my past. There is nothing here but memories. Everyone I ever loved is dead. The house is as empty as my heart."

He rubbed his hand up and down her back. She leaned into him, laying her head on his chest and sighing.

"What are you going to do now?" he asked.

She stepped out of his arms. He let her go because he couldn't hold on to what wasn't his. The ranch. The house. Her.

He'd been an unwilling and unwitting participant in her uncle's scheme. He'd have benefited from her death.

Knowing that now made him sick and tarnished Wolf Ranch in a way he'd never thought possible. Her father had chosen well when he picked this piece of land. He'd built an amazing home and filled it with family and love. He'd created an empire, but his greatest achievement stood before him, a mass of despair and determination all rolled into one. He had no doubt she'd take her uncle down.

"My plans are complicated, but they end with Uncle Phillip in jail."

"What can I do to help?"

"This is my fight. I'll take care of it."

"Not on your own, sweetheart. I've got a stake in this to protect too. Besides, you don't have a car, or a change of clothes."

That earned him a short-lived smile. "I guess you're stuck with me a while longer."

"At least until we can get the proof you need against your uncle. I won't let that bastard get away with hurting you."

"Yeah. I've got to find concrete evidence against him before I go to the feds."

"Then let's get started. I'll follow up on the land deal. You track down the paintings. I can't really help you with that."

He opened the truck door and held it for her. He took her arm when she stepped up on the running board, and helped her into the seat. Settled, she gave him another of those elusive smiles. He wondered if she tried to hide her awareness of him this close as much as he tried to hide it from her. The last thing he needed was to fall for a woman who was completely out of his league, had no intention of staying in Montana, and grieved the loss of her sister with every breath she took.

"Ready?" she asked.

"Let's pay Travis a visit and get your stuff back."

"Why does that sound more like a threat than a plan?"

"You're getting to know me better by the minute."

"I'm liking you more by the minute."

This time, he smiled and let out a short laugh. Because he liked her, too, he gave her hand a squeeze to let her know he understood how she felt about Travis and wanting retribution for what he put her through last night.

She pulled at him, and he didn't know if he wanted to get closer when he'd already been burned by one member of her family. He didn't know if he trusted her to do the right thing or not. In the end, even if he got his money, he'd lost the one thing he'd wanted more than anything. A chance to live his life the way he wanted on the land he'd hoped to make his. He'd had everything worked out in his mind. Well, the best-laid plans . . .

Time to move on and help Ella clean up the mess.

Travis better not piss him off.

CHAPTER 9

Gabe didn't turn on any music on the ride over to Travis's place. Ella's thoughts grew too noisy, so she focused on the scenery. Snow-dusted plains gave way to towering mountains. She loved the expanse of it, almost as much as the feel of Gabe's hand holding hers. As before, he took it when she went quiet on him. She didn't mean to close him out, it just happened when her mind drifted to her sister. She wondered what her uncle was doing right this minute, probably playacting for the cameras while plotting her demise.

The smell hit her first. The putrid scent of cows and manure. She held up her hand to cover her nose and mouth, but ended up with the back of Gabe's hand to her face. "Oh. My. God."

"It's something, all right." Gabe scrunched his nose.

"You have got to be kidding me."

"Wait until we round the bend. You won't believe your eyes."

"How do you stand the stench?"

"I don't run my ranch this way." Gabe turned the corner and she understood.

Cows stood clustered together in large pens, barely

enough room to move. Manure and urine soaked the ground. Hay and feed were piled in the corner of the pens, not in feed troughs to keep the animals from stepping on and soiling their food.

"This is inhumane."

"Tell me about it. Travis has enough land to run the cattle, let them graze at will and feed them in the troughs out in the pastures, but he's too lazy and greedy to do it right. He's lost half his cowhands because of this crap. Some of the guys have worked this ranch for years, but after Travis's father died a year ago, this place has gone to shit."

"Literally," Ella finished for him. "This place is depressing. Look at that." Ella pointed out the window to one of the pens. "That cow is dead. Has been for a few days by the looks of it and no one has taken it out of there and buried it."

"That's not the worst of it. Don't turn around. One of the babies in that pen behind you got trampled."

Ella turned to look, but Gabe touched her face and turned it away.

"Just knowing is more than enough. You don't need to see it, too."

"Gabe, this isn't right."

"No. It's not. These are some of the purest bred cattle in the country. Prime beef. Black Angus. Worth a lot of money. Travis treats them like they're nothing."

"The same way he treated me last night when he dumped me in the snow. He's going to regret that."

"Oh, he'll pay," Gabe said, pulling the truck into the drive behind Travis's old truck. They got out and rounded the hood to meet in the middle.

Travis stepped out of the nearby barn with a shotgun

in his hand pointed at the truck. "Why the fuck did you bring her 'round here?"

Gabe took her hand and held it tight. Travis took three quick, menacing steps closer. Gabe stepped in front and blocked her from Travis.

"Put that fucking gun down before you accidentally shoot yourself, pal."

"I'll pump you full of holes for trespassing. Now, I'll ask you again, why did you bring that bitch here?"

Gabe turned and whispered over his shoulder, "He doesn't know who you are?"

She shook her head. "No one can know. If it gets back to my uncle that I'm here, he'll send someone after me."

"This is a complicated mess, you know that?"

"Thanks for summing it up."

Gabe frowned but turned back to face off with the gun-toting asshole.

"Travis, all I want is her suitcase. Give me her belongings, and we'll be on our way."

"Get off my land."

Ella couldn't see Travis while standing behind Gabe, so she stared off to the side at the sad cows, their black hides crusted with dirt. She raked her gaze over their lean bodies, looking for other signs of abuse and neglect. They were dirty and probably hungry, but she tried to tell herself it wasn't as bad as it seemed. Still, something about the animals nagged at her. She pulled her hand free from Gabe's and limped toward the fence line.

Gabe caught her by the arm. "Where are you going? The muck is calf-deep."

"I need to see something."

"Stop right there," Travis shouted, swinging the gun at her.

"I wouldn't do that if I were you." Gabe spoke with controlled calm, but something in his voice hinted at iron.

Travis hesitated a moment before lowering the shotgun with a snort.

Ella hiked her good foot on the rail and examined the cows more closely. The smell really couldn't be described, though the longer she lingered in this god-awful place, the less the stench overwhelmed her.

"What are you looking for?" Gabe called, exasperation plain in his voice. "Come down from there before you hurt yourself more."

Angry beyond words, Ella forgot about her sprained ankle and jumped down. She yelped in pain, took two steps, and found herself grabbed by the arms, hauled up and over the worst of the muck, and landed inches from Gabe. How did he move so fast? The flash of intensity in his honey brown eyes only increased her dizziness. She swallowed hard and refocused on the dirtbag three yards away.

"Get off my land," Travis bellowed.

"Shut the hell up," she snapped. She rose on her good foot on tiptoe and leaned in close to Gabe's ear. He held her hips to steady her. She braced herself against him with her hands on his wide shoulders, without considering how natural it was to hold him and be held by him. Good God, he smelled good, like leather and soap and something earthy and uniquely Gabe. "Those cows have the Wolf Ranch logo."

"It's your brand. One that commands a high price," he whispered back.

"It did, but if these animals aren't treated better, the reputation will be ruined."

Gabe held her away and frowned, glaring at her and then resting his gaze on the sad animals.

"My first and last priority is their care and well-being. I needed to be sure they're mine, so I can do something about it."

"Travis's father ran this ranch, and ran it well, up until his death. The animals were treated right, and your family made a lot of money off these animals."

"Enough said. Thank you." She tried to pull away, but he held her close. Her gaze locked with his. They stared at each other, that strange awareness they both didn't acknowledge existed pulling at her and him. "What?"

"How much pain are you in?"

"Not enough to stop me from putting ol' Travis in his place."

"You two need to get a room," Travis called, still pacing erratically. His impatience making him even more cranky. "What the hell do you want with me?"

"I'm fine," she said to Gabe, stepping out of his embrace and ignoring the look that said, *Yeah, right.*

She pivoted around, set her hands on her hips, and stared Travis down. "I want you to use that shriveled, beer-soaked brain of yours for something other than directing your hand to scratch your hairy ass."

Gabe let out a full belly laugh, which made it impossible to hide her own smile.

"No one disrespects me on my own land."

"You're doing a fine job of that all on your own. This ranch is a disgrace."

Travis made a sound like an angry bull. "I'll wrap

my hand around your scrawny neck and choke the life out of you."

"You're not the only one who wants me dead, so get in line. In fact," she walked right up to him and yanked the shotgun out of his hands, "put that down before you hurt someone. I swear to God, five-year-olds have more common sense than you."

"Hey, give that back."

She expertly emptied the spent rounds from the chambers, slammed the gun back together, turned, and shoved the gun stock into Travis's nuts. Travis dropped to his knees, both hands on his crotch.

"You didn't even reload after you shot the thing last. Idiot."

"Hey, city girl, give me that." Gabe took the gun from her, but she continued to stare down Travis. "Where'd you learn to do that?"

"Dad taught us how to handle guns on the ranch. He had a beautiful Winchester."

"It's in the inventory."

"A girl out on the town in the big city needs to be able to protect herself. They teach all kinds of martial arts and kickboxing classes at the gym. Guys jump at the chance to roll around on the mats with a girl." She narrowed her gaze on Travis. "They call me Ball-buster."

Gabe's hand clamped onto her shoulders and he gave her a friendly squeeze. "You're more than meets the eye, city girl."

"You ain't seen nothing yet."

"I'm curious about the rest."

That was a definite innuendo. In other circumstances, she wouldn't mind getting an up-close look at the tall, well-built rancher. She appreciated his good-natured attitude and the way he defused a situation. Those broad shoulders and contoured biceps sweetened the deal. Something to think about later. Well, she couldn't stop thinking about him, but now was not the time, and she refocused.

Travis kicked a rock across the yard, looking more nervous than pissed.

He thought her some low lackey like him, working for the company, here to check on Wolf Ranch for the family. He'd been nervous when they met that she'd come to look into something more. He didn't want anyone to see this place and the sorry state of this ranch and the cattle. He wouldn't report her to anyone in the company. He couldn't. Not without alerting them to a problem here, so she went with her gut and tried to set things right for now, until she could implement a permanent solution.

"Now, listen here, Travis. Maybe I didn't make myself clear last night. I work for Wolf Enterprises. Those are Wolf cattle. You will remove your head from your ass and move those cattle out of those damn pens and transfer them to the pastureland for them to graze and roam. You will feed and water them the proper way and dispose of the dead carcasses immediately."

She turned to Gabe. "Am I missing anything?" Before he answered, she turned back to Travis. "Oh, quarantine any sick animals away from the herd. Call the vet to check on them and get them well. I think that's all. You know your job. Do it."

"You're not the boss of me. You can't come in here and order me around like this."

"You will do as I say or face the consequences a hell

of a lot sooner than what's coming down the road. You got it?"

"Who the hell are you?"

"The woman you dumped on her ass in the snow in the middle of nowhere. The biggest mistake you ever made in your miserable good-for-nothing life."

"I'll call the company and get you fired. No one likes a pushy bitch."

"Call Jim Harrison. I dare you."

"How did you know . . ."

"I know a hell of a lot more than you. You underestimate women at your own peril. Let's go, Gabe, I'm done here."

She limped over to Travis's truck.

"What the hell do you think you're doing now?" The words came out whiny, like a kid who didn't get his way.

"Getting my bag. Lord knows, you're too lazy to have even taken it out of your truck."

Sure enough, her sister's bag sat on the floor of the passenger side. She grabbed the bag and hauled it out. Travis lunged, grasped her shoulder, and spun her around. She twisted her ankle and yelped out in pain, collapsing against the truck door.

Gabe grabbed Travis by the back of his jacket. Travis turned and caught a right hook in the jaw and fell backward and landed on his ass in the dirt.

"Bowden, this is none of your concern," Travis yelled, holding the side of his face.

Gabe loomed over Travis, hands fisted at his sides and fury in his eyes. "You made it my concern when you dumped her on that road, asshole. You left her out there to die. What is wrong with you?"

"She deserved it."

"Why? Because she's got better taste than to find anything appealing about you. Seems to me, her instincts were dead-on."

"You want her, keep her." Travis spat, climbing to his feet. "She's not worth the trouble."

"She's not yours to give away, you idiot. But thanks, I will keep her." Gabe scooped her right off her feet and carried her to his truck. She pulled the door open and he set her inside the cab. "Stay put."

Gabe took her bag and carried it to the truck, setting it in the bed and opening the driver's door. He didn't get in, but stared at Travis. "Don't make things worse for yourself. Do what she asked. Take care of these animals, or I'm coming back to take care of you."

Gabe slid behind the wheel, started the truck, and turned them around. He sped down the dirt road and took the right onto the main road back to his place.

"How'd you know Travis's contact at Wolf?"

"Jim is the head of Western Operations. It was a good guess he'd oversee anyone responsible for the cattle business. I'll look into it, and Travis will get what's coming to him."

"The company isn't exactly known for cattle."

She stretched out her leg and tried to adjust her foot to take the pressure off her ankle. "No. Not really. Which is why I don't remember seeing anything about the cattle."

"Not exactly up your alley, city girl."

"No. It's not. Small appliances make up the major portion of the company. Dad dabbled in other ventures. Farm equipment. Manufacturing machines. He pretty much had his hand in a lot of mechanical things. He liked to tinker."

"Like the puzzle sculpture."

"Exactly. Mechanics was his kind of fun. Lela and I recently diversified the business and added a botanical cosmetics line."

"I don't know anything about makeup." Gabe shook his head. "I do know you guys make a killer combine and rototiller."

"Do you own one of ours?"

"I wish. I guess I won't need either, or the field topper for that matter. My small tractor is enough for my property. I don't have the Wolf land."

"Yes, I guess it would take a great deal of equipment to run cattle on the ranch again."

Gabe nodded and got this far-off look on his face, thinking about all he'd lost. All the dreams her uncle made him believe in.

"I'm sorry, Gabe. I'll make it right."

He took her hand the way he seemed to do so easily and squeezed her fingers. "Not your fault, city girl. I should have seen the lie. No deal that good can be true."

"I was thinking the same thing about you."

"What?"

"You can't be real. No guys are as nice as you are and look like that." She held out her hand and swept it up and down to indicate his strong, toned frame and that gorgeous, rugged face. She loved the way he cocked back one side of his mouth and laughed under his breath, dismissing her words. He had to know women drooled over him, but he didn't use his looks to his advantage. Comfortably easy with who he was, he didn't need to do anything but be himself to disarm strangers and make them feel relaxed with him.

"I'm far from perfect, honey. Ask my brothers."

She sighed, and the grief threatened to drag her under when she thought of her sister and what she'd say about Ella riding around with a virtual stranger, confronting gun-toting wannabe cowboys, and trying to take down their uncle by herself.

"How many do you have?"

"Three."

"Wow. No sisters?"

"Just us boys."

"I always wanted a brother."

"I imagine having an identical twin was a lot of fun. You two must have spent your schooldays fooling your friends and teachers, making them think you were the other one, like you did with me."

"All the time, but not anymore." She leaned her head against the side window and stared off into space.

"I'm sorry. You must miss her a lot."

"More than my heart can take." She sucked back the tears and held tight to Gabe's strong hand. They pulled into the yard, and Gabe stopped the truck in front of the house. She stared at the simple wood two-bedroom structure. Dark brown, cream trim, a small covered deck off the front. She liked the stone path. The snow from the night before clung to the ground and tops of bare branches on the trees and plants. The roof held a thick coating, making the house seem cozy and inviting beneath the white blanket. "How did I end up staying with you?"

"Because when you're left on your own in Montana, you piss off cowboys, who dump you on your ass in the snow, you pull shotguns from the same idiot cowboy with no regard for getting shot, and though you haven't

said it, sticking with me is a hell of lot safer than confronting your murderous uncle."

"I see your point," she said, hiding a smile.

"You really scared the hell out of me, pulling that
gun from Travis like that."

"He didn't have his finger on the trigger. He's all
bluster."

"Yeah, well, next time someone's got a gun on you,
do me a favor, don't rush them and grab it."

"What would you have me do, stand there and get
shot?"

"Stay away from people with guns," he ordered, getting disgruntled.

"Is that possible in Montana?" she asked, checking
out the gun rack behind her that held two rifles.

"Smart-ass."

"Top of my class," she teased back.

"Not you, party girl. You probably cut more classes
than you attended."

That sparked her anger. For whatever reason, she
wanted him to see her, not the made-up person on TV
and in the papers. "Right. You hear the gossip, see
a bunch of pictures of me out with friends, and you
think you know me? I'm just some party girl. Another
spoiled rich girl, wasting my life on booze and drugs.
No dreams. No aspirations. Nothing I want to do with
my life. Not a care in the world, because I only care
about myself, spending my dead parents' money, and
having fun. Right? That's the woman you saw on TV
this morning. The woman the whole world thinks they
know."

"Hold it right there, city—"

Wound up, she let her anger reign. "Well, let me tell

you something. You don't know me. You don't know anything, except for the hundreds of seconds captured by the camera flash out of the billions of seconds they didn't capture or care about.

"You think I'm just the party girl out for a good time and a wild fuck?" She leaned up and kissed him hard. With cold and impersonal calculation she took the kiss deeper. She didn't expect the connection they'd both tried to ignore until now to flare and race through her system, making her want to draw even closer to the fire.

He tore his mouth from hers, grabbed her by the shoulders, and set her back, but didn't release her. "I am more than willing to kiss you senseless when the time is right, but not like this. Don't kiss me like that, just to prove a point. It's not you."

The kiss forgotten, her hurt and anger flashed again. Better to be angry than engulfed in her sadness. "How the hell would you know? You don't know who I am. You don't know anything. You didn't watch your sister die right before your eyes and stand there helpless to do anything. You didn't run away and leave your other half lying dead and bloody on the floor while your uncle plotted your death with a cop who should have protected an innocent woman.

"So don't act like you know. You don't know. No one knows." The tears filled her eyes and spilled over and down her cheeks.

Damn it to hell, this woman had been to the devil and back. "You never said you were there when he killed your sister." He held her shoulders and made her look at him. "Does he know you're here? You asked if he sent me to find you. Is he coming for you?"

"No." She tried to pull away, but he held firm. "I paid cash for the ticket and used a fake ID."

Relieved beyond measure, he wrapped his arms around her, and pressed his cheek to the top of her hair. If her uncle didn't know where to find her, they still had time to sort this out. He hoped.

CHAPTER 10

Gabe held Ella close. She buried her face in his chest and sobbed so hard, he felt every wracking breath reverberate through his ribs. The breakdown was inevitable. Still, he had no idea what to do with a beautiful crying woman. He had brothers. If one of them broke down, he'd slap him on the back, tell him to suck it up, everything would be okay, and they'd drink until they were numb and bottled their feelings again.

Heartsick, frightened, and in pain from her injuries, she needed time to process, heal, and grieve without all of this hanging over her head.

He got out of the truck, scooped her into his arms, and carried her up the icy walk to the front door.

"Why are you always picking me up?"

"Easiest way I could think of to get my hands on you." Okay, maybe that was more truth than the moment called for, but he'd never had good timing with women. Probably why his bed remained empty the last eight months.

"I need to find the papers for the missing paintings." She settled her head on his shoulder.

God, the way she smelled, so sweet, like spring wildflowers . . .

Yeah, she needed those papers, some kind of proof her uncle had been stealing from her. He needed to talk to her more about her sister's murder and the cop who helped her uncle cover it up.

He shoved open the front door, walked through, and kicked it closed with his heel. He walked to the couch and sat down with her in his lap. He gathered her close, pressed his cheek to her soft hair, and held her, letting her know without words she wasn't alone.

Time ticked by and his mind spun thoughts of her returning to New York to face her uncle with the proof, not knowing who to trust. He formed one plan that turned into several variations. No matter what happened, he swore he'd keep her safe.

Her tears faded and she settled against him, drifting into the sleep she desperately needed. Gabe's gaze swept the room and his comfortable furnishings. He'd made a good place for himself here, but he'd reached for more. He'd reached too high, thinking he'd move into the Wolf place, run the ranch, grow the business, and one day be worthy of that house and land and what it stood for in this community. Wealth. Prosperity. Hard work to build something to encompass that vast land and large house. All of which belonged to the woman in his arms.

He wanted that place, but damn if he didn't want the woman in his arms more. If she noticed how much, she'd ignored it the way he tried to ignore the state of his hard cock pressed to her hip. Fresh and lovely. Too wealthy and educated. Too much the city girl to his backwoods country boy. It could never work in the real world. Still, he couldn't help wanting the fantasy.

He hated seeing her cry, knowing how deeply she

hurt. He admired her spunk and determination. While he enjoyed watching her put Travis in his place, he didn't like her impulsive move to disarm him. That smart, sharp mind of hers probably got her into all kinds of trouble. She'd keep him on his toes.

But she wasn't staying. He had to get that through his head. Once she had the proof she needed, she'd go back to her life. The life that suited her. She had a company to run, a family dynasty to uphold. No way she chose a life out here in the middle of nowhere on a cattle ranch. After everything that happened, she'd probably sell Wolf Ranch for the money it was worth and forget she ever stepped foot in Montana.

With a heavy sigh, he gave in to stupidity and hugged her close. She moaned in pain when he crushed her side too tight. He smoothed his hand over her hip, soothing the small hurt, and she settled against him again.

He couldn't sit here all day, even though that was exactly what he wanted to do, not when he needed to feed the horses and go to town to get her father's papers. The sooner he helped her clean up this mess with her uncle, the sooner she'd go back home and stop unknowingly torturing him.

He indulged in one last sweet smell of her soft hair and shifted her off his lap and onto the leather sofa. He pulled the dark pillow beneath her head and settled her legs on the couch as he slid off to stand beside her. Careful not to jar her sprained ankle, he unzipped her worthless boots and placed them on the floor. He propped her bad foot on another pillow and tucked her coat around her to keep her warm while she got some much needed sleep. Satisfied he had her settled for at least a couple of hours, he leaned down and kissed her on the head. He closed his eyes, holding back the urge to lie down with her and hold her in his arms.

He stepped away, but stopped when she reached out and grasped his jeans at his thigh. He knelt beside her and brushed the hair from her face. "What is it?"

"I'm sorry."

"Nothing to be sorry about. Just don't grab guns from people anymore."

"No. For what my uncle did to you."

He traced the tear that escaped her lashes and rolled over her soft cheek. "I'll figure something out."

"I'll make it right. I promise."

"Get some rest. I'm going out to feed the horses."

"I'd like to see them."

"Later. You need some sleep."

Her lids slid closed despite how hard she tried to stay awake. He stood and stared down at her peaceful face, thinking of how young and sweet she was with so much weighing on her shoulders. Still, she thought of him and wanted to make things right. If he hadn't been such an idiot, she wouldn't need to make things right. Nothing for her to do anyway, except hopefully get his money back. Even then, what could he do? Buy another piece of property? He'd have to spend some time researching his options. Nothing compared to Wolf Ranch, but if he reevaluated his needs and found something to fit, it might take him only a few months to close the deal.

What if he didn't get his money back? That thought didn't even bear thinking about right now. He'd be ruined. He didn't have money to hire a lawyer to sue Phillip Wolf, who could probably use his vast wealth to fight Gabe for years, making it impossible to get his money and costing him a fortune in legal fees.

"What a fucking mess." He stepped out into the backyard and made his way over the five inches of snow to the stables. His boots crunched on the ice. The yard would turn to a muddy mess if the weather warmed up a few more degrees. Of course, this time of year they'd probably get more snow. He felt the chill of it in the air and looked north to the building gray clouds. Yeah, they'd get more snow soon. Should have checked the weather reports, but he'd been distracted by a green-eyed beauty.

He liked her a lot. She wasn't callous and frivolous. The sad and disgusted way she looked at how all those cows were treated told him she cared about their well-being. While the smell made her wrinkle her cute nose, she didn't go all girly on him and whine about leaving that place immediately. No, she'd been more concerned with helping those animals than preserving her sense of smell or her ruined boots that probably cost someone's monthly salary.

Gabe walked into the overcrowded stables and shook his head. He'd hoped to get the twenty-seven horses into the Wolf stables, spread them out, give them the room they deserved. He thought it'd be only a matter of weeks. Now he'd have to come up with another place to house the horses he'd doubled up in the stalls. He'd have to build a temporary shed. He hated leaving them out in the weather, especially with more snow coming.

Mentally making a list of things he'd need to do and change because of the circumstances, he fed and watered the horses. With the snow coming, he'd have to run into town and get supplies. No telling how long he'd be stuck on the ranch with Ella.

The thought appealed a lot. More than he'd like to admit.

He worked for an hour in the stables with the horses. Being with them calmed his mind, and the physical work helped relieve the stress. He didn't think about the bogus contract, or how much he wanted to kill Phillip for signing those worthless papers when he knew his signature was meaningless.

See, he wasn't thinking about it at all. He dumped the pitchfork in the wheelbarrow full of horseshit and straw, planted his hands on his hips, stared at the ground, and shook his head.

Everything he'd worked so hard for, all down the drain.

He walked down the center aisle toward the door and gave Sully and Winnie a pat on the head before he left. He loved being with the horses. If things got any worse, he'd lose them, too.

He thought of the woman in his house. Not going to happen. He'd protect her and everything he'd worked so hard to build.

CHAPTER 11

Ella woke up in the dark, momentarily disoriented. She focused on the stone fireplace with the chunky wood mantel and the pictures of Gabe and his family. It wasn't hard to imagine him on a bucking bronco or bull, winning those buckles and trophies.

A warmth spread through her chest when she thought about him. Strong. Kind. A physical powerhouse, he'd punched Travis like he was flicking an annoying gnat. When she broke down under grief's strain, he held her protected in his strong arms.

A piece of her connected with Gabe and refused to let go.

She had to fix this mess before any more of her uncle's evil deeds touched his life.

The anger in his eyes, she'd recognized. She felt the very same, but the death of his dream for his future tore at her heart. A hardworking man, he'd earned the money to buy Wolf Ranch with the sweat off his back. No one handed him anything. Well, her uncle handed him Wolf Ranch on a silver platter, complete with a ridiculous price tag.

Which begged the question. Why did her uncle want

to sell the property for so little when it was worth so much more? Why sell it now? To hide the art theft? It didn't make any sense. If he planned to kill her and Lela—which it seemed clear he had—why did he need to sell the property to cover up something so small as theft? In the grand scheme of the Wolf fortune, those paintings were a drop in the bucket. Yes, they were worth a small fortune, but nothing compared to the other assets held by Wolf Enterprises. The paintings, especially the one her mother painted, were more sentimental than anything. A reminder of happier times they'd spent at the ranch.

Why did her uncle need the money? Maybe if she discovered that, everything would finally fall into place.

She didn't know where Gabe had gone, but the house felt empty and cold without him. She stood, wincing at the ache in her ankle. She limped to her room and sifted through the sparse contents of Lela's suitcase. She pulled out her sister's favorite pair of black leggings. Lela liked to wear them on the plane for comfort. She *used* to wear them. Ella held back the tears and chose the lavender pullover tunic. Soft, warm, it reminded her so much of her sister's simple, yet elegant taste.

She held the sweater to her nose and inhaled her sister's scent. God, she missed her.

She drew the line at borrowing her sister's underwear, but snagged the lavender lace bra and a pair of black socks. Based on the contents, she had two more outfits. As pretty as her sister's clothes were, nothing she packed would keep her warm outside.

What were you thinking?

Probably that she'd come here, get the proof, and be home in no time to take her uncle down.

"Why didn't you come to me for help? Why did you do this on your own?"

Ella didn't have the answers to those questions and had to respect her sister's choices.

"You were supposed to do it with me, Lela. Side by side like always. You and me against the world."

With a heavy heart, she searched all the pockets and compartments in the suitcase for more clues. Nothing.

She scooped up the clothes and her sister's toiletry bag and limped across the hall to the small bathroom. She closed the door and set her things on the toilet lid. She stripped, turned on the shower, and stepped under the spray, welcoming the warmth and massaging effect on her back and head. Clean and feeling human again, she stepped out of the shower, pulled the rolled-up tan towel off the pile on the shelf under the sink, and patted herself dry. She felt bad rooting through Gabe's things. She didn't want to take advantage, but took one of the three toothbrushes from the cabinet drawer along with the travel size tube of toothpaste and brushed her teeth. Dressed in her sister's clean clothes, she applied tinted moisturizer on her face to improve her sallow appearance.

She tossed her dirty bra and panties into the sink, washed them with the hand soap, and hung them next to her wet towel on the bar next to the shower. She hated to leave her things strung over Gabe's bathroom, but what choice did she have at this point?

She pressed her thighs together, thinking of Gabe and the warm way he made her feel when he looked at her.

She thought of him wrapping his arms around her from behind, and sliding his hands over her taut belly and lower, to pull the towel up and touch her where she burned.

Stop. You've got things to do.

Still alone and not knowing when to expect Gabe home, she grabbed her tote off the table by the front door, set the heavy bag on the dining table, and pulled out her laptop and notebook.

She opened her laptop, but froze before turning it on. What if they could track her Internet access and emails?

Frustrated, she opened her notebook and concentrated on making a list. She thought of her sister. What could she do for Lela?

Check on funeral arrangements. Maybe her uncle already made them, but Ella wanted Lela buried at the ranch with their parents. *Plan memorial service. Find proof against my uncle. Find someone I trust to help me arrest my uncle.* She wrote: *State attorney? FBI?*

Who was she kidding? Without Internet access and the ability to hide her identity, she couldn't accomplish anything.

The desk across the room caught her attention, but she hesitated to use Gabe's laptop. She'd imposed so much already, she hated to use his things without asking. Still, she couldn't sit here and do nothing. Too much time had passed already.

Set on accomplishing at least one of her tasks, she limped over to his desk and sat in his chair. She opened his laptop and the screen lit up. No password protection; several spreadsheets and documents popped up. She tried not to snoop, but they were right in front of her face. His plans and calculations for the ranch, the cattle, his breeding program, cost estimates, land allocations. More stuff she couldn't decipher. Smart, well-thought-out plans for a man about to embark on a new venture. He'd outlined the steps he needed to take, timelines for different aspects of the business, and forecasts for the next five years.

She touched her fingertips to the screen. "You worked so hard to set this up." She'd learned a thing or two about finance in school and working her way through the many departments at the company. If his projections were correct, and she had no reason to doubt them based on what she'd seen, he'd be profitable inside a year and making better than decent money in five. More than enough for him to live at Wolf Ranch and support a family.

Her gaze went to the photos on the mantel. Family was important to him. Naturally, given his age and a prospering business, he'd want to settle down, get married, and have a family of his own. She thought of dark-haired, brown-eyed babies in his strong, protective arms and sighed. Such a pretty picture.

She shook it off and stared at his spreadsheets again, more plans forming in her mind. More she needed to do to make this right for him.

With Gabe's pages minimized, she opened his browser and typed in the New York City morgue they'd mentioned on the news. She jotted down the number on her pad. With a few more keystrokes and searches, she found Heaven's Gate Funeral Home in New York. She'd ask Mary to make arrangements to have them prepare her sister's body for burial and ship it to a funeral home in Crystal Creek.

Warm hands settled on her shoulders and kneaded her tight muscles. Gabe. She hadn't heard him come in or walk up behind her. He worked her shoulders with his big hands, easing her mind as well as her body. She looked up at him upside down, and he traced his finger along her cheek, wiping the single tear away. The moment stretched, their gazes held, and he combed his fingers through her damp hair to let her know he felt the pull between them too.

Unable to decide on a casket on Heaven's Gate's website, she'd been staring at the photos for ten minutes. Gabe's body brushed against her back as he leaned over, took the mouse, and clicked on the screen. She stared at the wood coffin with the white satin interior. A vine of roses carved into the wood. His hand settled on the rose pendant on her chest.

"That's the one," he said simply, his fingertips brushing up her neck and through her long hair. Shivers danced up her spine and his hands settled on her shoulders again.

She jotted down her choice—the perfect choice, thanks to Gabe's help—on her notepad and sighed.

"You can't make that phone call."

She ignored the order in his voice, knowing he was only trying to protect her.

"I'll contact the house staff and instruct Mary to complete the arrangements."

"What if the phone is tapped, or she tells your uncle where you are?"

"My uncle would never expect me to call. The servant extension is a different number from the house. I'm not going to tell her where I am. And she won't say anything. She works for me, not my uncle."

"Is there a difference?"

"Yes. Which is one of the reasons my uncle is doing this."

"It's too great a risk."

"I have to do this. My sister deserves to be buried with dignity, not left in some cold morgue."

She leaned back in the chair and stared up at Gabe. He leaned against the desk, his hands stuffed in his pockets. He gave her a nod that he didn't like it, but he'd drop it.

"You look better and worse all at the same time," he said, not smiling.

"Thanks. You're a real sweet-talker."

"That's why the place is crawling with women," he teased back, letting go of the tension between them from a minute ago.

"Um, I guess I never thought about it. Is my being here a problem for you and your girlfriend?" He didn't wear a ring and the house definitely shouted bachelor with its sparse furnishings and decorations, but a man like him probably had a girlfriend somewhere. Or maybe ten.

"My fiancée—"

"Oh shit. I'm sorry. I kissed you. I'll explain to her that it was my fault."

"Ella. Stop. She left me years ago. She never stayed one night in this house."

Since he started this conversation, she waited, feeling as if he wanted her to know what happened.

"It's no big deal. I met a girl in college."

"Good ol' Texas A&M."

"We were together three years. I asked Stacy to marry me junior year. She said yes. We graduated. I bought this place and brought her home to marry her and build a life, starting on this small spread. I brushed off her complaints about living this far from even the smallest town, and how she'd never find a job, friends, how she'd be stuck out here with me, as nothing more than wedding jitters. Hell, I was nervous too. I figured once we settled in, she'd make this place hers, and we'd have some kids, and she'd be happy."

"This place wasn't what she expected?" Ella guessed.

"Let's say she was a bit high-maintenance from the get-go. She grew up in a middle-class home in a good-size town in Texas. All the plans we talked about at school sounded good. She went along, swearing she loved me and couldn't wait to be a rancher's wife."

"You brought her here, and the reality of living in the country on the ranch with the animals set in."

"A tiny house in the middle of nowhere, limited access to shopping malls, the movies, restaurants—fun—wasn't exactly what she had in mind."

No. Ella imagined she'd wanted something grand, like Wolf Ranch, and located closer to a big city like Bozeman.

"What happened?"

"She left me standing at the altar, staring at the house and land and the life she didn't want."

Ella had seen the beautiful wood arch out back down by the creek, under two towering trees. She bet it was beautiful in the spring and fall with the grass and wildflowers. The perfect spot to get married.

"I'm sorry, Gabe. No one deserves to be abandoned like that."

She understood all too well the kind of hurt that caused. Her mother loved her father and couldn't overcome her grief at losing him after the plane crash. She'd gone to their New York estate, the place they used to go to be alone and ride the horses, and hung herself, choosing death and an afterlife with her beloved rather than a life with her daughters. Loving someone that much was dangerous. A broken heart could break you.

"Yeah, well, after that, I left this place and followed the rodeo circuit to earn the money I needed to buy a bigger place and set up the ranch I really want."

Yes. Wolf Ranch. Gabe had jumped at the chance to buy it when her uncle presented a deal too good to be true, because he needed the house and land to prove himself worthy.

"I rode broncos and bulls and any woman I could get my hands on."

To prove he didn't need Stacy and could have any woman he wanted. Blunt, but she appreciated his honesty. She'd bet everything she owned all he had to do was smile and they jumped into his bed. The thought brought on a wave of unfamiliar jealousy and anger. She barely knew him, but thinking about him with another woman set off a bunch of emotions she didn't want to analyze too closely.

"Did it help you forget Stacy?"

"Nope, but it passed the time, and I made a lot of money." He might have stopped sleeping with random women to prove he was over Stacy and what she did to him, but he still needed the big ranch to prove he had something to give a woman who shared his dream.

Gabe's gaze met hers. "Stacy showed up about two years ago. She wanted me back. Said it was a huge mistake to leave me, that we could make a life together work."

"Must have made you feel good to see her come crawling back."

"Not like I thought it would. She gave me all the words I thought I wanted to hear, but I didn't feel anything inside. Nothing. I'd made a mistake, thinking she'd be happy living the life I wanted. I never considered the life she wanted. I deserved what I got, standing alone at that altar, waiting on a woman who only existed in my head. A woman I thought I loved once but didn't. I won't make that mistake again."

"You made a name for yourself and a lot of money on the rodeo circuit. She thought you'd have the life she imagined." She pointed to the buckles and trophies.

"Something like that. But I still live here, and her picture of our life still didn't match mine. Although I still wanted the wife and family, the life my parents showed me, I didn't believe her smile."

"I know the one."

"I bet you do. Men probably smile at you all the time and want only one thing."

"Two. Money and sex. The first is a great aphrodisiac for the second to some people."

"How many men have asked you to marry them?"

"None. I rarely date someone more than a few weeks and never let things get that far. Like you, I never quite believe the smile."

"The pictures on TV prove you hardly ever stay home alone."

"Partners in fun are one thing. A partner for life is quite another. Love is dangerous. It makes people lie to make someone else happy, but in the end it only hurts them more when that person discovers the truth."

"Exactly what Stacy did."

"It makes people grieve so hard when they lose it that they'll do anything to get it back."

"Your mother."

"She loved my father so much, she couldn't live without him. The vows say till death do us part. My mother believed that in death she'd be with him again."

"Were they happy together?"

"They were made for each other. They smiled and meant it every day."

"Don't you want that for yourself?"

"My life is complicated. They met before all the money came into play. I've got that and an uncle who wants me dead."

She pointed to the mantel. "Home. Family. Seems I don't have either anymore. My family is all dead, and I can't go back to my house in New York where my sister died."

"We'll find the evidence you need to put that bastard behind bars, so you can go home."

Funny, she didn't want to go anywhere. She liked it here. Even with everything hanging over her head, she still felt life was simpler here.

"Um, I hope you don't mind I borrowed your computer."

"Help yourself. Lord knows everything on there is a whole lot of nothing now."

"Your projections and business plans are well thought out."

"They won't be executed. Not in the same way. I'll have to figure out what to do with my limited resources."

He stood and took two steps away, ending any further conversation about how much this place and reaching for more had cost him.

He turned back to face her. "I got you a present."

Surprised, she opened her mouth, but closed it again.

He shook his head. "It's nothing big, just something you need."

"Thank you."

"Don't thank me yet. You might not like it."

"Gabe."

He closed the distance between them, reading in her the importance of what she wanted to say. He crouched in front of her, one hand on the arm of her chair and the other on the desk.

She leaned in close because the moment called for it. "Thank you for saving me out on that road and letting me stay here. I don't know what I would have done without your help. You're a good man, who didn't deserve any of this."

His steady gaze told her he understood she meant what Stacy and her uncle both did to him. His hand clamped on to her leg, and he massaged his way up over her knee to her thigh and hip. Heat spread like wildfire through her system.

"You'll be okay."

Hearing him say it made her feel better. A spark of belief flamed to life.

"You're tough. You've had to be to grow up without your parents, just you and your sister, no one else to rely on or help you when you needed it."

"How do you know that?"

"Because your uncle killed your sister for something as stupid as money."

"It's a lot of money."

"Nothing is worth taking someone's life."

"Yeah, well, I want to kill him for what he did to her."

"I know you do, but you'll do what is right and make sure your sister gets the justice she deserves."

"I'll make sure you get the justice you deserve. He shouldn't have made that deal with you."

"Stop worrying about me."

"I can't," she confessed.

His eyes narrowed and blazed with heat. He leaned in close, or maybe she leaned into him. No, they'd met in the middle, that strange connection between them pulling them in. Their faces remained an inch apart. His breath whispered over her skin, smelling of the wintergreen mints he kept in his truck. She thought he'd kiss her and held her breath.

His big hand reached up and held the side of her head, and he pressed his forehead to hers and closed his eyes like it hurt to be this close to her. He stood, breaking the intimate spell, and stared down at her with the same need she felt reflected in his eyes. He didn't give in and neither did she. They let the moment, the feelings and emotions simmer.

"I've got to bring the stuff in from my truck." He turned back before he went out the door. "Can you cook?"

"I can make reservations and order take-out."

He laughed. "City girl. I've got to feed the horses and do some chores. I'll make you something to eat when I get back. You must be starving."

"I haven't eaten all day."

"Damn, honey, I'm sorry."

"Not your fault. I wasn't really hungry anyway."

"I know you're grieving for your sister, but you've got

to eat. Especially if you're taking those pain pills." She shrugged that away. "You didn't take them, did you?"

"No. I'm fine."

"Why don't you take them?"

"I don't like them. They make me feel not myself. I don't like feeling that way."

He tilted his head and studied her. "You're not what I thought you are."

"Ditsy spoiled rich girl?"

"I think that's just another lie you let people believe."

"What are you talking about?"

"You know what I'm talking about." With that bombshell hanging between them, he walked out the door, a blast of cold air and snow blowing and whipping the door shut.

So, he'd decided the news reports he'd seen about her and Lela that morning might not be all true. Most people didn't look close enough, or care one way or the other. Her close friends laughed at what reporters said about her. Lela used to think the absurd stories were funny.

She used Gabe's cordless phone and called the penthouse staff extension.

"Wolf residence."

"Mary, it's Ella."

Mary knew her and Lela better than anyone. She'd cooked for the family for years and had become more like an aunt to her and Lela. Mary sniffled and stammered out, "Ella, do you know? Has someone told you?"

"Yes, Mary, I know all about Lela. I'm so sorry you were the one to find her."

"I can't believe someone murdered my beautiful girl in her own home. Your uncle is going insane looking for you. Where are you, dear? Come home. We'll get through this together."

"I can't. Not yet. Please, whatever you do, don't tell Uncle Phillip you spoke to me."

"He asks about you every five minutes."

"Please, Mary. It's important."

"Why are you calling?"

"I need you to do something for Lela."

"Anything, dear."

"I want you to tell Uncle Phillip you'd like to oversee the funeral arrangements."

"Come home. We'll do it together."

"I can't. Not yet. Write this down." Ella rattled off the names and phone numbers for the funeral homes in New York and Crystal Creek, along with her selection for the casket. "In my closet near the back is a navy blue garment bag. Inside is our mother's white lace dress. The one she wore on her honeymoon with Dad. Lela cherished that dress. Grab the pretty glitter You You Louboutin heels in her closet. Lela always loved those shoes."

"I know the ones. She wore them to her graduation."

Ella sighed and pinched the bridge of her nose, thinking of all Lela accomplished, but never got to see bloom into her bright future. A future that had been snuffed out, never to shine again.

"Yes. Please take her things to the funeral home so they can prepare her for burial."

"I know just what to do. I did the same for my mother just last year, remember?"

"Yes. I do. I'm so sorry to bring up sad memories and ask you to take on this task for me."

Mary sniffled back tears. "She was a beautiful girl

with a big heart. So tragic to see her die that way. I hate what they are saying about you on those tabloid shows and in the news. It's disgusting the way they make up stories and tell lies. They don't know you or her."

"What is Uncle doing?"

"He's holed up in his library with that detective. Those two have been going back and forth about something since this happened."

Gabe walked in with bags of groceries gripped in both his hands, a dusting of snow covering his black ski cap and wide shoulders. He smiled and gave her a questioning look, wondering why she stared at him so intently. She couldn't help herself.

"Do you need me?"

Yes stuck on the tip of her tongue, but she shook her head no. Gabe must have sensed her indecision and hesitated a moment longer before turning and walking into the small kitchen.

"Mary, please, just do as I ask, and delete this call from caller ID too. I don't want Uncle to know where I am or how to get in touch with me."

"I'll do all you asked. What about your sister's funeral? We need to make plans. People are calling, asking about the service and you."

"I'll prepare a press release. The funeral will be private. Family only. A memorial will be held later."

"But, Ella—"

"That's what I want. You'll understand why soon. Trust me, Mary, what I'm asking is necessary. Uncle Phillip cannot be trusted."

"I have to go. Your uncle is bellowing for me. Take care, my dear. I'll do everything you asked. You can count on me."

"I always do."

Ella put the phone on the desk and scrubbed both hands over her face. When she finished, she stared at the box and bag Gabe set in front of her.

"What is that?"

"Your present."

"Gabe, you really didn't need to—"

"I really did. Open it."

She smoothed her hands over the shoe box, caught the edge, and lifted the lid, revealing the pair of black boots. Sturdy. Warm. Perfect for the winter weather and the snow.

"Your foot should fit in there with the brace. When you lace them up, they'll give you extra support for that ankle until it heals. The best part, they're waterproof. For the most part. Believe me, you spend any length of time in the snow, they'll get wet. But they should do the trick for the next few days while you're here."

"Trying to get rid of me so fast."

"Yeah, that's why I bought you shoes to wear here. You'll look ridiculous in New York with those and your designer slacks."

"I love them."

"You mean you'll tolerate them while you're here."

"No. I really love them. They're perfect. Thank you."

He gave her a skeptical look, but reached out and handed her the bag. "This one I owe you."

"What is it?"

"You're really bad at opening presents. You're supposed to tear into the thing."

She held the paper sack and pulled the tissue out, tossing it up in the air with a touch of flair. Gabe smiled and shook his head. She reached inside and pulled out the contents and set them on the desk and just stared at the pretty sweaters he'd bought for her.

One, a soft, thick cable knit with a V-neck in a deep purple. The next, a softer knit with a V-neck in a turquoise blue. The last, a tunic much like the one she wore but heavier in weight, in a beautiful raspberry pink. She loved them and let it show in the way she ran her hands over the material, admiring the texture.

"I hope I got the size right. I didn't know what you'd like, and they certainly don't cost anywhere near what your sweater probably cost, but I thought they'd look nice on you." Gabe could barely look at her, nervous and unsure of his purchases and whether she'd like them.

She couldn't help it. The tears glistened in her eyes. No one had ever done something so nice for her for no reason. Spontaneity won out over propriety and she leaned up and gave him a quick kiss. This time the kiss was much different than the one she'd pushed on him earlier. That time, she'd let her anger rule her emotions. This time, she felt the heat spread through her whole system. Everything inside her wanted to dive in for another, deeper kiss. After the way he'd reacted the last time she kissed him, she stuck to the present and not the tension crackling between them.

"Thank you. I love them." She didn't really look at him, but picked up the pink sweater and held it to her chest, checking the size and admiring the way the material hung just so to the tops of her thighs. Perfect.

Acutely aware of Gabe standing motionless beside her, she glanced up and sucked in a deep breath. The intensity in his eyes made her hesitate.

"Gabe, really, I love them. Thank you so much. You didn't have to do this, but I appreciate it so much."

"I ruined your sweater."

She reached out and grabbed his bare forearm. His warmth seeped into her skin and set her body ablaze. She leaned in, but caught herself before she rubbed up against him. "It's no big deal. You didn't have to buy me anything."

"I wanted to." His words came out soft. His gaze fell to her hand on his arm. She pulled it away. Something in his eyes told her he wanted her to touch him again. More. The heat of his stare pulled her in, but he turned away first and walked over to the boxes he'd dragged in while she was on the phone. He took the long, thick down coat from the top of them and came back and handed it to her.

"I pulled this out of one of the boxes from your mother's closet. I didn't think anything from yours would fit after all these years. You probably don't want to wear your mother's clothes, but I thought this jacket might suit you. You need something better than the one you brought. Plus it's another thing that got ruined in the snow."

She took the deep purple coat and held it to her chest, smelling it and rubbing her hand over the material. She remembered her mother wearing it, cheering and clapping her hands together as Ella raced Lela down the mountain on sleds.

"Thank you. Purple was my mother's favorite color."

"I gathered that from your parents' room."

"That's right, you oversaw the people who packed everything. Thank you, Gabe, for everything."

He turned and walked into the kitchen.

"What are you doing now?"

"Making dinner. If I don't feed you, I'll need to buy

you a smaller size. Lord knows there's barely anything of you to look at as it is."

She laughed and retorted, "Is that why all the sweaters have V-necks, because I've got nothing for you to look at?" She pointedly looked at her full breasts and up at him.

His gaze blazed a trail from her face to her breasts. "Sweetheart, I like looking at everything there is about you."

The heat in that look promised a hell of a lot more than looking.

CHAPTER 12

Gabe watched Ella from the kitchen while he prepared dinner. Nothing special, just a couple of pork chops he picked up at the store. He put them in the cast-iron skillet to fry along with the onions he'd chopped earlier.

He could still feel the heat of her touch on his arm. The kiss surprised him. Not that the simple kiss sparked something inside him, but the intensity with which it spread through his system and made him crave more. It took everything he had not to grab hold of her and crush his mouth to hers. She tasted sweet, like his favorite strawberry pie.

He bought Stacy a pair of gold earrings once. Something special for her birthday. He didn't remember feeling this damn good about giving her the present as he did seeing Ella's eyes light up when she saw the boots and sweaters. Nothing special. Just what he owed her and something to protect her feet. Still, you'd have thought by the look on her face he bought her diamonds. Men probably had in the past. She said she liked to have fun with the guys she dated, nothing serious. Judging by the photos of her out on the town on the TV news reports, he had no doubt she didn't spend many nights alone. That thought stopped him cold. Then he thought about it again and the shy way she'd kissed him and touched his arm. Not practiced or seductive, but a real and true show of affection for what he'd done for her.

He thought of their argument earlier and the angry kiss she planted on him, a strange punishment for the stupid thing he said. Every minute he spent in her company, he got to know her better, and with every new thing he learned, he wanted to know more. He'd even told her about Stacy. He'd never talked about what happened with anyone. Not even his brothers.

The longer she spent with him, the more she let her guard down and began to trust in him. She'd have plenty of time to get to know him over the next couple of days. One hell of a storm was rolling in and they'd be lucky if the snow didn't bury them up to their necks. He hoped the satellite didn't go out, but with thick clouds covering the sky, no doubt they'd lose service. He hoped to keep track of what was happening with the murder investigation through the news and Internet. He didn't want to get caught in any more of her uncle's surprises.

The salad went together in a matter of minutes. He flipped the pork chops in the pan and grabbed the cornbread muffins he bought at the store. He turned the oven to warm and put four muffins on a baking pan and set them in to heat.

Ella surfed the Web, looking for information on the detective and ties he had in the department and community. She moved her back this way and that to ease the pain etching lines in her forehead. Her discomfort disturbed him on a level he didn't want to evaluate too close. The whole thing with the sweaters already made him think he'd gone mad.

Unable to watch her squirm in pain, he pulled the jug of iced tea from the fridge and poured her a glass. He went to the cabinet by the phone and pulled out the bottle of ibuprofen he kept there for those nights when working in the stables left him aching and sore.

She stood and limped toward him. He met her halfway in the dining area. "Here. If you won't take those pain meds, take these. They'll take the edge off."

"Thanks." She popped the pills in her mouth and downed three quarters of the glass of iced tea and let out a huge sigh. "I was really thirsty."

"Let's get something straight. You've got nowhere else to stay because your house is empty. I'm happy to let you stay here as long as you like. This is the kitchen." He indicated with a sweep of his arm. "I keep the food in here. If you're thirsty, get something to drink. If you're hungry, grab something out of the fridge or cupboards. For God's sake, help yourself to whatever you want."

"Why are you mad at me?"

"I'm not," he snapped. "I'm mad at me. It's nearly seven at night, and you've had nothing to eat or drink all day. How do you exist without any coffee in the morning?"

"That accounts for the raging caffeine withdrawal headache."

He swore and went back to the fridge and pulled out a soda. "Drink this. It's full of caffeine and should help."

"Thanks."

"Stop thanking me. If you want something, don't stop to ask, just grab it." *If you want me, grab me. I won't mind.* He'd never wanted any woman as much as he wanted her.

"Thanks. I took one of your spare toothbrushes already, but the soda and that food are really what I need."

"I should have fed you."

"It's not like you stopped to eat today either."

"I ate a huge breakfast before you got up and drank three cups of coffee while I waited for you. I ate a sandwich and half a bag of chips on my way home from the store."

Gabe went back to the stove and took the meat off the burner. He pulled the pan of cornbread from the oven and set it on the stove.

"That smells like heaven. You're a really good cook."

"You haven't even tasted it yet."

"If it tastes half as good as it looks, I'll love it."

"So you really don't know how to cook?"

"Not really. We have Mary. She's an amazing cook. And I eat out a lot."

He wanted to ask her with whom. Thoughts of her out at the nightclubs flashed in his mind, those skimpy outfits he'd seen her in on TV this morning. But he remembered what she said about how he didn't know her, so he asked, "Really? I bet they've got some great restaurants in New York. Got a favorite?"

"Several. My sister and I loved this Italian place called Mama's. This little hole-in-the-wall most people would walk right by, but we loved it there. Family-owned, Mama's cooks the best lasagna in the city. The Florentine fettuccine Alfredo is to die for."

He smiled, liking her this way. "What else did you and your sister like to do?" Genuinely interested, he kept his gaze steady on her, prompting her to keep talking.

"Broadway."

"Really?"

"We loved the plays. Our mother used to drag our dad, but I think he secretly liked it. They took us all the time. We still go. Kind of a tradition. Especially the Radio City Christmas Spectacular with the Rockettes. Every year. We never miss it."

She caught herself talking about her sister in the present tense. Like they'd go see a show next week.

"Sit at the table, sweetheart. I'll just be a minute with the rest of dinner."

She took the seat facing him in the kitchen and put her sore foot up on the chair across from her. He grabbed a plastic bag from the drawer and went to the freezer. He filled the bag, took it to the cutting board, used the meat tenderizer to smash the ice cubes into bits, sealed the bag, and took it to the table.

"Here, I can do that."

"I've got it." He reached under the table and undid the straps on the brace and carefully slipped it off. He placed the bag over her swollen ankle over her sock. "Better."

"Yeah. Thanks."

"You're welcome. According to the news this morning, Lela attended school. Something about getting her MBA from Columbia, right? What about you?"

"I finished mine through the University of Indiana's online business program last month. I've taken a few more classes at NYU."

"Seriously? The University of Indiana?" He set her plate and his on the table and went back to the kitchen and grabbed the silverware and napkins.

"Don't turn your nose up at Indiana, Mr. Texas A&M. They are the top-rated online business program in the country. It may not be Columbia, but it's a great program."

"Why do it online? I imagine you went to the same private schools with your sister and got a top-notch education."

"All true, but Lela went right out of high school. What can I say, I like having fun with my friends, but it's not like the press makes out. Plus that life gets boring real fast. I was eighteen, young, and having fun. Then I remembered Lela and I are a team and I owed my parents better than that, so I went back to school and spent most of my time trying to catch up to her. You see, in order for us to inherit at twenty-five, we each have to have either an MBA, or have worked for the company full-time for five years."

"So your sister went the traditional college route, attending classes and working part-time at the company. You worked full-time at the company and did your classes online."

"Exactly. My sister attended school and worked in the executive offices. She played the part my parents wanted for us and my uncle expected. Over the last five years, I've worked in almost every department from the mailroom up. Never more than three months, I take whatever position is open in the other department that would be a step up from the last. That way, when we took over, we'd understand how the company worked from the ground up. We'd go to dinner once a week and talk about the company, how things were being run by the managers in place, what needed to be changed or tweaked, and we'd bring those items up to the executive staff. We never wanted to take over the company from the people my father left in charge of running it, we wanted to contribute and be a real part of the team."

"That sounds like a very good plan for learning the business and understanding all the working parts."

"Exactly. How could we spend all our time in school and then take over one day, having no idea what the company did and how to manage it? Just because we had the degree didn't guarantee we knew what we were doing. Our father worked hard to build the company out of next to nothing. He deserved for us to take the opportunity he gave us and do it right. We owed that to the people who have worked for him and after him to keep the company running and prosperous. Everything we have is because of them and we didn't want to walk in one day, take over, and make anyone think we didn't appreciate everything they've done.

"People in the company are skeptical when I start in a new department. I mean, I don't give them a choice about my taking the job, but once they see I'm serious about learning how to do it and how they run the department, they come around and are encouraging."

"Do you tell them why you're working in all the departments?"

"No. Not outright. At first they think I can't make up my mind about what I want to do. That, or that I'm just doing the bare minimum to get what's mine."

"They don't believe that for long, though, do they?"

"No. I seem to have a hard time pulling back from doing what is necessary. I take every job seriously. I want to do it right. Mediocre just seems . . ."

"Half-assed," he supplied.

She smirked and nodded her agreement. "Yes. Still, my uncle thinks I'm nothing but a waste."

"When you take over, is he out?"

"No. That's the thing. Nothing would have changed for him, including the massive salary he's paid. He'd still answer to the executive staff. We join that team, but no one person holds all the power in the company. This whole bizarre plot is about money and power and control. It's just so stupid and ridiculous. If he wanted more money, Lela and I would have given it to him. He sold the paintings probably for millions. He stole the money you paid for the ranch. Why? How much is enough? Does it have to be everything?"

Gabe didn't get it either. Ella and Lela by all accounts were kind women. He believed if their uncle wanted more, they'd have given it. For nothing more than because he was family.

He changed the subject back to the business. "Is the company public?"

"No. It's privately held. We own more than seventy percent of the business."

"How is it that your company does small appliances; restaurant, farm, and manufacturing equipment; and botanical cosmetics? That's an odd mix."

"If my father had lived, I don't doubt he'd have added several other odd enterprises. He bought the restaurant appliance business a couple of years after he started running it for my mother's family businesses. You know all those coffee houses with cappuccino machines that spit out lattes and caramel macchiatos? My favorite, by the way. Well, most of those machines are Wolf. We also make ovens, freezers, refrigeration units, stuff like that. My father expanded the business by partnering with another company that made small appliances. They made quality items, but lacked the business leadership to mass-produce and market their goods."

"Your father steps in and Wolf appliances are sold in every major department store in the country. I have one of your can openers and a coffeemaker."

"I noticed."

"Yet you can't cook."

"I can make the coffee and open a can. I know how to use every product we sell."

"What about the makeup stuff?"

That earned him a smile and a giggle. "We started the makeup *stuff.* I vacationed in Vermont with friends and found this cute little shop in a small town. I needed some lotion and lip balm. It's cold there, like it is here."

"Dries out the skin," he finished for her.

"Exactly. I loved the products and spoke with the owner. Turns out to be two sisters who started the company, making the products in their kitchen. Everything is organic, high-quality, natural ingredients."

"The two sisters reminded you of you and Lela, so you made them an offer," he guessed, earning him another of her elusive smiles.

"Yes. They didn't have the capital to bring the business into the mainstream and compete with other major companies. We launched the products in a few markets last year and sales are booming in those areas. We have a huge marketing campaign and rollout of the products scheduled for the week of our birthday."

"Your coming-out party." Gabe hated the way her eyes went soft and sad, filling with more unshed tears, thinking about everything her sister would miss. They'd worked together to create their own niche in the company, add to it like their father did before them. Just when they were about to announce their new product and take their place at the company, Lela was murdered, leaving Ella to uphold the family dreams by herself.

"You wanted that business."

"I like it and enjoy working on the products. The colors and scents."

"Seems right up your alley. The news showed you at Fashion Week in New York and Paris."

"With my friends, it's hard not to get caught up in fashion and makeup and all the trends."

Yeah, in her circle, all of that would be important. Still, she didn't seem quite that shallow.

"The thing is, Lela and I wanted the cosmetics business to prove to our uncle that we deserved to run the company. He was always so hard to please. Nothing we did ever seemed good enough."

"So you divided to conquer. Lela would have the school background and you'd have the company experience. Then you decided to get the MBA too. When you took over in a couple of months, you'd show him you earned it just as much as Lela."

"With my parents gone, I wanted him to be proud of us." She laughed bitterly.

Gabe rubbed his hand up and down her forearm. To keep her from falling back into despair, he changed the subject. "Can you run a combine tractor?"

Pride lit her eyes. "Yes. I can. I spent a month at the plant in Indiana."

"Where you now attend school." He put together the pieces.

She laughed, and this time the smile brightened her eyes. "Yes. I worked at the plant, and test-drove all the equipment."

"So you could be a farm girl after all."

"I said I test-drove it, so I'd know how to operate it. I didn't say I was trading in my Manolo Blahniks for rubber boots."

That made him laugh. "City girl."

"Cowboy."

"Hey, you own over one thousand head of cattle. That's more than me."

"I didn't know about them, which is odd because I worked in that division and audited everything they oversee. If the cattle fall under Jim, why didn't I find any records on them?"

"Maybe that's what your sister discovered in addition to the missing paintings. Maybe your uncle has been supplementing his income with the money you make on the cattle."

"Maybe. Are those the boxes of paperwork from my father's office?" She cocked her head in the direction of the front door.

"Yeah. That's everything. The thing is, I packed up those boxes myself. I didn't see anything about paintings or the cattle. Most of it is the bills and insurance on the ranch. Nothing stood out."

"Well, I'll take a look and see what I find. I might notice something you didn't. After all, you weren't looking for anything."

"No, not specifically, but I tried to scan all the files in case something important popped up. Your uncle wanted the stuff in storage, and he didn't seem inclined to want to go through anything, so I thought to let him know if something important needed his attention."

"His MO is to let others do things for him. He'll

probably send someone to go through the contents of the storage locker at a later date."

"Lockers. The house took up five huge lockers."

"Um, okay. I forget how big that place is. I haven't been there since my father died in the plane crash." Her eyes went blank on him.

"Hey, sweetheart, where did you go?"

"Why would Detective Robbins cover up a murder for my uncle? What else has he helped cover up?"

"Maybe the sale of the paintings. I imagine it's easier to find a buyer in New York than out here."

"I searched the Internet for any news reports that tie the detective to the art world. Nothing. None of the newsworthy cases he's worked have anything to do with that scene according to what I found, but that doesn't exactly rule it out."

"Let's start with what we know and work from there. Tell me what happened to your sister." She needed to talk about it, but he hated to make her relive it.

Ella told him the whole story, her voice soft and infused with anguish. His heart throbbed with the pain he felt in every detail she described from the horrendous images in her mind. "My uncle stood there, my sister dead at his feet, and told the detective to find me, put me in a hotel room, and stage an overdose. Everyone would believe it, right?"

"Except you don't do drugs. The people who really know you wouldn't believe it."

Her eyes went wide with surprise that he'd know that as the truth. "No, they wouldn't."

He reached out and swept his thumb over her wet cheek, cupped her face in his palm, and stared into her lovely, sad eyes. "I'm sorry, Ella. I like your sister. She had your strength and grit."

For a moment, she leaned into his touch, then pulled away, her eyes reflecting her guilt. "I'm hiding in your house. I haven't done anything to see that he gets what he deserves."

"You found out about the paintings. The cattle business. The sale of the ranch. We'll find the proof you need."

"We?"

"No one fucks with my life and gets away with it. Besides, you keep holding on to me, and I'll keep holding on to you." He squeezed her hand to indicate their connection.

"Why?"

"Because I don't want to let go," he admitted. Feeling exposed, he added, "Not until I know you're safe."

The silence between them stretched, but it never turned uncomfortable.

"They talked about her murder like it was nothing."

"They talked about killing you like it was nothing," he reminded her. "Are you sure he doesn't know where you are?"

"I can't be a hundred percent sure, but I've turned off my cell phone. I used cash at the airport, and haven't used my credit cards since I left New York. I used your phone to call Mary to make the funeral arrangements. Mary will erase the caller ID and keep that a secret."

"But you're having your sister brought here to be buried."

"Yes, but what difference does it make if her body is stored here or in New York? She can't be buried until the thaw anyway. My parents are buried on the ranch.

It would be strange if she isn't brought here and buried with them."

"You're taking too many risks. He'll find out and send someone after you—or even come here himself."

She knew the risk and took the chance anyway to see her sister buried, resting in peace with their parents. Gabe didn't like it, but changed the subject. What was done was done. He'd watch out for her if Phillip's henchmen came calling.

"How will you prove he killed your sister?"

"That may be a bit more difficult, but not impossible. I have a couple of ideas. Also, my uncle took something from my sister's body. I want it back."

"What if he got rid of it?"

"I don't think he did. There was something in the way he looked at the necklace and tucked it away in his pocket. I don't know how to explain it."

"Like he needed to keep it and remember what he did?"

"Yes. Something very nearly like that. Odd. Disturbing, but he seemed to covet that item."

"Your uncle is a psycho. What was he like to you growing up?"

"Distant. Uninterested. We lived in the same house, but you'd think we didn't know each other at all. The only time he took an interest was when I was in the papers and tabloids."

"He didn't like your public image."

"He believed what the papers wrote about me and my sister. When we were younger, she was by my side at most of the events before school took over her life."

"Maybe your public life will save you."

"Why would you say that?"

"Look at the media surrounding your sister now and the elaborate means he's had to go to cover it up. You've got wealth and status. The longer you stay missing, the harder it will be for him to pull off his plan to get rid of you. I caught a couple news reports on the radio. People are already speculating about your absence in New York."

"I didn't think about that. My friends would expect me to step up and make a public announcement of some sort."

"The people you know would look for you, try to contact you. They'd raise questions about your sudden disappearance, especially after your sister is found murdered."

"My voice mail box and email are probably full of messages, but I can't check them. They're probably tracing my phone. They've got my name and face splashed all over the TV. They need to find me and eliminate me to get away with Lela's murder."

"Which is why you were so cautious when we met. You were afraid I'd turn you over to your uncle and the police."

"You suspected last night that I wasn't Lela, even before you saw the news this morning, didn't you?"

He sat back in his chair and smiled. "It started with little things. The way you reacted when I called you Lela. You didn't remember meeting me. You played it off, but not well enough. It piqued my curiosity, so I paid attention. Your eyes are close, but just different enough that I noticed. You don't smell like her."

That earned him a smile and a halfhearted laugh. "I don't smell like her? Why are you smelling us?"

"Don't be shocked, but I like beautiful women."

She gave him a mocking stunned face with her eyes wide and her mouth open. It only made him smile more. He liked this playful side of her. Relaxed with him, she settled into the conversation and opened up.

"When I met Lela, the wind kicked up. I smelled her perfume. Most women smell good. You smell amazingly good."

"You liked her perfume?"

"Hers I liked. Yours is addictive."

"Are you flirting with me?" she teased.

It surprised him too, because she wasn't his type. Beautiful, smart, sexy as hell, yes, but a city girl at heart. Not the country girl he wanted. Still, he couldn't seem to help himself and continued to hold her hand firmly in his. Lost in the conversation and the connection they shared, she didn't realize her fingers rubbed against his skin in a hypnotic way that pulled him under her spell even more deeply than he cared to admit.

"I'm working on it. Maybe I need more practice."

"Um, so you knew I wasn't Lela because of my eyes and the way I smell."

He took her change of subject in stride. They'd get to the personal stuff over time. Right now, they had bigger things to talk about and clear up.

"I didn't know anything, except it seemed odd. I saw the news report this morning and it made sense. I met your sister, but I didn't get to know her. I'm sorry for your loss and everything you're going through. Whatever help you need, it's yours, because your uncle will go down for what he's done."

"You mean that."

"My father says if you aren't a man of your word, you aren't a man at all."

"I like your dad."

"I like him too."

"Do your parents live around here?"

"About forty miles away on the family ranch. Dad's getting older. He'll retire soon and travel with Mom. We're trying to convince Dane to come home and run the place. Blake lives a bit farther away. He's a world-class racehorse trainer. Caleb just got married last month and lives with his wife on her family's ranch in Colorado."

"Where is Dane?"

"Last I spoke to him in Nevada checking on the cattle I bought."

"I'm sorry, Gabe."

"I know you are. You'll make it right, but now we have bigger worries than my lack of funds and potentially losing my cattle, the horses, this place. You know, everything."

"I won't let that happen."

He wanted to believe her. Part of him did, but if her uncle succeeded in killing her, he'd be screwed. No way he let anything happen to her for that reason, and some others he didn't want to name right now. "How about we brighten things up? Dessert?"

"I loved dinner. I can't imagine what you've done for dessert."

"I picked up a double chocolate fudge cake from the bakery."

"Well, now you've found my weakness."

"Careful, I'll exploit it," he warned.

"By all means, I'd probably give up my fortune for chocolate."

"I don't want your fortune."

"What do you want?"

"To get to know you better," he answered honestly. "Looks like I'll get the chance." He cocked his head toward the window behind her.

"Oh my God, look at that snow."

"We're due for a couple of feet over the next three days."

"Are you serious?"

"I never joke about snow."

CHAPTER 13

Phillip sat behind his desk in the library now that the police had released the scene of the crime, his hand wrapped around a tumbler of bourbon, even though he'd like to wrap it around the cook's scrawny neck.

"Mary, you took some clothes and shoes to the mortuary."

Her gaze shot from the glass to meet his. "Yes, sir."

"I'm still not clear what prompted you to take such initiative."

"I've been with the girls since the day their parents brought them home. You are dealing with so much, what with the investigation into Lela's death and Ella's disappearance. It's not right to leave Lela at the morgue. Friends and distant relatives have called asking about the services. I needed to do something."

The tears gathering in Mary's eyes didn't affect him.

"Yet you didn't set up a service. You instructed them to send the body to Montana when it's released. Why?"

"Mr. and Mrs. Wolf are buried on the ranch property. It's only fitting Lela is buried with them. I thought it better her body be stored at a mortuary in Montana rather than New York, so we can bury her as soon as her grave can be prepared after the thaw. Besides, we can't have the service with the ongoing investigation and without Ella."

Made sense, but she was still lying about something.

"Have you spoken to Ella?"

"No, sir."

The lie rolled off the old bat's lips so easily. She'd always been protective of the girls.

"You'd do anything for them."

"Of course. It's my job," she added.

"And you want to keep your job and the sizable pension set aside for you when you retire from your position here. That pension goes away if you're fired."

The doorbell rang, saving her from answering his warning. Ella was too smart to tell the cook anything important, but he had to try just in case she might actually know something.

"Get that. If it's anyone but Detective Robbins, send them away." Before Mary exited the library, he said, "You should consider what will happen to you if I find out you're lying."

Her head came up and her steady gaze met his. "I do not know where Ella is." She left to do her job and see who was at the front door.

Phillip believed her. Oh, she'd spoken to Ella, but she didn't know where the girl was hiding. Which begged the question. Why was Ella hiding? All she had to do was come forward and accuse him of murdering Lela. He had made sure the evidence was stacked against her, but she'd, at the very least, raise suspicions about Lela's death.

Only one answer came to mind. Ella was coming after him and he'd better be ready. He needed to find her and teach her a lesson about going up against him.

Detective Robbins knocked on the open door to get his attention before closing it and walking over to take the seat in front of the desk. He eyed the glass of bourbon, the only outward sign Phillip remained nervous about this situation. Phillip normally didn't drink this early in the day, but he needed it to calm his nerves.

"Did you find out where Lela went those three days?" Phillip took a sip of his drink, trying to keep calm.

"She's as cagey as her sister. There's nothing on her credit card. She withdrew two thousand dollars from her bank the day she disappeared." Detective Robbins rubbed his hand over his brow. "I'm still checking video surveillance at the airport, but it's a lot of footage to comb through. In the meantime, I'm being pressured to bring Ella in for questioning. My superiors want to see progress on this case. I've tied the gun to Ella and can present the evidence to my superiors when we're ready. The press reported the possible motive. We either see this through or come up with another plan and shift the focus somewhere else."

"We can't. We need to move forward, find her, and shut her up immediately. Give another press conference. Offer a reward for information to locate her. When you find her, kill her and make it look like she resisted arrest and tried to flee. You had no choice but to shoot her."

"That will get my superiors off my back, but bring in internal affairs."

"I'll handle that for you. I have someone in the department." Phillip didn't say who.

"I don't like putting my ass and career on the line, or all these loose ends."

"Then do your job and find her and tie this up."

"It's not exactly that easy when the girl's got more money than God. She could be anywhere."

"How far can she get without accessing her accounts?"

"With friends as rich as she is, pretty damn far."

"Check with them."

"I have. None of them has heard from her. They are all worried and anxious, demanding I find her. They think whoever killed Lela may have abducted her. Even the press is suspicious about her disappearing from the public eye."

"If you believe her friends haven't been in contact with her, then she's out there on her own. Find her before this all blows up in our faces."

"If it does, don't expect me to cover your ass."

"Don't expect me to help you. I'll be out of the country, living the good life, while you rot in a cell if it comes to that."

The detective knew when to cut his losses. He rose from his chair and walked out of the room without another word.

Phillip downed the last of his bourbon, spun his chair around to stare out the windows at the afternoon sun bathing Central Park in golden light and tried not to think about what might happen if Ella uncovered all his secrets.

CHAPTER 14

Ella bolted upright, pulled from the nightmare, the blood spreading over her sister's chest, Lela's lifeless green eyes staring at her, begging her to do something, by a hand touching her shoulder. She grabbed hold and looked up, ready to fight off her attacker. Her breath came out in a whoosh.

"It's me, Gabe. I'm here. You're safe."

She sank back against the dining chair and let out a ragged breath. Gabe set a coffee mug on the dining table in front of her on top of one of the stacks of papers she'd spent most of the night going through with a fine-tooth comb.

"Are you okay?" He ran his hand down the back of her head to her neck and rubbed at her stiff muscles. The butterflies in her belly took flight into a whirlwind of awareness. The ruggedly handsome man standing this close to her sent a wave of heat rolling through her system. Like gravity, he drew her in.

"I'm tired and frustrated and pissed off. There's nothing here." She'd spent the whole night crossing her eyes looking at the papers, only to come up empty.

"If we have to go through every box in the storage lockers, we'll find the evidence."

"That's just it. I don't think it's there."

"Where would Lela hide it?"

"If I knew that I'd go and get it." She leaned her head against his arm. "Sorry."

"Don't be. You've been up all night."

"That's no excuse for snapping at you."

"Yeah, well, you need to let go of my hand now. I'm a nice guy, but I'm not dead."

Ella dropped her gaze to his hand lying on her chest, his fingers spread wide over her breast. Both her hands locked around his wrist. The sight of his big hand touching her so intimately sent a shaft of heat and electricity rushing through her system. Her nipples tightened and heat shot through her veins and pooled low in her belly. Her face and ears burned with embarrassment.

She loosened her hold, and his big hand swept up her chest and neck, his warm fingers cupping her chin and tilting her face up to his. He leaned down and kissed her softly on the forehead and met her gaze. Surprised and touched by the sweet gesture, she could only stare when he smiled.

"Sorry."

"I'm not. You look good in my shirt."

Time stopped. The moment stretched. Neither of them moved.

The Led Zeppelin T-shirt had become her favorite sleep attire over the last few days. She'd given him back his sweatpants after tripping one too many times on the long legs. She wore her sister's leggings.

His gaze dipped to her mouth and back to her eyes.

She thought he might kiss her. The last kiss she gave him had been too quick, but it packed a punch. She'd meant it as a thank-you for helping her and never expected it to mean so much more. Even in her dazed and sad state, she'd recognized the unique and overpowering attraction between them.

His fingers smoothed over her cheeks. "Go to bed. You need your rest."

"What time is it?" She grabbed his hand, turned his arm so she could look at his watch, and jumped up from her seat to grab the remote for the TV. She forgot about her ankle, stumbled, and tried to take the weight off her foot, but only managed to throw herself off balance even more. Strong arms locked around her waist and hauled her upright before she took a nosedive into the wood floor.

"Whoa now. Where's the fire?"

"It's almost seven. Top of the hour of the national news. Lela will be one of the first stories. I need to find out what my uncle is doing now." She turned her head to look out the window. A light snowfall fell from the sky. Nothing like the whiteout from last night. "Do you think the satellite is working?"

"Should be. The snow's not that thick right now. Give it a try."

She tried to take a step, but he held her close against his chest. She settled into him and looked over her shoulder and up at his handsome face.

"Slow down. Be careful."

Was that a warning about her ankle, their budding relationship, or for himself where she was concerned? She didn't know. Didn't care. It had been too long since anyone took care of her. Without her sister to look out for her anymore, she had no one left. No one but this strong and steady cowboy who went out of his way at every turn for her.

She shifted in his arms, facing him. He never let her go, but held her in a light embrace, his gaze steady on her face, waiting to see what she'd do. She wrapped her arms around his neck, went up on tiptoe, and laid her chin on his shoulder and hugged him close. The sense of warmth and safety she always felt around him amplified. "Thank you for taking care of me."

"I'll never let you fall, Ella. I won't let anyone hurt you."

"You're not like any man I've ever met."

Which was why she was drawn to him. He didn't take anything for granted. Spoke his mind and meant what he said. Protected what he loved and the principles he believed in. He didn't have an ulterior motive for the things he did for her. He just wanted to help someone in need. Generous and kind. Yeah, she didn't know many men like him.

She settled into him again. "I still haven't found what I need. I don't know what to do." Comfortable in his arms, maybe she had found one thing she needed. She didn't know what to do about him either.

His hands swept up her back and down, settling on her hips. He gently set her away and stared down at her. "Turn on the TV. See what that bastard is up to now. One step at a time. We'll figure this out."

The strange pull between them sent her back up on tiptoe, but this time, Gabe leaned down to meet her halfway. His lips met hers and settled, their gazes locked. She pulled back an inch, watching him, his eyes filling with passion like she'd never seen in any other man she dated. She brushed her lips against his again. Felt that pull turn to demand. She sank into him, opened to him when his tongue touched her lips in a soft caress that asked so much without a word spoken between them. Words weren't needed, not when everything inside her sighed and said, *This is where I'm meant to be. Right here. Right now. Always.* She never thought anything like this would happen to her. She'd never trusted fully in the people around her, who always seemed to want something. Wealth gave her opportunities and things, but it kept her lonely, especially after a few incidents where friends turned out to be leeches, taking and taking and giving nothing significant back.

Gabe swept his hand up her spine and pulled her closer, banding his other arm around her waist. She gave herself over to the kiss, his taste, his strength wrapped around her, and the knowledge that this man wanted only one thing—her.

Dangerous ground. Her mother had loved her father so deeply, it consumed her. When she lost him, she lost her will to live. Ella usually kept men at a distance and never allowed herself to feel anything more than lust the few times she found someone appealing enough to date.

With Gabe, she felt the rush of blood heating her body, the need to be closer, and the affection in her heart and mind for the man. The weight of grief lifted, the anger subsided, the frustration over not finding the evidence waned, and all she knew was she and Gabe locked in this moment. The kiss, the way he made her feel, she sank into both, absorbed it all and sighed, settling into him—them. Connected in a way she'd never felt, he ended the kiss with a brush of his lips over hers and a sweep of his hand over the side of her face and into her hair, pushing it back over her shoulder.

"God, you're beautiful."

She'd heard similar compliments from countless others, men she'd dated, women at parties and get-togethers, said with a smile and air kisses next to her cheek, but little sincerity behind the words. Gabe's softly spoken declaration sank into her heart, took root, and wrapped her in such a sense of belonging she found herself at a complete loss for what to say.

She reached up and touched her hand to his hard jaw and leaned her forehead to his chin. His arms contracted around her.

"It's going to be okay."

She believed him. It wasn't okay right now. It wouldn't be for a long time. But somehow, some way, she'd make it to okay again. When she did, she'd stand in this man's arms and feel all the wild emotions she felt right now for him without all the pain and heartache, and she'd finally be okay again.

Gabe did something that went against every command of every cell in his body and set Ella away from him, instead of pulling her closer. He held her by the shoulders and stared down into her upturned face. He traced his finger across her brow and drew her long bangs to the side and tucked the strands behind her ear like he'd seen her do a dozen times. He thought the gesture sexy as hell. Everything about her appealed to him, but he found the odd things she did—like scrunching up one side of her mouth when she didn't like what she was thinking—stuck with him. They made him smile on the inside and want to draw closer to her, know her better. He'd never cared enough about anyone besides his family to wonder what made her scrunch her face like that, or to want to make her happy, because he couldn't stand to see her so sad. Worse was listening to her cry in the night. He hated feeling so inadequate to heal her pain and make her smile. He wished he could bring her sister back, stop all this madness with her uncle, and keep her safe. Always.

If he thought he'd loved Stacy, and his need to protect and hold on to Ella was a hundred times stronger than anything he'd felt for Stacy, then what was this thing he had with Ella?

Dangerous. He knew how it would end, but didn't have an ounce of self-preservation. He let it ride, because any amount of time he spent with her was worth it, even when he knew it would end in pain and loss. Again. But this time would be worse, and still he gave in to the compulsion to be with her.

"Turn the TV on before you miss the news."

"Um, yeah, right."

He liked the way she hesitated to leave his side, but she refocused with a determination he had grown to admire more and more over the last few days. She felt things were moving too slowly, but she never stopped. She'd never back down. Not until she avenged her sister. He had no doubt she'd do it too. That said more about who she was than a thousand pictures of her walking out of a nightclub, or vacationing in some exotic location, wearing outrageously expensive dresses and shoes. Young, she should be out having fun with her friends.

Hadn't he done practically the same thing, riding the rodeo circuit from town to town, sleeping with random women, drinking, and having fun with his friends?

Those thoughts brought several others. Like maybe she was too young for him. Six years her senior; what the hell would she want with a guy his age, living in the middle of nowhere? Same story, different woman. The best he could do for a nightclub was the honky-tonk in town filled to the rafters with drunk cowboys, who outnumbered the women by at least four to one. She'd certainly have her pick of the litter. Not that she'd be interested in a bar full of rowdy cowboys when she was used to the jet-setting crowd. Still, it wasn't like they had nothing in common. She loved the horses and the quiet solitude of the ranch. They had the same taste in movies and music. Over time, he bet they'd find all kinds of things they both liked. If she stayed with him long enough to do that. Which wasn't likely, he reminded himself.

"What's that strange look on your face?" she asked, standing by the sofa, staring back at him. "Are you upset with me?"

"No." The edge to his tone made her frown and narrow her pretty green eyes on him. "Sorry. I'm fine. Just thinking." Distracted by his own thoughts, he hadn't paid attention to the TV. "What's on the news today?"

"A thirty-seven car pileup in New Hampshire killed eight people."

"More good news, huh?"

"The NASDAQ is up nine points."

"I'll call my accountant and tell him to sell. Oh, wait. I don't have an accountant or a 401(k)."

"What's the matter with you?"

"Nothing. I've been cooped up in the house too long."

"You just came back in after spending an hour out in the stables with the horses."

"So. Winter isn't exactly my favorite time of year. Too much snow and bad weather keep me indoors when I'd rather be outside."

"Then why don't you move?"

"This is home. I love it here."

Her lips tilted in a half smile and she shook her head at his contrary statements and mood.

The paper towel commercial ended and the reporter appeared on the screen again. "In other news, Phillip Wolf has offered a one-hundred-thousand-dollar reward for information leading to the whereabouts of his niece Ella Wolf, who has just been named a person of interest in her sister Lela Wolf's murder. Wanted for questioning, the New York socialite hasn't been seen in three days, causing speculation as to where she is and why she hasn't come forward to make a statement about her sister's death. Sources tell us the twins were due to inherit their parents' estate, including Wolf Enterprises, on their upcoming twenty-fifth birthday if they met the terms of the will.

"Inside sources confirm the police have evidence that shows the sisters fought and Lela Wolf was upset her sister wasn't living up to the terms. Lela recently earned her MBA from Columbia University and graduated summa cum laude, while Ella earned high marks for fashion and late-night partying."

"If you have any information regarding the whereabouts of Ella Wolf, you're asked to call the number on your screen."

Ella turned from the TV and faced him. "He put a bounty on my head. I can't go anywhere now. Someone will recognize me. How the hell am I supposed to figure out where my sister hid the evidence with the entire country looking for me?"

"Maybe it's not that bad." Gabe tried to sound convincing, but even he couldn't pull it off with the worry and fear building in his gut. Some people would do just about anything to get their hands on that money. People like Travis, who had seen her and knew she was with Gabe. He kept those thoughts to himself, but the smart woman was two steps ahead of him.

"Travis will contact the company and tell them I'm here. They'll send people to scour Montana to find me. He'll want the contents of the house, thinking Lela came here and found something. I'll never have a chance to go through everything now."

"First, Travis isn't likely to watch the news." She nodded, agreeing to his assessment of Travis and his TV-watching priorities. His preference probably leaned more to pay-per-view porn. Lord knows, the only person he'd get lucky with was himself. "Second, I'm telling you, there isn't anything in that stuff that pertains to the cattle or the paintings. Unless you found something in those papers, there's nothing to find."

"There's something. There has to be. This is the last place she came. She spent two days here. Where did she go? Who did she see? What did she find? That's what I came here to investigate and now I'll never have the chance. He wins."

"Wait. Stop. His plan is unraveling. If you come forward and tell the police he killed your sister, they'll have to investigate, and he won't be able to stage a drug overdose for you and make it look convincing."

"I don't have any proof. It's his word against mine.

He's got a detective who can make the evidence lab falsify reports on his side. How many other officials are in his pocket who can cover this up and make it look like I murdered my sister?"

"Then we stick to the plan. Find the evidence and bring it to the authorities. There has to be something you missed. You knew your sister better than anyone. You share the same DNA. You know how she thinks. How did she find out about your uncle and what he did? What would she do to find the proof? Where would she start?"

"Not here. Not at the ranch. Something prompted her to come here?"

"Okay, so what brought her here?"

"I don't know."

"Think. Something he said to her. Something he did at your house, or at the company that piqued her interest. What changed about her over the last few days you saw her?"

"Nothing. She worked as usual. Then she disappeared for three days. I thought maybe she found someone special and ran off for a lovers' weekend."

"Wouldn't she tell you about that?"

"We shared everything, but I thought maybe she'd fallen for a guy and wanted to keep it private until she knew for sure. I thought she wanted to keep it for herself for a little while."

"Because you shared everything and something like that she'd want to hold on to because it's hers," he guessed.

"Yes. We only know what it's like to be identical twins and have our experiences and lives so intertwined that nothing is ever really just ours. I thought she'd found something special. Someone that was hers to share her life outside of sharing mine." Choked up, a tear rolled down her cheek, followed by a dozen more. "She'll never fall in love, get married, and have a family of her own. I'll never have nieces and nephews to spoil. We were supposed to grow old together. I don't know how to live without my other half. I turn to tell her something ten times a day and she isn't there." Ella started to cry and fell into his arms when he reached for her. Her hands clutched his shirt and she buried her face in his chest. "I'm all alone, and I don't know how to be just me when it was always us."

Every heart-wrenching word tore at his heart. The depth of her sadness made him ache to his bones. He didn't know what to do, or what to say. Nothing would bring her sister back, or make her feel better.

She exploded out of his arms and paced away and turned to face him. "I was too late. I should have run faster. Gotten there sooner. I left her there. I didn't do anything!"

"You lived. And that's okay, Ella. It's what she wanted."

"I was right there. I should have saved her."

"How? Your uncle wants you both dead. What were you going to do, walk in there so he could kill both of you and make it look like a murder-suicide? Stop beating yourself up and thinking you deserved to die in her place. You knew each other better than anyone. She knew you'd finish this, so think like her and tell me, what would Lela do if she discovered something about your uncle?" He hadn't meant to yell at her, but she needed to focus on what she could do, not what she didn't do and couldn't have prevented in the first place.

Ella sucked in a ragged breath and focused on him. She wiped her wet eyes with the backs of her hands. "She is . . . was . . . meticulous about her schoolwork and job. She took notes. She kept her files and homework organized. She researched everything like crazy. If she found something that didn't fit, she'd investigate and figure out how it did, or why it was out of place."

"So she probably found something at the company and it led her here."

"That's the only thing that makes sense, but I don't know what she found." Ella stared off in the distance, her gaze on the window and the snow-covered fields outside. "She discovered the cattle. That's the only thing at the company that ties to the ranch. But it's not enough."

"What do you mean?"

"It doesn't account for how angry she was about what my uncle did. So he kept the money earned from the cattle. That's small compared to what the company makes on the whole."

"What if the cattle is the tip of the iceberg? The cattle led her to investigate further and she found something else."

"Possibly. Yes. It had to be something more to make her that outraged and to tie in to the fact that Uncle Phillip admitted he and the detective had covered up a hell of a lot more."

"So Lela discovered the cattle scam and started going back in the company records to see how far back your uncle's deceit went. What else did he do?"

"I don't know. But I'm going to find out."

CHAPTER 15

Ella had spent some quality time in the IT department at the company and became fast friends with a very interesting employee, who had a talent for coding. The company wasted Chris's talent on menial tasks. She and Lela promoted him. Their systems had never been more secure and their databases had not been used more productively in years. They'd reap the benefits for years to come with targeted marketing campaigns and improved customer service.

Right now, Ella needed Chris's skill set for an entirely different reason.

She used the prepaid cell phone Gabe picked up in town that morning when the snow had let up for a bit. She texted a message to the private number Chris used for family and friends to contact him when they crashed their computers, needed to install a new program, and just messed up something and couldn't figure it out. Chris cursed people for clicking on every emailed link, unknowingly opening themselves up to spyware and viruses. He joked that even his mother contacted him more for technical support to get her back on her beloved cooking websites than just to say hi and catch up.

Ella: I need your help. Lela needs your help.
Chris: What is going on? No way you killed Lela.
Ella: No. Someone just as close to her did. Help me prove it.

Ella held her breath, waiting the thirty seconds it took Chris to make his decision. Did he believe her?

Chris: What do you need?
Ella: UNTRACEABLE access to the Wolf Enterprises database systems.

Ella bit her thumbnail. Gabe's hand settled over hers and made her stop. The seconds ticked by, turning into minutes with no message.

"Why doesn't he answer already?" Gabe asked.

"I just asked him to commit what is probably a felony."

"It's your company. Your data."

"If I'm convicted of my sister's murder and he helps me, he could be in a world of trouble."

Chris: Access the system using the link I'm sending you. Log in under the admin account I showed you, using the PW I gave you.

"Do you know what he's talking about?" Gabe asked.

"Yes." She stared up at Gabe, unable to hide her excitement. Finally, a chance to do something to avenge her sister.

Ella: Thank you, Chris.

Chris: I'm sorry about Lela. I hope you find what you need.

Her phone beeped again with the URL. She typed it into Gabe's laptop. "I'm in."

"Start with the cattle business. See where that leads you," Gabe suggested.

"I'll do that right after I check my sister's emails, files, and calendar to see if she left any more clues."

It took Ella twenty minutes to discover the only thing out of place in her sister's organized electronic world.

Friday—2:30 PM—Mechanic—27 Elk Rd., Crystal Creek, Montana.

No name. Her fingers flew across the keyboard for another ten minutes, digging for anything she could find on the address. Frustrated, she slammed her hands on the table, startling Gabe watching TV on the couch.

"What's wrong?"

"I found an appointment for Friday with an address here in Crystal Creek."

"Really? Who'd she meet?"

"I'm not sure. Everything tied to the address is in Tom Wright's name, along with three other addresses."

"Rental property," Gabe guessed.

"Right. We need to go and see who really lives there." Ella stood to grab her jacket.

"Hold on. We can't go now."

"Why? This is a lead. A place to start. If my sister met with someone at this address, we have to check it out."

"Ella." Gabe dragged out her name. "Look out the window."

The whiteout snowfall that started last night, but had waned this morning, thickened with every passing moment. Dark, ominous clouds in the distance promised even more. She turned back to Gabe just as the "Severe Storm Warning" alert flashed across the TV screen.

"We caught a lucky break after breakfast when I went to get you that phone, but in another hour, we'll be lucky to have power, let alone a satellite signal. So, if you want to keep searching the company records, you better hurry up. We're about to be stuck here for at least a couple of days."

"No." Her voice rose with her conviction. She attempted a more rational tone. "We have to go now."

"It's not safe. But you will be for the next few days, because if we can't get out, no way anyone comes here for you either."

She held his intense stare. "Gabe." She pleaded with her gaze for him to understand the urgency building inside of her bones to do something. Now.

"I give you my word, as soon as the storm passes and the roads are safe to travel, I'll go to that address and find whoever lives there. I'll make them tell me what they know about your sister."

"You swear."

"I don't break my promises."

He was right. Frustrated, but resigned, she sat back at the computer determined to find anything else tied to her uncle.

Over the next two hours, she discovered a few more interesting facts. The cattle business contracts were buried in the system. Money got paid out to the Dorsche Ranch, but no income came in, which could only mean the income went to an account outside of Wolf Enterprises. Probably directly to her uncle.

She checked on Jim Harrison, the guy in charge of Western Operations. Interesting that his salary increased ten percent every year with a substantial bonus, when the company's employees' raises averaged five percent. Bonuses were given to key employees, but Jim received the largest, besides the executive staff. Reading between the lines, she guessed Jim overlooked the lack of income from the cattle business, orchestrating her uncle's embezzlement.

Her uncle hadn't started with the cattle, though. Gabe had been right about that. His deceit went further back. All the way back to two years before her parents died. Once she knew what to look for, or rather what wasn't there, namely income to match the orders going out, it was easy to follow the trail and uncover who else in the company covered it up.

"What's with the big sigh?" Gabe asked from the sofa, his arm draped along the back. Casually handsome, yet she felt his interest and restraint while he waited out the storm and the tedious computer investigation she performed despite the fact they both wanted to act on the one lead they had that might actually end this for her uncle.

"My uncle's embezzlement goes all the way back to when my father ran the company. It's more than him taking the income from the cattle business, despite the company paying Dorsche Ranch. Take the small appliances division. Deliveries went out to two particular distributors, but payment didn't come in. Same thing on the restaurant side. They aren't huge accounts, but still, the balances don't add up. In some cases, the price of stock going out doesn't match the income coming in. Some accounts get heavy discounts because of volume, but nothing like this."

"Why didn't your accounting department find these discrepancies?"

"Because my uncle had the accountant in his pocket. The person in charge of these accounts gets a very high salary and bonus each year. Like Jim Harrison, who runs the Western Operations division the cattle ranch falls under."

"So Lela found the embezzlement and came to check on the cattle business?"

"No. According to her search history, she didn't access any of these files."

"You're sure?"

"Yes. She came to meet the mechanic. But why?"

"I'm as antsy as you to find out." Gabe changed the subject back to what she could focus on. "What about audits of the accounts?"

"I'm going to check that now."

"Hurry. Snow's getting thicker. The TV is getting fuzzy. We'll lose the signal soon."

With another heavy sigh, she got back to it and followed the audit records, or lack thereof to the personnel files. Why hadn't the audits been done? Because the auditor died before he could do the job, according to his file. She looked up his replacement.

"Huh?"

"What?"

"Do you find it odd that just after my uncle started stealing from the company two auditors died?"

"Definitely a strange coincidence. How'd they die?"

She typed the man's name into her search engine

and checked the various links that came up with that name. One stood out. She opened the news article and read.

Gabe must have felt her surprise and dread. He rose and came to stand beside her. "What is it?"

"Mr. Trahan worked for my father. He died in a car accident. Run off the road at night. No witnesses. Do you think . . . No!" The TV went blank and she lost her Internet connection. Her gaze shot to the windows and the near-impenetrable wall of snow falling from the dark sky. "Damn it."

Gabe settled his hands on her tense shoulders. "Time's up. Satellite is out."

She slammed the laptop cover and let out a disgruntled huff, falling back against the chair back and crossing her arms under her breasts.

"I think you're right."

"About what?" She snapped the words out in a huff.

"If your uncle could shoot your sister and calmly discuss how to cover it up and murder you, I think he's killed before."

"He killed that auditor." Ella's mind filled with scenarios and possibilities. She spoke the one question that had circled her mind since her sister's death. "How many other people has he murdered?"

CHAPTER 16

The oil lamp's bright flame lit Ella's face across from him. Gabe studied the light and shadows as they shifted and changed her beautiful face, trying to figure out what it was about her that held his attention and made him yearn with a need he'd never felt for anyone. They'd spent the last three days cooped up in the house, snow falling so hard outside it had become treacherous to even make it out to the barn to feed the horses.

Distracting Ella from her dark thoughts had become his pleasure and torture. He wanted to get closer to her, but held himself back, knowing this thing crackling between them, hot as the flames in the fireplace, would never go any further than the short time she'd be here. Once she uncovered all her uncle's secrets, she'd walk out of his life.

Gabe tried every second to block out the fantasy Ella would ever want a country kind of life. No way he'd turn this place into a cage that held her from the city life she already lived in New York. He'd been down that road and had the road rash on his heart to prove that asking someone to go against who they are and what they wanted only ended in a tangle of wreckage.

"I raise you fifty cents."

Ella tossed two quarters on the coffee table between them. The fireplace at her back, legs folded in front of her under the table. When he shifted forward from bracing his back against the couch, their knees touched. Her eyes dilated with awareness and arousal. The same way they did whenever he accidentally touched her. He tried not to, but the pull between them was like a black hole, sucking them together.

Sometimes he had to touch her to draw her out of the quiet solitude that pulled her away from him and reality. With each passing hour, trapped in the house with nothing to do but think about her dead sister and how she'd gotten no further in taking down her uncle, her mood turned as gray as the gloomy sky. He didn't like those long periods she sat alone, her thoughts turned inward and her lovely eyes filled with so much hurt, loss, and sadness, his heart ached along with hers. Like they shared the same pulse.

Gabe checked his cards, figured she probably had better than his pair of sixes, but tossed in two quarters anyway. The girl knew how to play poker better than anyone he'd ever met. "Call."

She set her cards on the table with a smirk. "Three queens. Beat that."

"As usual, you've got me." He tossed his cards face-down.

"I can't possibly be whipping you this badly. You're losing on purpose just to make me feel better."

Ella turned the cards over. Her gaze swept up his chest and face to meet his. The heat spread through him, beckoned him to draw her close, kiss her, and feel the fire spread and make them both burn. He didn't move, but savored that tense moment they shared staring at each other, both knowing what the other wanted, but not willing to make that leap. Not yet. But how long could he hold out? If he gave in, would he ever be able to let go? No. So he held himself back.

"Wow." She shook her head before letting out a chuckle. "You really are a horrible cardplayer."

That made him laugh. "Normally, I'm the one sweeping the pot my way. I should take you to Vegas, give you some money, and let you win me some big bucks to cover my recent losses."

"Anytime you want to go, I'm in."

"If it meant you'd be safe, I'd take you right now."

Her gaze went to the windows and the snow falling in a cascade of white flakes.

"I feel as though I've been cocooned in here these last days. Safe. Protected. I think about what will happen when the storm passes, I find the evidence, and I emerge. What happened changed me. I'm no longer Ella, Lela's twin. I'm just me, and I don't know who that person is without her."

Gabe reached across the table and took her hand. His thumb swept over the back of hers in a hypnotic sweep of his skin against hers. The warmth of it seeped into her skin and spread up her arm and through her whole body and deep into her heart.

Sometimes a simple touch holds more meaning than any words offered to fill the space that remains empty no matter what is said. Sometimes having someone beside you in the quiet solitude is enough.

Sometimes all you need is a friend who knows you, sees you, cares enough to be with you when there really is nothing left to say.

Gabe had become that person for her over the last few days. Such a short time for them to settle into such an easy relationship. One that felt old, comfortable, like they'd read each other's souls and said, *I remember you.*

Gabe rose, keeping her hand in his, and pulled her up. He leaned down and blew out the lamp's flame. The fire had dwindled to red and black coals. Just enough to cast a soft glow over the hearth. With no other light, she depended on Gabe to lead her through the house he knew even in the dark. He stopped beside her outside her bedroom door. Like the last three nights, the connection they shared sparked like lightning up a Jacob's ladder.

They stood inches apart, her hand held in his. Neither of them breathed. They stared at each other in the dark, wanting, needing the other, but neither of them moved.

Gabe leaned in, his mouth a breath from hers, but he stopped, his eyes searching hers in the dimness that could hold their secrets if only they'd give them up, give in to this desire pulsing between them.

Gabe pushed the door open behind her, released her hand, and stepped back still staring at her for a heartbeat. Two. Then he turned and walked down the hall to his room and closed the door between them.

She crawled into her cold, empty bed. She wanted to go to him. Be with him, but that wasn't fair. To either of them. He didn't want to take advantage of her grief. She wasn't sure what she felt went beyond needing his comfort and strength to see her through these dark days.

The thought of never being held by him in the night, never knowing what it felt like to make love with him made her heart ache. When this was over, could she leave, go back to her life and run the company, never knowing?

No.

Because it was more than attraction. Gabe was a man worth knowing. He was a man worth taking a chance on.

CHAPTER 17

Phillip answered his cell phone on the first ring. "Tell me the reward worked and you found her," he barked to the detective.

"We've received numerous calls, but nothing checks out. The surveillance videos are taking too long to go through, so I came down to the company to check out Lela's computer. I found an odd calendar entry for Montana."

The library walls closed in on him. "What?"

If Lela and Ella went to the ranch, they might have discovered the missing paintings and cattle business. Impossible that they found anything more—unless they discovered the sale of the property. He'd under-sold it by a substantial sum. He needed the cash. Bribes to grease wheels were expensive, and he lived a rather extravagant lifestyle. His mistress cost a fortune, but she was well worth it. He'd finally found someone who understood what he needed and liked. The money he gave her and the apartment he maintained to keep her set him back plenty, but he didn't care. He deserved her.

"Why would she have a meeting scheduled with a mechanic in Montana? There's no name, just an address."

Phillip's stomach tightened with dread. He slammed his fist down on the desk and swore. So Lela had found it all.

"Hire men to check that address and the ranch property for Ella. Send them immediately. Find that fucking mechanic. Find Ella. Kill them both."

"Consider it done."

CHAPTER 18

Gabe parked in the dilapidated mobile home's driveway. As promised, he'd check out the "mechanic's" place and find out who really lived here before he went to the property owner, Mr. Wright, asking questions. He didn't want to bring Lela's name into it and cause any suspicions that would lead the cops straight to Ella.

A car engine drew his attention down the short driveway. The mail truck lumbered along the road and stopped at the line of mailboxes. Gabe rushed down the drive to intercept the mailman.

"Howdy," the mailman called, stepping from the truck, his hands loaded with mail.

"Hey there. Do you know who lives here?"

The mailman's eyes went soft and his gaze drifted to the beige mobile home. "This is ol' Jarrod Finney's place. Too bad what he done to himself."

"What happened?" Gabe asked, trying not to sound overeager for the answer.

"Shot himself dead. I tell you, I never seen nothing like it."

"You found him?"

The mailman frowned and stared off in the distance.

"Mail was piling up in the box, so I went up to check on him. He'd been dead a couple days by then. Smelled something terrible. I called the cops out. They took care of him from there. Must have been all those medical bills piling up. I don't know what he had, but the bills just kept on coming. Must have been too terrible a burden for him, especially after his wife was found shot dead in some seedy motel room outside of Bozeman."

"When did that happen?"

"Oh, years ago. Probably ten or more now."

"What did Mr. Finney do for work?"

"As far as I know, he didn't work much at all anymore, but once he was a mechanic. He said something about working at the airport when his wife was killed."

Gabe sucked in a breath. Not an auto mechanic. An airplane mechanic.

He needed to get back to Ella, so they could zero in on Jarrod Finney. Gabe didn't believe in coincidences. Ten years ago, Stuart Wolf's plane crashed.

Gabe's mind spun with questions and speculations.

"Thank you for the information." Gabe left the mailman to finish putting the mail in the line of mailboxes and hightailed it back to his truck. Scrapes on the front door by the knob caught his attention. Maybe they were from the police getting into the place after Mr. Finney took his life. Maybe not.

Gabe climbed the wood steps. They creaked and bowed under his weight. He went to the dirty window, cupped his hands on the grimy glass, and looked in. Mail and papers littered the dining table and floor. The kitchen cupboards stood open, the contents pulled out and tossed on the counter and floor along with the papers. Drawers hung from their openings or sat stacked and battered on the floor. The living room had suffered the same ransacking as the kitchen. He bet the back bedrooms hadn't fared much better. Not messy house-keeping. Not the cops. Phillip's men had been here. They were closing in. He needed to get back home to Ella.

He ran for the truck and jumped into the cab. He turned the key, revved the engine, and threw the truck into drive. He rolled down the driveway, turned onto the road, and pointed the truck toward home. Toward Ella.

A black Escalade pulled out of a side road and onto the road behind him. His gut tightened with dread. Too far back to see his plate, but way too close for comfort.

Gabe hit the gas, lengthening the distance between him and what had to be Phillip's men. He took a long, roundabout way to the back road that led across the south side of his ranch and allowed him a clear view of the road behind him and Wolf Road ahead. All clear.

No way he'd lead them to her.

Ella sat at the dining room table, staring out the window. Today, though the sky might have cleared, her mood remained as turbulent as the storm that passed.

Gabe came up behind her, smelling of hay, horses, and the cold, crisp wind outside. He'd been a beacon in her dark world, drawing her close, teasing, and coaxing her out of her moods. Still, living with the sexy rancher made her palms itch to touch him. Just looking at all those rippling muscles made her want to crawl up him and kiss him. That thick mass of hair made her want to slide her fingers through it and grab hold and never let go until their bodies came together and burned up all this pent-up desire building inside her the longer she spent in his company.

Did the man have to look that good in a pair of jeans and boots?

She thought about the almost kiss when he left her at her bedroom door last night. The way he looked at her and made her feel. She wanted to kiss him right now, just to feel his lips pressed against hers again.

She gave in to need and her heart's demand and stood and wrapped her arms around him. "Are you okay?"

"Fine." The word didn't match the way he squeezed her to him and the sigh of relief he let out.

"You're not telling me something. What happened?"

He hesitated and held her tighter. "I almost got caught by your uncle's men."

She gasped out her surprise. "What? No." She stepped out of his arms, wishing she'd stayed enclosed in all that strength and protection. "Did they see you?" Worry knotted her gut.

"I took the long way home, up the back pass. No one followed me."

"You're sure."

"Yes. I'd never let anything happen to you."

"What did you find?" she asked, still peeved Gabe had refused to let her accompany him to follow up on the only clue her sister left in Montana.

"A man named Jarrod Finney lived at the address you gave me. He wasn't an auto mechanic, but an airplane mechanic. He worked at the Bozeman airport. The mailman didn't have a lot of information on the man, but he did say that Mr. Finney's wife was found dead in a motel room about ten years ago."

Ella's heart lurched as pain gave way to fury. The coldhearted bastard ripped away all her happiness and everyone she loved. She wanted to put him down like a rabid dog.

"My father's crash was no accident." In the last few days, with everything she'd learned, this had niggled the back of her mind, and yet she had pushed the thought away. Her uncle had killed his own flesh and blood, and yet the murder of his brother seemed impossible.

"Did you talk to him?"

"I'm sorry, Ella, but he committed suicide. If my guess is right, the same day your sister showed the meeting with him on her calendar."

"If he confessed to a plot to kill my father, we'll never know now. He and Lela are both dead and the information is gone with them. Another dead end." Literally. "More mysterious deaths that tie to my uncle but I can't prove he orchestrated or committed them himself." Her heart sank. She planted her elbows on the table and held her head in her hands, trying to sort out all she knew, but couldn't prove. She wanted to fight and scream and make someone understand what she couldn't put into words.

"What other mysterious deaths? What more have you found?"

"You know about Mr. Trahan, the auditor who got run off the road and died. The audit was never completed the year my father died, or the next. Then the executives must have noticed. Our CFO ordered the audit. Again, the man in charge . . . a Mr. Reiser"—she held up one of the articles she'd printed out—"met with an untimely death."

"What happened to him?"

"Shot during a mugging."

"What the fuck?"

"There's more. The police arrested the CFO who ordered those audits. Turns out he and another woman ran a high-priced call girl service. Someone tipped the cops off that he was involved."

"I bet I can guess who," Gabe said.

"It makes sense. I was in high school when this happened, and my uncle hired a new CFO—a longtime friend of his from college. The person who completes the independent audit each year since my uncle's hand-picked CFO came on board is listed in the payroll system as a contractor. He's paid monthly for his services. The thing is, he only works for about two months for the company."

"The rest of the time he's being paid off." Gabe ran a hand through his hair.

"What if these men didn't have accidents at all? What if my uncle killed them?"

"Jeez, Ella, that's two men at the company, possibly the mechanic's wife, Lela, and your father, all tied to your uncle."

"I know. I don't have any proof, just the embezzlement and my suspicions."

"What about your mother's death?" he asked, his words soft.

"She loved my father in a way I can't explain. They were like two puzzle pieces. When they found each other, they locked and did everything together. The one thing they loved more than anything was riding. My father kept several horses at the New York estate. They went there all the time to be together, ride, have picnics. It was their place. She hung herself in the stables. She couldn't live without him. She didn't live for us."

"Ah, Ella, I'm sorry."

She didn't want his sympathy and pushed forward. "I found a few other threads leading me in other directions, but they require phone calls and possibly visits in order to actually unravel this ball of lies and deceit."

"Lela told your uncle she had proof he did something. So the mechanic must have given it to her. We still need to find it. The embezzlement will put him in jail, proof he committed murder will keep him there. I have something else to show you." He grabbed the large envelope he must have set on the table when he walked in and pulled out some papers.

"Before I checked out Finney's place, I stopped by the courthouse and asked the clerk to pull all the records in your father's name and regarding Wolf Ranch." He set the papers in front of her. "Turns out, the property is much bigger. In actuality, it's just over twenty-three thousand acres. Your father bought the original property and built the house." He pulled the second deed out of the pile and set it on top. "Two years later, he made an additional land purchase when prices dropped drastically. Over time, the land has become worth a hell of a lot more."

"How much more?"

"With the additional wells, grassland, and rangeland, about sixteen-point-nine million. Your dad was something else."

"Yes, he was. He bought low and sold high. My uncle sells things that don't belong to him way below market value and thinks he's doing good business because he's got cash in his pocket."

"I thought you should know. The language in the purchase papers states all of Wolf Ranch, which technically includes this additional land. If the deal went through, your uncle would have cost you more than fifteen million dollars."

"With this and the paintings and cattle we're no longer talking a drop in the bucket of the Wolf assets, but a downpour."

"You've uncovered a lot of things you can use against your uncle. Because of that, I contacted someone I know at the FBI."

"What?"

"Hear me out. My brother Caleb's wife has a brother in the FBI. Sam's in Virginia. He's agreed to help you whenever you're ready to go up against your uncle. He'll remain on standby, until we need him. In the meantime, he's quietly putting together a case against Detective Robbins, the lawyers who set up the ranch deal, and your uncle. It's just preliminary stuff, but put together with what you've found, you've got a case to arrest your uncle."

"I don't have all the proof to back this up."

"We'll find it."

"What if I don't?"

"You will."

"Do you trust Sam?"

"Absolutely."

"You're sure?"

"I'd have to be to trust him with your life." He held out his hand to her. "Come on. You need a break. Get dressed. You're coming with me."

"Gabe, I can't go anywhere. Someone might see me."

"We're not going to town, just out for a walk. It's

sunny. We'll keep it short, so you don't hurt that ankle. You need to get out of this house."

"I need to keep working."

"It will be here when you get back."

"Gabe."

"Ella, I want to spend time with you outside these walls. Come to the stables. See the horses. You'll feel better."

The thought of seeing the horses appealed to her on a deep level. She hadn't been outside in days. As much as she'd uncovered about her uncle, she had a lot more work ahead of her. She needed a clear head, some time to let what she'd learned settle.

"That look on your face tells me you want to go. So, come on, city girl."

CHAPTER 19

Gabe waited in the kitchen for Ella to get ready to go out. She didn't look good. Dark circles marred the undersides of her eyes. She'd barely slept the last few days and when she did, she had nightmares that made her scream out in the night. He wanted to go to her, wrap her in his arms, and make it all go away. As if he could make her forget, but he'd work damn hard to distract her. Oh, the many ways he'd distract her. He'd start with another kiss, his lips pressed to hers, his tongue sliding in to taste and tease. They'd end naked and happily exhausted, because if he had to walk around much longer in this hyper-aroused state he'd explode.

The kiss they shared played in a loop in his mind. He could still taste her. He thanked God and the universe this morning for clear skies. If he had to spend one more day in this house alone with her and nowhere to go, he'd grab her and take her to bed because the wanting was killing him.

She needed time and he needed to decide if he could let her go if he did sleep with her, because there was no way in hell she'd stay with him when she had so much waiting for her in New York. Her friends. A company to run. A life he couldn't give her here. He came up with one reason after another for why he shouldn't sleep with her. She was too young. Too rich. Nothing like any of the other women he dated.

That one actually appealed to him more than anything else. He liked her. Admired her courage and determination. The woman refused to quit.

She amazed him with her insights, computer skills, knowledge about finance and how her business ran. Her uncle underestimated her. If he'd let the twins take over the company as planned, he'd have reaped the benefits of their combined talents. Now it was left to Ella to right the wrongs her uncle instigated and take the company into the future on her own. A monumental task, but he didn't doubt for a second she was up for the challenge. He only hoped she remembered to take care of herself. Right now, grief held her captive. Until she had time to process the loss of her sister and the loss of the dream they'd shared for their future, she'd stay in this depressed state that took over her and stole all the light he saw inside her when she forgot everything else and was just with him. Those moments were rare, but something to hold on to. He'd tuck them away, pull them out someday soon when he missed her, and remember he once lived with a remarkable woman.

"Gabe. I'm ready."

He wasn't. Not for the punch to the gut that hit him when he turned around and saw her wearing one of the sweaters he bought her. He'd never bought a woman clothes. It made him feel strange to see her in something he picked out especially for her. He'd never tell her he stood in front of the displays agonizing over which ones to get her because he wanted her to like them, despite his limited choices and lack of experience. She looked good. She had worn the dark pink the other day. It made the gold highlights in her light brown hair stand out. Today she wore the dark purple. He loved the way it made the green in her eyes glow.

Nervous because he hadn't said anything, just stared, she ran her hand over her stomach and asked, "Does it look okay?"

"You're beautiful. The fit's perfect."

Yep, the sweater hugged her curves and made his mouth water. He wanted to get his hands on her, slide them up and under the sweater, and feel her smooth, warm skin against his palms. He wanted to mold her full breasts in his hands and feel the weight of them when he kissed her long and deep. He wanted her with a passion he'd never felt.

"I really love it." Her words came out soft and shy. Her head dipped to the side, her gaze on a spot by his feet. Probably because he couldn't hide how much he wanted to kiss her again. "It's very soft."

Like everything about her. Her hair. Her skin. Her sweet flowers-in-spring scent. Her eyes when she stared at him without thinking about it. Her lips when he kissed her.

"We should go." Maybe he said that too abruptly.

"Gabe, are you mad at me?" She shifted her weight.

"Nope. Just need to get out of this house." He needed to put some distance between them, but couldn't manage to put actions to thought because it went against everything else he felt inside. Ignoring the warnings in his head, he took her hand and led her to the front door. He helped her with her coat and checked out her feet. "The boots fit okay?" She'd only worn the brace and her socks in the house. He found it cute. He never thought anything cute, except maybe puppies, kittens, and foals.

I'm losing it.

"They feel great. Heavy. I'm sure they'll keep my feet dry and warm."

"Let me know if they don't and we need to come back. Can you walk on that ankle, or does it still hurt?"

"It's much better. A few days off it did wonders."

"That and the ice I kept making you put on it."

"No more ice. I'm tired of being cold all the time."

Happy to warm you up. He left that thought unsaid. "You're walking better, that's what matters." He took her hand again and opened the door and ushered her out with him. He slowed his pace to match hers. She favored her right foot, but it barely slowed her down. "How's your hip?"

"Sore, but better. The bruises are fading."

The image and the memory of all that creamy skin stretched out below him from his dream last night filled his mind. The thought of making love to her, kissing every inch of skin from her rosy lips to her little toes, nearly made him groan.

"Good. I'm glad you feel better."

"Hard not to when you take such good care of me, cooking every meal, cleaning up, and making me take a break a split second before I throw my computer out the window."

"I'm worried about your blood pressure," he teased.

"Yeah, well, you should be more worried I'll take one of the guns from your house and shoot my uncle."

"I'll load it for you."

They might both be joking, but her uncle deserved it and more.

Gabe opened the stable door and let Ella go in ahead of him. He stopped short before he slammed into her back. "What's the matter?" he asked, wondering why she didn't go in.

"Oh, Gabe, look at them."

Gabe followed her gaze and smiled. At least twelve of his horses stuck their heads out of the stalls and some whinnied to greet him. He stared down at her and caught his breath. Her whole face lit up with joy, seeing all the horses. He put his hands on her shoulders and gave her a squeeze. "That's the first real smile I've seen from you." Her happiness made him feel lighter, so he kissed her on the side of the head and nudged her forward. "Go see them. They're bored in here. I've got to let them out into the pastures later, but I thought you'd like to see them first."

Ella didn't need coaxing. She took off down the aisle and greeted the first horse she came to with an affectionate pat on the head and a vigorous scratch behind the ear. He'd prepared for her to come, so he grabbed the bag of sliced apples from the table next to the sink and met her five doors down the aisle.

"She's beautiful." Ella referred to the palomino mare.

"Her name is Winnie. I got her two years ago as a foal. She's my girl." Winnie stretched and nuzzled his neck, then tried to steal the whole bag of apples. "She loves her treats." He handed a couple of slices to Ella to feed Winnie.

"I miss my horses."

"How many do you have?"

"Two beautiful Arabians. A black and a white. Bentley and Mercedes."

"Even your horses have expensive names."

"That was a joke." She laughed and smacked him on the arm. "You are so easy. Try Angel and Belle."

He had to admit, she got him. She held Winnie's head in both hands and laid her forehead to the horse's.

"They are my babies. I miss them. I don't spend nearly enough time with them at the estate outside the city these days."

"You should make time. They obviously make you happy."

"When things got tough, or I needed time away from the city to think, I'd go to the estate and ride for hours. I always felt closer to my parents there. I'd spend time brushing down the horses and pampering them. They help me relax and think clearly again."

Gabe handed her a brush from the table, unlatched the door to Winnie's stall, and held his hand out to indicate she indulge her need to be with the horse.

"Winnie loves to be spoiled. You hang out with her. I'll let the others out into the pasture. Careful on your ankle."

She readily went into the stall and started working the brush over Winnie's golden coat. He walked to the stall next door, but stopped from going inside to get Sully when Ella walked out of Winnie's stall and stopped him.

"Gabe."

"Yeah?"

"Thank you for understanding."

Yeah, he understood how much she needed a distraction, one she loved and helped her settle her mind.

He went to her, cupped her face, and tilted it up. His lips touched her forehead in a soft kiss. He'd like to kiss her in a different way, but she needed the comfort and he needed to give it to her. Anything to make her feel better, because seeing the sadness come back into her eyes tore at him in a way that connected him to her even more.

"You're welcome, sweetheart." He stared down into her beautiful face and bright green eyes. "It'll take me about half an hour to get these guys out to the pastures. Winnie is all yours."

She reached up, wrapped her hands around his neck, and pressed her body down the length of his. He reined in the urge to crush her to him and take her mouth in a deep kiss. The hug ended far sooner than he'd like. No amount of time with her would ever be long enough.

That thought hung with him for the next half hour as he let the horses out into the fields. He left three of the horses that weren't feeling well in the stables, along with Winnie. He'd kept his eye on Ella. She'd kept her eye on him, glancing his way whenever he came back. He caught the glimpses of interest in her when her eyes roamed over him, heating his body.

The play of emotions on her face shifted and changed the longer she spent with the horse. Sadness overshadowed her earlier joy at seeing the horses. At one point, she broke down and cried again. He kept to his chores and let her work out her thoughts and memories and grief in her own way and time.

The tears had dried and she set the brush on the table and went back to Winnie and gave the big horse a hug. He smiled, knowing exactly how she felt. Sometimes, you just needed someone to hang out with, who didn't say anything while you worked out your shit.

Ella stood back, gave Winnie a scratch behind the
ear and down her neck, and let out a heavy sigh. His
cue to step in and change her focus again, or she'd just
go back to poring over files and not take the time she
needed for herself. Sometimes stepping away from
things helped put them into perspective.

Gabe came up behind Ella and clamped his hands
on her shoulders, working his fingers into the tired and
sore muscles.

"Thanks."

"You're welcome."

She surprised him and turned, going up on her toes
to kiss him softly. A touch of her lips to his. Far too
short and lacking the passion they both felt in the jolt to
both their bodies. The intensity in her eyes matched the
need gnawing at his gut to pull her close and devour,
but he left his hands where they were on her hips,
loosely holding her close, but still too far away. He'd
paid attention to this woman over the last few days, and
the tilt of her head and the set of her mouth told him she
had something to say, something important weighing
on her mind.

"I mean it. Thank you for making me come out here.
I needed this."

"I know you want to find the truth, but you've got to
take care of yourself. You'll figure this out."

"It's taking too long. I feel like I'm missing something important. Like she told me something and I
didn't hear it."

"Let's take a walk. Clear your head. Take a look at
everything again with fresh eyes." He set her away and
took a step back. He needed the space, or he'd do something stupid. Like pick her up and carry her over to the

pile of hay bales and set her pretty bottom on them and strip her bare and make love to her right here in the stables. That would knock some of the city girl right off her. Of course, she seemed just as comfortable here as she did there.

"What's that look?" Ella tilted her head and studied his face.

"What look?"

"That one. Where you shake your head and look at me like I'm a strange bug."

"You are strange."

"I'm sorry."

"You are everything you are, but then you're not."

"Well, that explains it."

She didn't get it. He didn't really get it, but it appealed to him in a weird way that made him think about her more and more. Everything about her didn't add up to what people knew about her, but in a strange way, it did.

"You're a city girl."

"I live in New York City, but I've been to many places over the years, including Montana," she pointed out.

"Yes. That's it."

"What's it?"

"You fit in just about anywhere."

"I don't know about that."

"You fit here. You're just as comfortable living in the city, going out to clubs, and shopping in Manhattan as you are brushing down the horses and staying with me in my little house. You are everything the public sees about you, but then you're so much more they don't even begin to guess."

"You aren't only a cowboy. Sure you've got the

horses and the cattle. The spread you've set up here, but you're much more than that. You're a college graduate with spreadsheets that put some of my project managers to shame. Statistics, financials, genealogies for the animals, projections, and forecasts. While that is what you do, you are grounded in family and tradition. You didn't want my ranch to show off that you live in that big house. You wanted it for the land, the stable space you so obviously need for all the horses you adore like a father does his children. You wanted it to build something lasting. Something you can pass on the way your father will pass on his ranch to you boys. Your brothers are everything to you. You'd drop everything this second and go to them if they needed you."

"So. They're my brothers. That's what you do for family."

"No. That is what *you* do for family. Some of us aren't so lucky to have that kind of bond. Some of us had it and lost it. You hold on to it, to them, because they are important to you. I look at the pictures in your house, hear the way you talk about your brothers and your parents, and I envy you.

"I think about what happens after I take down my uncle. What then? Everything I planned with Lela is gone. What am I doing all of this for? Yes, to see my uncle pay for killing my sister, but once that's done, it's just me."

"You'll run the company. You'll go back to your friends in New York. You'll have your life, and you'll live it for you and Lela."

"What if that isn't the life I want? Not without her. I thought the next chapter of my life would be running the company with Lela. Now it seems like a lifetime of work and no fun. What would I be working for? The satisfaction of taking what my father started and making it more successful. Why? So I can have more money? For what? To buy more stuff I don't need or want."

"Ella, you're not thinking straight. Once you finish this with your uncle, you'll settle into your life again the way it is now."

"Right. The way it is now."

Her gaze went unfocused. She stared at nothing past his shoulder and he felt the weight of her loneliness. He didn't know what to say, because she was right. She'd go back to New York, take over the company, and do it alone. Of course, she'd rise up out of her grief, her friends would circle around her, and eventually she'd start living her life and find someone to share it with her. The overwhelming urge to punch something, or whoever had the audacity to be with her when he wanted her this bad, stunned him. He'd never been a possessive man with any woman who came into his life. Probably why he let them go so easily. Letting go of Ella wouldn't be easy. In fact, the longer he spent with her, the harder it got to think about his life, the next steps he needed to take without her.

This time, he did reach for her and wrap his arms around her and pull her close. He held her tight, so she felt how much he needed her close. He pressed his cheek to her head and gave her as much truth as he could speak aloud. "You are not alone. I will be with you every step of the way until your uncle is behind bars. I'm here as long as you want me."

Her head came up and her expressive green eyes filled with a longing that matched his own. Her gaze dipped to his mouth and back up. He read the need in her eyes, but still tried to fight it. For her. For him. "Tell me to go and leave you alone."

"I don't want to be alone. I want to be with you."

He wanted to ask her for how long, but stopped himself, because soon she'd leave and go back to that life she thought she'd outgrown, but would want back because it was familiar. She'd need it back to regain some of the normal from her past in her new life without her sister.

Way past saying anything, he let loose the reins on his need and pulled her close. He dipped his head, his gaze on her rosy lips. They parted on a sigh, and he pressed his mouth to hers for a deep kiss. He held nothing back this time and plunged in, giving everything and taking all she offered. His lips fit to hers, and she opened to him without reservation. He swept his tongue along hers, melding his mouth to hers. His fingers gripped her hips, let loose, and swept up inside her sweater and up her smooth spine. When his fingertips touched her skin, she sighed and pressed closer. He spread his fingers wide and smoothed them down her back and over her bottom, gripping tight, he pulled her up to her toes and pressed her hips to his, letting her know in blatant reality how much he wanted her. She rocked her hips against his hard cock, and he groaned, breaking the kiss to move down her throat and kiss that sweet spot between her neck and shoulder. "God, you always smell so damn good."

Her head fell back, and he kissed his way back up her throat to her lips again for another searing kiss.

"Don't stop," she said against his mouth. "Don't ever stop."

"I'm just getting started." To prove it, he sank his tongue deep in her mouth and tangled with hers in a sensual kiss that rocked him hard.

Ella gave herself over to Gabe. Everything in her mind disappeared except for one thought. She wanted him. When she was with him, she believed everything was going to be okay. When he kissed her, she felt a connection as deep as the one she'd shared with her sister. Different, but just as strong.

Her back hit the stable gate. He lifted her leg and held it against his hip, sliding his hand up the length of the outside of her thigh to her hip, dipping low over her ass. He pressed his hard shaft to her lower belly. She angled her hips and rubbed against him. His mouth blazed a trail up her throat to her mouth. She opened for him, meeting every thrust of his tongue with her own. She gripped his jacket in her hands, held on while they went at each other in a frenzy. Too much separated her from him, so she slid her hands between their bodies and unzipped his jacket. He barely gave her enough room to do that before her hands went around his back and up under his thermal shirt and slid over the strong muscles in his back, up his spine, and back down again. His warm skin slid against her palms. She brought them around his sides, spread her fingers wide, and mapped his stomach up to his chest. Nothing but a wide expanse of tight muscles and warmth she wanted to sink into and hold on to forever.

Gabe must have felt the same way as she did about getting her hands on him. He grabbed hold of the bottom of her sweater and stopped kissing her long enough to yank it up and over her head. His eyes locked on her breasts and the heat in his eyes flared. She shook out her hair, fisted his shirt in her hand, and pulled him back close to keep her warm. His big hands spread over her back and down to her hips, pulling her close. She gasped when he touched the still healing bruises and her aching hipbone. Gabe mumbled, "Sorry," against her lips and softly rubbed circles over her battered muscles and bones. The caress sent a shaft of heat to her core.

Ella faltered on her tiptoes due to her sore ankle in the lighter hold Gabe kept on her. Frustrated his massive height kept her at a disadvantage to explore all she wanted, she gripped his shoulders and jumped up, wrapping her legs around his waist. Surprised, he immediately clamped his hands on her ass to hold her in place. She cupped his face and kissed him, sliding her tongue over his in a deep kiss she desperately needed. He backed her into the gate again. His hands came up to grip her rib cage and push her higher. His mouth trailed kisses down her throat to the edge of the lace bra. He swept his tongue over the swell of her breast, then clamped his mouth over her hard nipple despite the barrier. She sighed and arched her back, offering up her breasts for him to feast.

Winnie stuck her head over the stall door and nibbled at the side of her head and hair, making her laugh.

Gabe's head came up and his gaze locked on her face. "Aw, God, Ella. This is not good."

"It will be in a few minutes."

Gabe leaned forward and rested his forehead on her chin. Winnie nudged her big head against hers, trying to get to Gabe. "I'm not making love to you in here."

"With a few less clothes, I'm pretty sure we can manage it."

"Damnit, this is the stables and you're freezing. You've got goose bumps all over you."

"I'm hot for you."

Gabe's head came up again, and he smiled and let out a soft laugh. "I want you in my bed where I can treat you right."

She grabbed the back of his jacket in both hands and pulled herself off the gate, away from Winnie, and Gabe followed her movement and moved back, taking her with him. He stood in the middle of the stables with her in his arms, her legs wrapped around his waist, and his hands gripping her thighs to hold her steady. He gave her the smile she liked so much and had grown accustomed to over the last few days whenever he tried to tease her out of her bad mood.

"This is ridiculous, but God, I want you." His admission came out on a gruff exhale.

"Take me to bed, cowboy. Giddy-up." She nudged him with her legs and he headed for the door without another word. The minute they left the stables, the sun hit her, but didn't do anything to ward off the freezing cold. Gabe wrapped his arms around her to keep her warm, but she distracted herself by sliding her hands inside his jacket and over his strong, wide shoulders. She kissed him once, twice, and again.

"Can't see," he muttered against her lips.

She left his amazing mouth and kissed her way along his jaw to his ear, tracing the edge of it with her tongue. Gabe groaned and his fingers contracted on her bottom, bringing her closer. He used his strength to lift her a few inches, then let her slide down his hard shaft, creating a delicious friction against her core. She smiled against his neck a split second before she bit

down on his skin, then soothed the small hurt with a
lick of her tongue.

His stride lengthened out and sped up. "The house
is too damn far."

She smiled and licked him again, kissing her way
down his throat, peeling away his shirt with her hand
to kiss the muscles running along his shoulder. She slid
her hand up his shoulder and into his thick, dark hair.
The silky strands spread between her fingers, and she
gripped them tight, kissing his neck and hoping he got
them to the house faster.

"Hurry. I need you," she whispered in his ear, and
sucked his earlobe.

He took the steps up to the porch without slowing
down. They went through the front door, and he kicked
it shut with his foot without stopping and headed down
the short hall.

"My room's closer."

"Condoms." He passed her door and rushed through
his. He walked straight to the bed, leaned down, and
pressed her into the mattress, planting his mouth over
hers and sinking into her once again. She pulled him
even closer with her legs, and he grinded his hips to
hers.

"Too many clothes," she mumbled as his lips left
hers.

His hands slipped around her back to unfasten her
bra. He pulled it off her arms in one long fluid motion,
his mouth clamping onto her breast. He sucked hard,
and she arched off the bed for more, her hands going
into his hair to hold him to her. He swept his hot tongue
over her hard nipple and along the underside of her
breast.

"God, you taste so damn good. Even sweeter than you smell."

Her laugh turned into a heavy sigh when he paid equal attention to her other breast. She let him have his way, but wrestled his jacket off his arms and pulled his shirt over his head. Her hands slid down his bare back and up again. Gabe kissed his way down her belly, his hands sliding down her sides to her pants. He stood at the end of the bed and grabbed her knee, pulling her leg up so he could unlace her boot and pull it off. He did the same with the other, but never took his eyes off her. His heated gaze swept from her face to her breasts and back. Everything inside her went molten.

Shoes gone, he reached up to grab the sides of her pants and gently pulled them down her legs. Since she didn't want to wear Lela's underwear, she didn't have any on. His eyes narrowed and a half smile tilted his mouth in the most adorable way. She raised an eyebrow, daring him to come to her. He worked off his boots and socks in seconds, but didn't strip off his jeans. Instead, he came back to her and planted his knee between her thighs.

"Scoot back, sweetheart."

She did as he asked and he pursued her up the bed, his hands planted on either side of her as he stared down at her from all fours. She expected him to lie on top of her, for the dance to start all over again, but he didn't. He took his time, looking his fill at her laid out below him.

"You're so beautiful." He leaned down to kiss the worst of the bruises on her hip and down her thigh. It didn't hurt. Every soft kiss relaxed her, made her melt and fall under his spell. Soft afternoon light fell over them, highlighting the rich brown tones in his hair. She watched him loving her, sighed, and closed her eyes, letting herself just feel.

He kissed his way up her entire right side, making her forget about her aches and pains and feel nothing but ripples of pure pleasure. One big hand cupped her breast and molded it to his palm. His tongue swept across her right breast and his mouth settled over her tight nipple, and he sucked softly, keeping to this new lazy pace. Everything in the stables had been hot and fast. This was relaxed and sweet. A slow burn that settled her, centered her, and drew her deeper into Gabe's amazing spell.

Gabe craved this woman. He wanted to take and devour, but something about the way she looked at him, sighed, and lay beneath him so trusting made him take his time. He didn't need to rush. They had all the time in the world. Still, a part of him knew his time with her was ticking down, but still he touched and tasted and learned all the things that pleased her and made her sigh that way like he had forever.

Her hands slid over his back and shoulders, down his arms, and up his chest. She never stopped touching him, even when he lay down by her side and stripped off his jeans and boxer briefs. She turned into him, mapping his taut stomach with her fingers, kissing his neck and down to his chest. Every flick of her tongue and press of her lips to his skin sent a spark of lightning through his veins. Her small hand smoothed over his belly and lower to his hard cock. She wrapped her fingers around him and stroked down and up again. Her fingers went wide, her palm rubbed over his hard flesh, and she clamped her fingers over his balls. She worked her hand over him, making him groan.

Unable to take the sweet torture for long, he pulled her hand away and kissed her, long and deep. She held him close, and he pressed his aching cock into her thigh, sweeping his hand over her smooth skin, her belly, dipping his fingers between her thighs. She rocked her hips into his palm, and he slipped one finger into her slick core. Hot. Wet. Ready for him to love her. He slid his finger deep and pulled it free, rubbing against her soft folds and making her moan.

"Gabe."

His name on her lips in that breathy voice made him want to do anything she asked. He knew exactly what she wanted, because he wanted it too.

He grabbed the condom out of the bedside drawer, tore it open with his teeth, and sheathed himself. He shifted on top of her and she welcomed him into her arms, pulling him down for a searing kiss. His cock's thick head pressed against her entrance and she shifted her hips to take him in. He sank into her in one long, slow, fluid motion, and with his whole body pressed to hers, something inside him shifted and aligned and felt so damn right he lost all thought, but to have her. Keep her.

"Ella."

He kissed her and made love to her like he'd never get the chance to do it again. He needed to prove a point. What he wanted to show her, he didn't know for sure, but he had to get her to understand what he couldn't seem to think or say with any amount of clarity. His body knew what it wanted to say. He took possession and loved and caressed every inch of her.

Her open response drove him on. He thrust deep, and she met him, holding him close, her hands sweeping over his heated skin to soothe and coax him on. He took his time loving her, soaking up the connection they shared and the feel of her against him. He needed only her. Lots more of her.

Her fingers dug into his hips and pulled him closer. He grinded his hips to hers, and she bit her bottom lip and moved against him. He loved watching her expressive face. He pulled out and sank back into her again, making that same move. Her body contracted around his, and he did it again, this time thrusting faster and harder. She planted her heels in the bed, and he rocked against her. She tightened around his hard shaft, and he let himself go. Her nails bit into his skin, and she pressed her head into the pillow and exploded beneath him, taking him over the edge.

He collapsed on top of her, lying in her arms, her fingers tracing circles on his back. He breathed heavily into her hair and neck and kissed her softly. Completely content to stay right here for the next fifty years of his life. She shifted under him, in pain from his weight pressing on her hip. He slid his hand down to her bottom, held her tight, and rolled to his back, taking her with him. Not exactly a smooth move, she settled mostly on top of him, her leg over his hips, her head on his chest. He hugged her close and kissed the top of her head. She snuggled close like a contented cat, curling up for a nap. When she yawned, he remembered she'd barely slept last night at all.

He brushed his fingers up and down her arm, hoping she drifted off to sleep. She never slept long or well. He wanted her to relax and sleep all she needed. Besides, it kept him from having to say anything. He didn't know what to say after everything they shared.

His fingers brushed up her arm to the soft skin between her shoulder and neck. She cocked her head and giggled at the light tickle. He did it again. She laughed harder and pushed against his side to get away. He held her close.

"I love it when you laugh."

She laid her chin on his chest, staring up at him, her eyes bright with mirth. A pretty smile on her face that withered with the sheen of tears filling her eyes.

"What is it, sweetheart?"

"I feel so guilty for being this happy."

"Ah, honey, you have nothing to feel guilty about. Your sister loved you. She wouldn't want you to give yourself over to grief and never find any happiness for yourself."

"I'm supposed to be finding the evidence, not falling into bed with you."

He shifted away, feeling like all they'd shared hadn't meant half as much to her as it did to him if she thought it was just a distraction from her real purpose here. He sat on the edge of the bed, his hands braced at his sides. He gripped the mattress and stared down at his feet.

He tried to stand, but she wrapped her arms around his shoulders and locked her hands together at his chest, holding him down. Her chin settled on his shoulder, her breasts pressed to his back. Warm. Soft. Her flowery scent wrapped around him. Damn if he didn't inhale her scent and feel that much more connected to her. But she didn't feel the same.

"Wait. Don't go. I'm sorry that came out wrong. What I meant is, you make my heart feel so full, but at the same time, it's still so empty.

"Everyone I've ever loved is gone. Taken away from

me far too soon. I watched him kill my sister. He swore he'd see me dead too. What if he makes that happen and there's nothing I can do to stop him? What if he finds me here? I couldn't bear it if something happened to you because of me."

And there was the real truth. "Nothing is going to happen to me. I will not let anything happen to you. Don't you get it? I can't imagine a world without you in it."

"Then you know how I feel about you."

Her forehead pressed to his, and he reached up and cupped her face in his palm, her tears wet against his fingers.

"I am so afraid that what I feel for you will only lead to something terrible."

Meaning her uncle might hurt him to hurt her. "You know me. I hold on. I'm holding on to you."

"For how long?"

He laid her back onto the bed, their foreheads still pressed together, his body covering hers. "I'll hold on as long as you want me."

"I do want you."

The depth of emotion in her eyes told him just how hard that admission was for her to make. It wasn't exactly what he wanted to hear—he wanted more—but he'd take it for now. They had something worth keeping, and he'd hold on to it, and her. Forever, if she let him.

CHAPTER 20

"**H**ow the hell is she sending emails when she isn't even here? Why can't you trace her?" Phillip demanded of the head of the IT department. He'd forgotten the guy's name, but remembered Ella and Lela had promoted him after Ella worked in that department for some months, until she got bored.

"Mr. Wolf, I can assure you the police and our team have checked the system and at this time are unable to determine her location. It changes from server to server all over the world. She's purposely concealing her location."

"How is that possible?"

"She's savvy, or she's hired someone who is to help her do it. It isn't difficult if you know what you're doing."

Phillip had a feeling this man was hiding something, like he might be the one helping Ella get into their systems. Why? What did she have planned?

He didn't know, and the not knowing was driving him crazy.

"Has she opened the email that has the tracking program the police gave you?"

"No."

"How is that possible? You concealed it as an ordinary file, right?"

"I did, but unless she opens the file, or clicks on the link, there is nothing else I can do."

"So she knows it's a trap."

The IT man didn't answer the implied question, telling him without words their ploy to find her wouldn't work. He also didn't say he'd tipped her off.

"You're still working with the police forensic team?"

"Detective Robbins asked them to stay and go through all our systems, but the legal department stopped them. Unless and until they present a warrant, I'll provide them with information regarding Ella's email account and her access to the company system, but that is all."

"That is not all. You will give them access to everything so they can find her."

"I'm sorry, sir, but the legal department determined that access is too broad. We are a privately held company. Our records are proprietary and contain information that could be leaked to our competitors. Legally, without a warrant, we don't have to tell them anything."

"I want you to tell them everything you find out about her interactions with the company."

"I'm sorry, sir, I'm following the legal team's advice. If she's done something illegal and there is documentation of that in the system, you don't want to open the company to a lawsuit."

Phillip considered that, wondering if that warning was for him specifically. The longer this went unresolved, the more paranoid he became that everyone was working against him, and at any moment this could all fall apart, and he'd end up in jail. He couldn't let that happen.

"Keep at it. Find a way to track her down."

"We're doing our best, sir."

Yes, but was he doing his best to find Ella, or hide her?

CHAPTER 21

Ella slept beside him. Gabe indulged his need to stay close, brushing his fingers through her long hair, feeling her skin pressed to his as she lay down his side, her leg thrown over his, and her face snuggled in the crook of his shoulder and neck.

Like most every time she slept, she had a nightmare. Her body went rigid and still beside him, her breath caught and stopped, and she let out a distressed sound and suppressed scream. Her hand curled in a ball on his chest, and she mumbled incoherently. The only word he recognized was Lela's name. He wished he understood the rest, so he could find a way to help her cope.

He folded her into his arms when the worst of the nightmare took hold. She woke with a start, the words "the cave," sputtering from her lips before her eyes went wide. She pressed her hand to his chest to push him away, but stopped the second she realized it was him and not her uncle trying to hold her down before she flailed herself right out of bed.

Someone pounded on the front door three times. Both of them stilled. Eyes wide and filled with fear, she stared at him. Her body shook down the length of his.

"Stay here. No matter what, do not come out of this room. I'll see who it is."

The front door slammed, making him less nervous. In fact, he had a feeling one of his brothers had come calling. He kissed Ella, rolled out of bed, and snagged his jeans off the floor and pulled them on. He stuffed his feet into his boots without putting on his socks and found his shirt lying on the floor, half under the bed. Dressed, he went to his open bedroom door and turned back to stare at Ella in his bed, the blue sheets and tan blanket pulled up to her chest, covering all that beautiful soft skin.

"Gabe," Blake shouted from the front room.

"I'll be right there, Blake."

Ella registered his brother's name and fell back into the pillows with a sigh of relief. He couldn't leave her without some reassurance. He walked back to the bed, leaned over, and kissed her again. He rose up far enough to see her expressive green eyes.

"I'll get rid of him. Stay here." He tugged the sheet down just enough to plant a kiss between her breasts, right over her heart. "I'm not done with you yet."

She gave him a soft smile. Satisfied the last of the nightmare and fear had faded, he left her in his bed and went to kick his brother out of his house. He didn't know what brought Blake here, but he needed to get rid of him fast. He felt like if he didn't, the outside world would intrude and the fragile balance they'd found, which hadn't had nearly enough time to settle into a solid foundation for what he wanted to build with her, would crumble.

"Have you seen this?" Blake tossed a newspaper and two tabloids on the counter. "Were you asleep? Your hair is all messed up."

"No." Gabe wasn't about to explain the woman in

his bed had a thing for running her fingers through his hair when they made love. He raked his fingers through the disheveled mess and put it back to rights—mostly.

Gabe moved closer and scanned the many photos of Ella from her nights out with friends in the city, to vacation photos of her in sundresses and bikinis on gorgeous beaches. The scenery didn't hold his attention. He knew every inch of that body now, and he craved it with every breath he took. He tossed the tabloids aside and stared down at the photos of her friends standing outside the police station, looking their best in dresses and suits. The caption read, "Ella Wolf's longtime boyfriend, Michael Henry, and friends meet with police to discuss Ella's innocence and demand the police investigate her disappearance."

He wanted to tear the paper to shreds and never look at the man who claimed to be Ella's boyfriend. The thought of him touching her, kissing her, making love to her burned in his gut.

"Did you know about this? Lela died the day after you met her."

"Yeah. I know."

"I saw Joel in town. He said her body is at the mortuary. What the hell is going on? You meet Lela, she tells you to stay away from her ranch, someone murders her, they think her sister killed her, and you send me an email that the deal is off. What the fuck is going on?"

Gabe paced into the open living room, turned, and took two steps back. Blake turned to keep track of him.

"Phillip Wolf signed the contract with me to sell the house and property. I transferred the money to an escrow account. On March twelfth the deal was supposed to close."

"Right. What changed? You have a contract with him."

"He doesn't own the property and can't sign off on the sale unless Lela and Ella Wolf are both dead. Which is exactly what he plans to make happen so the deal can close on that date. Their birthday. The day they turn twenty-five and take over control of their inheritance and the company."

"Are you shitting me? You think he killed Lela. But the papers suggest Ella killed her."

"I have no doubt Phillip killed her."

"That is some fucked-up shit. So Phillip's signature isn't worth spit on the contract?"

Gabe shook his head no. "Someone also transferred the money out of the escrow account."

"Where the fuck is it?"

"Gone."

"Gone. Did you call the real estate agent who brokered the deal? Did you call a fucking lawyer to sue his ass?"

"No. I'm handling it."

"You're handling it," Blake parroted him again. "Phillip offered a reward to find Ella. Why? So he can kill her."

"Yes."

"What are you going to do? What about the cattle you bought? Not to mention the hundred head of cattle you already have here. The money you've put out? The horses you've got stacked up in that tiny barn you've got outside. You can't fit all of them on this place."

"I'll figure it out."

"That asshole royally screwed you." Blake put his hands on his hips, shook his head, and frowned. "You don't have the money to pay back the loan. You'll have to sell off the cattle and most of the horses at a loss. You might lose this place. This will ruin you, Gabe."

"Yes, I know."

"Why aren't you going out of your mind? Why aren't you as mad as I am about this?"

"Because he knows I'll make it right."

Gabe stepped to the side and stared past his brother, who'd blocked Ella, standing in the kitchen door, her shoulder propped against the frame, arms crossed under her breasts. She'd dressed and combed her hair. He noted she stood on her good foot, the other tucked into the brace. Since he carried her back to the house half naked, the purple sweater still lay on the floor in the stables, and she'd put on one of Lela's blouses. She looked pretty and fresh from her short nap. She'd taken a minute to clean up to meet his brother. It made his heart melt a little that it mattered to her.

Blake turned his back on Ella again and faced him. "You've got Ella Wolf stashed in your house." He glanced at Gabe's head again and added, "You slept with her after what her uncle did to you? What the hell!"

Gabe walked past Blake and took Ella's hand and drew her into the kitchen with him. He put his arm around her and faced his brother. "Blake, meet Ella Wolf. Ella, my brother Blake."

"Nice to meet you," Ella said, but Blake just stood there staring at her, disbelief clouding his eyes. "You two get angry exactly the same way. You crinkle up your brows and start cussing."

"You're about to lose everything, and you're still willing to hide her here?" Blake asked him.

"I won't let anything happen to her. Ever."

"You'll give up everything? For her?"

"He's not giving up anything." She turned back to Gabe, the paper in her hand as she read. "Ella Wolf enjoyed lavish parties and vacations. Her extravagant lifestyle afforded her entry into the most exclusive circles in New York and L.A. Known for her chic style, she graced many best-dressed lists from coast to coast. Her friends say she's warm and funny with eclectic taste in movies, music, and art. They defended her, saying she could never kill her beloved sister."

Ella turned the paper to show him and Blake. "I sound like some brainless Barbie. I have an MBA. I graduated summa cum laude. Half these pictures are of me at charity benefits. This picture of me shopping is at the cosmetics boutique I own."

She shook her head at the paper and looked up at him with a silent plea to understand the dichotomy of the life the press made it seem she lived versus the private life she actually lived. No one wanted to see past the sparkle and shine of her public life to discover the true woman she'd become over the last few years. She'd changed, grown, and didn't fit that mold the press, her friends, and even her uncle wanted to keep her in.

They were talking about a woman who didn't exist.

Gabe gave her the only words he had to make her understand he got it. "I know you."

He snatched the paper from her and pointed to the photo of the guy he wanted to destroy and the caption below. "This is just another lie, right?" He didn't really need to ask. She'd never cheat on a boyfriend, or use him to abate her grief, but he needed to hear her say it.

Ella read the line he pointed to and smiled. "He's gay and getting it on with my hairdresser, Mario. Neither of us was interested in dating. He's hiding his true identity so his very staid and old-fashioned father doesn't disinherit him. We pretended to be together when we went out to make things easier on both of us. He's a really nice guy with a closed-minded father, who cares more about money and appearances than his son's happiness. He and Mario are really cute together."

"Is there anything about you that's real?" Blake asked.

"Stick around. Find out. Ask me a question, and I'll give you a true answer."

"Are you going to let your uncle screw my brother out of everything?"

"No. Gabe will get everything he wanted and more."

"More? Ella, what are you talking about? I just want my money back." Well, Gabe wanted to keep her too, but didn't know how to make that happen. Or if he could make it happen at all.

"Do you trust me?"

"Yes."

"Just like that?" Blake asked. "You barely know this woman. Sleeping with her doesn't mean she's telling you the truth."

Gabe slammed both hands into Blake's chest and shoved him back two steps. "Don't. Not with her. You don't know her. I do." He grabbed the papers and tabloid rags off the counter and scrunched them in his fist and held them between him and Blake. "This isn't her. Not the way it looks, or how they say it is. She came here to find the evidence to prove her uncle is a dirty, rotten bastard and put him away. She could have hired a dozen high-priced lawyers to do it for her, but she did it for her sister and parents, and the legacy they left her, and she's trying to protect and preserve. She's hiding from a man who wants her dead. So shut the fuck up, get a beer, sit down and get to know her, or get the fuck out of my house. She's got work to do, and I aim to help her and keep her safe until she gets it done."

Blake gave him a knowing smile and pulled out his phone and hit a number. He put the phone to his ear and said, "Hey, Mama. Gabe's fine. He met someone. Yeah, the ranch deal fell through, but looks like he might have something better going." Blake glanced at Ella, who nodded her head up and down.

"Ella, what are you going to do?" Gabe asked. Several times she'd alluded to making this right in some way, but she never said how. He wanted the property and the dream, but he'd settle for getting his money back. It'd go a long way to helping him settle somewhere else. He'd done some backbreaking work and rodeoing to get that money. He'd earned it with his sweat and blood.

"You'll see. Trust me. A couple of phone calls, and I'll make everything right."

"I just want my money back."

"You'll get it," she promised with a soft smile.

"I'm hanging with Gabe and his girl for another hour or so, then I'll head home," Blake said to their mother. He held the phone out to Gabe. "She wants to talk to you."

"Thanks." Gabe took the phone and shoved Blake again. Nothing but brotherly love and ensuring Blake remembered the pecking order. He was the oldest and Blake would pay for putting him on the spot like this.

"Hey, Mom. So you got my message and sent Blake to check on me."

"I didn't like the way you sounded. I worry about you no matter how big and grown you are."

"I'm sorry I made you worry. Tell Dad everything is fine. The deal went south, but I'm working on getting the money back. I'll probably have to sell the cattle at a loss, but I'll figure it out."

Ella sat at the table in front of her computer again. Her head came up and she shook her head side to side.

"Or maybe something else will come along," he said, with more of a question in his voice directed at Ella. She smiled and nodded yes.

"Who's the girl?" his mother asked.

"Her name is Ella."

"Just like the girl all over the news."

"Yeah. Her."

His mother didn't understand he literally meant her. "How'd you meet her?" His mother tried to sound casual, but a hint of more than curiosity filled her voice.

"I found her on the side of the road and decided to keep her."

Blake had his beer bottle to his lips, taking a deep drink. He choked and coughed, but managed to swallow.

Ella laughed and shook her head at him again.

"It's a long story. You'll like her."

"I get to meet this one?"

"I hope so," Gabe said, giving away far too much to his all-knowing mother. Those simple words told her everything she needed to know, because the only girl he'd ever brought home to meet his parents was Stacy after he asked her to marry him.

Maybe he should take a minute and think about what that meant. But he didn't and went with his gut and the pull that tugged at him even now to close the distance between him and Ella just so he could be close to her.

"What's she like?"

"She's beautiful. But when you tell her that her eyes fall away because she's been told that her whole life and doesn't really believe it." Ella's gaze fell away from him, but snapped back when he added, "She's got a beautiful heart. She loves her sister the way I love my stupid brothers. She believes in doing what's right, even when it's hard—or dangerous. She's really smart. She's got an MBA and runs her own businesses. She's got this cosmetics company that makes all these botanical lotions and perfumes and makeup. She smells really good." That made his mother and Ella laugh. "She blushes and the faint freckles on the top of her cheeks stand out. She makes a killer cup of coffee and can drive a combine tractor. She talks to the horses like they're people. She's got a drive and determination that makes Dad and all four of us boys look lazy."

"Does she make you smile?"

As the oldest, he'd been the most serious of them. Always taking on the chores his little brothers couldn't do to help out his dad. He'd been the one they counted on to always look out for Blake, Caleb, and Dane when they couldn't, and he'd taken working with his dad and watching out for his brothers seriously. He was the one who gave up Friday night football games in high school, or going to a dance to stay home and help out. Not that his brothers hadn't stepped up as they got older and shouldered their load, but he'd been doing it so long, he had a tendency to drop other things in favor of doing his work. Yeah, maybe he'd given up some of the fun, but he'd learned a hell of a lot working by his father's side.

"She makes me smile every time I think about her, or look at her."

"Bring her to supper," his mother coaxed, trying her best to hide how much she wanted to meet Ella. She didn't want him to pull back, now that he'd admitted so much.

He surprised everyone when he asked, "Ella, Mom wants us to come to dinner soon. You up for it?"

Ella's eyes went wide, and she stared at her piles of papers in front of her. The paper trail of her uncle's deceit. She had a job to finish, but she needed to find a way to see a future for herself. He just gave her something to think about and plan for the future where her uncle was behind bars, and she was with him. He held his breath and hoped she said yes.

"Dinner would be lovely."

"She's in, Mom, but it's going to have to be down the road. Ella has some business that may take her back to New York soon. So I'll let you know."

"Are you putting me off, Gabe Bowden?"

"Not at all. I can't wait for you and Dad to meet her. Until then, you can grill Blake for information about her. Now that Blake's settled down, he can't stop staring at her."

Blake quickly looked away when Ella looked up from her computer screen. "What? I'm just trying to figure out what the hell she's doing with you. There's got to be something wrong with her. But you're right, she smells really good."

Ella laughed again. "Okay, stop, it's just getting creepy now with you guys smelling me all the time."

"Can't help it," Blake said. "I spend my days with horses. You don't smell anything like them."

"Thank God," Ella said, rolling her eyes and staring back at her computer, making Blake laugh.

"I'll talk to you soon, Mom. Say hi to Dad."

"I will. And Gabe?"

"Yeah?"

"I'm really happy for you."

"Thanks, Mom."

Gabe handed the phone back to Blake and smacked him on the side of the head.

"What the hell was that for?"

"Coming out here to spy on me."

"You knew someone would show up when everything you've been working your ass off for goes up in smoke."

"Can we stop talking about it already? It's bad enough I can't stop thinking about it. I need to figure out what comes next, and what I'm going to do."

"Don't make any plans yet," Ella said. "I've got something in the works that might suit you better."

"What's that?" he asked, and Blake turned in his seat to face her for the answer.

"You'll see."

"That's not an answer."

"I'm working on it, but first I need to do something else." She held her hand out to Blake. "May I use your phone, please?"

Blake handed it over. "Who are you calling?"

"Hey, Cheryl, this is Ella. Yeah, I borrowed a friend's phone. Thank you. I miss her so much," Ella said, her eyes glassing over, a single tear slipping past her lashes and rolling down her cheek. "I know he and the police are looking for me, but I'd appreciate it if you kept this call confidential. I hate to put you on the spot, things are happening right now that I need to handle privately. Yes, we'll hold a memorial service as soon as I return. The bastard who killed her will be put in jail very soon."

Ella raised her shaking hand to push her hair out of her face, trying to keep her composure. Gabe circled the table and clamped his hands on her shoulders and leaned down and kissed her on the head. "Listen, I need you to put together a gift basket and send it to Montana. Include the moisturizing body butter and a variety of the other lotions, cosmetics, and include the Serenity perfume."

"Oh God, please don't make my mother smell like you," Gabe pleaded, giving her shoulders a squeeze.

"That's just creepy," Blake added.

Ella laughed and the tears in her eyes cleared. "Change the perfume to one of the others. Something soft and light. Yes, the Primrose is perfect."

Gabe and Blake both sighed with relief, and Ella let out a soft laugh.

"Make it really big and beautiful. Maybe get some chocolates from the confections shop next door. Lovely. Please send the basket to Mrs. Bowden. I'm handing the phone off to my friend, he'll give you the address. I'll be in touch soon. Right now, keep doing what you're doing, and we'll talk soon about the big launch in March."

Ella handed the phone to Blake, who rattled off their mother's address and said goodbye.

"That was a really nice thing to do," Gabe said.

"It's nothing," she said, looking away from both of them. "You guys are really close to your mother."

"Have to be. She gets really pissed when we don't call and sends Dad after us," Blake said.

"Must be nice to have family who cares about you like that."

Blake gave him a look that said he got it. Ella didn't have a mother or a father, and she just lost the only family who cared about her.

He brushed his hand down her hair, leaned down, and kissed her on the head again. She fell back in her chair and took his hand, holding it against her chest. Her heart thrashed against his hand. She wasn't as calm as she appeared.

"So, are you making dinner?" Blake asked Ella.

"The only thing she makes is reservations. Dinner's on you and me. Come on. Let's get it done."

Gabe filled Blake in on Ella's story and how her uncle killed Lela and the plot he hatched to frame and then kill Ella too. Ella worked quietly at her laptop, head down, following her uncle's trail, hoping it led to the evidence she needed. Blake kept eyeing her, looking at her in a whole new way the more Gabe told him about her. When they all sat down to dinner together an hour later, Ella put away her past and her plans for the future and focused on the present. Before they ate, Gabe stopped beside her chair and leaned down and gave her a soft, lingering kiss. She smiled up at him, her eyes filled with such warmth and affection he swallowed back the lump in his throat.

"So, you like the horses?" Blake asked to start the conversation with Ella.

"I love them. Gabe's got some real beauties out there."

"Do you ride?"

"As often as I can. I've got two horses at my country estate in New York, outside the city of course."

"Tell him their names," Gabe coaxed, hoping she took the hint.

"Cristal and Jimmy Choo. Arabians. You'd love them."

"You named your horses after champagne and shoes. Rich women really are different."

Ella laughed, but Gabe about lost it when he saw the look of disbelief on his brother's face.

"Their names are Angel and Belle. One white, and one black."

Blake laughed, knowing the joke was on him. "Are you going to bring them here and live on your ranch?" Blake asked the one question Gabe wanted to ask Ella since the day he met her.

Her gaze found his, and they stared at each other for a long time. "Maybe," she finally said, tying him in even more knots. She turned back to speak to Blake. "If I'm not dead by my birthday, and my uncle is behind bars, I'll definitely have to do something with all those cattle and the ranch."

Her gaze found his again, but he couldn't read the look.

Gabe got the hint when she didn't give either of them a straight answer. She didn't know what she was going to do. Despite the fact he wanted her here with him always, stuck in the back of his mind was the reality that she didn't fit on a ranch in Montana, and he'd never fit in a big city. The thought gnawed at him, making his insides raw, but he couldn't pull back. Not when everything inside him wanted to hold on and keep her. For as long as he could.

"Some of the pictures in the papers showed you at the Oscars in L.A. Do you know a lot of celebrities?" Blake asked her.

"Some."

That line of questioning and the stories Ella told took them into the evening. By the time Blake left, she had him eating out of her hand. Gabe liked seeing her this way. Joking, telling stories about her life—which was way different than the papers portrayed it—and giving him an in-depth glimpse at the life she'd led. So different from his, but rooted in longtime friendships with people who were more like family.

When he thought of the pictures he'd seen of her with a crowd of people sitting around a table filled with food and wine, he thought of a family gathering now. The same faces surrounded her, not random people she met out on the town, but the usual crowd. Out here, you had potlucks and community meetings where people gathered. In New York, he guessed, you had dinner out with friends at a swanky restaurant. Instead of barn dances and saloons, you went to a club.

"What's that smile?" she asked, when he stared at her too long, letting his thoughts spin out to find a way that she wasn't so different than him.

She grabbed his beer and took a sip. He'd offered to get her one of her own, but she'd spent the night sipping off his. Even his brother noticed.

"You keep stealing my beer."

She pulled the bottle down from her lips and swallowed. "Sorry."

"I don't mind."

"My drinking your beer makes you smile."

"Yes. And the fact that you're happy to have steak and lobster with five-hundred-dollar bottles of wine with your friends and have Southwest chicken with rice and black beans and drink my beer with me and Blake."

"Dinner was really good. The company even better," she said, winking at Blake. His brother was lost. So was he. She hadn't flirted. Not her style, but somehow she'd endeared herself to both of them with just her sweet, open, and honest personality.

He and Ella saw his brother to the door. Blake turned and took Ella's hand. "I'm real sorry about your sister. I hope I get to see you again soon."

"Thank you, Blake. I really enjoyed meeting you and the stories you told about Gabe when he was little."

"I've got lots more embarrassing stories to tell."

"I look forward to hearing them." She smiled at his brother with such genuine affection and sincerity Gabe hoped she meant that she'd stay long enough to do it.

Blake released Ella and gave him a bear hug. He stood back and stared at him before walking away. "She's not what I expected for you, but she's perfect."

Gabe understood exactly what he meant. Ella wasn't the kind of woman who'd stay at home, cooking his meals and raising his kids, content to live on a working ranch with the cattle and horses. The kind of woman he thought he wanted until he met her. That wasn't Ella. Would probably never be Ella's way, but she fit him perfectly. He just didn't know if he fit her.

CHAPTER 22

Gabe's mouth covered hers, swallowing her gasp as he pulled her out of yet another nightmare and straight into a fantasy come true. His warm, hard body covered hers. His hips pressed snugly between her thighs. The thick head of his penis nudged at her entrance, but he didn't fill her. He used it and his mouth to get her attention and draw her to him and out of the depths of her despair.

"Gabe, honey, I'm awake."

"Good. That makes this fun instead of creepy."

She giggled, but it turned into a deep sigh when he blazed a trail of kisses down her neck and over her breast and took her hard nipple into his mouth. She combed her fingers through his dark hair, kept her eyes closed, and enjoyed every touch, lick, kiss he lavished on her body. His big hand slid down her side. She relaxed into the moment again and ran her hands over Gabe's shoulders and down his strong back.

"Everywhere I touch, you're hard."

"I am for you, darlin'."

She loved the rumble in his voice when he teased her like that. Even more, she loved the way he played her body like an instrument, knowing just when to speed up and slow down. Like last night after Blake left. Gabe knew she missed her sister and the connection they'd shared. Gabe left the dirty dishes and took her to bed, loving her long into the night with soft kisses and sweet words that made her melt and fall so hard for him that she'd cried. Not for her sister and all she'd lost, but because of the depth of emotion this man evoked in her, something no other man had ever done. While her mind worked on the problem of finding the evidence and taking down her uncle, her heart conjured dreams of being with this man, and how she'd make that work.

She couldn't stop thinking about taking down her uncle, running the business, doing the huge national launch for her cosmetics company, dealing with the ranch and the cattle, and finding a way to keep Gabe and have it all. Did she even want it all?

Right now, she wanted him.

"Stop thinking," Gabe said, a second before his mouth pressed to hers, and his tongue dipped into her mouth to taste and tangle with hers.

"Make me," she said against his lips.

He joined their bodies in a slow glide. "My pleasure."

No, it was all hers. The man had a way of reading her, anticipating her, and knowing just what she needed most. Right now, she needed him close.

His chest pressed to hers. Their bodies moved together in a push and pull that created a lovely friction between them that stoked the fire and sent out ripples of heat through her body. She wrapped her arms around his back and held tight, his hips pumping into hers as they made love with soft kisses and warm caresses. Her thoughts melted away with the heat between them intensifying. She spread her thighs wider, took him in deeper, pressed her aching breasts to his hard chest, and gave herself over to this man, whose heart beat with hers.

"Gabe."

She called his name, and he answered, thrusting hard and deep. She spread her fingers wide on his back and dragged them down over his ass, pulling him close again and again. His breath came out hard and fast at her neck. She pressed her cheek to his and let go of everything but the feel of this man pressing down on her, covering her, keeping her safe and showing her heaven.

Gabe's big hand clamped onto her thigh, shifted it higher, his hips grinding into hers as he thrust deep again and sent her flying. He followed her with his body vibrating against hers as he let go and held on all at the same time.

His weight on her felt like a safe harbor. Someplace she could rest and feel safe from the turbulent seas she faced in her life right now. But was she hiding away, getting lost in this man and the easy relationship she'd found with him? *No*, her heart shouted. It went deeper than distraction and holding on to someone who made her feel so much more than the pain, fury, and loneliness of losing her sister. His lips touched her neck just below her ear in a soft kiss, and her heart swelled and sank on a sigh. Somehow, in the middle of all this madness, she'd found a man she could love. She did love him. In all her grief and despair, there'd been this rising tide of something that kept her going and made her believe that when all this was over, she wouldn't be alone.

Gabe rose above her on his hands and stared down at her, a lazy smile on his face. "Good morning, sweetheart."

She stretched her arms up over her head and pulled him close with her feet hooked over his thighs. His eyes went soft when the motion brought him deep inside her again. She set her hands on his shoulders and slid them down his arms, squeezing his massive biceps. "Morning."

"You keep doing stuff like that, and we'll never leave this bed."

She raked her fingers back up his shoulders and down his chest. "Promise?"

He leaned down and kissed her, letting her know how much he'd like to stay right here with her. He pressed back up on his hands. "I need food and so do the horses and cattle. Want to come out and help me feed them?"

"Sure."

Gabe settled beside her on his side, his head propped on his hand, and stared down at her. "What's that face?" He used his free hand to cup her cheek and turn her head to face him.

"Will you take me to see my sister this morning?"

"Is there any way I can talk you out of that?"

"No. I need to see her."

"Ella, it's too dangerous. I don't want anyone to see you and turn you into the police for the reward. What if your uncle's men are watching the place, hoping you'll show up?"

"I'll be careful. I need to see her. Maybe if I do, it'll help me understand what she wanted me to know."

"What do you mean?"

"We had that twin thing. We could say so much with a look or a few simple words. We finished each other's sentences. I knew how she felt just by seeing her. Sometimes, I'd come home and she'd be waiting for me, saying she had a weird feeling I needed to talk to her. I did the same to her many times. When my uncle attacked her, I know she was trying to tell me something. I just can't seem to figure out what it was."

"You saw her die, honey. That's traumatic in itself, but to watch your uncle kill her, that's something you'd never expect or accept. Family is supposed to protect each other."

"Maybe in your family. My uncle has never been anything but a man who lives in my house, uses my father's things, and only took an interest in my and Lela's lives for appearances' sake, but nothing more. The whole time he's been stealing from us."

"Do you think he planned to kill Lela?"

"Not in that way. Shooting her was impulsive. He wanted the location where she hid the evidence and lost his temper."

"So where would she hide the evidence here?"

"On the ranch, but you cleaned out the house and didn't find anything."

"I cleaned out the house, but I never touched the stables, the guesthouse, or other outbuildings on the property. Maybe she hid it somewhere else."

"We used to love to play in the barn loft. Maybe it's up there. Dad built us a tree house on the property in the woods. I'm not even sure I could find it at this point, but it's worth a look."

"We're in for a warm spell over the next few days."

"You mean it will get up in the forties." Her words came out overly bright with faked enthusiasm.

Gabe shook his head. "City girl. You are so pampered."

"Lela and I planned a birthday trip in May after the cosmetics launch to go to Bora Bora. Nothing but white sand beaches and crystal-clear water for a week."

Gabe swiped the tear rolling down her cheek with his thumb. "I hate it when you cry."

"You make me smile."

"Then don't make me take you to see your sister."

"Let me borrow your truck, and I'll go alone."

"I may not want to take you, because I hate to see you cry, but I'd never let you face that alone, sweetheart."

She rolled into him, and he wrapped her in his arms. Safe. Warm. Protected. So much comfort and support offered up without any expectation of getting anything in return. He simply wanted to be with her. Such a nice change from what she knew in New York where people tried to come into her circle of friends in hopes of using her name and theirs to move up in the world. She'd tired of that game long ago. Gabe was a breath of fresh air when she could barely breathe at all.

I love you, her heart whispered, but she couldn't find the words to say that to him. Not yet. Not when her life was in such turmoil, her future uncertain. But she'd find a way to be with him, because she didn't want to lose anyone else she loved.

Gabe patted her on the ass. "Get up, lazy. We've got horses to feed and places to go."

"Gabe."

"Yeah, honey?"

"I wish I could stay right here with you forever."

He traced her forehead, pushing a lock of hair off her face and behind her ear. "You can if you want."

He gave her another of those soft, sweet kisses she'd become addicted to, rolled out of bed, and walked into the bathroom, her gaze following his very fine ass. God, the man was gorgeous.

She lay in his bed and thought about what he said. The shower went on in the other room. The monotonous sound relaxed her. Did she want to stay here with Gabe? Well, not in this room. The walls were a faded and drab off-white that made her feel morose. She liked his simple furniture. Clean lines. A nice deep, rich brown to contrast with the light blue sheets and sand-colored spread on the bed. She stared at the rodeo plaques and buckles around the room. He'd been one hell of a rider, winning all those awards. She thought of the scars on his body and guessed how he'd gotten them. He sometimes favored his right leg. Especially when he spent any length of time outside in the freezing temperatures. He probably hurt it riding bulls or broncos, earning the money to buy Wolf Ranch. She hated that she'd left the house sitting because of ghosts who didn't live there but in her heart. Yeah, she wanted to stay with Gabe, but she could do a hell of a lot better than the twelve hundred square feet they'd been sharing the last week.

A smile spread across her face. She looked around the room again, noticing this and that of Gabe's style. Yep. The man liked simplicity, but he might also like a woman's touch of comfort and beauty mixed in.

"What are you smiling about, sweetheart?" Gabe

walked out of the bathroom with a towel around his waist, his dark hair dripping water onto his massive shoulders.

"Just plotting. And seeing you naked always makes me smile."

Gabe pulled the towel free and held his arms wide, the towel dangling from his fingers. "Look all you want, honey, if it makes you smile like that."

She laughed and rolled out of bed, walking right into his open arms. She hugged him close, her bare skin pressed to his. "You're wet."

"Give me two minutes, and I'll say the same about you." His big hands brushed down her back and covered her ass.

Flirting back, she did the same and squeezed his in return. "You have a very fine ass."

"You have the prettiest smile I've ever seen and gorgeous green eyes."

"Here, I thought my boobs held your attention."

He stared down between them at her breasts pressed to his chest. "Oh, they do, but I really like your legs."

She chuckled. "Is there anything about me you don't like?"

"Your uncle. I really hate him."

"The feeling is mutual. I'm taking a shower, you make the coffee."

"I thought you'd make it while I showered."

"Sorry. Guess I'm too used to Mary doing those things for me. And now you." She gave his butt a smack and walked into the bathroom smiling.

"Can we call her and ask her to come and cook and make the coffee for us?" he called to her from the bedroom.

Just to see if he'd say anything, she shouted back, "I'll set it up."

Maybe he didn't respond because he thought she was kidding, but he'd learn she meant what she said soon enough.

CHAPTER 23

Gabe handed his black ski cap to Ella two miles before they reached town. "Put that on now, sweetheart. I don't want anyone to recognize you."

"I'm starting to think you're ashamed to be seen with me."

He didn't care what she looked like, so long as she stayed out of her uncle's grasp. With a detective in his pocket and any number of others who helped Phillip cover up Lela's murder, no one who discovered Ella could be trusted to keep her safe.

"I'll do everything I have to, to keep you safe." Gabe vowed. "I spoke to Mr. Henighan, the funeral director. I've known him forever. He's a good and honest man. He's expecting us and promised no one else will be there. No one has tried to see Lela, or come in asking about her besides a local reporter. That doesn't mean your uncle doesn't have someone watching the place, hoping you show up."

She stared out the side window and didn't look at him, but her hands remained clutched tightly together in her lap. He put his hand over hers.

"Ella, sweetheart, it's going to be okay."

"I hope so. I know it's a huge risk going to see her, but I have to." Her eyes pleaded with him to understand.

"If it were one of my brothers, I'd feel the same way." They entered the outskirts of town. He turned onto First Street and made a left on Webster. "Stay with me the whole time. No matter what, you stick by my side. If someone asks you to leave me for any reason, you say no."

"Gabe, I won't do anything stupid or reckless. Besides, anyone takes one look at you and they aren't coming anywhere near me."

"What's that supposed to mean?"

"Looked in a mirror lately? You're huge. The dirty look you gave Blake when he pissed you off was enough to make anybody think twice about getting too close to you."

"I'd never give Blake a dirty look and mean it."

"You did yesterday."

He traced a finger over her cheek and down her neck and settled his hand on her chest above her heart. "No one says or does anything that makes you unhappy."

"I'll remind you of that when you do something that displeases me."

"Listen to you, city girl. Displeases you. Huh. I've been nothing but nice."

"You're a prince."

"Have you ever dated a prince?" he asked, just to tease.

"No, but I met one once."

He took his eyes from the road and stared at her in shock, then quickly looked back. "I was joking."

"So was I," she said, laughing. "You've got a really warped sense of who I am."

"You're not like anyone I've ever known," he said, pulling the truck into a parking spot in back of the funeral home, backing in just in case they needed to make a quick getaway.

"Same goes for you, cowboy."

He brought her hand to his mouth and kissed it. She tried to pull away, but he held tight. "Wait." He scanned the parking lot. Only two other cars. Mr. Henighan's and the mortician's, Joel Snell. He watched the street and studied all the parked cars along the road and in nearby parking lots. Nothing caught his attention, or seemed out of place. No ominous black Escalade tucked in among the many trucks and SUVs. "We go in together. We come out together."

"You and me."

He turned to her and met her steady gaze. "You and me."

Gabe got out first. Ella scooted along the truck seat to exit on his side. He blocked her from view until she stepped down to the pavement. He closed the door behind her, hit the lock button on the key fob, and escorted her quickly across the parking lot to the back door. Mr. Henighan expected them, so the door remained unlocked, per his instructions when they spoke on the phone.

They entered the building and stood inside a hallway that ran to the front of the building. Several doors opened on the right and left side. Gabe had been here several times for family and friends' funerals since he was a little boy. He always hated this place. It made him sad. The cream walls, dark wood, and quiet were supposed to make people feel comfortable and lent a sense of solemnity to the space, but the heavy scent of fresh flowers nearly choked him.

"Mr. Henighan," he called out.

The tall, thin man came around the corner at the front and walked down the hall toward them. "Gabe. Good to see you again, son. How are your folks?"

"Good. I really appreciate you doing this for me."

"No trouble at all. Your mother and I go way back."

Gabe didn't want to think about his mother dating in high school, so he changed the subject. "This is my friend, Ella Wolf."

"Ms. Wolf, my deepest condolences for your loss. Please, come this way."

"Are we alone?" Gabe asked.

"Yes, of course. Just to be sure you've got all the privacy you need, I've sent Joel on break. He's gone to the coffee shop."

"He'll keep quiet that she's here," Gabe said, his voice holding a hint of danger if he didn't like Mr. Henighan's answer.

"Gabe, relax. I'm the only one who knows she's here. I'm on your side."

Cautious, he tried to believe Mr. Henighan wouldn't sell them out for the reward Phillip offered. A lot of money; most people wouldn't hesitate to turn Ella in, but in these parts, you took a man at his word until he proved his word wasn't worth shit. Mr. Henighan hadn't given Gabe any reason not to trust him.

"May I see her?" Ella asked, her voice soft and sweet and so filled with sadness he wrapped his arm around her and pulled her close.

"Come this way. I'll show you the flowers while I prepare her for you to see."

They followed Mr. Henighan into a room. Huge bouquets sat on the floor, towered toward the ceiling, and sat on every available table around the room. Mary must have directed everyone to send them here.

Ella held her locket in her hand against her chest. "It's beautiful." Ella stared at the outpouring of love from friends and colleagues. It meant even more because they hadn't even scheduled a memorial yet.

"I've kept all the cards and well wishes. I'll give them to you whenever you're ready to leave. Please excuse me for a moment, and I'll make your sister ready."

Mr. Henighan left them alone.

"This is quite a display, honey. Who knew there was this many different kinds of white flowers in the world." He tried to brighten her mood with a little levity, but she continued to stare.

He let her go when she walked up the aisle between the chairs to an overflowing basket of flowers and smelled the roses. He didn't understand why she needed to get that close. The whole room was filled with their sweet scent. "I'm not even twenty-five and I've buried both my parents and now my sister."

"You'll bury your uncle next." That earned him a halfhearted smile.

"It's not fair, Gabe. It's just not fair."

"No, honey, it's not. But you'll get through this."

"I will, because I have you."

"For as long as you want me."

"I might just keep you."

"What's with the *might* crap?"

That earned him a giggle and a smile. Maybe she thought he was teasing, but at this point, she had to know there was a hell of a lot more truth to his words than playing. She gave him a look, and they stared at each other across the room, some silent conversation that he understood. She didn't think he was teasing, and he knew she meant to keep him, but her gaze drifted to the casket behind her, and he got that message too. If things didn't turn out well for her, he might bury her, rather than marry her. The thought made his gut go tight and a deluge of thoughts swamp his mind.

What if something happened to her? No one knew they were together, except for his family. Would he have a chance to say goodbye, or would her lawyers, business associates, and friends step in, take over, and nudge him out? He didn't like the thoughts running through his mind and vowed he'd make himself a permanent part of her life. Somehow. Despite all the obstacles.

"Relax, Gabe. Everything is fine."

"Not if something happens to you. What do I do then?"

"You give Caleb's brother-in-law Sam the information I've dug up so far. He can start asking questions and hopefully solve this whole thing."

"I meant . . ."

Gabe shut his mouth when Ella's gaze shot to the door. Gabe turned to protect her from whoever was coming in, but relaxed when he saw only Mr. Henighan.

"Ready?" the staid man asked.

Gabe wanted to walk Ella right out of there and spare her any more pain. He wanted to finish his sentence and tell her he meant, how was he supposed to live without her? Instead, he took her hand and followed Mr. Henighan back down the hall to the only open door. They entered the room where they kept the bodies in refrigerated storage lockers, like in a morgue. Hard to bury a person in the dead of winter out here when the ground was frozen solid under several feet of snow and ice.

One of the storage lockers stood open. The table pulled out. Lela lay there, a sheet covering her body. He couldn't really see her face, just the back of her head. It looked like she slept, staring into the storage locker. Ella's hand gripped his, her nails biting into his skin. She didn't speak. Probably couldn't, so he did it for her.

"Mr. Henighan, we thank you for setting this up. Please, may we have a few minutes alone."

"Take all the time you need. Um, Ms. Wolf, Dr. Fortner left this for you." Mr. Henighan tried to hand her a large envelope from the desk in the corner. "He sealed it himself and told me to tell you if you have any questions or concerns to please contact him."

Ella didn't move to take the envelope. She stood beside him staring at her sister's lifeless body. Gabe took the heavy envelope. He wondered what this doctor left for Ella. It felt like some kind of hard case inside along with the papers he expected in the envelope.

"I'll leave you. If you need anything, please don't hesitate to call for me. I'll be in the office two doors down."

"No one comes in here," Gabe said.

"You have my word," Mr. Henighan assured him, making a quiet exit behind them.

He stood beside Ella and waited for her to make the first move. He'd stand there all day if that's what she needed.

"I don't want to remember her like this." Her voice came out quiet and sincere.

"All you have to do is look in the mirror and remember her."

"But I'll grow old and my face will change, but she will always be twenty-four and gone far too soon."

"And when that day comes, and you look in the mirror, you'll know what she'd have looked like, and you'll know you lived for the both of you because she wanted you to live."

"How do you always know the right thing to say?"

"Because I know you. You feel guilty about what happened, but, honey, you didn't do anything wrong. You couldn't save her. If you went into that room, he'd have killed you too. She called you for backup in case something happened."

"It did happen."

"And she knew if it did, you'd finish it. I've seen you, working all those hours at the computer. You're not just digging for information on your uncle. You've been working at the company. You've done everything you can, but the one thing you need to do."

"What is that?"

"Say goodbye to your sister."

"I can't."

"You have to, sweetheart. She's gone, but she'll always be in your heart."

Ella reached for her heart-shaped pendant, like she always did when she thought of Lela. Gabe was right. She needed to say goodbye.

It wasn't easy, but she let go of his hand and walked to the bank of refrigerated lockers and sat on the rolling stool Mr. Henighan left for her. She dropped Lela's purse beside her and pulled the ski cap off her head and shook out her hair. Hot, she peeled her mother's heavy coat down and let it drop behind her as she sat on the bottom of it.

Gabe leaned back against the closed door, standing sentry for her, so no one came in and disturbed this solemn moment.

"Take all the time you need, honey. I'm not going anywhere."

She believed him. The look in his eyes said he meant those words for a hell of a lot more than the time she needed with her sister. No, he meant he'd wait as long as it took for her to decide to be with him. Always. Well, she'd already decided in her heart. She just had to finish this and make it happen.

For the first time, she looked at her sister's beautiful face. Passive. Calm. Serenity embodied.

She reached out and brushed the backs of her fingers over her sister's soft cheek. "It wasn't supposed to be like this. We were supposed to grow old together. You're supposed to be my bridesmaid and my kids' favorite aunt. Who is going to spoil them rotten now? Who am I going to spoil now that you're gone?"

She glanced over at Gabe. His intense brown eyes stared back at her. Reading his thoughts, she'd spoil her own kids. With him. She'd have nieces and nephews to spoil. The man had three brothers.

Thinking about Gabe was far easier than saying goodbye to her sister, but she turned back to Lela and tried.

"Why didn't you tell me what you were doing? Why didn't you let me help you? Why did you come to the ranch?"

Ella leaned back against the other locker and stared down at her sister, remembering what happened that morning in the penthouse. She forced herself to go back and remember the call. Something nagged at the back of her mind, but she couldn't put her finger on it.

The longer she sat, the more memories that surfaced. She tried to make herself remember the good times. Like a slideshow in reverse, their lives together played out. She went back to the week before Lela died and the lunch they shared at the office, talking about the promotions they had set up for the cosmetics company launch. Back further to them sharing a bottle of champagne when the deal closed, and they owned the business. Dinners on their birthdays. Sleepovers as teens and children. Conversations about boys. Sharing all the good times and bad. Every achievement and loss. Every day of their lives.

The vacation they took together when they turned eighteen. Ten days in Europe. Not nearly enough time to see everything, but enough to finally stretch their wings and experience freedom out from under their uncle's thumb. Trips to Italy and Spain. Lela loved exploring Australia. Every year, a different place.

She remembered them as little girls, holding hands on the first day of school. Sitting on horseback, Lela's hands wrapped around her waist. She'd never been as fond of the horses as Ella. Both of them bundled up in snowsuits on tiny skis sliding down the mountain. Lela helping her write a paper in high school for a book she hadn't read. Ella helping Lela with the math she hated. "Why do they put letters in math?" she'd grumbled.

When Lela smiled, it made Ella want to smile too, even when she'd had a bad day. Her laugh made you want in on the joke. She loved to read and draw and watch black-and-white movies on Sunday afternoons.

Ella pulled the slip of paper out of the purse and stared at the last drawing her sister ever did.

"When we were kids, teachers would send home

notes to my parents requesting that they please tell
Lela to stop doodling all over her homework. She never
did. They'd mark her down for neatness and sometimes
give her points for creativity." She laughed and held the
paper up to Gabe. He walked over, knelt in front of her,
and looked at the picture.

"She's a good artist. Is that what you meant by the
cave?" Gabe pointed to the arch over the picture of her
and Lela's lockets, with the rosebush on either side, and
it all came back to her.

That something nagging her intensified. "What do
you mean?"

"When you sleep, you have nightmares, and you're
always saying, 'The cave.'"

The cave.

Ella's heart soared as recognition slammed through
her. She smiled and turned to Lela. "*That's* what you
meant. You'd never *cave*. The truth will *roll* out, not
come out. You told me where to find it, I just didn't
remember."

"Remember what?"

"Lela and I were five when we moved into the
ranch. My mother shooed us out of the house while the
movers were unpacking. We went to find our father in
the garage. We loved it out there. Our voices and foot-
steps echoed off the cement floor and walls."

"It's a six-car garage, honey, it's like a cavern."

"We pretended we were wolves howling in a cave."

"There is nothing in the garage. I watched them
clean out the toolboxes and miscellaneous stuff. It was
mostly Christmas and house decorations. No papers."

"Did you move the big heavy workbench with all the
drawers?"

"No one could move that thing. It's somehow bolted to the wall, despite the fact it's on wheels."

"Dad found us in the garage, and we told him it was our cave. He asked us if we wanted to see something, but we had to keep it a secret. We loved playing games with Dad, so we followed him over to the big cabinet. He showed us the secret code, the lock popped, and the cabinet and part of the wall rolled open."

"You're kidding me."

"Every house we lived in had a secret place. A vault." She smiled remembering her father. "Every Wolf needs a cave to keep his secrets."

"Do you think she hid the evidence there?"

"I'd bet my life on it."

"Don't say that."

She leaned forward and pressed her forehead to his, closing her eyes, and breathing him in. "I'm not ready to say goodbye."

"You can't stall much longer. We need to go to Wolf Ranch and open that vault."

"I know."

"It's only goodbye for now. You'll finish this, and we'll bury her with your parents on the ranch. You'll take her home." Gabe kissed her, stood, and walked back to his position by the door.

Ella put her hand on her sister's head. "Isn't he great, Lela?" The thought that her sister had sent her to Montana, to Gabe, and had somehow found her the perfect man from heaven made her smile. "Thank you, Lela, for always being my friend, for always having my back, and loving me with your big, beautiful heart. I will finish this and live my life for the both of us. I love you." She leaned over and kissed her sister on the forehead.

Ella stood behind Lela, grasped the table, and pushed it back into the locker. She touched her sister's soft hair one last time and closed the door. She planted both hands on the bank of doors and hung her head between her shoulders, letting the tears roll down her cheeks.

"Ella, honey, come here."

She pushed off the doors and ran into Gabe's open arms. He hugged her close, kissed the top of her head, and whispered, "You are still loved."

She felt her sister's presence in that room. She felt Gabe's warmth and kindness wrapped around her. Not exactly a declaration that he loved her, but again, exactly what she needed to hear.

CHAPTER 24

Gabe played with Ella's hair, rubbing her head softly. She leaned against him as he drove the truck down the icy road he'd cleared that morning before they left the house. With the sun up and the temperature in the high forties, the snow melted into a slushy mess. The white-capped mountains loomed all around them. Strange weather for this time of year, but he'd take the warmer temps as long as they could get them.

"What's in the envelope Mr. Henighan gave you?"

"The autopsy report and Dr. Fortner's recording of his analysis of Lela's injuries."

"Who is Dr. Fortner?"

"He's the top forensic pathologist in the country."

"You hired him to do an independent autopsy of your sister?"

"Insurance," she explained. "I heard a struggle on the phone. I think he hit her. I wanted Dr. Fortner to confirm her time of death, any other injuries or bruising. The angle of the shot. I'm shorter than my uncle, so the bullet trajectory will be different if I shoot versus him. I can't be sure exactly what they'll falsify against me, so I covered my ass."

"Smart."

"With this, everything I've gathered, and whatever Lela left at the ranch, I feel a sense that everything will work out. I can't explain it, but I felt her in that room. She brought me here for a reason, Gabe. I think that reason has a lot more to do with you than just finding the evidence."

"I don't care what brought you here, I'm worried that someone or something will take you away." The admission made him feel vulnerable and open in a way he'd never been with anyone else. With her, he felt he had to lay it all on the line. Time passed, but it felt like a clock ticking down, rather than time stretching out into their future. If he didn't tell her now, he might not get the chance. That scared him more than anything. Losing her because he hadn't said enough, done enough to show her he wanted her. Here. With him. Always.

Ella reached over, rubbed her palm over the back of his hand, and laced her fingers through his when he turned his hand over to hold hers. She gave him a soft smile, and his heart felt lighter.

Gabe rounded the bend in the road approaching his place and slammed on the brakes. The truck tires slid and the backend swung to the right, nearly colliding with the snowbank.

Ella sat up straight next to him. "Why are we stopping? I thought we were going up the road to Wolf Ranch."

"Look at the road."

"What about it? It's covered in ice and snow."

"And fresh tire tracks."

"So."

"No one lives up that road but you."

Ella stared straight ahead, eyes glued to the ominous sight. Fear paled her skin and made her hand tremble in his.

"We can't go up there now. Your uncle's men are probably waiting for you."

"I have to do this. We need that evidence."

"Let's call the sheriff. He can meet us at the house."

Her lips pressed into a thin line, and she shook her head. "After what happened, I won't trust anyone to see this through to the end. Not until I have the evidence in hand." She pleaded with her eyes for him to understand.

"Fine." He eased the truck forward, taking the turn-off for their place. "If someone is up there, I'm not driving in and giving them a free shot at you. We'll saddle a couple of horses and ride over. It'll take longer, but we can hide in the trees and get away a hell of a lot faster on horseback."

While he saddled Sully and Winnie, she grabbed their warmer gear from the house and met him in the stables. She didn't hesitate to give Winnie a soft pet down her long neck, stick her foot in the stirrup, and boost herself up into the saddle.

He held her thigh, feeling the connection between them pulse. Everything inside him told him to grab her off the horse, take her inside, and lock her away forever where she'd be safe. Instead, he silently swore he'd protect her, or die trying.

Ella stared out across the snow-covered field to the house rising up ahead on a hill overlooking the tree-lined valley she rode up. Behind the house, the white-capped mountains towered to the sky. She'd waited while Gabe circled the house, looking for any sign someone was inside. She'd promised to stay hidden, but the fear in her gut nearly made her leave the protection of the trees to go after him.

Gabe whistled to her from atop his horse on the rise, leading to the back gardens and patio. She rode up the hill and stopped near him. He didn't give her time to dismount, but grabbed her by the waist and lifted her from the saddle, bringing her down in front of him. Her body slid along his until her feet hit the ground. She stayed close and glanced up, wondering about his odd behavior. On the ride over, he'd constantly stared at her, but she didn't know why.

"Someone's been here. At least two trucks or SUVs based on the tire impressions and width of the wheels. The side door on the garage has a busted window."

"They went inside?"

He nodded. "Probably to check the house for you. Does Phillip know about the vault?"

"No. The lawyers only had the information on the penthouse safe. Not the ones in the other houses." She glanced back to the huge, empty house. "I never expected to come back here alone."

"You're not alone," he reminded her, taking her hand. "I don't know how long ago those people left, or if they are coming back. If they do, we get to these horses as fast as we can and head for the trees."

"Okay."

"Promise you'll stay by my side."

To ease his mind, break the tension, and make him relax, she closed the distance between them, pressed her hip to his, and said, "Let's go, cowboy."

Gabe planted his hand on her ass and pushed her

forward. They walked across the back patio and circled the house. Gabe pulled the keys from his pocket and unlocked the side door. She took a step to go in, but he grabbed her waist to stop her, leaned in, and whispered by her ear, "Let me go first in case someone is inside."

He took her hand and they cautiously walked down a short hall that opened into the living room. The house stood still and silent around them.

No sound or sign of her uncle's men. She didn't feel anyone else in the house, just the massive emptiness. Like her heart that had once been filled with love and family, it now felt hollow and cold. Nothing but a cavernous pit of grief and despair.

Gabe stopped and turned to her. He tugged on her hand to get her attention. "What's wrong?"

Her gaze roamed the massive room, the empty walls, bare windows, and cold fireplace, and settled on Gabe's handsome face. His warm brown eyes stared back at her, filled with concern and patience. Her chest went tight, and her heart stuttered when he looked at her like that. The need to be close to him, and the easy way she accepted that was where she always wanted to be, surprised her.

Under all the pain, love grew each and every minute she spent with this man. He was right. She'd never forget her sister, or the life they shared together, but Ella was alive and needed to find a way to live. Out of her sadness, love sprouted and reached for Gabe like a plant reaching for the sun.

Did he feel the same way?

Maybe. Why else would he help her like this?

She smiled, feeling lighter. "I'm fine."

Gabe followed her through the kitchen. When she

reached the garage door, he pulled her back and went out first.

She stepped out into the huge open space and walked into the center. Nostalgic and thinking of her sister's secret message, she opened her mouth and let out a loud wolf howl.

Gabe shook his head. One side of his mouth cocked back in a half grin, squinting his eye a bit. So cute. "You're probably a lot of fun at a party."

"You've seen the pictures, I am the life of the party."

"You're the glue."

"What?"

"You gather people around you and they stick because you're fun and kind and you take care of the people around you. I looked at some of those photos again. Most of them were you with friends out to celebrate a birthday or other special occasion. Not for you. For them. You threw the parties. You celebrated them and their accomplishments because you know what it feels like to not have someone do it for you. After your parents died, it was you and Lela out to dinner together for your birthday. High school graduation, you and Lela on a European vacation. Turn twenty-five and take over the company, it's you and her off to Bora Bora together."

"Yeah, well, now it's just me and this mess and nothing to celebrate."

"Promise me, Ella, when this is done that you will celebrate. You've earned it. Don't let your uncle take one more thing from you. Don't let him steal the fun-loving, joyful woman in those pictures. As much as I like the strong, confident, sentimental, kick-someone-in-the-balls-when-they-cross-you you I've gotten to know, I want to meet her too."

Ella laughed, but guessed he was right. She hadn't been herself. She'd never be her old self again. Too much had changed. She'd changed, and she was beginning to like the new Ella.

"I'll take you to one of my favorite places in the city. We'll celebrate." She held her hand out with his and stepped close, dancing side to side. He joined her with a smile. "We'll dance."

Ella spun away from Gabe and came face-to-face with the cabinet she hoped held all the Wolf family secrets.

CHAPTER 25

Ella stood in front of the metal cabinet and stared at the drawers, her mind taking her back years to a time when she felt safe and loved and didn't even know it because it just was her life. She traced her fingers over the drawer handles and metal numbers.

"Remember how I told you my father liked to tinker with things?"

Ella pulled out the number four drawer and heard the slide and click. Number two came next. Forty-two, her father's favorite number. Another soft snick.

"It's a puzzle lock." Gabe smiled and stared in awe at what looked like a tool cabinet, but was so much more. Kind of like Ella.

"He loved puzzles." She sighed and thought fondly of her father. God, how she missed him. "Some he made, others he bought. He'd spend hours trying to solve them. It helped him think, strategize, see things in a new way."

Number eight stuck a bit from disuse, but she tugged it open, hearing the distinct sound of a lever scraping and catching. Last, she pulled out number twelve. This time, a heavy bar clinked open and the cabinet and wood pegboard behind it snapped loose. She pulled on the cabinet. It rolled easily open and she stood staring at the shadowed room inside, filled with stacks of papers and files; cash; an orange metal box; jewelry and watch cases from Tiffany, Bulgari, Cartier, and Rolex; and other miscellaneous items she'd have to sort through to discover the contents.

She ducked under the door frame and entered the steel four-foot by four-foot box. "Watch your head," she warned Gabe as he planted his hands on both sides of the entrance and peeked inside.

"I should have brought a flashlight."

Ella grabbed the lantern off one of the shelves and turned the knob. The LED lights came on, brightening the whole room. She set the lamp on the shelf and turned back. Gabe stared at her, so much sadness filling his eyes, her heart sank. "What?"

His gaze fell to the file box at her feet and the white folded piece of paper on top with her name scrolled in her sister's handwriting. The hairs on the back of her neck stood on end. Her spine tingled with dread.

Ella snatched the paper up and unfolded it, her eyes watering when she saw her sister's pretty script and the doodle of a rose on the top.

"Ella Bear," she choked out, trying to read the letter to Gabe. *"If you're here, and I'm gone, you must finish this. It's all here. Uncle Phillip killed Dad. You know what to do. You always know what to do. I tried to do this for Mom and Dad and for you. Where I failed, I know you'll succeed. You'll have everything we both dreamed. Finally, my twin sister, you won't have to share."*

Ella choked back a sob. "She put a smiley face." Ella

turned the paper to show him. Sympathy radiated from his warm eyes and it nearly sent her to her knees. "We shared everything: our birthday, toys, clothes, friends, secrets. When you're twins, it's just how it is. I never minded sharing. Not with her."

"She calls you Ella Bear?"

"When we were babies and toddlers, we refused to sleep in separate beds. Mom and Dad gave up trying to separate us. Every night they'd come to tuck us in and kiss us good night. My mother would make sure I had my favorite bunny and always offered a stuffed friend to Lela, but she'd push it away and say, 'I seep with my Ella Bear,' and she'd hug me close, press her face in my hair, and fall asleep."

The sob wracked her whole body, and she fell to her knees, clutching the paper in her hands with her head down, tears dripping onto her hands.

Gabe crouched in front of her and pulled her close. "It's okay, sweetheart. That's a really great memory. She loved you so much."

"I loved them, and they are all gone." She tried to catch her breath, but couldn't.

Gabe dragged her into his lap, wrapped his arms around her, and held her close. She pressed her face to his coat and let the tears fall and the pain wash over her. She didn't know how long she cried all over him. He didn't seem to mind, but crooned sweet words and brushed kisses against her head.

She regained control, calming as Gabe rocked her in his arms, and they sat in the quiet. "I'm going to make him pay for taking them from me."

"Does she say anything else in the letter?" he asked.

Ella raised the crushed note and read the final lines.

"Take control of everything he wants. Be everything you are and ever wanted to be. Find someone you love to share your life with now. I will always be with you, Ella Bear. I love you. Lela."

"You had an amazing sister."

Ella sighed, turned in Gabe's arms, and hugged him close. "Yes, I did." Ready to face the reality of what her uncle did, she let Gabe go and scooted off his lap to check the contents of the vault.

"This is sweet." Gabe pointed to the picture of the two full-bloom roses facing each other off one stem Lela drew next to her name. "It matches the tattoo on the back of your neck."

"When we went on our trip to Europe, we decided we'd get a tattoo in France. Lela drew that. Identical roses separated from one stem. I got the tattoo, but when Lela saw how much it hurt me, she backed out.

"Let's see what Lela left me." She opened the lid to the box and smiled. "My sister was anal retentive about organization."

"And you're not?" he shot back. "You reorganized the silverware drawer, alphabetized my DVD collection by movie genre, reorganized the bathroom, and if that wasn't enough, you completely overhauled the files on my computer, putting everything into separate folders."

"It makes things easier to find."

"It makes you obsessive."

"I found your missing Jason Statham movie, didn't I?"

"Yes, you did. Thank you, sweetheart."

"You're welcome. Now, let's see just how much shit that bastard did to my family."

"Let's take it with us and go through it at my place."

"No. It's safer here. That's why she didn't bring

it with her. She knew he might do something to her. That's why she left me the letter. What I can't figure out is why she confronted him, even with the cop there. Why not just go to the authorities with all of this?"

"Passion."

"What?"

"If she's like you, she'd have been passionate about everything she did. He pissed her off and she went in there ready to make him pay and give him a piece of her mind."

"It got her killed."

"Which is why we're going to handle this another way."

"What did you find?"

Gabe flipped through the spreadsheets. "I think your father was on to your uncle before he died. These are the financial statements for the company. Your father made notes all over them, accounting for lost revenue and missing income."

Ella looked through another set of papers. "These are more of the same."

Gabe pulled out a CD with a slip of paper attached with a binder clip.

"What is that?"

"A receipt for drinks for two the same day Lela has in her calendar to meet the mechanic."

Gabe checked the box for any more papers, but only found a small handheld digital recorder. He pushed play.

"What happened to your wife?"

"That's Lela," Ella said.

"Phillip Wolf killed her. He kidnapped her from our house while she was out hanging the laundry on

the line. I was at work, checking over your parents' plane."

"Was there anything wrong with it?"

"No, ma'am. Good as new. Your father paid good money to keep that plane in top condition. I did my inspection and he did his before he flew it every time."

"Did you inspect the plane the day of the crash?"

"I went over it from nose to tail. Checked everything out. But then a man stopped by the hangar. He handed me a picture of Marjorie, sitting in a chair, a gag in her mouth, the morning newspaper against her chest."

Ella reached for Gabe's hand and held it tight.

"What did the man ask you to do?"

"Sabotage the fuel gauge to make your father think he had more fuel than he did and swap out the black box for one that didn't work to cover it up." The words came out choked and halting. Ella felt his pain. *"I did it to save her, but I couldn't. He killed her anyway."*

"How did you disable the black box?" Lela asked.

"I didn't. I swapped it the day after the plane crash."

"How? Weren't there a ton of NTSB and police?"

"They were everywhere. The guy in charge, Eardly, the one who came with Marjorie's picture and the order to kill your father, asked if I did my job. I told him I did it and begged him to tell me where they took my wife. He said that part wasn't his job, handed me an envelope full of cash, and dismissed me, telling the others he'd questioned and released me. I hoped they'd release my wife, and I'd find her at home. Before I left the hangar housing all the wreckage, dinner arrived for the investigators. They were distracted just long enough for me to switch out the black boxes and take the faulty fuel gauge."

Ella and Gabe both stared at the bright orange metal box and gauge on the floor beside them.

"Is that what's in the bag?"

"After they killed my wife, I took that money, the evidence, and I took off until the coast was clear. They got what they wanted. If I came forward, they'd pin the whole thing on me. I'd go to jail. I couldn't sit in a box the rest of my life, going mad with grief. You have to understand, I did it to save her. I've lived with this for ten years and it's eating me alive. I deserved to lose my wife for what I'd done and now cancer is slowly killing me.

"They had my wife." His voice cracked.

The sound made Ella's heart ache, but he'd killed her father and never came forward. Maybe if he had, her mother and sister would still be alive today.

"You take this to the right people. Make him pay for killing my wife."

"What about you? You killed my father."

"I paid every day. No one could be more sorry than I am for what I've done. God has sealed my fate. It's nothing less than what I deserve. I'm not long for this world."

The anguish in his voice wasn't enough to make her sympathize. He'd killed her father, which led to her mother's suicide. Yet he'd only been trying to save his wife. The fury swept through her. Gabe's hand settled over their joined ones, her nails biting into this skin. She loosened her grip, but didn't let go of him, or her rage. She'd make her uncle pay for ruining so many lives.

"How do you know my uncle is responsible?"

"The black box and gauge aren't the only things I

kept. I took the photograph. I stared at that picture every day, reminding myself of what I'd done and what it cost me. Every day I made myself look at her face and apologize for what I'd done. The other day, tired from the chemo and dying, I lay down with the picture and my eyes watered up and I saw something I'd never seen before. Here, look." Something rustled. *"See, right here. In the reflection of the picture on the wall. He didn't just take Marjorie's picture. He took one of himself."*

Gabe pulled the picture out of the envelope that had held the recorder. He held it between him and Ella. They both stared at the image of Phillip, taking the photograph reflected off the glass. If you weren't looking for it, you'd probably miss it overlaid in the framed art on the wall, but once you saw it, there was no mistaking Phillip Wolf.

"After all these years, I finally know and can prove Phillip Wolf killed my wife."

The rest of the tape was nothing but them saying goodbye. "I'll listen to the whole thing again, but my uncle will probably say I fabricated the conversation."

Gabe held up the CD marked "Surveillance, The Rise, Bozeman, Montana."

"Your sister didn't leave anything to chance. She recorded the conversation and got the meeting on video." He held up the restaurant receipt. "She's got proof of the date and time of the meeting, which I'll bet matches the time on the video."

"This is what brought her here. The meeting to get the evidence that Uncle Phillip killed our father. She came to the ranch and discovered my father's stash of evidence against him too."

"You've uncovered even more. The ongoing embezzlement, the missing paintings; and he killed those auditors."

"He won't kill anyone else," she vowed.

"Were you supposed to be on the plane with your father?"

"No. If I remember right, my parents had a long, private conversation in the study right before he left. Lela was fighting a cold. I wanted to stay with the horses. Mom stayed with us, and my father went alone. He promised to return in a few days."

"He didn't want to take you with him. Your father went back to confront your uncle, but Phillip had already set up his death."

"Because he knew my father was on to him about the embezzlement."

Ella sighed and stared at the black box and the files of evidence against her uncle, and thought of the morning her sister confronted their uncle. Triumphant. Full of righteous indignation, and emboldened by the presence of a detective she thought was on her side, Lela marched into the penthouse and swore to take him down.

Ella wouldn't be that reckless. She needed to verify everything and leave nothing to chance.

"Check this out." Gabe held out a legal-size folder.

Ella opened it and gasped. "My father wrote out a new will." She sorted through the papers, found the old will, and started comparing it to the new one. Gabe sat beside her in silence until she finished deciphering all the legalese.

"Fucking asshole, dickhead. Jail is too good for that murderous bastard. I'm going to dump his ass in a vat of acid and watch him writhe in pain."

"I'm right there with you. I want to rip the guy limb from limb for what he's done to you and your family." The anger in his voice matched the fury in her heart. "Tell me what the papers say."

"My father was not only on to what he'd done, he'd made sure my uncle never received anything if something happened to my parents. The will my uncle is using now was made when Lela and I were born. My father changed the will two months before he died. My uncle isn't our guardian. My parents name my mother's distant cousin. I remember meeting her a few times. She was really nice. She and my mother were great friends. They spoke on the phone and exchanged letters often. After my parents died, she came to see me and Lela several times, but then she stopped."

"Your uncle must have made her stop coming around. If she and your mother were close, she might have asked questions about why you girls were with him and not her. Your mother wouldn't have left you girls to this woman without at least talking to her about it first."

"That's my guess, but that's not all. The terms of the will are completely different. Lela and I never had to get our MBA, or work at the company. They left it all to us, to do with as we pleased." A tear rolled down her cheek. "The will states that if Lela and I wanted to pursue other interests, like art or veterinary school, we could sell the company, or keep it and hire managers to run it."

"You wanted to be a vet?"

"I was fourteen and in love with the horses my father bought me."

"What dad doesn't want to buy his princesses ponies?"

"My father spoiled us every chance he got. My mother too. They'd each scold the other for doing something for us. Then they'd smile at each other like in the grand scheme of things it didn't really matter." She ran her fingertips over the papers.

"When you were babies, the MBA and running the company seemed a good idea. Then, you grew up and your parents wanted you to find your own path and do what you loved."

"I miss them so much."

"I know you do, sweetheart. They've given you everything you need to finish this and do what they wanted for you."

"What's that?"

"Live the life that makes you happy. Whatever kind of life that is."

"Everything could have been so different if that bastard hadn't meddled in our lives."

She leaned back and scanned the contents of the vault. "I finally have all the proof I need to take my uncle down. It's time to contact Sam."

Gabe's silence spoke volumes. Once she called Sam, everything would change. She'd go back to New York and do what she had to do.

"Come on, let's close this up and get back to the house. We'll call Sam in the morning."

Ella wanted to call Sam immediately. Still, she nodded and silently agreed to wait until the morning. They'd have tonight together, just the two of them, before everything got even more complicated and her life intruded on his again.

Gabe closed the vault and all the open workbench drawers. The locks clicked back into place. The evidence remained inside. Safe, until they handed it over to Sam. Gabe took her hand and led her back through the house to the side door leading out to the patio.

"Where the hell did you leave your phone?" A deep voice echoed through the kitchen. Someone must have come in through the garage side door just after they left. The men her uncle had sent to find her. Her heart slammed into her ribs, then raced, sending an adrenaline rush through her veins.

Gabe opened the patio door and shoved her through.

"Probably in the bathroom." The second voice sounded closer as the men moved through the house.

"Go get it. I wish this fucking house wasn't so damn cold. I'm going out on the patio to stand in the sun for a smoke."

Gabe pulled her close. "Get to the horses. Ride for the trees. Hide. Now."

"Come with me."

Gabe gave her a steely look that said, *No way.* "I'll get rid of them. Go. Quick. Before they see you." He gave her a quick kiss and shoved her bottom to get her moving.

She scrambled around the side of the patio and out of view from the windows that lined this side of the house.

Gabe didn't waste time and snuck back through the living room and around a huge pillar and came up silently behind Phillip's man. He snatched the gun from the guy's waistband holster and pressed the steel between his shoulder blades. "Don't say a fucking word."

The guy was smart enough to keep quiet. Gabe grabbed him by the neck and dragged him backward toward the bathroom off the stairs. The second guy came around the corner, his lost phone in hand, and halted dead in his tracks.

"If you want your friend to live," Gabe said in a low, even voice, "take your gun out nice and easy, drop it to the floor, and kick it my way."

The guy complied with a murderous look. "Who the fuck are you?"

"The owner. You're trespassing. Not to mention breaking and entering."

"Phillip Wolf sent us. He owns this place, not you."

"Wrong. He sold me the property. I don't know what you're doing here, but you need to get the hell off my land."

"We're looking for Ella Wolf."

"As you can see"—Gabe swept his gaze over the empty rooms—"she's not here."

"You seen her?"

"The only people sneaking around this place are you two."

"Come on, man, you're not going to pull that trigger."

"'Round these parts, we shoot strangers first and ask questions later." The deadly serious note in his voice got their attention. "Now, get the fuck out of my house." Gabe shoved the guy he held the gun on toward the front door. The other guy scampered after him. Gabe snagged the other gun off the floor and kept the ends of his barrels trained on both men. He walked them to the black Escalade out front. Probably the same one he saw at Finney's trailer home.

"How the hell did you even know we were here?"

"Called the alarm company to put the service in my name. They told me about the alarm going off when you two yahoos broke the garage window. If Phillip

Wolf sent you here, why didn't he give you a key or the alarm code?"

The two men stared at each other, clearly at a loss for an answer. They'd simply taken the easy route and broke in instead of going through the hassle of contacting Phillip over such mundane details as keys and codes.

"Right. Maybe I should call the sheriff. Let him check you two out. Make sure you're legit," Gabe suggested.

"Look, man, take it easy." One threw up his hands in protest. "The woman isn't here. We're leaving. Just give us back the guns. We don't want trouble."

"You've already got it. Get in the car and drive away. Don't come back, and we won't have a problem. Got it?"

The men tore out like the devil hunted them. He waited for them to turn the bend out of his sight. Still, he waited a couple of minutes more to see if they were stupid enough to come back.

His heart pounded. Had Ella remained out of sight? That encounter was too close for comfort. He dreaded what came next. Facing off with Phillip would be far more dangerous than going up against his goons.

Satisfied the men had left without further incident, he went back through the house, locked everything up, and set the alarm. He ran around the back to his horse, stuffed the guns in his saddle bags, and got up in the saddle. He turned and headed back down the hill toward the tree line, following Ella's horse's tracks.

Just outside the trees, he whistled for her to come out. "All's clear, sweetheart."

Smart woman that she was, she came out fifteen feet down, closer to the wide valley they came up earlier. A much easier spot from which to ride hard and get away.

"I can't stay here anymore. I've put you in danger."

"You're in danger every second that bastard isn't behind bars."

"Yes, and now I've brought that danger to your door." She leaned forward as if the weight of all she had to do now settled on her shoulders. "It's time, Gabe."

CHAPTER 26

Gabe knelt beside Ella sitting at the kitchen table hours after they returned home. He ran his hands up her thighs to her hips and grabbed hold to get her attention. "Come to bed, Ella."

"I'm so tired."

"Let it be. At least for tonight."

"I don't want to leave."

The burden of having to fix everything weighed on her when all she wanted to do was grieve for her family. He hoped a part of her wanted to stay because of him.

"I want you to stay."

To prove how much he meant that statement, he pulled her sister's letter that she'd been staring at for the last hour from her hands and set it on the table. He reached up, cupped the back of her neck, and drew her to him for a soft kiss that coaxed her to set her sorrows aside and find some happiness in his arms. If that was all he could offer her right now, he'd give her everything.

Her lips were soft against his. He stood, pulling her up with him, their mouths still pressed together, and he sank deeper into the kiss and her.

God, how he needed her. He dipped his hands low over her hips, bringing her up to wrap her legs around his waist. Her arms encircled his head, and he buried his face in her neck and kissed and nipped, hungry for her in a way he didn't want to evaluate too closely.

With his long strides and determination to get her into his bed, he had her in their room in seconds, but the short walk didn't distract him from kissing her, or rubbing his hands over her bottom, dipping deep, to tease her soft folds.

His legs hit the bed, and he bent forward, letting her fall on her back onto the mattress and rumpled sheets. She bounced and smiled up at him.

"I like seeing you in my clothes," he said, staring down at her in his Led Zeppelin T-shirt and Texas A&M sweatpants. Her favorite outfit to lounge around the house while she washed her clothes. "But I prefer you out of them."

He put actions to words, peeling the sweatpants down her legs. Since the first time they made love, and he discovered she didn't wear any panties, because she didn't have any but the original pair she arrived in, it had become a torture to see her each and every day, knowing she was bare under her clothes.

She pulled the shirt over her head and tossed it over the side of the bed. His eyes devoured every inch of her soft, creamy skin.

"Love me, Gabe."

He wanted to tell her how much he already did, but showed her instead. He leaned over and planted soft kisses down the center of her chest and over her belly. Her fingers slid through his hair and she sighed softly into the night. He detoured from her stomach

and planted a kiss on her hip. He slid his hands up
her thighs and back down, grabbing her knees and
spreading her legs wide, opening her to him. He laid
a trail of kisses up the inside of her thigh and buried
his face in her heat, sweeping his tongue deep into her
core. Her fingers clenched in his hair and she moaned.
The taste of her shot through him in a blaze, making
his cock jerk and the need to be inside her intensify,
but he wanted to please her, make her forget everything but him and the way he made her feel when they
were together. He wanted her to know how much she
meant to him. How much he couldn't live without her.
What he couldn't bring himself to say with words, because he couldn't find any that expressed the depth of
what he felt, he showed her with his body.

He nibbled and sucked, then swept his thumb over
her clit in soft up and down sweeps, creating just the
right amount of friction to bring her to the brink. He
didn't let her fall. He wanted to be inside her when she
came. His own release rode him hard, but he fought it
back, wanting to prolong her pleasure as long as possible. His lips pressed to the inside of her thigh again,
and he thrust two fingers into her slick sheath. Her hips
rolled against his hand, and he worked his fingers in
and out of her. He kissed his way up her stomach to
her breast and took her rosy nipple into his mouth and
sucked hard as he thrust his fingers deep. Her hand slid
over his head and down his neck to his shoulder. She
grabbed it tight, and he did it again.

Desperate to have her, he gripped her hips and shifted
her higher on the bed. Her hands never left his bare
chest, sliding over his muscles even as he reached for a
condom on the side table. He grabbed it, but somehow

she pushed him onto his back and ended up on top of him. She straddled his hips, planted her hands on both sides of his head, and bent to kiss him. She pressed up and stared down at him, a seductive smile on her face.

"My turn."

He didn't know what she had in mind, but he sure as hell liked looking at her. Her brown hair hung just past her shoulders. Her breasts were full and tipped up with her rosy nipples, hard and begging for his mouth. His gaze dipped lower, over her flat belly, to the barely there strip that led straight to heaven. He wanted to bury himself deep, but lost all thought when she leaned down, kissed his neck, and her hand wrapped around his balls. She slid her hand up his aching cock and squeezed, sweeping her thumb over the thick head, her fingers working up and down it.

She pulled his boxer briefs down, freeing his swollen flesh. Her breast brushed against it as his boxer briefs swept down his legs, and he kicked them away.

Her hands swept up his thighs, and he wanted her to straddle him again, so he could bury himself inside her. He wanted to watch her ride him hard and fast.

She had other ideas.

Her hair brushed against his stomach, tickling him and making his muscles taut. Her tongue swept over the head of his cock, licking away the bead of liquid a second before she took him into her mouth, sliding down and back up, her tongue gliding along the length of him. At that moment, he lost all thought and gave himself over to the sweet torture.

So close, he called to her, "El . . ." But her name died on his lips when her hand wrapped around the bottom of his dick and her mouth came down on him, and she bobbed up and down, using her hand and mouth to drive him insane with pleasure.

"I'm so damn close. I want to be inside of you."

She reached up his chest and snatched the open condom from his hand. The sexiest damn thing he ever saw was her licking her lips and sheathing him. He reached for her, dragging her up his body and pulling her head down for a deep kiss. He reached between them, found her hot, wet center, and sank his finger deep. She found as much pleasure in loving him as he'd found in pleasing her.

Desperate. Out of his mind. He held her hips and brought her down hard on top of him. She rolled her hips to accommodate him and they found the easy rhythm they always found when they came together like this.

She rode him hard and fast and he held on as long as he could, reaching up to stroke his hands over her breasts, squeezing her tight nipples between his fingers. She arched into his hands, offering up the bounty to his touch.

On the edge, he reared up, wrapped his arm around her waist, and rolled her under him. She landed on her back, her arms coming up to encircle his shoulders. Her fingers dug into his back, nails biting into his skin when he thrust into her hard and deep. He grinded his hips to hers, pulled out, and sank back in to do it again. Her hips moved with him, against him, away from him. They matched each other in every way. He gave himself over to her and felt the way she gave herself over to him.

Her fingers raked down his sides and her hands settled on his hips. She pulled him close, and he rocked against her hips, riding her hard, and creating a sweet friction against her clit just the way he'd learned she liked it. Her body tightened around him. He pulled out and thrust deep again, sending her over the edge on a ragged sigh, her body holding his in a tight fist that convulsed and drew from him an orgasm so intense he closed his eyes, tossed back his head, and let himself go with a satisfied groan.

Gabe fell on top of her and pressed her into the mattress. She didn't mind his weight. In fact, she needed it. Ella wrapped her arms around his back and hugged him close, knowing exactly how he felt and why. He'd just shown her how much he loved her, but he knew she had to go and wanted to give her a reason to stay.

He must realize how much she wanted the same thing. Hadn't she shown him?

"Gabe."

"I don't want to talk about your family and what you need to do. Not now. Not tonight."

He rolled to his back, separating himself from the intimacy they'd shared but moments ago. He didn't let her go entirely and kept his big hand splayed over her thigh. She rolled toward him. He shifted and pulled her close to his chest in the crook of his arm.

"Gabe . . ."

"Not now. Just be with me. Here. Nothing else between us."

She kissed her way up his chest, neck, and jaw to his lips, sliding her naked body against his. She kissed him and felt the simmering heat she always felt between them pulse. She pressed her hand against his strong jaw and made him look at her. "I am here. With you. Where I always want to be."

His arms banded around her in a fierce hug. He rolled to his side and they lay face-to-face, his forehead pressed to hers. He kissed her again. Soft, warm, sweet, and enticing, but not the start of something, just a show of love and affection and connection.

"I don't want to let you go."

"Then hold on."

CHAPTER 27

Ella wanted to scream. Gabe refused to speak to her about leaving for New York. *Damn man*. Instead, he spent the entire morning in the stables with the horses. Understandable; they needed to be fed, their stalls cleaned, but he didn't have to find any and every excuse not to come back to the house.

After a quiet breakfast, he called Sam at the FBI to go over what they found yesterday, and how it all tied together and led to Lela's murder. Ella took the phone to go over the rest with Sam, and Gabe walked out the door.

Well, ignoring the situation wasn't getting them anywhere. She tapped her fingers on the table with impatience. Her uncle would pay, but she couldn't let his comeuppance happen at the expense of her relationship with Gabe. She couldn't leave so much unsaid between them.

The front door creaked open. *Finally*, Gabe came to talk to her. She rose from the table and turned and came face-to-face with Travis. His lips pulled back in a feral smile, and his eyes narrowed. He rushed her, his determined strides clearing the distance between them in seconds, arms outstretched to grab her. She screamed and tried to back away, but he caught her by the arm and spun her around. Her back slammed into his chest and his hand clamped over her mouth, practically blocking her nose too.

With his arm banded around her stomach, he dragged her out the front door. She tried to kick him and struggled to get free. Her muffled screams barely made any sound. Frantic, she swept her gaze over the yard and barn for any sign of Gabe, but she didn't see him. She tried to bite Travis's hand, but he only pressed harder, hurting her face and jaw.

"Stop fighting me, you uppity bitch. Who the hell do you think you are, ruining me. I found out who you are from the men your uncle sent to find you. I'm taking you to the sheriff and collecting that reward your uncle put up for you."

She planted her feet, trying to keep him from getting her to his truck. She twisted her sprained ankle, fighting to get free of his punishing grasp, and yelped in pain. Her breath sawed in and out from the small gap between his hand and her nostrils. Pissed off, she screamed again, hoping Gabe heard her.

Travis jerked behind her, pulling her off balance. He let loose, and she fell to the ground and twisted around, ready to defend herself. No need. Gabe punched Travis right in the nose, breaking it with a sickening crack. Travis ended up on his ass in the snow and bellowed out an obscenity.

Gabe grabbed him by his coat, lifted him off his feet, and slammed him into the side of the truck. "Don't you ever fucking touch her again."

All hell broke loose, four cars pulled into the driveway, two of them with red and blue flashing lights swirling. A man who looked very much like a younger version of Gabe jumped out of an old Ford truck and came running. Gabe's brother Dane.

An older man slid from another beat-up truck with "Crystal Creek Veterinary" on the door. The vet she'd hired to check on the cattle at Travis's place. The officers were right behind Dane, but she reached Gabe first.

Gabe flipped Travis around to face the truck and wrenched his arm up behind his back, his hand pressed between his shoulder blades.

"You're going to break my arm."

"I'll kill you if you ever lay a hand on her again."

"Gabe, honey, let him go. The cops are here."

He didn't let up his hold, but glanced over at her. "Are you all right?"

"I'm fine. Let him go." She limped forward to touch her hand to his shoulder and reassure him.

His eyes scanned down her body and narrowed on her hurt ankle. He turned back to Travis. "You bastard, you hurt her."

The rage that came over Gabe's face stunned her. He let go of Travis's arm and hauled back his big fist to punch him in the ribs, but Dane rushed in, grabbed Gabe by the arm, and hauled him away from Travis.

"Hold on now, bro, let the cops take care of him."

"I'm going to fucking kill him."

Dane pushed against Gabe's chest, holding him off. Not an easy task. Gabe really wanted to kill Travis, who leaned against his truck, holding his bleeding nose and wailing about cows and stupid women.

"That fucking reward is mine," Travis yelled. "Don't even think about taking it for yourself. I saw her first."

Gabe went ballistic, pushing against Dane's hold. "You say one fucking word about who she is and I'll kill you."

Ella shook her head and pushed herself between Gabe and Dane. Grabbing hold of Gabe's coat, she shook him to get his attention. "Listen to me. Stop."

Gabe finally took his gaze from Travis and stared down at her. He dropped to one knee and reached for her leg, massaging her calf and checking her ankle with a soft squeeze. "Are you okay?"

She put her hands on his shoulders to steady herself. "I'm fine."

"You're limping again."

"I jarred my ankle and hip when I stumbled."

"You going to introduce me, or what?" Dane asked from behind them.

Gabe held her leg and leaned his head against her belly and let out a heavy sigh.

"I'm okay," she repeated, because he obviously needed to hear it.

Gabe stood and pulled her to his side. "What are you doing here?" he asked his brother.

"She contacted me two days ago and told me to bring your cattle. She hired me to bring her cattle to her ranch."

Gabe stared down at her. "You did?"

"Did you think I forgot about them?"

"No. It's just . . ."

"Everything. I know. But I did not forget what that asshole did to me, or the fact those animals were not being cared for properly. I told you I just needed to make a couple of phone calls to make it all right.

"I called Dane, and then I had the vet set up the men

and trucks to move the cattle off Travis's ranch this morning. The sheriff was supposed to arrest Travis."

The vet, Dr. Potts, stepped up next to her and offered his hand. "It's nice to meet you, Ms. Wolf." She shook it. "Travis was already headed in this direction when we arrived. The sheriff's men arrived moments later, and we followed Travis here, though not in time to stop him from pushing you, and Gabe from tearing a strip off his sorry hide. I only wish we'd been a few minutes longer so Gabe could finish the job after the way Travis has neglected and mistreated those animals."

"What the hell is going on?" Gabe asked.

"I've tried to talk to you all morning, but you shut me out." Tears welled in her eyes.

"Sweetheart, I'm sorry." Gabe tried to step toward her, but the officer stepped in, took his hands, and handcuffed him.

"What the hell," Gabe said, his voice tinged with suppressed anger.

"You can't go around punching people—even if they deserve it," the officer added under his breath. "Let's go. We'll take this down to the station and sort out who instigated the fight. Travis is bellowing about pressing charges for assault."

Travis kicked and bucked in the backseat of the other car, cussing and carrying on, his shackled hands holding a wad of bandages to his bloodied nose. "The reward is mine," he wailed.

The officer turned to her. "Meet me down at the station. I'll need your statement. I spoke with Special Agent Sam Turner earlier this morning. He assured me you are headed back to New York to meet with authorities in connection to your sister's murder and that you had nothing to do with it."

"I'm leaving as soon as I clean up this mess with Travis and Gabe."

Satisfied, the officer walked Gabe to his car and helped him into the backseat.

Strong hands clamped onto her shoulders and squeezed her tense muscles. Dane stood behind her, staring at Gabe from over her head. "I'll go get him."

"You take care of that." She pointed to the massive semitrucks driving past Gabe's house, headed up to her ranch. Gabe stared at the trucks going by, hauling her sick cattle. She didn't know how many trips it would take to move them all, but she'd have them safe and in her pastures soon. They'd be well fed and tended to properly thanks to Dr. Potts's help, and the men she'd hired to help Gabe. Now, all she had to do was convince Gabe to take over her ranch the way he'd planned, but on a much larger scale. "I'll handle Gabe. And Travis."

"Go get 'em, honey."

She shook her head. "You're a lot like your brother."

"He's not going to be happy you kept him in the dark about this."

"I wanted to surprise him."

"We live a simple life. Surprises like this don't happen every day."

The sheriff's vehicles pulled out of the driveway. She never stopped looking at Gabe until the cars disappeared out of sight.

Dr. Potts walked back to his truck. "I'll follow them on down the road and make sure they get settled."

Dane remained behind her. "Now what?"

"I finish what I started."

"So, back to New York?"

"For now."

"What about Gabe?"

"What about him?"

"The way I heard it from Blake, Gabe is in love with you."

"I don't know about that."

"Yes, you do."

She turned to face him and stared up at his dark eyes, so close to the familiar ones she'd grown used to giving her that same penetrating look.

"I have something I need to do. Because of that, Gabe and I have left talk of the future for later."

"Is that why you did this, because you want a future with him?"

"I set him up at the ranch because it's his dream, and I understand that. My father had a dream and worked to build his legacy, and it was taken from him far too soon. I won't let that happen to Gabe. He wanted it. He'll have it. I told him I'd make it right, and I will."

"So, not the spoiled rich girl you try so hard to get people to believe you are."

"I don't really care what people think."

"No. But you care what he thinks."

"Gabe knows who I am."

"Maybe he does. I bet you terrify him."

"Why is that?"

"Because he's probably thinking what I'm thinking. You won't last one year out here before you're begging to go back to the city to shop, order take-out, catch a movie, eat at a fancy restaurant, anything to be away from here and the isolation that is a part of life living on a ranch."

"Yeah, well, you don't know me, or what I want."

"Just let him down easy, that's all I ask."

"I would never do anything to hurt Gabe. He saved my life." In so many ways he'd saved her. From that deserted road. From the life she thought she had to live to meet everyone's expectations. From herself for going along with everything and never once taking a second to discover what she really wanted and why she hung on to pieces of the life she'd had with her family on the ranch. She loved her horses, going to the country music bar, staying home over going out. Would she miss her life in the city? Probably, but that didn't mean she couldn't go back once in a while, because what she'd really miss was her friends. But she'd keep in touch through email, texts, and phone calls.

"I hope you mean that. I'd hate to see yet another woman make him a promise she doesn't mean."

"Not going to happen. Now, please, take care of the ranch and let me take care of Gabe."

"When will you both be back?"

"I'm not sure. Gabe will want to return as soon as possible. It might take me a bit longer."

Dane frowned and gave her an exactly-what-I-thought look.

"I have employees and responsibilities." That didn't seem to appease Dane, who continued to frown at her. "As much as I want to be with Gabe, it's a massive undertaking to run an entire company, but I owe it to my sister."

"Gabe will help you."

"It isn't for Gabe to do. He'll have his work here. The work he loves in the place he wants to be with his family. I can't ask him to leave all that for me."

"What if you're what he wants?"

"He might say that, and even believe it, but I know he'll never be happy anywhere but here."

"The choices you face aren't fair or easy. I'm sorry about that, but I'm looking out for my brother."

"That makes two of us. I know him, Dane. I can't change who he is. I don't want to."

Dane gave her a hug and stepped back. "Blake was right. You're nothing like that woman in the pictures and on the TV. I hope you two figure this out. You're not what I expected, but you might be perfect for him."

"Blake said something very similar."

"We're brothers, and obviously brilliant." Dane shrugged and headed for his truck. "I'll take care of Gabe's place and yours until you get back. Don't forget, Mom wants to have you over for dinner. She told me to remind you."

Ella shook her head, turned, and went into the house to get the keys to Gabe's truck, his cell phone, and her purse. She made a quick call to the new lawyers she hired right after she spoke to Sam this morning, telling them to meet her at the sheriff's office in Crystal Creek. Who knew she'd have to use them so soon? She packed up all the papers and files she had strewn everywhere, tucked them and her laptop back into her tote, and carried them out to the truck. She went into the bedroom and packed all her clothes. She rummaged through Gabe's closet, finding a suitcase and packing him enough clothes for a week.

She loaded everything into the backseat of the truck and turned the key. The engine hummed, but she didn't back out of the drive. She sat staring at the house, wondering if everything would ever be like it was last night with Gabe when he made love to her. She hoped it would be for both their sakes.

Instead of turning right out of the drive, she went left, up the road to her ranch. The trucks unloaded the cattle into the pastureland on the east side of the property. Dane saw her coming and waved for her to stop.

"Where you goin', honey? Town's the other way."

She laughed and shook her head. "I need to get something from the house."

"Need help?"

"No, I've got it covered. How's everything going here?"

"Travis should be shot."

"Yeah, well, short of that I've got two lawyers ready to put him in his place."

"Go get 'em, honey. I'll see you at dinner at Mom's."

With that, Dane went back to directing cattle traffic with the men up on horseback, driving the cattle further along into the pastures.

It didn't take her long to retrieve the boxes of files and the black box from the airplane crash. She waved to Dane on her way back down the pass to town. On her way, she called to have the plane ready and spoke with Sam to make sure everything was in order.

Time to finish this. But first, she had to get her man.

CHAPTER 28

Ella walked into the sheriff's office, feeling more like her old self. Confident. In control. Ready to take on the job ahead. She scanned the room, noting she'd beat the lawyers to the office. Not surprising since they were coming in from Bozeman.

"Thanks for coming down, Miss Wolf," the officer who handcuffed Gabe said from his desk behind a short wall that separated him from the entry area.

"I'm here to press charges against Travis Dorsche and get any charges against Gabe Bowden dropped. Travis deserved the broken nose and a lot more, but we'll get to Gabe as soon as my lawyers arrive. For now, what do you need me to do to press charges against Travis for attempted sexual assault and attempted murder to go along with the animal abuse and neglect he's already facing?"

"Those are big accusations."

"Those are the facts. Let me tell you all about it and you can write up the report. My lawyers will have a discussion with Travis about the way he treated me and whether or not Gabe was protecting me when Travis grabbed me and shoved me to the ground."

"I'm starting to get a clearer picture of what happened," the officer said.

"I thought you would, but that is what happened, so we'll just play this out and see how far Travis wants to take this."

"Travis really made an enemy of you. I'd hate to be in his shoes."

"Damn right." Her uncle thought he could go up against her. Well, he'd discover, just like Travis was about to find out, that she wasn't an easy target. She'd stand her ground and use everything at her disposal to do what was right and see them behind bars.

Filled with the confidence she hadn't felt since her sister's murder and her spiral into depression, she dictated her statement about what happened with Travis. By the time she finished, the officer was frowning and shaking his head. She hadn't even gotten into the animal neglect and abuse she'd witnessed. She had the documentation and the sick animals to prove it.

Gabe sat on the cot with his back to the wall, legs stretched out. He'd replayed last night in his mind all morning, and let the scene play out again. Ella and him together in bed, making love, completely connected in a way he'd never been with any other woman. God, the way she made him feel. Then he woke up this morning, knowing that their time in seclusion together was up. They needed to go to New York, and she needed to avenge her sister and take down that bastard once and for all.

The thing was, playing house was one thing, but Gabe couldn't shake the fear that Ella would get justice, and then discover how much she missed her familiar life. The country might be good for grief, healing, and hiding out, but was it an existence she could ever truly lead. Not a weekend here or there, but days that stretched into weeks that encompassed a lifetime. God, he wanted a lifetime. But she had responsibilities to her company and the people she employed. If he knew one thing about Ella it was that she looked out for her own. What chance did this fantasy of her living in Montana have in the face of her reality?

The days they'd spent together would go down as the best time of his life. He'd spend the rest of his days loving this woman. As much as he wanted to ask her to stay with him on the ranch, he hoped she wanted just as much to ask him to stay with her in New York. Yet neither of them would be happy living the other's life. So how could he ask her to do something he couldn't do for her? It would end in disaster. He'd rather let her go now, his sweet memories of their time together happy moments he'd pull out every time he missed her. Which would be every second of every day.

Look at that. He finally fell in love and lost her before he ever really had her. From the moment he'd met her, she'd always been passing through his life.

"Hey, cowboy, I came to bust you out of this joint. I've got two horses saddled out back. Let's make a quick getaway and ride off into the sunset together."

He wanted to smile, but couldn't find one to give her. "Where are we off to, city girl? The Big Apple?"

"I've got the jet waiting on the tarmac."

He slid from the cot and stood in front of her next to the bars. "It's very strange that you mean that."

"I'm sorry, Gabe."

"For what? Being who you are? I like who you are."

She averted her face, her expression covered by a curtain of light brown hair. "It gets in the way sometimes."

He shrugged that away. Ever since she found the evidence, things between them had gotten weird.

"I'm sorry I didn't tell you about the cattle and the ranch. I wanted to surprise you."

"You surprised me, all right. I left you alone to do what you needed to do. I never realized how much you can get done in a short amount of time with nothing more than a phone and a computer."

"I'm a resourceful girl." She turned her head away to glance at the two men in suits who walked into the holding cell area. "I couldn't leave those cattle with Travis. The man has no regard for decency. They need to be taken care of properly. It's a good business that makes a lot of money. You wanted the ranch. You paid my uncle to buy the place. I told you I'd make it right."

"I never thought you meant to hire me as an employee to run your ranch."

"Not my ranch. Our ranch."

Too much to hope she meant she'd live there with him and be a rancher's wife. Yet, for a brief moment, he let the wave of anticipation wash over him before becoming more practical. "What exactly do you mean by that?"

"I'm a businesswoman, and I'm making you a business proposition."

Of course. "Is that why you brought the suits?"

"I couldn't trust the lawyers at the company or the family attorney, so I hired Mr. Crawford and Mr. White out of Bozeman."

"You're serious?"

"They are here to get you out of this trouble with Travis and facilitate our new business arrangement."

So this is how it would end. He'd get the land, but not the woman. If he thought it hurt the first time, it was nothing compared to the crushing grip around his heart now.

He leaned his shoulder against the bars and studied her. The woman he knew, but didn't quite get at the moment. "Explain this arrangement?"

"Okay. Well. You paid my uncle one-point-five million for the whole ranch. As you discovered, the current market value of the ranch is about sixteen-point-nine million."

"So, what are you offering me? A job?" The anger simmered in his gut.

"A partnership. Your million and a half buys you a twenty percent interest in Wolf Ranch. Still, an amazing deal. You will live in the house, oversee the cattle business, grow it as you planned, and run it as you see fit. I've hired some men temporarily to help you get started, including Dane to oversee things until you get back."

"You hired my brother?"

"He's the only man I knew you'd approve to look after the cattle and your horses."

"So I do all the work and get twenty percent."

"You own twenty percent. We'll split the profits twenty-five, seventy-five."

"So I do all the work and you get the lion's share of the profits too?"

"No. You do. You do the work. You build the business, and you'll earn the profits. I'm just supplying the land and the initial startup with the cattle. What you do with it is up to you."

"You once warned me about taking deals that are too good to be true."

"Take this one. You won't find anything better. Besides, I've already moved the cattle. The contents of the house will be moved back in tomorrow."

"So I get the ranch and a furnished house. What's the catch?"

"Angel and Belle."

"Your horses."

"Blake is on his way to get them and bring them here. It's not right to leave them at the New York estate all alone."

There it was. Once she returned to the city and took over the business, she'd have no time for her beloved horses. No time for him.

"Jeez, Ella. What else have you done with your spare time?"

"Learned that when something really terrible happens, something even better can show you the way back to happiness. Thank you isn't enough for all you've done," she said.

"So you practically gave me your house and turned everything we had into a business deal?" He couldn't help the anger in his voice.

"You know that's not true. What we have is special, but it doesn't change what I have to do. I promised I'd make things right, and I have. Now I'll always know where you are and that you're happy."

That sounded too close to goodbye. It tore his heart to shreds. He wanted to ask her how he'd ever be happy again without her, but he couldn't put her on the spot like that. Not with the suits standing there discreetly acting like they weren't seeing and hearing everything he and Ella said.

"This isn't over." He'd stay by her side until her uncle was behind bars no matter what. The business deal pissed him off, because he wanted a hell of a lot more. He wasn't stupid enough to turn it down. Not when it kept him connected to her—even if only in this small way.

"I hope not."

"Bust me out of here, city girl."

She reached up and touched her hand to his face, giving him a soft smile. "Mr. Crawford has some papers for you to sign on the ranch stuff. Mr. White has brokered a deal with Travis. He won't press charges for the assault—"

"Mostly because you were clearly defending Ms. Wolf from further attack and she had every reason to believe Travis would harm her due to their previous encounter where he attempted to sexually assault her and left her for dead on the side of the road, in freezing temperatures, with no means of reaching safety before she succumbed to the cold."

"Thank you, Mr. White." She rolled her eyes at Gabe, which made him even more crazy for her, because although she'd called in the cavalry, she still found the stuffed shirts irritating.

"Travis drops the charges against you in exchange for lesser charges for what he did to me."

"That sucks. You almost died out there."

"Yes, well, I may have to thank Travis for leaving me out there."

"Why the hell would you do that?"

"If not for him, I might not have met you."

Those words went right to Gabe's heart. He squeezed Ella's hand, drew her close, and whispered, "Get me out of here." His voice came out gruff. He needed her in his arms. Right now.

"Crawford, the papers." She held out her hand for the contract. "Sign these."

"You aren't letting me out of here without signing those?"

"It's a great deal. Take it."

"What if I want more?" He didn't want twenty percent of this and seventy-five percent of that. He wanted it all. Her. Even if it did seem impossible.

"I want to give it to you, but I can't. Not yet." Her gaze fell to the floor. "My uncle."

She needed to finish things. Put it behind her and stand on her own for the first time without her twin backing her up. She needed to know she could. A woman of integrity, she wouldn't make him promises now when her world was still in chaos and she might not be able to keep those promises. She'd never hurt him on purpose and refused to open the door to even the possibility she might.

He wanted to build a life with her. A simple plan, complicated by geography, lifestyles, and circumstances beyond their control.

"Is Sam ready?"

"Everything is in place. I need to bring what I have and finish it."

Gabe narrowed his gaze. "We will finish it. I'm going with you."

"I hoped you'd say that."

He smiled. "You knew I'd say that."

"I packed you a bag. We're leaving now."

"I hope your digs in New York are better than this."

"I think you'll like the penthouse."

"Ah, well, if that's the best you can do."

That earned him a dazzling smile. One that squeezed his heart and refused to let go. He took the papers and signed them, trusting in her completely that they said what she outlined and with no hidden tricks.

The lawyers had disappeared moments ago and returned with an officer. The minute the cell door opened, he reached for Ella and pulled her into a tight hug, lifting her off her feet.

"Are you okay?"

"Right now, I'm perfect."

He hugged her tighter. Yeah, right now, this second, when they were in each other's arms, everything was perfect. But would it last?

His doubts grew when they reached the Bozeman airport and they drove to the hangar and the private plane she'd chartered to take them to New York. Far beyond anything he could imagine or afford. They barely spoke during the flight. The stewardess served them the meal Ella ordered, including his favorite amber beer. She sat beside him, her head on his shoulder, hand in his, lost in her own thoughts of what was to come.

When the pilot announced they'd land in twenty minutes, she pointed out the window, and he stared at the New York City lights. He'd never seen anything like it.

"So many people."

"Welcome to New York."

CHAPTER 29

Touchdown made all of Gabe's protective instincts kick in. This was Phillip's home turf. He had people in his pocket, including the police, but Gabe swore he wouldn't let anything happen to Ella. He didn't make promises he didn't intend to keep.

The pilots opened the plane door. He helped Ella gather their stuff. They exited and Gabe gaped at the black SUV, complete with driver, waiting for them. The back door opened, and Sam got out.

"Is that him?" Ella asked.

"Sam," Gabe called, setting down his bag and Ella's to take Sam's outstretched hand. They'd met only a few months ago at Caleb and Summer's wedding, but he liked Sam and accepted the hug and slap on the back like he greeted one of his brothers. "This is Ella Wolf."

"Nice to meet you in person, Ms. Wolf."

"I told you on the phone, it's just Ella. Nice to see you too. How are we on time?"

"If you'd been any later, we'd have had to do this without you."

"Sorry. I had to bail Gabe out of jail."

Sam eyed Gabe with a cocky grin. "Really? What happened?"

"I clocked the asshole who nearly killed Ella."

"Travis," Sam guessed. "Ella told me all about him. We're up to speed on this end. I've got agents on all the key players. We'll start rounding them up about the same time we get your uncle."

"Great. Let's do that now and get this over with."

Ella walked to the SUV, and the driver held the door for her. Sam grabbed one of the bags at his feet. "She's even more gorgeous in person," Sam commented. "The pictures don't do her justice."

"Hands off. She's mine."

"I got that loud and clear by the way she looks at you. Is she moving to Montana?"

"No. Yes. I don't know. We haven't gotten that far yet." Frustrated, Gabe changed the subject back to the matter at hand. "How long is this going to take?"

"If she's got the evidence she says she does, not long at all. We'll wrap this up tomorrow, once everyone is in custody. Charges will be filed, and depending on how many cut deals and plead guilty, it's only a matter of letting the system work over the next couple of months. Her part will be done once we arrest everyone, and she turns over the evidence."

"Will she have to testify?"

"Depends on the evidence and if he pleads guilty or innocent. Her testimony will sway any jury to convict."

"She told you what happened."

"The whole gruesome tale. I talked to her for about an hour this morning. I'll go with you to her place and look over all the evidence. We'll all go to the police station in the morning and question her uncle."

"Is this a problem for you, working this case with the NYPD?"

"They'll get the credit for the bust. They're happy I'm handing this to them, especially since it involves several corrupt cops."

"Is she in danger?"

"Not with you by her side, knocking out bad guys. Plus I've brought some other agents as added security."

Gabe stared at the big man, putting the boxes of evidence into the back of the SUV. "Good. I don't want anything else to happen to her."

"Come on, let's get this show on the road. I've got a bad guy to take down."

"I kind of hoped to do that myself," Gabe admitted.

"We need to do this by the book. We've got a long list of charges against him. I want to nail his ass for every single one of them."

"Gabe," Ella called from the car. "Are you guys coming, or what? Let's go."

"Bossy," Sam teased, smiling at him.

"A woman on a mission."

"Let's see if we can get this done."

"I'm pretty sure she can do anything she sets her mind to."

"When you've got her kind of money, I don't doubt it."

Gabe never really thought about her money in terms of anything bigger than the massive ranch she owned. He thought of her working for the business, but not in terms of the wealth she held.

"It's not a competition. You two live very different lives," Sam said, reading his expression.

"Get out of my head."

"Screw it on straight. She is who she is. You are who

you are. If you two really have something together, all
the rest doesn't matter, unless you make it matter."

"I live in Montana. She lives here."

"Why can't you live in both places?"

"The ranch, for one."

"Seems to me your brothers are taking care of that
while you're away. It's not like that has to be a onetime
deal."

"They have their own lives."

"Yeah, but you've got men who work for you to oversee things when you're gone."

"Seriously, you two, time is ticking by while you two
have a tea party and play catch-up on the tarmac," Ella
called out to them again; this time she stood next to the
SUV, hip cocked, hands on her hips.

"God, she's something." Gabe stared, a slight smile
on his face. Why couldn't they live in both places?
Maybe it wasn't the way he pictured his life, but she
wasn't exactly the kind of woman he pictured living
that life with him. Maybe neither of them had to give
up everything to be with the other? Maybe all they had
to do was find a middle ground they could both live
with?

Ella picked up Gabe's hand again and checked the time
on his watch. The press set up twenty minutes ago. The
podium and microphones were in place on the steps
of the courthouse. Reporters eyed the SUV with the
black-tinted windows, wondering who might be inside.
Well, they'd come for a show and she planned to give
it to them. She'd revel in seeing her uncle's face when
Sam arrested him.

"I cannot believe your uncle is holding a press conference, naming you the suspect," Gabe said for the third time.

She smiled and shook her head. "I can. This press conference is as much to name me the suspect in my sister's death as it is to draw suspicions away from him even more. Too many people are asking questions. Reporters are wondering why none of my friends believe I killed my sister, or can come up with a single occasion that we fought, let alone argued about something."

Gabe held up several recent local papers. "Your friends defend you vehemently and are asking for further investigation."

"My friends and the people they know have a lot of influence. If they make enough noise, someone in the police department is going to question Detective Robbins's investigation. My uncle can't let that happen."

Gabe nodded toward the window. "The bastard is ready to start the party."

"Good thing I brought the fireworks." She put her hand on the door to exit, but Gabe reached across and stopped her before she got out.

"Are you sure about this? How do you know he's not armed?"

"I don't." Ella opened the door and stepped out.

She smiled at Gabe's descriptive string of swear-words, but didn't wait to find out if he'd really, *"Stuff her pretty ass back into the SUV,"* as he'd threatened.

"You can play with my ass later," she teased.

Gabe growled under his breath, but shot back, "Damn right I will as soon as I get you alone."

"Looking forward to it. Oh, and honey, if it comes to it, I'll bail you out again."

Gabe laughed. "Damn right you will."

Several reporters spotted her coming. They swatted at their camera crews to turn in her direction. Photographers snapped pictures of her and Gabe.

Her uncle stood at the podium, looking over the eager crowd, though he hadn't spotted her yet. The family lawyers, Detective Robbins, several other high-ranking officers, and the medical examiner stood around him, looking important, waiting to take their turn to prove she'd done the unthinkable.

"Ella Wolf has been missing since Lela's death—" Her uncle began his string of lies, but she cut him off.

"I'm not missing, Uncle," she called out across the lines of reporters with their recorders in hand.

She took Gabe's hand and led him straight through the throng to her target. With six-foot-two of solid muscle beside her, she stopped next to her uncle.

The shocked look on his face disappeared so quickly she wished she'd snapped a picture to replay it later and gloat. That was probably the first time his face contorted into any kind of honest expression in years. He'd miss his dermatologist in prison. She wondered what he'd really look like in another year when his face unfroze. Maybe she'd send him a gift basket of wrinkle cream from her new cosmetics line just to piss him off.

She had to give him credit, he recovered from the shock quickly. "Ella." Her uncle's eyes darted to the reporters hanging on every word. "The police want to talk to you. They know you killed your sister."

"You paid them to falsify evidence and point the finger at me. You killed her."

"You don't know what you're talking about, my dear. You're confused."

"I stood outside the library door, and I saw you murder my sister."

"Ella, why would I do that? I loved her like my own child."

"You wanted what will never be yours. You tried to take it once before, but just like this time, you failed. You killed my father, you greedy son of a bitch, and Lela found the evidence to take you down." She took the recorder from her pocket, pushed play, and set it on the podium in front of the microphones.

"What happened to your wife?"

"Phillip Wolf killed her . . ."

She let the recording play to the now hushed crowd of reporters standing stunned with their recorders in hand raised to capture every damning word.

"Those are lies. You fabricated the tape. You killed Lela." Sweat poured down the side of his face. His mouth drew back in a tight line. He grabbed her by the front of her coat and hauled her up against his chest and got right in her face. His eyes were filled with fear and fury. "You're sick. You need help."

"This isn't the first mistake you've made."

Gabe swung his arm down onto Uncle Phillip's hands and broke the hold he had on Ella's coat. Sam pulled her back a few steps for safety, and Gabe grabbed her uncle with one hand and punched him in the face with the other, sending him to his ass on the ground in front of everyone. "Keep your fucking hands off her."

Photographers and reporters crushed in, snapping photos of her uncle on the ground holding his bleeding nose and asking questions over one another.

"I'll have you arrested for assault," her uncle bellowed through his cupped hands.

"Won't be the first time today," Gabe shot back, making Ella laugh.

Agents rushed forward and took her uncle into custody, bringing his arms behind his back and arresting him.

"Read him his rights." When the agent finished, Sam said, "You're under arrest for the murder of Lela and Stuart Wolf, a string of other murders, fraud, embezzlement, art theft, and any number of other things I have yet to unravel."

"Detective Robbins will tell you she killed her sister. The rest is her drug-induced imagination."

"Look around you, Uncle, Detective Robbins and some of his cohorts are also under arrest. Wait until they get him in an interrogation room. He'll probably sing like a bird about what you did, how much you paid him to do your bidding, and name names of all the other people you've got on your payroll using my money."

"You have no proof."

"Lela discovered you killed the airplane mechanic's wife and set up our father's plane crash. I bet it pissed you off that we weren't on that plane too. I found the so-called accidental deaths of Wolf employees." His eyes went wide with undiluted fear. "Bribes. Embezzlement. Falsified records." She made a tsk, tsk sound and shook her head. "You've been busy. I wonder what I'll find in the penthouse vault."

Uncle Phillip ducked his head like a mad bull and tried to come after her again, but the FBI agents restrained him. Camera flashes went off like a strobe light, blinding him and everyone around them.

Ella grabbed the recorder off the podium, handed it to Sam, and turned her back on her uncle. She walked toward the car with a throng of reporters crushing in on her, yelling questions, Gabe by her side, an FBI agent covering her back, and her uncle yelling obscenities.

A woman fought her way through the crush of people and blocked her path. Ella stopped. Gabe stepped in front of Ella to protect her.

"Wait. Please. You can't do this."

"Who are you?" Gabe asked.

"I am Rose. Phillip's girlfriend."

"Rose, leave now," her uncle barked.

Rose, short for Rosalind. Her mother's name. Her father had called her Rose affectionately, but she never permitted others the privilege reserved only for her beloved husband.

Something about the woman bothered her. Ella stared, not caring that it made the other woman uncomfortable. She resembled her mother, with her dark hair hanging in waves past her shoulders to the middle of her back. The wind whipped and made her coat flap open, revealing a gorgeous green beaded dress Ella remembered her mother wearing long ago. Eyes narrowed, she scowled at her uncle, then looked back at the brunette, studying her closer. Yes, the resemblance was there, but it was more the clothes, the jewelry. All her mother's. He'd found a way to re-create what he'd lost.

Could his jealousy toward her father have run deeper than his success? Maybe he'd killed her father over a lot more than money. The thought turned her stomach. Another item to add to her uncle's list of sins. You shall not covet your *brother's* wife.

"You're sick, you know that. You'll get what's coming to you. I'll make sure of it," Ella vowed.

Her uncle's eyes blazed with rage that she'd discovered yet another of his secrets. Again, she ignored his obscenities.

"Wait. You can't do this. What will I do now?" Rose asked. "Phillip, you swore you'd take care of me."

Ella turned to Sam. "Arrest her. She's wearing my mother's clothes and jewelry. Get a search warrant for her place. I bet you'll find more of my mother's things there."

"I haven't done anything," Rose pleaded.

"We'll see about that," Ella shot back. If Rose was associated with her uncle, no doubt she was guilty of something.

Agents moved the press back nearly fifteen feet to give them space.

Gabe wrapped her in his arm and close to his side and walked her to the car. He slid in beside her. The agent closed the door and stood guard, though that didn't deter the reporters and photographers from yelling out more questions and taking photos of them through the dark glass, since they were now well away from the FBI agents completing their arrests.

"He's really pissed."

"How's your hand?" she asked concerned about his bruised and swollen knuckles. She pulled the makeup wipes out of her sister's purse and wiped away the smeared blood.

"Not so bad. I'll live. Unfortunately, so will your uncle." Gabe flexed his hand, stretching and clenching his fingers before he settled it on her thigh. She covered it with hers.

"You have a real gift for breaking noses."

"I got into a fight when I was about seventeen with this really big dude at school."

"Let me guess, over a girl."

"Can I help it if she preferred me to the dickhead? Anyway, no matter how many times I hit the guy, he kept coming at me. I punched him hard in the face, broke his nose, and it stopped him cold. Lesson learned. Someone comes at you, pop them in the nose. Hurts like hell and bleeds like a son of a bitch. Makes it hard to breathe with all that blood pouring out your nose and dripping down your throat."

"Okay, yuck. Stop talking."

"Good idea." He turned into her, cupped her face, and leaned down, kissing her with such tenderness and love that tears stung the backs of her eyes. "I am so proud of you."

"I'm not done yet. There's still so much to do."

"It's getting late. Aren't you tired?"

"We're heading over to the penthouse once Sam gets here. He'll execute a search warrant and try to find the evidence from Lela's murder."

"Your uncle is one twisted sick bastard."

"Tell me about it. Want to see my house?"

"Is it anything like your ranch?"

"Our ranch. You own part of that now, you know?"

"I'm still getting used to it."

"You belong there."

Gabe went quiet on her. He always did when even the hint of their future came up, as if he didn't want to say anything to upset the balance between them.

The look on his face when he saw the jet, the lights when they flew over New York City, the SUV and the man she'd hired to drive her. Just a small glimpse of her life and already he felt uncomfortable and out of place.

"The penthouse is nothing like the ranch. It's extravagant, which is why Uncle Phillip loved it. My father used it to impress business associates. My mother liked to dabble in decorating. Lela and I grew up there and to some extent simply didn't notice that we lived differently than others." Gabe didn't say anything. "You'll like the staff—Mary, Lee, and Felicity."

"You mentioned Mary."

"She's been with us for years. Amazing cook. Great listener. Doles out advice with dessert."

That made Gabe smile. "Did you pour your heart out to her about boys who did you wrong?"

"Always."

"Let me guess, she told you they were all wrong for you and if they didn't like you it was their problem."

"No. She told me to stop being so picky and orchestrating everything to my liking. Boys like to be in charge. I'm not very good at that."

"I got that when you made me sign a contract for part of your ranch and told me to take care of the thousand head of cattle that started arriving this morning, along with my brother and the cattle I already bought."

"Are you complaining?"

"Not at all. I got what I wanted, right?"

She nodded, but wondered why it didn't sound like he was very happy about getting what he wanted. She wanted to ask him, but Sam opened the car door and got in.

"The detective is in custody and trying to make a deal before your uncle sells him out. We've got the lawyers who executed the update to the will in custody. They will make a deal and probably pay you a huge settlement for withholding information. We'll have to wait and see if they get disbarred. Thanks to your evidence and IT guy, we've got several of your executive staff and a couple managers in custody." The car pulled into traffic and headed toward Central Park. "Once we cleaned house, you've got fourteen employees we've linked to illegal activity connected to the embezzlement and another nine we found to be loosely connected, but they didn't necessarily do anything illegal."

"In other words, they followed directions from the fourteen when they should have questioned what they were asked to do."

"In most cases, they went along in order to keep their jobs. They felt coerced to help."

"Either way, they're all fired."

"That's up to you," Sam said.

"Great. I'll take care of it. Probably need to bring extra security to the office and make some kind of announcement to the staff."

"No doubt the press and paparazzi will be at your building before we get there," Sam pointed out.

"Great," Gabe said, not looking happy at all.

"I'm sorry. I should have thought about that." Ella touched his arm and stared up at him. "Hey, you've punched out two guys today, why not a few more paparazzi to add to the mix."

"You just love bailing me out of jail," he teased back, making her feel a bit better that he was taking some of this in stride.

"I paid those lawyers a fortune. They should at least earn it."

Gabe leaned down and kissed her. "How about we just ignore whoever shows up at your place and finish what we came here to do."

"I don't really want to go home," she admitted.

Gabe hugged her to his side.

"Sam, I want to know everything that you find at Rose's place."

"Agents are on their way over with a warrant now. We'll know soon."

Gabe touched her cheek. "Do you think that's why he didn't get rid of your mother's things when he moved in?"

"He's one sick son of a bitch," she confirmed. "Lela and I stayed clear of his room, so I assumed the stuff was still in there. I never guessed he had a real-life Barbie to play my mother."

After that bombshell, everyone in the car remained silent for the rest of the ride.

Sam scanned the crowd in front of her building and swore. "Gabe, you ready for this?"

"Do I have a choice?"

"You get out first, followed by Ella. I'll come out behind her and follow you into the building. The other agent will make sure no one follows us in. Keep moving through the crowd to the door. Don't stop."

"Got it," Gabe confirmed.

"Okay, here we go," Sam said.

Ella was used to photogs taking pictures of her out with friends, but this was altogether different. They shouted questions and crushed in on them the moment they got out of the car. Gabe kept a firm grip on her hand and led her through the throng of people.

She stopped on the steps and tugged Gabe's hand to make him stop with her. Sam slammed into her back. "Wait."

"Ella, this is not a good idea. This is an ongoing investigation. You don't want to say anything that might compromise the case," Sam said.

"I won't, but they need to get one thing straight." She turned and faced the crowd. Gabe stood at her back, giving her all the support she needed to do this one small thing for her sister.

The shouting continued. One question after another, no one really understanding what was going on, but speculating about the stunning scene she'd made at the press conference. Gabe let out a screaming whistle behind her and everyone shut up, stunned to silence.

One reporter she recognized from a local TV station, who hadn't quite made her mark and reported on some rather mundane fluff pieces. Ella focused on her.

"Is it true your uncle orchestrated your father's plane crash and killed your sister?" the reporter boldly asked. At least she was up to speed on what happened at the press conference.

"Yes. My uncle murdered my sister, Lela. He, law enforcement, and other key people covered it up and tried to frame me for her murder."

"Where have you been? Why are you just coming forward now?"

Ella ignored the question of where she'd been, well aware of the interest everyone showed in Gabe. Several people shouted questions, asking about him over the reporter she spoke directly to.

"I returned home today with the evidence I uncovered over the last weeks. More facts will come out tomorrow, but I want people to know my sister was a beautiful, kind, gentle woman who didn't deserve what happened to her, or the brutal way my uncle killed her."

Choked up, she turned into Gabe's chest. He immediately wrapped her in his arms.

"Sir, what is your relationship with Ms. Wolf?"

Gabe stiffened. She leaned back and looked over her shoulder at the reporter who'd been interested in the facts of her sister's murder, but knew viewers would want the dirt on the gorgeous man with her. "He's my . . ." "Boyfriend" didn't encompass what Gabe meant to her. He was so much more than someone she dated. Which they hadn't really done. He wasn't just a lover either. "He's mine," she said, looking up at him. His dark eyes narrowed with an intensity that made her breath catch. His arms pulled her tight to his big body and she melted against him.

The throng of paparazzi exploded with another round of questions, but Gabe pulled her through the front door of her building and into the lobby. The doorman, Sam, and the other agent stood in front of the doors, blocking everyone else from following her inside. Gabe hit the button for the elevator and held her close. She wiped the tears from her eyes. Ever the gentleman, Gabe let her enter the elevator first. She hit the button for the top floor.

The second the doors closed, he pulled her into his arms. This wasn't a kiss. It was a devouring. By the time the elevator doors opened they were completely lost in each other.

Gabe wrenched away and allowed her to pass him and step out of the elevator. Her breath came as short as his. She led the way to her door. He stopped her with his hand over hers on the knob.

"Did you mean what you said downstairs?"

She smiled and looked up at him, placing her hands on his chest. "With my whole heart."

He opened his mouth to say something, but stopped himself.

"Don't worry, Gabe. It's going to work out. I just need you to hold on longer."

"Always," he said, taking her hand.

Ella stepped into her home for the first time since she'd left. She stood in the marble entry with the bright crystal chandelier overhead and stared past the men sitting on the living room sofa drinking coffee, and Mary and Felicity, sitting in the two chairs adjacent to the closed library doors. She froze, the memories flooding her mind. She took a step back and slammed into Gabe's chest. His strong hands clamped onto her shoulders and squeezed. His warm breath fluttered across her cheek and he whispered, "Breathe."

She sucked in a ragged breath, and the overwhelming fear and anguish subsided.

"Your house is amazing, sweetheart. The view . . . there aren't words."

Ella stared across the room at the massive windows that overlooked Central Park. She stared at the stars and sucked in another breath, leaning back against Gabe, taking in the strength of him backing her up.

"Ella," Mary said. "You're home."

Yes, where Lela died in that room. Gone. Forever. The tears came again.

Mary came forward with Felicity on her heels. They hugged her, despite the fact Gabe still held her hand. She took in their comfort, but couldn't return it, completely lost in the misery of what happened.

Mary and Felicity stood back, staring at her. Gabe

turned and stood in front of her, blocking her view of the room. His warm hands came up and cupped her face, making her look at him.

"You're okay, sweetheart. Lela isn't here. Your uncle is in jail. Breathe."

She clamped her hands on his wrists and held tight. "I'm okay."

"You sure?"

She gave him a quick nod. "Don't let go."

"Never."

"Um, Ella, who's your friend?" Felicity asked. The young woman had been on the household staff for several years. She kept the house clean and ran errands for her and Lela.

Ella never took her gaze from Gabe. "This is Gabe Bowden. I brought him back with me from Montana."

Gabe smiled down at her. "Am I like a souvenir?"

"More like a dream come true." Her words came out soft, just for him.

His gaze blazed down at her, and she felt the heat.

"Ms. Wolf. We're with the FBI. Sam Turner asked us to meet him here with the warrant," one of the men from the sofa stepped forward to address her.

"Ready?" Gabe asked, kissing her on the forehead.

Yeah, she was ready to keep going and get this done. She gave Gabe's wrists another squeeze. He let her go, stepping back and allowing her to take the lead again.

"Felicity, our bags are down in the car. Please bring them up and put them in my room. Mary, Gabe and I haven't eaten in some time. Please make him a snack and get him a beer." She turned to the men waiting. "May I please see the warrant."

Felicity went out the door. Mary rushed back to the kitchen.

She read the warrant. Sam came in behind her with several other people with forensics patches on the back of their jackets.

"Ella, can you get us into the safe?"

She turned for the stairs. "You bet your ass I can." She marched up the stairs and down the corridor, only hesitating a moment outside Lela's open bedroom door.

"Your room?" Sam asked.

"No. Lela's," Gabe said, taking her hand and leading her on. "Which one, honey?"

"Past my room at the end."

With everyone focused on her, she stood before the massive ornate wood doors and closed her eyes, thinking of her parents' room, the way it looked before her uncle came here, and remembered how she and Lela would run down the hall, throw the doors open wide, and run in and jump on their parents' bed to wake them up. Each of them would be pulled down between their parents, hugged, and tickled. They'd giggle and laugh. She'd felt so loved and safe.

"Ella?"

"I haven't been in this room since my parents died."

"You can wait out here if you'd like," Sam suggested.

"You can do this, Ella," Gabe encouraged.

She put her hands on the knobs, turned, and pushed the doors wide. "Oh. My. God."

"What?" Gabe asked.

"Nothing has changed. This is exactly what the room looked like when my parents lived here. Well, almost."

Ella stared at the lavender walls, deep purple cover on the four-poster bed, the antique dressers, and her mother's collection of antique mirrors. Several ornate silver hand mirrors lay on the dresser along with her mother's crystal perfume bottles. No fewer than ten pictures of her mother were scattered about the walls and tabletops.

"Honey, I know you said your dad adored your mother, but seriously, this is a bit much," Gabe said, staring around the room.

"Uncle Phillip's obsessed with her." She could not believe her eyes. "Jeez. This is just bizarre." She turned her focus back to the daunting task ahead. "Sam, there are several missing watercolors worth a fortune."

"I'll need the paperwork."

"It's with the insurance stuff. Let's check the safe." She walked to the closet door and hesitated, turning to glance at Gabe. "I'm afraid what I'll find in here."

"More creepy," he suggested. "It can't get worse than him killing your sister, dating a woman who he dressed up as your mother, and sleeping in a room where no matter where you look your mother is staring back at you. Didn't Felicity or Mary say anything to you about this?"

"No. They weren't allowed in here. Lee worked exclusively for my uncle. He preferred it that way."

"To keep his secretes. Where is Lee?"

She turned to Sam. "You might want to find him."

"On it," one of the other agents said, leaving the room.

Ella sucked in a deep breath and opened the double doors to the walk-in closet. The air whooshed out of her with relief. Nothing strange awaited her. Her mother's cheval mirror stood in the corner. An ornate decorative wood carving stood atop a chest of drawers. Her uncle's suits and clothes hung around the room, his shoes lined up on the shelves. Her mother's things were in fact missing.

"Where's the safe?" Sam asked.

She walked to the six-foot-tall painting on the wall.

"At least your uncle kept one of the paintings," Gabe commented.

"He couldn't get rid of this one. It's bolted to the wall." She opened the drawer next to the painting and rubbed her finger along the upper edge of the frame, feeling for the button. She pressed it and the lever behind the painting clicked and the painting popped from the wall on the left side. She swung the frame wide, revealing the huge safe behind it.

Sam opened a folder behind her and stepped forward, pointing to the combination noted in the papers from her lawyer about her parents' original will. He spun the dial and stopped at each of the three numbers, turned the handle, and opened the heavy door, revealing the contents inside. Stacks of cash, files, her father's watches, cuff links, and tie tacks and clips. Sam pulled out the trays to reveal her mother's jewelry, but most of it was missing. She remembered the trays full of sparkling gems in a rainbow of colors.

"Lela and I used to love to play dress-up in our mother's clothes and jewels. Now, some bitch is doing it and acting a part for that bastard." She turned to Sam. "I want it all back."

"You'll get it," he assured her.

"I don't see the locket he took from my sister's body. It's got to be here." She left the small room to the FBI agents and stood in the middle of her parents' old bedroom.

She stared around the room at all the photos of her mother, which led her to the ornate carved box on the table by the window. She opened the lid and discovered her mother's collection of drawings and paintings she and Lela had done as children. Tears spilled down her cheeks as she sorted through the pages. "She kept them. It makes me sad and happy at the same time to know she kept these."

"She loved you and Lela. I'm pretty sure my mom has a bunch of my school stuff too." Gabe hugged her from behind and glanced at the pictures with her. "I don't think any of mine are of flowers."

"No, cowboy, they're probably all of horses."

"Like yours," he pointed to the picture she'd drawn in probably second grade, of her atop a brown horse. She'd drawn a tiara on her head.

"Most girls dream of a knight in shining armor atop a horse come to save them. Not you, honey, you're already a princess, ready to ride off all by yourself. You don't need no stinkin' knight."

Unable to help herself, she laughed. "Doesn't mean I don't want a cowboy all my own." She turned and kissed his cheek, but caught the worry in his eyes that despite all they shared, they still wouldn't be together.

She put the pictures back in the box and closed the lid. She turned and stared at the room again and tried to think like her uncle. By all outward appearances, everything looked in its place. Like him. Perfectly crisp suit and shirt with ties that gave him just enough flair. Cuff links and tie tacks to showcase his wealth, but not too much to put people off. The outside hid what was within.

Drawn to the French wardrobe, she pulled the double

doors open. Here was the man within. Several candle holders surrounded a picture of her naked mother, standing by a bank of windows, the light highlighting her body. She had her arms raised to her hair, a clip in her fingers.

"Wow! How do you think he got that shot?" Gabe asked.

Ella pushed the framed photo over, hiding the picture. "I don't want to know. If memory serves, that is the master bedroom in the Paris apartment. It looks like she was putting her hair up to take a bath."

"Peeping through the door and taking pictures of her."

Outraged, she clenched her fingers into tight fists at her sides. "There's got to be a special place in hell for someone like him. Jail is too good for that asshole. How dare he do that."

The photo might have caught her attention, but the wood box with the solid gold wolf on the lid held it. "Sam, check this out."

Sam stepped around her and pulled the box out with his gloved hands. He set it on the table next to the bed and a vase of her mother's favorite white lilies. He tried to open the lid, but it wouldn't budge.

"Puzzle box?" Gabe asked.

"I think so," she said. "It probably belonged to my father, though I don't remember it."

"You guys have a screwdriver or something we can use to pry this box open, Sam?"

"No! I'm not ruining this box. Give me a second to figure it out."

"Ella, it's just a box."

"It was my dad's."

Sam handed her a pair of latex gloves. "Put these on.

Anything you find in there is evidence. I don't want you to compromise it."

Ella put on the gloves and studied the box. In the end, she found the box gave up its contents easily by pushing the wolf's tail down. A latch clicked open and the top popped. "No wonder Uncle Phillip used this one. It's probably the simplest puzzle box my father owned."

Ella lifted the lid, knowing what she'd find, but feeling the punch to the gut all the same. She pulled out her sister's bloodstained locket.

Gabe wrapped his arm around her shoulders and pulled her close.

Ella placed the locket in the evidence bag Sam held out to her. She reached in and pulled out the silver and black Beretta twenty-two pistol, removed the magazine, pulled the slide, and checked the chamber. She counted three bullets in the magazine.

"Sam, how many times was Mr. Reiser shot in the mugging?" she asked.

"Four, why?"

"Plus one used to shoot the airplane mechanic's wife in the head. Three bullets left in the magazine that holds seven." Ella sighed.

"Plus one in the chamber," Gabe added. "There's your five shots. That's the murder weapon."

"I'll have the team run ballistics to verify the bullets from those two murders match the gun," Sam said.

Ella put it in the evidence box Sam handed her from one of the evidence techs.

The purple leather-bound book drew her attention. She pulled it out and opened the cover, her mother's pretty script scrawled across the pages.

"Your mother's diary?" Gabe asked.

"Yes." Ella flipped through the pages to the end. She turned the book toward Gabe.

"What's with all the gibberish?"

"Code."

"Another puzzle?"

"My parents had a secret code to write love letters, so no one but the two of them knew what they said."

"Can you decipher it?" Gabe asked.

Sam handed her his small notebook and a pen. It took her several tries to remember the key to the code, but once she got it started, the rest came easily.

"Phillip wants to own me as he wants to own all Stuart built. He killed my husband. He'll kill me, too, to get what he really wants. But it will never be his. I will lure him to the estate, and I will finish him to save my girls. I love you Ella and Lela with my whole heart."

"That's it? That's all she wrote?" Sam asked.

Hard to read through her tears, but she skimmed the last several journal entries. "She writes about his growing interest in her and how uncomfortable it makes her. She says he talks about running the Wolf empire with her by his side as it should have been all along."

"His obsession for her drove him over the edge," Gabe said, taking her hand and bringing it to his lips, kissing her palm.

"It's insane that he thought he even had a chance with her. Anyone who saw my parents together knew she loved my father. He adored her. If she discovered Uncle Phillip killed my father, she'd have wanted revenge."

"From the note she wrote, it sounds like she meant to kill him," Gabe said.

"If he was obsessed with her, she'd have been able to get close to him. So, she lured him to the estate, knowing he'd come like an eager dog ready for a pet. Whatever she tried to do—poison him, shoot him, whack him in the head with a shovel—he turned the tables." She pressed a hand to her sour stomach. "He hung her. I can't imagine all her fury unleashed to kill that bastard turned to agonizing fear when Uncle Phillip's so-called love turned to murderous rage. To do that to the woman he supposedly loved . . ." Reality hit her like an elbow to the gut, it stunned and hurt her. "I wish she'd killed him." She slammed the diary down on the table, letting her rage reign. "All these years, I thought love killed her. I thought she loved Daddy more than she loved us."

"No, Ella. Never. Even if she'd killed herself, that was her grief, not her love for him that drove her to it."

The guilt ate a hole in her gut. "He made me hate her for leaving me." She'd never allowed herself to grieve her loss and miss her. Those feelings swamped her now, threatening to drag her down into a pit of despair. The tears rolled down her face, but she held back the screams of agony.

Gabe cupped her face and swept his thumbs over her wet cheeks. His gaze held hers. "She didn't abandon you, sweetheart. She tried to protect you."

"He took them all away. My father, mother, sister. All of them gone, and for what? Money," she spat out, like it meant nothing, because it didn't compare to the people he took from her.

"He'll pay, sweetheart."

"The book doesn't prove he killed your mother," Sam said. "Unless he confesses, I can't charge him. We could exhume her body and do another autopsy."

"No. Leave her to rest in peace with my father. Soon I'll bury Lela beside them. They'll know I finished it, the way my mother and Lela both tried to do for me."

Sam took the wood box from her lap. Gabe pulled her close and walked her out of the room and down the hall and back to the stairs. They walked through the living room to the dining area. Mary came out a door, carrying a tray.

"Mr. Bowden, I have a beer and a sandwich for you. Ella, dear, I've made you a vanilla latte, some fruit, and a chicken salad."

Tears and her emotions back under control, she said, "Thank you, Mary. We'll sit here at the table while the FBI finishes their work. Please make sure there is coffee and a snack for them if they'd like it."

"Of course. I'll take care of it right away."

Gabe waited for Mary to go back into the kitchen to make more coffee for the ten cops upstairs. He reached over, plucked Ella from her chair, and set her on his lap. She immediately settled into him and reached for her coffee. She drank it absently, resting her head against him.

He picked up his snack and stared at it. "Did she seriously make me a filet mignon sandwich?"

Ella glanced at it, stole it from him, and took a bite. "Yep. With cheddar, Dijon mustard, and red lettuce with red onion. It's very good." She held the sandwich up to him, and he took a big bite.

"Damn, that's good."

Gabe set the bowl of fruit on her belly. He snagged a strawberry and popped it into his mouth. The blueberries were fat and huge. He pressed one to Ella's lips, and she grabbed it with her teeth.

Sam came up behind them. "Ella, we're ready to do the library."

"She's not going in there, Sam. Do your thing, but leave her be."

"Gabe, man, it would be easier if she set up the scene for us and . . ."

"She's not going in there. She needs to eat and take a minute for herself."

Ella didn't contradict him. Sam sighed and headed for the library without her.

"I can't."

"I know," he said, hugging her close. "Eat." She'd already eaten most of the sandwich and half the bowl of fruit. He didn't mind sharing. Once he finished his half, he started on her salad. He loved the strange green dressing and pumpkin seeds with the shredded chicken and greens. "I need to hire a cook. This is really good."

Ella laughed and shook her head. "Either that or you'll have to cook, because you already know I don't."

Such a telling statement that she meant to live with him, but he didn't dare take it as her intent.

"So, it's left to me to take care of you."

She leaned up and gave him a quick kiss. "You do it so well."

CHAPTER 30

Gabe walked out of the bathroom dressed for the day and still feeling exhausted. He'd barely gotten three hours' sleep. He stared at the rumpled bed and figured Ella probably got one. He wanted to pack her bag, put her on a plane, and take her back to Montana and away from this mess. Not going to happen, but that was exactly what she needed. He hated finding her crying in Lela's room in the middle of the night. He'd done everything he could to show her how much he loved her and that she'd never be alone again, but it hadn't been enough to make her smile and ease her grief. Part of him knew she needed to work her way through it in her own time and in her own way, but it still left him feeling inadequate. He needed to do something, because seeing her like that ate away at him and broke his heart.

She was a good, kind, loving, decent person who didn't deserve any of this. He hated Phillip for what he'd done to her, to her family.

Gabe made his way down the stairs, amazed at the extravagance of her home. He'd seen pictures of places like this in magazines, but never up close. He glanced out the windows at the park and knew this neighborhood was probably the most expensive real estate in the country. Ella was used to this lifestyle. He was still trying to get used to it and felt like he should put his hands behind his back and not touch anything.

He walked through the living room and found Ella at the dining room table with Mary and Felicity, bent over notepads. Ella looked up and smiled when she saw him. The doorbell rang and Felicity rose to answer it. Ella stood and came to him, wrapping her arms around his neck and giving him a sweet kiss. She tasted of coffee and a bit of desperation the way she held her lips pressed to his. He hugged her close, but didn't let go when she ended the kiss.

"I don't like waking up without you," he grumbled.

"I couldn't sleep. Too much to do."

"You need your rest."

"I just need you." She laid her head on his shoulder and sighed.

He kissed her on the head and glanced over her at Sam, who walked in the door, talking on his phone.

"Yeah, he's right here," Sam said, handing the phone to him.

Ella let him go. "Hi, Sam."

"You need to sleep," he said, seeing the same dark circles and bloodshot eyes Gabe saw this morning.

"Hello," Gabe said into the phone, not knowing why Sam handed it to him.

"Hey, man, it's Caleb."

"Oh, hey. What's up? Why are you calling Sam and me?"

"Good news. Summer and I are pregnant."

Gabe's heart soared. "Congratulations. To both of you. When?"

"Late September."

"That's great, Caleb. Really fantastic. I'm so happy for you."

"Thanks. We're really happy, too. Listen, I won't keep you, I know you're in the thick of it with your girl this morning, but I wanted to say I'm happy for you too. Blake and Dane rave about Ella. I can't wait to meet her."

"You will soon."

"Call me when things settle down. We need to catch up."

"Will do. And give Summer a big kiss for me."

"Definitely. Bye."

Gabe handed the phone back to Sam, unable to hide the huge smile.

"What is it?" Ella asked, looking from him to Sam, easily reading how happy they both were.

"My brother knocked up Sam's sister. We're going to be uncles." Gabe high-fived Sam and they both smiled like crazy.

Ella laughed at the two of them. "Congratulations. When's the baby due?"

"End of September."

"This is going to be one lucky baby. They already have an uncle to play cops and robbers and another to play cowboy."

He and Sam both laughed, but Gabe caught the sad look in her eyes that she'd never hear her sister say she was pregnant. She'd never get to tell her sister the same. They'd never share the experience of being pregnant and delivering their babies. So many things they'd never share, and all of them reflected in Ella's sad eyes.

"Maybe if this one wises up, the baby will have a rich aunt who takes her shopping on Madison Avenue."

Ella's gaze locked with his. She didn't say anything about becoming the baby's aunt, but gave him hope when she laughed and said, "What if it's a boy?"

"Can you buy a dirt bike on Madison Avenue?" Sam asked.

"I guess I better find out. Just in case," she added.

Gabe wanted to know if that meant just in case it was a boy, or just in case she became his wife. He didn't even question that's what he wanted. He wished he knew how to make that happen. Asking her was easy, but the reality of it seemed a lot harder to figure out, especially when he was standing in her multimillion-dollar home on 5th Avenue in New York City when he belonged on his ranch in Montana. Correction, their ranch. The one she owned the lion's share of because no way could he afford that house and massive piece of land. Despite all that, he wanted her, everything else be damned.

Sam broke the tension. "Shall we go see how your uncle is doing this morning?"

"Let's," Ella said, turning to the table and jotting down several things on the notepad Mary left.

"Ella, what were you discussing with Mary and Felicity?" he asked, seeing the long list of items on the paper, even though it was too far away for him to read.

"Packing up Rose's place and this one so I can sell them."

"Ella, isn't it a bit premature to sell this place? This is your home."

Ella turned to him. "I can't live here, Gabe. Not anymore. No by myself."

"But . . ."

"I've got the estate outside the city, and I can buy another place in the city, but not here. I don't want to be here anymore."

"Okay. If that's what you want."

"It is. This is just a place, filled with things. You know what I learned last night when I saw Rose? As much as I hated seeing her in my mother's things, they aren't as important as my memories of my mother, father, and Lela. Keeping this place or letting it go won't change my memories of them. They are so much more to me than this place, or the things that belonged to them."

"It's just, you may feel differently once some time has passed."

"Not about this place. I'm not getting rid of everything, but I need to do this."

"I just want to be sure you don't regret it."

"You were right. I've outgrown the life I'd been leading here. I intended to change that when Lela and I turned twenty-five and took over the company. A good time to start fresh and go in a new direction. After what's happened, everything has changed. I've changed. I want more than just running the company. I can't live in the past with my family's ghosts. It's too hard and it's killing me. I want a life worth living, filled with love and happiness and friends and hopefully family. I'm trying to get that, Gabe, but first I need to close the chapter on this part of my life."

Gabe took her hand. "Then let's do that. Let's finish this."

CHAPTER 31

Ella stood, staring down into her uncle's bruised face. His broken nose had been set and taped at the hospital. He looked ridiculous breathing through his mouth, sitting in the chair across the metal table from her in the police interrogation room with an air of confidence and arrogance that defied the situation. She'd remedy that right now.

"Ella, dear, you look tired."

"I am. Tired of you. But this will be the last time we speak or see each other."

"You think so?"

"Yes. You'll be tucked away where the only people you can hurt are locked up behind bars with you."

"I've got the best lawyers in the city."

Ella shook her head. "No. I have the best lawyers in the city. The ones you hired with my money were arrested last night too.

"You underestimated me and Lela. You thought you could get away with everything, but in the end your web of lies unraveled because of a man's conscience and cattle."

"What?"

Now she had his attention. "The man you coerced into sabotaging my father's plane stole the broken fuel gauge and black box and hid them away from you all these years, grieving what he'd done and the loss of his wife." She grabbed the sealed plastic evidence bag and placed the photo of Marjorie Finney, tied and gagged in a chair, on the table. She pointed to his reflection in the glass of the framed picture on the wall. "The woman you murdered. He went to Lela and told her everything and gave her the evidence to take you down. She found the records my father gathered before his death. The ones he planned to use to fire you and have you arrested. The reason you had him killed. Since I didn't know what Lela discovered, I started digging into the company records. You've been stealing from the company for a long time."

"You can't prove that."

"That was the easiest thing to prove. Records, or lack thereof, don't lie. The deposits to your Cayman accounts don't lie. The payments to your girlfriend Rose's apartment and for her rehab don't lie. The payments to Detective Robbins and your other coconspirators don't lie. The FBI was quite thorough in their investigation.

"It would have been much harder to prove you killed that auditor for the company. Mr. Reiser, who died in a tragic mugging. Let's not forget Marjorie. A picture speaks a thousand words, but it's not conclusive you shot her. Except you kept the gun used to shoot both of them. By the way, that's another charge against you. Illegally possessing unregistered firearms.

"Proving Mr. Trahan's car accident was murder might have been impossible if you hadn't depended on

Detective Robbins to dispose of the vehicle you used to run that auditor off the road. You really don't like auditors. Unless they work for you, that is. He kept it, by the way. The car. In a cousin's garage in Jersey. Locked away all these years. Insurance that you never double-crossed him. I suppose he probably would have black-mailed you for money for years if your crime spree hadn't kept him busy all these years, and you didn't pay him monthly already.

"Lela's murder would have been harder to prove. Even though I saw you murder my sister, it was still my word against yours, and you had people in your pocket all over this city. Well, not anymore. You may have wiped down the gun, but you forgot to wipe down your prints on the bullets and clip. Plus Detective Robbins copped to falsifying the report that says my prints were on the gun. Oh, and he told them you killed Lela. His account backs up mine. You also gave him Lela's jewelry in the handkerchief you used to wipe your face. They haven't had time to test it yet, but DNA doesn't lie."

Uncle Phillip stood and rounded the table to come after her, despite the handcuffs keeping his hands behind his back. Ella raised her foot and slammed it into his balls, kicking him back into his seat.

"Sit down. I'm not done talking."

He leaned forward and gritted his teeth against the pain. His face and ears turned red with rage. "Fucking bitch."

"You have no idea," she yelled.

Gabe burst through the door behind her. "I'm okay, honey." She gave Gabe a reassuring smile.

"Ballbuster." He shook his head and laughed.

"Damn right."

Gabe backed out of the room again, glaring at her uncle. She loved him for letting her do this her way. The cops weren't happy about it either, but Sam fought for her to have this time alone. After all, she'd uncovered several corrupt cops in the department. They owed her.

"What the hell are you doing with that rancher?"

"He's a better man than you will ever hope to be."

"Whatever. It doesn't matter what you think you have on me. My lawyers will keep this tied up in court for years."

Arrogant, but the cracks in his confidence made his words hesitant.

"I've had a judge freeze all your bank accounts. Based on the evidence, and how much you've stolen from me, when I'm done with you, you won't have a penny to your name. In fact, you owe me quite a bit. Which I will collect with every day that you spend in a cell wasting away as your life passes you by."

"You can't do that."

"I already did. So this is how things will go."

"You can't tell me what to do," he spat out.

"You're right, I can't. So here are your options. You choose. Plead guilty to all charges, and I will pay for a top attorney to represent you and make a reasonable deal with the state and federal prosecutors filing charges against you. You've been a very bad man and you are facing some serious charges and the rest of your life in prison."

"Don't talk to me like a child."

"Why not? You've acted like a spoiled brat, taking things that don't belong to you and lashing out at those who don't give you what you want.

"If you don't plead guilty to all charges, you can take your chances with a public defender."

"That's not fair."

"Grow up and face the consequences of what you've done. What I'm offering you is fair and just, and a hell of a lot more than you deserve. You killed my family!

"You killed my mother. She confronted you at the estate and called you out about my father's plane crash and your obsession with her. You wanted her, but all she wanted was my father back."

He slammed his shackled fists on the table. "She refused me. She tried to kill me."

The anger didn't completely mask the anguish behind those words he'd torn from his heart. He as much admitted to killing her mother. She didn't commit suicide and leave Ella and Lela on their own.

Ella shook her head, her heart heavy in her chest. "She loved my father. Not you. You killed your own brother to get him out of the way, then you made her pay for refusing you. You hung her, and it made you just a little bit happy because how dare she want another man over you."

"You don't know what you're talking about."

"No? I think that's why you slept in her room, all those pictures of her staring at you. You loved her, but you felt guilty that it made you happy to kill her. Maybe that's why you found a woman desperate enough to play your games and turned her into Rose. You wanted to have the fantasy you created in your mind. You needed her. Without her, all you had was the guilt that you killed the only woman you ever loved, and killing her made you feel good."

Silence. He couldn't even look at her anymore.

Strange, she felt a weight lift from her and a soft touch, like her parents' and Lela's hands on her shoulders, letting her know she'd done all she could for them.

She turned for the door.

"Where are you going? We aren't done here."

She glanced over her shoulder. "I'm done."

CHAPTER 32

Gabe stood at the windows in Ella's penthouse, staring out at the park. He stuffed his cell phone back in his pocket, his mind on the call with Dane. After a week, things at the ranch were settling into a routine. The men Ella hired with Dr. Potts's help were doing a good job. Several of them had moved into the bunkhouse on the property.

Ella's hands ran up his back to his shoulders. She squeezed and kneaded, massaging his muscles. "Longing for the great outdoors?"

She read him so well. The city and massive amounts of people were closing in on him. Claustrophobic, he longed to be out in the wide open spaces of Montana again, atop his horse, breathing the fresh air.

He pulled her around him to lean against his side. "I just got off the phone with Dane."

"How's the ranch?"

"Well, Miss Wolf, your cattle are getting fat and happy. The friend you sent to move me and unpack the contents of the storage lockers back into the house is all finished. Blake delivered Angel and Belle two days ago. They are settled in their stalls and under his spell. I think he means to horse-nap them."

"You'll break his nose if he tries, right?"

"Anything for you, darlin'." They'd come to a silent understanding these last days, keeping things light, neither of them discussing or even hinting that their time together was drawing to an end neither of them really wanted, but was inevitable all the same.

"How about something you want?"

Interested, he leaned down, nuzzled her neck, and whispered in her ear, "I always want you, honey."

She giggled, a genuine show of happiness. Closure with her uncle allowed her to find her comfort zone, running the company her way. She smiled more often, and it did his heart good to see the joy come back into her eyes.

"I'm taking you out tonight."

"You are?" he asked, surprised.

"To meet my friends."

"I heard there's something going on today." He dipped his hand in his pocket and pulled out the charm bracelet he bought her yesterday. He held it up and let the ruby heart charm catch the light. On either side of it hung a gold E and an L.

Ella gasped and covered her open mouth with her hand. Tears filled her eyes and spilled over.

"Happy Valentine's Day, sweetheart." He held the bracelet up and tapped the red heart. He'd already given her his, but this one she'd wear, a reminder of him and their time together, because soon all they'd have were their memories.

"Gabe, it's beautiful. It's perfect."

Ella held out her hand. He secured the bracelet around her wrist and kissed the back of her hand.

"Thank you." She leaned up and kissed him. "I have something a little different for you."

"What? No jewelry?" he teased.

"Come upstairs. We need to get ready to go."

"Honey, if I take you upstairs, there's no way we're going anywhere."

She pulled his hand and he followed her to the stairs. Smiling over her shoulder, she said, "We'll leave after we do that."

"What?" he asked, still teasing her.

She turned back to him before taking the stairs up and jumped into his arms, wrapping her legs around his waist. "We don't have much time, but take me to bed, cowboy."

"You city girls sure are bossy." But it was his pleasure to do her bidding, keep her in his arms as long as possible, because soon his arms would be as empty as the days stretching out in front of him.

She opened her mouth to protest his jibe, but he shut her up with a deep kiss and walked right up the stairs and into her bedroom. They landed on the bed in a tangle of arms and legs.

Gabe kissed his way up Ella's back. She lay on her stomach, her pretty face buried in the pillow. She didn't open her eyes, but rolled over, grabbed him by the back of his head, and kissed him long and deep, reminding him of last night and all the fun they had both in bed and out.

"Good morning, sweetheart."

Ella stared up at him, a soft smile on her face. "Hi. Did you sleep well?"

"I guess." After making love to her again, he spent most of the night staring at the ceiling, holding her close, and dreading what he had to do this morning.

"We had a late night, huh?"

"Well, that's what happens when you go out with a wild party girl."

After he made love to her yesterday evening, she'd rushed him through a shower, ordered him to put on dressier Western wear, and dragged him into a limousine that took them to a country bar she'd rented out for all her and Lela's friends. She stood onstage and gave a lovely tribute to Lela, telling stories about them together growing up as kids. Friends stood up with her and each one started with "Remember the time . . ." and told one story after another. Most of them were filled with fun and happiness, a few more poignant, but the thread throughout remained the kind and loving woman had left her mark on each of their lives and would be remembered as a true friend.

Ella made the last toast, making everyone tear up. Then she introduced the band, told everyone Lela would want a celebration, not a funeral, and she downed the shot of vodka like it was nothing. From that moment on, the drinks flowed, one of his favorite bands rocked the place, rattling the walls, and Ella and her friends had a blast.

Happy in her element and with those closest to her. By the end of the night, one thing was clear. Ella adored her friends, and they loved her. Not just friends, but family. She glowed. He'd thought Ella beautiful and strong from the moment he met her, but now she was thriving.

She belonged here. After all she'd lost, no way he could take her from everyone she loved and isolate her on his ranch in Montana. It would be too unfair. As much as he wanted her by his side, he wanted her happiness more.

She glanced at the clock beside the bed. "Why are you up so early? Come back to bed." She reached for him, and he willingly leaned down for a kiss, but pulled back far too early for her liking. "What's wrong? You've got a strange look in your eyes."

He desperately wanted to make love to her again, close out the world and the inevitable, but restrained himself, trying to make himself get what he had to say out.

"It's time for me to leave, Ella."

"Where are you going?"

"Home."

"Now."

"I've got a seven o'clock flight."

She sat up, the sheet tucked under her arms and draped across her chest. Sadness and fear lit her eyes. "I don't understand."

"Yes, you do. Just like me, you knew my coming here was temporary. As much as I hate to leave you, I have a ranch in Montana to run."

"So, what? This is it?"

"This is where we were always headed, city girl. You knew that as much as I did."

"I'm caught between angels and cowboys. The city and the country. Work and you. I owe my family for everything I have."

"You don't need to make excuses for doing what you need to do, Ella. They left everything to you because they knew you're strong and capable and smart enough to carry on all they started and hoped Wolf Enterprises would become. I know you're going to be a huge success. I am so proud of you for everything you did to avenge your sister and parents' deaths.

"You're an amazing woman, Ella Wolf. You're going to do amazing things with the company you now run. I've heard you talk about the projects you want to implement and the excitement in your voice about the launch of the new cosmetics line. You've found your place here, and that's okay. This is where you need to be."

"So, what, you don't want me anymore?" Tears glistened in her beautiful green eyes, making his gut go tight and his throat ache.

"I'll always want you, but I won't ask you to live a life you don't really want. I did that once, and it ended in disaster. I won't let what we shared turn into fights and resentments and anger and hate because we can't live with each other and have what we really want. I won't do that to you, to us, knowing in the end you'll hate me for it."

"Gabe, no, I just need more time to settle things here. We can be together."

"Ella, you and I both know your life is here, at the company and with your friends. This is where you belong, where you are your best, not on some isolated ranch in Montana. Even if we never said it, we both knew this day would come."

"We can make it work. I don't want this to be the end."

He tried to ignore the tears in her eyes and rolling

down her cheeks. He hated to break her already battered heart. She had to know that every one of those tears he caused tore his soul to shreds.

"We're partners in Wolf Ranch. Like you said, you'll always know where I am, but we have to face reality. You and me and forever was never meant to be." The words came out gruff, but he forced himself to swallow the agony and misery those words and the outlook of his bleak future caused.

He did the hardest thing he'd ever have to do and walked out the door, knowing he couldn't ask her to be someone she wasn't, and he couldn't be a different kind of man. It didn't bring him any comfort to know he'd done it for her, for him, and that it was the only way he knew how to preserve the love they'd shared.

The emptiness settled in his gut and spread through his heart and deep into his soul. The ache throbbed with every beat of his broken heart.

CHAPTER 33

Gabe stood beside Blake at the stall door, checking out the colt. Gabe's nemesis these last weeks. "Thanks for coming to pick up Pain in My Ass for training."

Blake laughed. "I thought his name is Bo."

"That may be his name, but that's not what he is," Gabe grumbled. He'd done a lot of that lately. "How're things with Bud and Dee at Three Peaks Ranch?"

"Get this, Bud found his granddaughter. She killed her father."

"No shit!"

"Bud's trying to get her to come home to the ranch."

"She's not in jail?"

"No. The way I hear it, it was self-defense. Her dad went drugged-out-nuts on her."

"I hope she's okay."

"I'll find out soon. She should be here in a week if things work out. Everything good with you?"

"Tell Mom everything is fine." Blake's eyes held the light of innocence, but Gabe didn't buy it. "Yes, I know that's why you came here to get the horse, instead of me bringing it to you tomorrow."

"Why the hell don't you just call her?" Blake asked.

"Leave it alone," Gabe warned.

"I don't understand why you broke things off with her. She's running around New York. You're here. You two own this place together, but you don't talk to her and she isn't here. It's been two weeks."

"Thanks for summing it up."

"Don't you love her?"

Gabe grabbed hold of the stall gate, gripping it so tight his fingers ached. Of course he loved her. More than anything or anyone, but he couldn't ask her to leave her life and live his. She'd resent him. Eventually, she'd hate him. The thought turned his stomach even now. Better to hold on to the beautiful memories of what they shared than to tarnish them with the bitterness that would build with each day she stayed with him when she'd rather be at work, with her friends, back in New York with everything and everyone that mattered most to her.

"Well, since you didn't go after her, looks like she came after you, big brother." Blake cocked his head toward the open barn door.

Gabe couldn't believe his eyes. The car skidded to a stop and Ella got out, slammed the door, and walked toward him with a pissed-off scowl and fury flashing in her eyes. She'd never looked more beautiful.

"I want to talk to you."

He wanted to grab hold of her, kiss away the feral look on her face, and never let her go again. But she didn't belong to him. She never really did. So why did she come back?

"City girl, what are you doing here?"

"I own eighty percent of this place, or did you forget?"

"Hard to forget when it's your name on the gate and the brand."

"Hey, honey," Blake said.

Gabe shoved Blake toward the doors. "Get out."

"You staying for dinner?" Blake pressed, smiling like an idiot.

Gabe almost cracked a smile when she opened her mouth to answer, but closed it and glared harder at him. Blake looked from her to him and shook his head, walking out the doors without another word.

"You left me." Some of the pain that flashed in her eyes wiped out the anger in her words.

"I didn't leave you. I came home."

That took the wind right out of her sails. He hated to see the uncertainty in her eyes.

"You said you'd always want me," she said more boldly than the unsure look on her face conveyed.

"I wanted you the second I saw you. I want you every second of every day." He wanted the truth from her, so he gave her the truth he lived with day in and day out missing her. "Doesn't change the fact this is never going to work, city girl."

"Stop calling me that. You don't understand."

"Oh, I understand. You don't belong here. Look at you. It's thirty-something degrees out and you're in a silk skirt, a short-sleeve sweater, no coat, and high heels that you ruined traipsing through the snow." Seeing the ruby heart bracelet he gave her for Valentine's Day on her wrist made his heart melt. "You're standing in the stables when you should be standing in a conference room conducting a board meeting." Gabe didn't want to say the words, but he did so anyway. "Go home, city girl. You don't belong here."

Tears welled in her eyes, but she didn't let them fall. Just the sight of them almost made him cave. Everything inside him ached, but his heart broke into a thousand pieces, a band around his chest tightened until he couldn't breathe, and he held his breath and waited. She didn't disappoint. Ella's fingers curled into tight fists, the unshed tears cleared from her eyes, and she took a menacing step toward him.

"Do you have any idea how many planes it takes to get here from Paris? How many hours it took me to cross half the globe? You tell me you'll always want me with one breath and tell me to go home with the next. Well, cowboy, I'm not going anywhere until you answer one question."

"What?"

"Do you love me?" Her voice went soft with the simple question that was more complicated than anything she could have asked him.

"Ella, what are you doing here?"

She threw up her hands and let them fall and slap the sides of her legs. "What am I doing here? You're here. Wherever you are is where I want to be. Don't you get it? I love you. I want to build a life with you. Here. With the horses and the cows and the children we'll have. I thought that's what you wanted too."

"I want that more than I can tell you, but let's face it, saying you want it is one thing. Making it happen— you living and working here and being happy—isn't exactly going to be easy for you. It'll be harder, especially when the power and Internet go down during a storm."

"Gabe, I have a battalion of people working for me. I am not the end-all-be-all at the company. I don't want to be. I want to have a full life. Yes, running the company, but also with the man I love and the children I want to share with you. What do I have to say to make you believe that the life we build here is what I want, what I need, what I long for every second of every day that we're apart? I love you. Isn't that enough to see us through whatever compromises we have to make?"

"My answer to your first question is yes."

"What?"

"I love you. I want you. Wherever you are is where I want to be. I needed you to make the choice on your own, without everything that happened with your family clouding your mind, or me influencing you. I needed to know that you aren't here for any other reason than this is where you want to be."

"It is. Why do you think I set this all up? Why do you think I brought Angel and Belle here? This is the life and home I want. With you."

"Then why are you still standing five feet away." He held out his arms. "Come here before I tackle hug you to the ground. I need you."

She flew into his arms. Her lips met his in a greedy kiss that nearly buckled his knees. Her legs wrapped around his waist and he slid his hands down her back to her hips.

Ella's hands came up to cup his face. She broke the kiss and stared into his eyes. "I've missed you so much."

"I can't sleep without you," he admitted, seeing the dark smudges under her eyes as well.

"Take me to bed, cowboy. Make love to me. I need you wrapped around me."

Gabe walked out the barn doors with her kissing her

way from his ear and down his neck. "The house is too damn far," he grumbled.

"I'll build a cottage out by the stables."

"Our love shack."

She bit into his earlobe. "Yes," she said, her voice all breathy. "My new office too, so I'll never be too far away from you."

Shivers ran down his spine. He squeezed her ass, raising her up the length of him and back down even as he walked the too long distance to the house. She sighed with pleasure and he desperately tried to reel in the urge to take her against the nearest tree. "You're killing me."

"You're going too slow." She clamped her legs tighter around his waist and grinded against him.

Gabe tried not to stumble, but the woman distracted him from walking to what he really wanted to do. Bury himself deep inside her heat.

Finally, he reached the front door, pushed it open, and kicked it closed with the back of his boot. He walked through the living room where Blake stood drinking a can of soda. Gabe didn't say anything, just kept walking down the hall to his room, Ella kissing his neck, her legs around his waist, completely oblivious to his brother's presence.

Before he kicked his bedroom door shut and made love to Ella the rest of the night, Blake's amused words made him smile. "Lucky bastard. I guess she's staying for dinner."

EPILOGUE

Ella used her key to open the front door and stepped into the dark house, exhausted and so happy to be home. She hated all the times she left Gabe, but it had been necessary to put her company and her life in order. She had sold the penthouse and bought a quaint loft that suited her and Gabe's taste for when she needed to be in New York. Her uncle didn't take long to accept her offer of a lawyer in exchange for pleading guilty to all his heinous crimes. He'd spend the rest of his life in jail.

She'd found something infinitely better than living in the past. She'd found a future with the man she loved right here at Wolf Ranch.

Over the last two weeks, she'd made it back to the ranch once. For a day. Gabe grew as impatient as she to make their living arrangement permanent. They filled those days apart with work and hours talking on the phone together, sharing their lives in a way that might not have happened if she stayed with him day after day.

She'd reached a turning point in her hectic schedule. Finally, she'd flip her long stays in New York with her short visits to Montana, and she couldn't be happier.

Used to sneaking into the house late at night, she found her way to the bedroom and Gabe without turning on the lights. She stripped her clothes at the end of the bed and dropped them one by one to the floor. Gabe lay on his stomach. She slid under the covers beside him and leaned down and kissed his shoulder, up his neck, to his ear, and whispered the same thing she always said to him. "I'm home."

His arm snaked out and wrapped around her, she landed on his chest when he rolled over.

"What time is it?"

"Just after one in the morning."

"I called you hours ago."

"I was on a plane."

"I missed you." He buried his face in her neck and inhaled her scent like he always did.

She smiled and held him close. "I missed you more."

"Happy birthday," he said, kissing his way down her neck to her breast, taking her hard nipple into his mouth.

"It is now." She gave herself over to making love to Gabe. His big hands swept up her back and down. He rolled her underneath him, his mouth on her breast. His hand swept down her side and thigh, pushing it out to make more room for his big body, though he remained at her side, brushing his fingers up the inside of her leg to the very center of her. His fingers smoothed over her soft folds; one dipped deep and pushed into her slick core, making her moan.

Neither of them wanted slow and sweet. They'd missed each other too much. Gabe took care of the condom, settled between her thighs, and thrust into her again and again. She raked her fingers down his back, over his hips, to his ass, and pulled him into her, deep. She loved the way he moved against her, creating that sweet friction, grinding against her until the heat pooled in her belly, the fire burned and flashed, sparking every nerve in her body.

Lost in his warmth, his body stretched over hers, his face buried in her neck, she held him close and sighed. He slid to her side, threw one leg over hers, along with his arm, and held her close, his face at her shoulder on the pillow.

"Promise me you'll be here in the morning."

"I don't have to be back in New York for two weeks, and then only for two days."

"Really?"

"Happy birthday to me, I'm staying with you. Right where I want to be."

Gabe rose up on his elbow and stared down at her. "You mean that?"

She reached up and cupped his face. "More than I can tell you with simple words. Besides, with two hundred pounds on top of me, where would I go?"

He kissed her. Soft and sweet, then lay beside her again, but didn't move off her. "This works perfectly with my plans."

"What plans?"

"Birthday surprise."

"What is it?"

"You'll see. I'm taking you somewhere later." He nuzzled her neck and squeezed her to his big body. "I'm so glad you're home."

"I keep telling you to get a dog to keep you company."

"You want a dog," he mumbled.

"You'd love a dog, too."

She felt his smile against her arm. She settled her hands on his warm skin over her middle and fell asleep.

Gabe helped Ella up into the truck seat, trying to hide his nervous excitement.

"You were really going to fly to New York to be with me tonight?" she asked for the fourth time that day.

"No way I let you spend your birthday alone." He gave her a quick kiss, closed the door, went around the truck, and slid behind the wheel. He drove them off the ranch and onto Wolf Road.

"I got your message. You were right. I was out to dinner with my friends."

"I saw the pictures on the Web."

"Checking up on me?"

"Making sure you were smiling and happy, not sad and missing Lela."

"I do miss her. I can't wait for the thaw so we can bury her properly."

"We'll do it soon, sweetheart. I promise. We'll bring her home."

"I can't believe you dragged me out of the house in the middle of that call. Where are you taking me? It's nearly dark."

"You'll see." He smiled and checked the road. They were just about where he wanted to be. "Did you hear that? I think the trailer gate is loose. Let me pull over and check it."

Gabe walked back behind the trailer and waited for Ella to get impatient and come check to see what was taking him so long. It didn't take long, but his gut tied in knots and his hands shook. Nervous, he hoped she liked her surprise. He hoped she said yes.

The minute she cleared the trailer and saw him on bended knee holding up a ring, she covered her mouth with both hands and let the shimmering tears fall.

"I found you on a deserted stretch of road. The second I saw you, I knew there was something about you I couldn't live without. I love you Ella Wolf, and I want to spend the rest of my life with you. Will you marry me?"

With each passing sentence she'd closed the distance and stood over him now, staring down at him, a soft smile on her face, her clasped hands pressed to her heart.

"Yes. Absolutely, yes."

Gabe slid the ring on her finger, shot up, wrapped his arms around her, and spun her around, his lips locked with hers. His heart soared and felt so full it might burst from his chest. The relief washed through him and made him laugh.

"I love you," he said, his forehead pressed to hers.

"I love you too. I can't wait to be your wife."

"Good, because we aren't waiting long." He didn't really need the promise that she'd stay with him always, but he wanted it.

A soft bark came from the back of the trailer.

"What is that?"

"Your birthday present."

"You got me a dog."

He smiled and brushed his nose against hers. "You wanted a dog."

She giggled, unable to disagree.

Gabe set her on her feet and took her hand, pressing it to his chest so she could see the ring. Two round diamonds in the center at each of her knuckles with a round emerald on either side where the diamonds met

in the middle, making a diamond shape out of the sparkling stones.

"I had this made for you. The diamonds are for you
and me. The emeralds for you and your sister. Green
stones that are very similar, but different enough if you
really look, like your and Lela's eyes."

The tears came again. "It's beautiful and perfect. I
love it."

"You're beautiful and perfect and I love you." He
held her close, taking in the moment. "Want to see your
puppy?"

"Yes!"

Gabe reluctantly let her go and opened the trailer
door. The furball rushed out and leaped into Ella's
arms, licking her face.

"He's potty trained and about four months old, so
he's got some manners."

"I love him."

"Good, because it's you and me and Bentley."

Ella laughed, trying not to drop the black and white
border collie. "Bentley?"

"I like it. It suits us." He gave her another soft kiss.
"Come on. Mom planned a birthday dinner with the
family. We promised, remember? We'll announce our
short engagement."

"How short?"

"We're getting married before our honeymoon trip
to Bora Bora."

The trip she planned with Lela, but he'd make just as
memorable when they went as husband and wife.

Eyes glistening with tears for missing Lela mixed
with her happiness, she leaned up and kissed him, then
pressed her forehead to his. "Perfect."

He took the puppy and walked to the truck and set him inside. He closed the door and walked Ella around the front, but stopped before going to the passenger side of the truck. He held her hand and stared up at the starry sky. "It's beautiful, isn't it?"

"I love it here."

He heard the truth in her words. She leaned into him, and he wrapped his arms around her and held her in front of him, staring up at the brilliant sky.

"Did you get everything you wanted for your birthday?"

"You're all I ever wanted."

Continue reading for a sneak peek at the second book in *New York Times* bestselling author Jennifer Ryan's thrilling Montana Men series

WHEN IT'S RIGHT

Gillian's turbulent life has never been easy, but nothing prepared her for the moment of violence that sends her and her little brother running from San Francisco to their grandfather's ranch in Montana. She learned long ago not to trust anyone, but she'll do anything to keep her brother safe and give him the happy childhood she never had.

When she meets Blake Bowden, a strong, silent, gorgeous cowboy who teaches her about the ranch and rescued horses—animals who have been through hell and back, just as she has—Gillian begins to feel happy and at ease for the first time. But in her world happiness has always been fleeting, and she's not sure she can believe in it or the man who has quickly found his way into her heart.

Blake has everything he's ever wanted: a partnership on a ranch that allows him to spend his day in the saddle training racehorses. His life is good, steady, uncomplicated . . . until the most beautiful, haunted looking woman arrives at Three Peaks Ranch. If he wants to keep his ideal life, his partner's granddaughter is

entirely off limits, but Gillian awakens a protective instinct in Blake that he can't ignore…and ignites a passion he shouldn't feel.

As Gillian heals and finds her way back into the
world, Blake knows that he's found the one thing that
he never knew he was missing. And when danger
comes close, he will do anything he must to keep Gillian safe…even if it means risking his life's dream.

COMING MARCH 2015

CHAPTER 1

San Francisco, California

"**H**elp me!"

Home late from her shift washing dishes at the Jade Palace, Gillian pounded up the two flights of stairs as fast as her legs allowed. She hit the landing and turned right, racing down the hallway past her apartment's open door to Mrs. Wicks's unit at the end of the hall. She'd heard the screams from outside. Not the first time she'd answered that call, but so help her God, if her father touched one hair on Justin's head, she'd kill him.

"I'm calling the police," the babysitter, Mrs. Wicks, threatened loud enough for her voice to carry down the hall.

"Damnit, woman, he's my blood," Gillian's father bellowed.

Gillian rushed into the apartment and spotted Justin with his arm cradled in his hand and pressed to his chest, tears shimmering in his eyes but otherwise appearing unharmed. She looked her father up and down, assessing the situation in a glance and the odds on talking him down from whatever ludicrous idea had taken root in his shadowed mind. Dressed in the same clothes he'd left in four days ago, his hair an oily mass hanging lank to his shoulders, he reeked of whiskey, cigarette and pot smoke, and acrid body odor. The wild look in his bloodshot eyes told her he hadn't slept in a good long while. Riding a meth high, he'd probably binged for days. Soon he'd lose all sense of reality and need more of the drug, which wouldn't give him the high he needed, since he'd overloaded his system. He'd crash, his body shutting down and putting him into a deep sleep for a day, or two, or three before he woke up miserable, needing more of what put him in this psychotic state in the first place.

Frustrated and angry, but resigned to this same worn-out routine, she shored up her resolve to get through this night, like she'd done too many times in the past, trapped raising a child with little money and even fewer choices. None of them good.

Her father paced, his movements jerky. He scratched at his arm, his legs, the back of his neck with his grime-filled nails. He slapped at his thigh, then bit at the tips of his fingers. A hint at how far he'd fallen down the rabbit hole. Not good.

"Dad, come on. Let's go home. I'll make you something to eat," she coaxed, keeping her voice calm.

A powder keg of roiling rage, he could blow any second. You never knew what would set him off.

Justin cowered in the corner of the couch, his eyes wide and watchful. He didn't move, afraid of drawing her father's attention. Even at six, he knew the rules of this twisted game.

Mrs. Wicks moved into the kitchen, leaving Gillian to handle getting her father out of there and back to their place. She'd done it before. Usually, he'd come looking for her, but she'd been held up at work, and he'd found little Justin alone. Gillian never left Justin with him if she could help it, especially over the last year, when her father spent more time strung out and paranoid on meth than comfortably numb with booze and pot, like he'd been every day of her life.

The last two weeks had been hell. Gillian's patience had worn thin days ago. If she could hold on, get her father out of Mrs. Wicks's apartment and into theirs, she could take Justin and crash somewhere else for a few days until her father came down and leveled off.

Then, joy, they could start this whole thing over again.

I wish Justin and I were anywhere else.

Inside, the pressure built. How good it would feel to open her mouth and unleash a string of curses, insults, and blame for what her father put her and Justin through day in and day out. She hated him for spending his life drowning in a bottle and doing drugs, his life going up in smoke. Her life went up with it. Justin's too. She wanted it to end. One way or another, just end.

Her father swatted at some imaginary bird, or butterfly, or dragon for all she knew. Only he saw the tormenting hallucinations. If he was this far gone, he was even more volatile and dangerous than usual.

"Dad, come on. I'll make you a burger and get you a beer."

"We have to go." His words came out rushed. He swatted at the air again, this time spinning around to the right before he stopped and turned the other way again, tracking his imaginary flying devils, waving his arms over his head to swat them away.

She shook her head, frustrated and tired of dealing with him. This. Everything. She wanted to run away, but where would she go? It was all she could do now to keep a roof over Justin's head and food in his belly with the diminishing help her father supplied. Out on the streets, or in a shelter, they'd be vulnerable to even more horrors. What kind of life would that be for Justin? Better than this one? Maybe. Maybe not. Still, she needed to find a way to give Justin better than she'd had growing up with a volatile drunk who could barely keep a bartending job and supplemented his income selling drugs to support his own habits.

"We have to go. We have to go. We have to go," her father chanted, getting agitated, hitting the side of his head with one hand and scratching at his leg and the imaginary bugs crawling under his skin with the other.

Fed up, she stepped toward him to grab his arm and lead him back to their place. He jumped out of her reach and laughed. The sound held no humor but a touch of hysteria in the odd shriek. Her father pointed at her, shaking his head side to side. "No. No. No. No. No." Again, his ominous giggle sent a chill up her spine.

Her father grabbed Justin's arm and yanked him off the couch. She stood her ground in front of him. No way her father left here with Justin.

"Let him go. He needs to finish his homework." She made up the excuse, hoping her father released Justin and she got the boy out of there.

"He's mine. He'll keep them away. He's got the light that turns them away."

Paranoid, delusional asshole.

She sighed, knowing just where this was going and not liking it one bit. Soon her father would spiral into a psychotic delusion no one could talk him out of.

Please, just pass out already.

Not that lucky, she tensed and waited to see what

came next. Her father pulled Justin in front of him, held him by both arms, and turned him this way and that, a shield against an enemy only he could see.

"Ow!" Justin cried out when her father's fingers dug into his thin arms.

"Keep them back." Her father tugged on Justin again. Hurt and scared, Justin planted his feet and pulled away, trying to get free. Her father held tighter and spun Justin around to face him. When Justin fell to the floor, tears spilling from his eyes, Gillian couldn't take the ache in her heart. Her anger exploded.

"Keep them back." Her father shook Justin again.

Gillian lost it. "I warned you, if you ever touched him . . ." She lunged for her father, striking him in the arm, breaking his hold on Justin. She shoved her father two steps back, and Justin ran for Mrs. Wicks in the kitchen. She rattled off the building address to the police on the phone. Not the first time someone called the cops on Gillian's father, and it probably wouldn't be the last. No way they got here in time to stop him now. Whatever happened next, Gillian would sure as hell make sure her father never got anywhere near Justin again.

Her father came after her in a drug-hazed rage that gave him strength and sent him into a mindless attack. All other thoughts disappeared behind the fury filling his mind. Her father only knew how to hurt. She'd been through this too many times to count and braced for the impact when his fist came at her, straight into her eye. Pain exploded in her head. She shoved him in the chest, but he came back with a slap to her jaw that stung something fierce. She kicked him in the shin and shoved him again. He fell back two steps, his hand coming up from behind his back. Momentarily stunned, she didn't move, but stared down the gun's black barrel in disbelief that he'd actually pulled a weapon on her. She didn't know where he'd gotten it, only that this added a whole other level to what had seemed like just another rotten night in her life.

Her father held the gun steady, even when he swatted the imaginary devils pestering him. His eyes narrowed on her, and in that moment she joined him in the madness she saw swirling in his gaze.

You or me?

One of them wasn't leaving that room alive.

Justin needs me.

You.

She rushed him, grabbed the gun, and spun her back into his chest, the gun in both their hands pointed to the window. He tried to wrench it free, punching her in the ribs with his free hand. She jerked on the gun again and again and scratched his hand to get him to release it, until he finally let go and the gun thumped onto the floor and skittered across the scarred hardwood. He shoved her from behind. She stumbled forward, scooped the gun off the floor, and turned to face him.

Never turn your back on a psycho.

He leaned forward and charged her like a wounded beast, murder in his eyes and a guttural yell that made the hairs on the back of her neck stand on end.

She swung the gun up and fired. Once. Twice.

Mrs. Wicks screamed.

Blood bloomed on his chest. Still he kept coming. His hands fisted in her T-shirt. He lifted her off her feet and shoved her backward into the window. Her back and head hit the glass with a crack a split second before it shattered. Glass tore and bit into her skin, but she didn't feel the pain past the one thought in her head. *It's done.*

Justin screamed, "Gillian, no!"

I'm sorry.

She flew through the window.

Her father's dark form stood in the opening, highlighted by the lights behind him. He literally dropped to the floor out of her sight.

Be safe, Justin. Be happy.

Her body slammed into the roof of a car with a sickening thud. Everything went black.

CHAPTER 2

Three Peaks Ranch, Montana

Blake Bowden tossed a flake of mixed grass into Bingo's feed holder. He pet the Thoroughbred on the neck and walked out of the stall.

Dee rushed down the aisle, ignoring the horses sticking their heads out to greet her. Her brow creased into worry lines. She kept her steady gaze locked on him. "You have to do something. I've never seen him like this. He's on his third shot of whiskey."

Blake caught the urgent tone, and his insides knotted with tension. Something terrible must have happened to get his old friend drinking the hard stuff. The man barely had more than a beer or two in a given week.

"He's in his office. He won't speak to me." Dee's eyes filled with fear and worry. She twisted the dish towel in her hands. Blake had never seen her this out of sorts.

He touched his hand to hers to reassure her. "Okay now, I'll go up and see what I can do."

Blake rushed up to the house, Dee hot on his trail. She stopped in the living room and held her hand out to indicate her husband, sitting in his study, his head bowed. Blake walked in and stood in front of Bud's desk. Bud didn't look up but continued to stare at the newspaper. A bottle of whiskey sat on the desk by his elbow, next to a half-filled tumbler. The desolate vibes coming off him filled the room and nearly stole Blake's breath. He'd known Bud since he was a kid, long before Bud made him a partner in Three Peaks Ranch. He'd never seen the man this miserable in his life.

"Bud, what happened?"

Several long moments passed, but finally Bud's gruff voice broke the eerie silence. "He's dead."

"Who?"

"Ron."

Dee gasped behind Blake. He turned and met her watery gaze. Her hand pressed to her open mouth.

Blake knew all about Ron, the man who convinced Bud's only daughter to run off with him when she was just eighteen. Wild and unruly, they spent years moving from town to town, from one dead-end job to the next, drinking and doing drugs. Bud lost track of them years ago, until one day he received a letter from the coroner's office asking him to claim his daughter's body. Bud hadn't caught up to her, but the drugs had. By the time Bud picked up Erin's ashes, Ron had split town with their daughter. No forwarding address as usual.

"What happened?" Blake figured he'd finally up and died from an overdose.

"She shot him."

"What? Who?"

"My granddaughter. Gillian. Twice. In the chest."

"Back up. How did you find out? Did she contact you?"

Bud shook his head, but he never took his eyes off the paper. "I had some time to kill at the airport in Denver, so I went into the bar and ordered a beer and a burger, thinking I'd pass the time before my flight watching a ball game on TV. Guy sitting next to me swore and said, 'Some people deserve to get shot.'" Bud smoothed his hand over the paper and the photo Blake couldn't really see. "He got up and left, but didn't take the paper. I slid it over to see what he'd been talking about." Bud sucked in a deep breath and traced his finger over the photo.

Blake stepped closer to the desk. Bud spun the *San Francisco Chronicle* and scooted it toward Blake. The photo showed firefighters and police kneeling on top of a car, helping someone who'd obviously fallen onto the roof. Blake read the caption under the photo. " 'After an altercation with her father, Gillian Tucker was thrown through a second-story window. She survived. Her father, Ron, died at the scene from a single gunshot wound to the chest.'"

Fate's a tricky beast.

It could bring you something you most desired or dump you on your ass. Bud had been handed his ass on a platter.

The picture was black and white, an up close view of the gruesome scene. The only part of Gillian Blake could see was her feet. She'd been wearing a pair of well-worn canvas shoes with a hole near the toe. Two firemen, paramedics, and a police officer blocked the rest of her, swallowed by the now-concave roof. Blake couldn't take his eyes off her tiny feet hanging from the top of the car.

The image transposed with the nightmare in his mind of another woman's feet tangled in the limbs of a felled tree. But that was the past. Maybe the confusion in his mind between the past and the present explained his surging need to help that poor girl. Not that it would make up for what he'd done.

Bud's voice rang out like a gunshot exploding into the silent room. He spoke in his normal tone, but the room, the house, seemed so empty, as empty as the man sitting behind the desk. "I called the San Francisco Police Department. I wanted to be sure it was him. I had to be sure it was her. She shot him after he beat her. She fired twice into his chest. Completely out of his mind on drugs, he still had the strength to grab her and shove her through the window before he died."

"Did they arrest and charge her with murder?"

Bud took a sip of the whiskey and continued to stare into nothing. "They're still investigating, but it looks like a clear case of self-defense. The neighbors in the building confirmed this wasn't the first time he'd hit her."

Bud downed the last of his drink. "I changed my flight and went to San Francisco last night. She refused to see me. I never even got a look at her. I tried again this morning, but she didn't change her mind. The doctor said she needed her rest. She'd be there several more days, so I came home. What the hell could I do?" He slammed his fist on the desk. "He nearly killed her."

"What did the doctor say?"

"Nothing specific. Her injuries are extensive, but she'll survive. I wonder, Blake—how much has she survived already that she had to shoot her own father to stop him from killing her?"

Blake wondered the same thing. "The point is, Bud, she did survive. What are you going to do now?"

"Anything I have to in order to get her here. Since she refused to talk to me, the doctor will speak to her on my behalf. I'm waiting for him to call me back." Bud fell silent again, staring at the wall, waiting for the phone to ring.

Blake eventually left to find Dee in the kitchen. She turned the pieces of fried chicken in a cast-iron skillet. Cooking to cope. She and Bud married long after Erin left with Ron and several years after Bud's first wife passed. Dee's sympathy was for Bud, not the man who spent the last years making Bud's life a misery of worry, regret, and hope that one day the guy would clean up his act and bring his granddaughter home. "How long's it been since Bud heard from Ron?"

"Years. He hasn't seen Gillian since she was a toddler. Since I married Bud, long before then, actually, Ron's never called or come back to town." Dee set the metal tongs on the counter and turned to face him. "He blames himself."

"Bud had nothing to do with this. Erin and Ron made their choices."

"Yes, and that poor girl paid the price." Sadness infused Dee's words and filled her eyes with concern.

"We don't know everything that happened. The article is very brief. Yes, he hit her, and she shot him, but beyond that we don't know anything about what her life with him has been like," Blake pointed out.

"Bud tried to find her years ago now. He never felt right leaving her with Ron. What if she doesn't want to come? What if he never gets a chance to make this right?"

"She shot her father. Maybe she needs time to recover and come to terms with what she's done."

"Do you think she did it on purpose?" Dee's eyes filled with worry and uncertainty.

"If someone hit me in the past and hit me again, and I had a gun in my hand, I'd sure as hell shoot the bastard." The anger roiled in Blake's gut for the man who pushed his daughter too far.

Dee pressed her lips together and nodded, silently agreeing with him.

Blake didn't feel bad for speaking his mind. Ron turned out to be the worst sort of man. You do not hit girls. You certainly never beat your child. The drugs had warped Ron's mind, or maybe he was just rotten to the core. Either way, Blake hated him for treating Gillian so poorly.

"Well, I guess we'll get the whole story when she gets here."

Blake headed back out to the stables and his beloved horses, haunted by thoughts of the woman with the tiny feet lying atop the car's smashed roof. He hoped she was okay, because he knew after a fall, whether from a window or a horse, everything changes.